Please return on or before the latest date above.
You can renew online at *www.kent.gov.uk/libs*
or by telephone 08458 247 200

SPITFIRE GIRLS

SPITFIRE GIRLS

Carol Gould

WINDSOR
PARAGON

First published 1998
by Black Ace Books
This Large Print edition published 2009
by BBC Audiobooks Ltd
by arrangement with
The Random House Group Ltd

Hardcover ISBN: 978 1 408 45898 3
Softcover   ISBN: 978 1 408 45899 0

British Library Cataloguing in Publication Data available

Printed and bound in Great Britain by
CPI Antony Rowe, Chippenham and Eastbourne

To Bill Leith and Stroma Hamilton-Campbell

ACKNOWLEDGEMENTS

This novel is based on fact. Some of the characters are or were historically very real persons. Churchill and Beaverbrook, for example, would be difficult enough to disguise, let alone create. Other characters, and particularly the principal heroines of my story, are freely invented. Where a character is not recognizable by name, the reader can take it that no reference is intended or should be inferred to any real person, dead or living.

In the course of my research for this book I have found the following non-fiction works particularly helpful. *The Forgotten Pilots* by Lettice Curtis, A Story of the Air Transport Auxiliary 1939–45, second edition, 1982; *Golden Wings* by Alison King, the Story of Some of the Women Ferry Pilots of the Air Transport Auxiliary, C. Arthur Pearson Ltd, 1956; *I Couldn't Care Less* by Anthony Phelps, the Harborough Publishing Company Ltd, with the Drysdale Press, Leicester.

Finally, my special thanks are due to Vanessa Neuling of Random House, Hunter Steele of Black Ace Books, Nicola King Blackwood, Bill Leith, Stroma Hamilton-Campbell, Issy Benjamin, Ruth Winter, Annie Price, Neil Robinson, Collection Curator, Marylebone Cricket Club, Duncan Boyd, the late John Rosenberg—and the 180 real Spitfire Girls.

C.G., London, December 1997

*. . . Unfortunately I lived at a time
when girls were still girls . . .*
Amelia Earhart

Part I

Before the Storm

In 1933 an ex-convict with one testicle was catapulted to the leadership of the German people. He had been catapulted by his senile predecessors and at once set about transforming the lives of his nation's populace by providing uniforms and a new symbol. The senile predecessors wondered why their protégé, Adolf Schicklgruber, ranted and raved.

Adolf became more widely known as Hitler and, as the Uniforms began their Master Plan to annihilate Jewish businesses, Friedrich Kranz became impotent. To the men at his flying club the fact that he was a great Austrian industrialist meant nothing when all had gathered under the shower taps. In recent days a ritual had developed. One by one they would file out, disgusted. On this particular day he knew his disfigurement, shared also by ancestors like their Saviour, had become a special feature. Soon he would be banned from these premises and more appropriate showering facilities would be arranged for his race by the Uniforms.

Rich, educated Jew: he could fly aeroplanes and he could make aeroplanes, but the man with one testicle had cut off his capabilities. In 1937, after four years of growing terror, he would travel away from his blonde wife and brown children, trusting the Uniforms to leave them unscathed.

Friedrich Kranz, too frightened to know his own sex any more, boarded one of his last remaining aircraft, hoping that England, of all places, would bring back his virility.

*　　　*　　　*

'No-one wishes to confront a maniac. We put these people away from time to time. In Germany they become heads of state.'

Interruptions, all in condemnation, blurred the man's words.

'Has any one still living ever seen the likes of his assortment of scum running a country?' Sir Henry Cobb was also ranting and raving.

In the Commons he had become known as Valerie Cobb's father, due to the activities of his unmarried daughter. She had set up an air joyride service and now lived in a hut with another woman on a circus caravan site in his Norfolk constituency. Polite folk felt ill at ease with his talk, and most people preferred listening to Neville Chamberlain and to Hitler's admirer Joe Kennedy.

'In the space of one generation, we have lost a proportion of our male population fighting a race obsessed with Wagner.'

Gallery visitors half-listened and half-glanced at their newspapers, surreptitiously peering at the photograph of the disaster that had struck in America the afternoon before. Members of Parliament argued over Hindenburg's successor, and the press got excited about the doomed airship named after everyman's senile Wagnerian.

'Does the Right Honourable Gentleman seriously consider the German people a threat?'

As laughter rang through the halls, Cobb felt the same tightening in his chest as during weekly rows with Valerie. He gave up.

4

'Pinning your hopes on a war—because your little girl wants to fly in it?' Tim Haydon, Member for Suffolk North, made a ritual of grabbing Cobb after debate. He was a bachelor fascinated by others' manifestations of solitude. That Valerie shared her solitude with another woman meant she was alone. It had become somewhat of an obsession.

'If a war gets your beady eyes off my daughter, then yes: why not?'

'The big news is that the man from Vienna is trying to buy a space in your constituency.'

'Vienna would be a blessing in my patch. Those idiots in the parish haven't seen anything foreign since a nun visited.'

'You know, I have wondered at times about your allegiances.'

'Leave that to Hitler. In fact, Tim, I expect you feel warmed by his methods. You knew of a Viennese presence in my milieu before I did.'

'Funny, because he was seen coming out of a hut in Hunstanton.'

'Who? Hitler?'

Haydon did not laugh.

Cobb reflected fleetingly to himself that an absence of a sense of humour must be congenital.

'Everyone knows there is only one hut in your village—in fact, one hut in Norfolk.'

Cobb, facing yet another widowers' dinner, got into a taxi in silence, leaving Haydon to fantasize on two women in a hut.

*   *   *

Edith Allam had come to Lakehurst, New Jersey

5

to watch another momentous event amongst crowds of men. She had positioned her camera apparatus and was ignoring the curious looks from the career reporters and press photographers. Sadly, the only other girl butting in on the proceedings was a tiny German. They chatted, Edith in the natural tongue of her immigrant parents, or so she thought.

'What is this inflection of yours?' asked Raine Fischtal, distinguished film-maker for the Reich.

Edith had never experienced inhibitions about her German. Everyone on Ritner Street spoke Yiddish—except, of course, for the Irish. Still, to Raine it was not real German.

'Hitler wants perfect diction to go with the uniforms.' Raine wanted to make the girl feel uncomfortable.

'For perfect diction you have to go to Philadelphia Normal School.'

'Normal? Obviously you are not a Wagnerian.'

'On the contrary—I am. Can I see your camera?'

Raine handed over the apparatus with more revulsion than reluctance. In front of her stood a striking brunette with intelligent blue eyes set far apart.

'Wagner would have enjoyed being here today,' said Edith. 'Imagine his glee at the sight of a giant Tristan in the sky over the New World.'

'Please be careful with my equipment. Yours is rudimentary. Made for non-mechanical minds.'

'Wrong again. I'm a mechanic—the only girl in South Philly with a pilot's licence.'

For some reason Raine was filled with even more disgust and snatched her movie camera from Edith's gloved hand. Why did American women

6

wear gloves at all the wrong times? she muttered to herself. Out of the corner of her eye she sensed a deep hurt had set in, but felt nothing for the native whose ghetto tongue was gutter German. Her blue eyes offended her—how dare she? It was a freak of nature.

Edith stayed put, thinking of the simplicity of her parents' lives. A brain like Raine's left her excited and frightened. How easily it could enslave someone!

A commotion made both women move. One of the reporters, a radio man, was sweating and Edith laughed.

'I hate these things. Didn't sleep at all last night. What about you?'

'Other things scare me,' replied Raine.

'Like what?'

'If you look over there, a lady with a movie camera is filming, and she's even taking shots of us—samples of merchandise to show to her master—like fabric to a tailor. They call it cut-and-paste. That frightens me, much more than a news story.'

Eddie Cuomo tipped his hat at Edith and she watched him wipe his brow and talk into the microphone. The event was approaching—the landing of the giant airship 'Hindenburg'—and Raine straightened with the prospect.

A few moments later, men ran for their lives and in the stupidity that is often confused with patriotism, Raine Fischtal let the flames engulf her before fleeing with her Master's film. Edith ran and snapped, ran and snapped, watching the German lettering disappear along the side of the giant Tristan, and in the distance she could hear the frightened man screaming, 'Oh, humanity, humanity . . .' a display of emotion which would lose him his job in a land which still loved its Teutonic roots . . .

Later, people would say that the Hindenburg disaster at Lakehurst, New Jersey marked the end of innocence for millions of Eddie Cuomo's listeners. Edith Allam's picture made the cover of *Life*. She didn't even get her hands burnt.

With the money from the picture she would try to get airborne and find out if Raine and her film had survived the holocaust.

2

In 1937 birds were beginning to get used to their natural flying patterns being disrupted by air currents created by buzzing monsters.

Valerie Cobb had transcended that world created by men, and looked down from her single-engine Spartan at the beaters. They loved their lives. She loved hers. Her aeroplane was much cleaner, she suspected, than the bodies of the Lords of the Manor. At least the wildlife could feel safe up here, she thought, as her machine surged through their domain.

It was the end of the busy season and she was returning to Hunstanton from a taxi job. Autumn was well under way, visibility atrocious and as she cleared thick cloud her craft received a jolt. Struggling to regain control, and emerging into calm skies, she was alarmed to register another small craft closing in. She banked steeply only to find the other plane coming alongside. It was a moment she had endured before: yet another foolhardy male pilot 'getting a good look'. Eye to eye, he leered and she took avoiding action: he misjudged, the joke went wrong and he clipped Valerie's wing.

She would have to come down. Furious, and in a frantic search for a landing patch, she skimmed houses and found herself in a small field. As her aeroplane juddered to a halt the damage seemed to tap against her bones like an invisible set of fingers. The Spartan cried out to her.

'Damn them.' Her mind regurgitated the image of the leering pilot. 'God, how I hope he crashes and wets himself.'

Emerging from the cockpit she inspected the damage.

'He'll sit down to tea, smelling of pee . . .'

Expletives rolled out, hitting the fuselage and echoing back. When the echoes stopped she knew they were being absorbed. A warm coat stood next to her, then two.

'Your pilot bending the rules?'

Valerie looked in disbelief at the pair. 'Tweedledum and Tweedledee also came to tea. Can I help you two?'

'We'll need to see the pilot's licence, madam.'

'I *am* the pilot.'

They circled the aircraft as if a pilot more to their liking would emerge to assure them both they were once again warm in a secure world.

'There is a landing fee of three pence, which we require. Otherwise the aeroplane is impounded and your licence confiscated.'

'Do you need me to find you a man to pay the

money?' Valerie was flashing the smile her father referred to as 'the heavens opening'.

Present company remained unimpressed. 'What is your business?'

'Taxiing, transport, joyrides and aircraft maintenance.'

Now fear had set in. They wanted her out of their midst. The unknown, like the dark, always frightens.

'I was terrorized into landing here by an irresponsible idiot. Send me someone to help do the wing.'

Tweedledum was becoming aggressive. 'We can suspend your licence.'

'Whatever for? What *is* this place, anyway?'

'If you don't know, you shouldn't be flying.'

'Can I guess? Number one, it's in my father's constituency. Number two—'

Tweedledee, the one who had remained silent throughout, interrupted:

'Weston Longville, madam.'

'Close enough.' Valerie laughed.

She thrust a coin into one of the coats and they slunk off. In the distance she could hear Tweedledum muttering something about madam this and madam that. She knew they would find her a mechanic because fear had turned to libido and she had scored two further conquests.

*   *   *

Shirley Bryce watched with amusement as Valerie brought their battered craft in for a perfect landing. A crack ground engineer, she had A, B, C and D licences and was qualified to undertake

10

both airframe and engine overhauls of aircraft. She had read her partner's poetry during this morning's wait and looked at the figure emerging from the cockpit with even more of the uncomfortable affection she had tried so hard to bury.

'Take three pence out of that job, plus the cost of patching,' said Valerie. 'I got clipped again and found two potential lovers. Lucky for me I landed in a proper airfield.'

'Someone from Vienna came to see you today.'

'What did you think?'

'Of the man from Vienna?'

'My landing in an airfield. And the wingtip? Was he nice?'

Shirley climbed atop the wing and Valerie grinned.

'He was looking for lessons,' said Shirley.

'What sort?'

'Up-in-the-air kind. God, was he nervous.'

By now the ground engineer had found her way underneath the wing. She thought of her ancestors as she lay prostrate. Her voice was muffled.

'Val, what does Blood Libel mean to you?'

The pilot was bored. 'Nothing. Are you sure he was Viennese?'

'He told me a story about Norwich in the eleven-hundreds, and something called Blood Libel.'

Valerie had loosened her flying suit and was watching the circus performers readying their equipment for that afternoon's show. She wondered if they were part of a foreign invasion force.

'He came to see you because of the troubles he's been having at home. For some reason he wants a higher-class licence, and he thinks you can help.

Now he's here, and his family is out of reach. They were supposed to come over and now they can't get out—at least in the manner he'd arranged.'

'Why?' At times Valerie avoided confronting the disturbed histories of older cultures.

Shirley sat upright. 'Hitler will take Austria and go to work on the Jews. Apparently their businesses are threatened and even the most charming of Viennese are more ardent Nazis than the Germans.'

'They're proud of their native son,' said Valerie.

'Listen, this man needs help. When he got here, our geniuses confiscated his own private plane. If he can familiarize himself with an old heap like this, he can get his family out of the old country. You could enlighten him.'

'What did he say about libel?' asked Valerie.

Shirley was sitting with legs folded and her partner towered over her slight figure.

'His name was Franz, or something, and he explained the remarkable history of Norwich as the first setting for a Blood Libel,' explained Shirley.

'Should Dad know about this?'

'It was eight hundred years ago.'

'His mission, idiot.'

Shirley stood. 'I think you should meet him.'

Valerie was thinking of the men who had already filled her day. 'I came close to losing everything myself today—all because of some maniac. How different could I possibly look in the cockpit? Somehow they always know I'm not one of them, and they single me out for the torture treatment.'

'It must be animal instinct, Val.'

'This is incident number thirty-six this year. I seem to attract lunatics.'

'You have your own style of flying.'

'Maybe we should quit. I'm tired. Try and get Franz back, would you?'

'*K*ranz. Friedrich Kranz.'

Shirley put her hand on Valerie's shoulder. In her other hand was one of the many precision tools of Britain's sole woman ground engineer. As her partner went off to think, she resumed her bodywork. Kranz would come back. Things would be different.

3

Excellence in sport had been encouraged in school, but for English girls destined for the London Season delusions of a muscular career had to be dashed shortly after puberty. Barbara Newman, a Rothschild cousin, had befriended Sally Remington when they were in the hockey team and had taken her under her wing. Sally's parents had lost everything in the Great Depression, so Sally was poor and Barbara was rich, but both girls shared a fiendish devotion to the development of their physical skills, far beyond puberty and in defiance of the Season.

After many battles with her parents Barbara managed to continue in her pursuits, which led her to become Britain's greatest woman ice-hockey player. Sally had taken a part-time job in the local flying club, serving drinks to other girls lucky enough to afford the lessons. With the money earned she pursued a cheaper sport and soon became a top club tennis player and began travelling the world competing against the greats of her day. Occasionally she would encounter Barbara in an American town or a Canadian outpost, and on days away from competition they would loiter at flying clubs and take the odd lesson. Both girls had become world celebrities and wherever they went fans fussed and doted. They shared a private chuckle when, time after time, flying lessons were given free of charge because of their notoriety. Aeroplanes had begun to fascinate the pair, the hours they accumulated beginning to add up towards a real qualification.

By 1938 Sally Remington had hurtled to the top of world tennis. Barbara's career came to an abrupt halt with the threat of war, her family having involved themselves heavily in the financing of refugee airlifts from European capitals still free from Nazi control. Their daughter, whose ice-hockey trophies covered the shelves of one entire room in their spacious London mansion, devoted herself to flying full-time, amazing her club with daring aerobatic displays and loop-the-loops that defied the dynamics of traditional aircraft design. All breath would be held as the famous ice-hockey champion would wind through the air at a screaming speed and feign loss of control, only to level out and start the ascent all over again.

Bill Tilden was the greatest tennis player of his generation and considered Sally his female equivalent. Indeed, he had tried to talk her out of returning to England and had very nearly persuaded her to continue as his mixed doubles partner on the American circuit. Flying, however, had reached into her soul and on a glorious California morning she had kissed the legendary ace goodbye, promising him she would be back the day peace had been restored. Sally, her racquets and a framed photograph of her tall, glamorous figure tucked amongst Big Bill, Ted Tinling and René Lacoste were loaded on to a steamer bound for Southampton. It was a perilous journey, with rumours of German submarines heading for international waters, but luck travelled with the beautiful tennis player and she was reunited with her adoring parents.

When she had recovered from culture shock and settled back into the routine of self-denial that had become the norm in damp, sunless London, she headed for Maylands, where she knew Barbara would be misbehaving at 2,000 feet or less. Recently the world's press had latched on to the Rothschild heiress's antics, and on tour Sally had read more about the British aerobatic ace than about Amy Johnson or Edith Allam.

On this warm afternoon Sally itched to be on a tennis court but her mind switched over to aeroplanes when Barbara's short, stocky figure emerged from the cockpit of a Puss Moth, her broad grin a welcome sight.

'You're back!' Barbara exclaimed as an admirer aimed a huge camera towards the pair and the shutter snapped.

'Who's a legend, then?' Sally said, her height overshadowing the other girl.

'Oh, Sally, don't be ridiculous. You are the legend, not I. Imagine being photographed with Big Bill and one of the Three Musketeers—that picture has been in every paper in Britain.'

'That's only because Ted Tinling is in it, and he's English.'

15

'They should invite him back to design some gorgeous clothes for the flying girls.' Barbara and Sally had entered the flying club common room, where strange faces greeted the pair.

'Haven't you heard, Sally?' Barbara asked, throwing her goggles on to the card table. 'Valerie Cobb is being asked to recruit some girls to fly in a Civil Air Guard. Apparently Hitler means business. Daddy says Jews are being singled out and thrown out of top jobs in Germany—lawyers, doctors, scientists, industrialists, the lot. You know Stella Teague, that ballerina who mucks about in Moths? She's been flying over to Romania and rescuing these people. Some chap called Goebbels collects their life's savings in a barrel and then he lets them get on an aeroplane with the shirt on their back.'

'What about Valerie Cobb?'

'She has two thousand hours, and the Air Ministry wants her to find a handful of girls with hundreds of hours who are sound of wind and limb, to stand by for some sort of civil air patrol.'

'I've got three hundred hours, Barbs,' Sally mumbled, sinking into a chair.

'You never know—this Nazi Party may destroy us all.'

'Those Europeans need a good game like tennis to divert them,' said Shirley. 'If a sport took hold and everybody had to wear white pants they'd forget the swastikas and just start producing masses of little Tildens and Helen Willses. What do you think, eh?'

'Be serious,' Barbara said, pulling a cigarette pack from her flying suit pocket and lighting up mannishly. 'I don't know about you, but I want to

16

be there when Valerie needs women. Something tells me our knowledge will lead to bigger things. Look at the Poles—they've got girls in their Air Force. Daddy says someone like that Shirley Bryce might end up being Chief Ground Engineer to the RAF.'

'She's a bloody genius.'

'It's in the genes,' Barbara said, puffing furiously.

Sally waved at the smoke. 'Genius?'

'That's why Hitler wants the brilliant folk out.'

'Here we go again—the Jews are smarter than any other race!'

'We may not be smarter, but we've learned to use our attributes to the best advantage. Someday the Jews will have their own country, and when they start tilling the soil the rest of the world will find some reason to attack them. Anyway, Shirley is undoubtedly the best and the brightest—there is no-one in the RAF who can match her abilities.'

'How do we get Valerie to remember us to the Air Ministry?'

'We don't, Sal.' Barbara stubbed out her cigarette, ignoring the cluster of male fliers who had joined them at the table and were feigning a card game. 'You and I have to keep plugging on and accumulating hours until she starts recruiting.'

Sally leaned across the table to whisper in her ear:

'What is it about you? Those chaps are dying to have an audience with the ice hockey champion.'

'Nonsense,' Barbara hissed. 'They're drooling over *you*.'

Both girls rose, and as they passed the men an assortment of eyes lingered on Sally's exquisite figure, her athletic, almost masculine arms and legs

17

tempered by a supremely feminine bosom, and her bottom tightly clad in a Tinling creation that bordered on the risqué.

'Keep moving, Sally Remington,' Barbara muttered, swinging her goggles. 'You ought to be ashamed of yourself, dressing like that over here. This is not Hollywood.'

Moving in to the main entrance area, the girls stopped in their tracks.

'My God, it's the lady herself, in the flesh.'

Valerie Cobb stood in the fading sunlight and lit a cigarette, her gracefully shaped hands an elegant complement to a figure clad in perfect summer tailoring.

'Now or never,' Barbara said, squeezing her companion's arm. 'Hello, Val,' she said casually.

Turning around in a flash, Valerie's gaze took in the small figure and she smiled. 'Barbara Newman—proficient in all types of biplane, with two hundred and eighty-seven hours since first licence granted.'

'You remember me, Val?' asked Barbara.

'Good Lord—who could forget you? In any case, I have just been examining club records,' she explained, her glance moving to Sally Remington. 'The Ministry has given me permission to do so. Am I correct in thinking that lady is Sally Remington?'

'Yes!' Barbara exclaimed. 'Tennis champion.'

Valerie turned to Sally:

'Proficient in things like Spartans, if I am not mistaken?'

'We met when you and Shirley came to Wimbledon last year,' Sally squeaked in awe.

'Yes—our first day off since we joined forces in

18

1931.'

'Will you be able to use us, Val?' Barbara demanded.

'At the present time, I have a list of six girls who have five hundred hours or more. You haven't enough experience. For God's sake, please try to accumulate some more. Try for R/T, navigators' and instrument licences. In the meantime, until I can recruit, you could be helping the Army Co-op—they need anti-aircraft practice, and those hours count.'

'How do we keep in touch with you?' Barbara was eager, her face animated.

'No need. I shall be checking every girl's records week by week, from now onwards, and as your papers become more impressive, so you stand a better chance of war work.'

'Do you and Shirley still share that hut?' Sally asked.

'It will soon be empty. My father thinks civilized man is on the brink.'

'So does mine,' said Barbara. 'Do you still write poetry?'

'Not any more,' Valerie responded, smiling at the two athletes. 'Perhaps when the Nazis come over, none of us will have anything to do, and such pastimes will win a girl bread coupons.'

Nodding to the pair with the same abruptness as her manner of speech, she shook hands briefly and then was gone.

'That woman is a menace.'

Barbara and Sally turned around to discover Noel Slater, the flight engineer who virtually lived at Maylands and who had most recently fought a lone battle to prevent club funds being ploughed

19

into the building of a ladies' lavatory.

'Would you prefer Hitler?' snapped Barbara.

'She means to put the likes of you up against the man himself,' he said, leering at Sally's tanned legs.

'Better us than you, mate.' Barbara was relentless.

'So, Sally Remington is back!' he exclaimed, grinning.

'That's right, Noel,' she crooned, towering over the diminutive flight engineer.

'Why?'

'Talented fliers like myself are needed by that menacing woman.'

'What about Wimbledon, my dear?' His voice had taken on a whining tone, and he was standing too close to Sally for comfort.

'Because of my absence, Noel, the entire tennis season will be brought to a halt for the duration of the inevitable war.'

For once he had stopped chattering and seemed bemused.

Barbara grabbed Sally by the arm and ushered her away.

In the new lavatory the two girls laughed nervously. But when they had stopped, the reality of Valerie's words began to permeate their good humour.

'They've a thousand hours, most of those girls,' Barbara lamented, sitting on a polished ledge. 'Marion Wickham has about nine hundred, and she's the least qualified of Val's inner circle. They are all qualified instructors, and the boys are already training with them, seven days a week without a space free.'

Outside, the noise of a motor was carried on the

20

warm afternoon air, Valerie reversing rapidly out of the forecourt and blowing dust in through the lavatory window. Barbara Newman and Sally Remington wanted to be part of her contingent more than anything in the world, more than marriage and babies and more than peace in their time. Though their parents could not understand this passion and wished for a cure to come down— if not from Heaven, then at the Hunt Ball—the pair, like hundreds of women of all ages who in 1938 were the cream of the nation's aeroplane pilots, craved a war above all else. If they had to train men to fight in the air they would do so, and if they had to ferry Moths they would do that as well, but most of all they wanted wings on their shoulders and the licence that went beyond their A, B, C, and Ds and which only men could bestow—the right to fly war machines and perhaps come back alive for Olympic Gold and a Wimbledon Championship in the peace they had helped to win.

4

Shirley Bryce was in dirty overalls.

Infatuated with aviation, the well-dressed Austrian named Kranz sat in the hut listening rapt to her readings of Valerie's poetry. In between verses she would describe their enterprise to him, embellishing it with wild tales of narrow escapes.

'I see my next fortune being made from sleek war machines. Don't you?' said Friedrich Kranz.

Shirley looked up from the poetry book:

21

'Who knows? You fell out of the air and into our hut, so how would I know how you'll get rich?'

Friedrich laughed. 'At home I manufactured these things. It's interesting how acceptable they were until the new regime came along. They were regarded as the best machines in the world, and I designed them myself. Suddenly I am under the thumb of a maniac and must turn a life's work over to him.'

'I have Jewish blood too.'

Friedrich laughed. 'Here, thank God, it doesn't matter. At least, not yet.'

'You're wrong. It does matter.'

'If Hitler comes here, you'll wear two stars, including one for cohabiting with another woman. She'll wear a star for cohabiting with a Jewess.'

'Val and I don't cohabit,' snapped Shirley. 'We're just chums.'

'Dear lady, I've offended.'

'Well, I am very fond of her,' admitted Shirley, picking up Valerie's poetry notebook.

'That's strictly private!' Valerie had arrived. She grabbed the book, nearly striking her mate.

Freidrich rose. 'Kranz, Friedrich.'

'Yes, I know. You look very much like a Franz who wants to fly.' She was stunningly dressed, and he was thunderstruck. In a split second of rudeness Britain's top woman pilot had made yet another conquest.

Kranz gushed:

'May I tell you about some Polish lady pilots I have left behind?'

'Sit down first. My head aches.' She looked down at Shirley.

'Val, Friedrich wants to build aircraft here.'

22

'In Hunstanton? You'd have more luck applying to be Poet Laureate.'

Kranz sat. 'There are a number of Polish ladies ferrying aeroplanes to Bucharest. They are helping to evacuate undesirables. Soon they too will be outcasts. Could you use them?'

Valerie, still standing, paused and looked at a random page of her poetry. 'How is it that you have knowledge of undesirables, as you call them, in Romania?'

'These people are lawyers, doctors, scientists and industrialists like myself. It is still possible to reach civilisation from Romania, but not for long. Hitler is aiming to include every country in the world on his agenda.'

'Include them for what?' She shut the book loudly.

'Purification,' Kranz replied coldly. 'There is a creeping terror in the German-speaking world, and though your partner tells me such things exist here, I cannot believe you could imagine what true terror is like.'

Valerie turned on Shirley. 'What on earth have you been telling him?'

'We were reading your poetry.'

'And the rest? Mr Kranz, you need me for something.'

'I know you are amongst this country's best. The RAF is unprepared, and when Hitler comes it will all happen as a great surprise. Mobilization will be last-minute and planes like yours will be confiscated.'

'Thank you for telling me how we are running our lives. Why do I figure in your aircraft business? I can't save these people.'

Shirley made noise and tea, offering her two cents:

'Hitler can't be all that bad with so many German faces smiling out from the newsreels.'

'Mr Kranz seems to think he is—bad, I mean,' commented Valerie. 'He wants to save the faces that aren't smiling.'

Kranz took his cup, his hand looking old compared with the rest of his body.

'Is Sir Henry Cobb not your father?' he asked.

Shirley made more noise.

Valerie had had enough:

'Unless you want a joyride in a crippled Spartan, Kranz, your visit is over.'

Friedrich rose slowly, feeling an overwhelming hunger. 'I won't detain you any further. You and I will need each other again soon.'

'I never recall having needed you in the first instance.'

Usually the shrewd, sometimes flirtatious businesswoman, she felt a controlled fury overtaking her judgement. What did he want?

Shirley fussed and kept him happy on his way to the door, where a bitter wind tried to enter the hut. He tipped his hat.

Valerie turned her back on the handsome Austrian as he walked out into the Norfolk chill.

'You are a cow,' said Shirley, returning to her partner.

'People who bring Dad into things revolt me.'

'One can't blame them. Anyway, you liked him.'

'You showed him my poetry. Fool. He could be a Nazi spy. They probably torture poets,' said Valerie. 'Perhaps Dad sent him to spook us. Are you afraid?'

24

'He did make me realize how close everything is getting.'

'That's why I wanted to get rid of him. Here's the news. The Air Ministry is ordering all private flying clubs to reduce the cost of lessons from four pounds to two shillings and sixpence an hour. They're asking kids from all over to start learning.'

'Does that exclude Friedrich? He wants lessons—I told you last time.'

'Forget him. The government is subsidizing the cheap lessons—it will let in hundreds of people too poor to afford air proficiency. Shirley, that includes girls, and I'm damned if I'm going to allow the Ministry to keep them on the ground if war comes.'

Shirley became morose, pushing the tea things into a pile at the bottom of the basin.

'Your father could help us if we quit. I bet the RAF will be bleating for instructors on the ground and in the air—they might even need me and my spanner.'

'They'll need you, believe me.' She paused. 'God, that man made me cross.'

'Do you think we would be given important posts? You know all my dreams about Chief Ground Engineer Bryce.'

'I don't know all your dreams.'

Thinking only of Kranz but trying to appear as far from passion as she could, Valerie marched off towards the Spartan.

Looking on, bemused, Shirley wondered if any more poetry would ever be written.

In the neighbourhood Edith Allam called home, the Hindenburg Disaster had dominated conversation for weeks. Not since the 'Titanic' had so many couples lain awake at night speculating about the variables: 'If we had been on it, if we had taken a holiday, if we were rich, if we had had any money at all . . .'

On this burning day in a Philadelphia August, Edith had waited five hours for an opportunity to view footage on loan to her employer, Press-Shots Inc., and indeed she was one of only four staff allowed to look at the film, including her constant companion and soulmate, Errol Carnaby—the only coloured projectionist in the industry. Word had got about that at the beginning of Raine Fischtal's movie of the airship tragedy was a sequence showing other forms of death. Raine had not thought of this portion of her work as tragic in the least, and believed scenes of *Krystallnacht* coupled with the arrival of the 'Hindenburg' in New Jersey were not grotesque.

Press-Shots did, but took care not to say so. They had been offered a special showing and were gracious to the German lady, particularly in view of her horrific burns suffered at Lakehurst. Her hands had been damaged and Edith reflected, as she watched black-and-white books being thrown on to black-and-white bonfires on the screen, that Raine would never make movies again. She thought of how physically alike they were—small, compact women with competitive eyes and appealing bodies—but how appalling was the German's view of the world. She watched as Raine, oblivious to her pain, sat upright at the scenario of broken Jewish windows and Nazi boots taunting prostrate physicists. It was a scene Edith could not imagine in Philly, where tonight she would be going out with an Italian, a Negro and an Irish American for ice-cream sodas in an enlightened downtown Automat.

When the presentation had ended, Edith's boss Burt Malone took his beefy self over to Raine's chair and made the usual offer to buy the rights American-style. He would rather perish than see that canister leave this room.

'I refuse.' Raine smiled as she said it.

'Nobody ever turns us down, honey, do they Edie?'

'I'm not surprised.' Edith had to be frank.

Raine Fischtal was getting angry:

'These pictures belong to the Reich. My show was a courtesy. We are not selling anything.'

'Who's we?'

'The Reich, Mr Malone.'

'She means she doesn't work alone—like the Cosa Nostra, Burt.'

'This Reich, who's really in charge?'

Raine had taken on the look of a weary bird stranded on the deck of a destroyer in a strange sea.

'No one is in charge, if that is the description you wish to use. The Führer is Reichschancellor, and he controls all areas of government, as well as the arts. My film-making falls into the realm of art.'

'He runs the shop *and* cooks the books, Burt.'

'Cooks?' Raine was nonplussed and Edith was

loving it.

'Well, if you'll allow me, I'd like to contact your government regarding purchase of exclusive rights in this remarkable piece of cinema. We think it would raise a few eyebrows here.'

By now the projectionist, with a slight smirk on his attractive face, placed the roll of film into its canister and Raine pulled it from his brown hands, gritting her teeth. She walked with precision to the door. Burt had slumped in his seat and seemed helpless, while the other employees in the room reflected their country's isolationist apathy. Errol seemed invisible—even in time of war he would become separate from the rest. Only Edith was not disinterested.

'Why don't you come out with my friends tonight?' asked Edith. '*We* go to Fidler's—the Automat, renowned around the world.'

Raine paused and smiled at the American:

'I will already be making my way back home. You know, my hands will need proper treatment from doctors without mixed blood.'

Suddenly Burt came alive:

'Oh, come off it, sister. Don't dish out this racial purity shit over here. Our medics are about fifty years ahead of the rest of the world.'

'Mr Malone, it is important you should start learning our manifesto. It is important, too, Miss Allam, that you should start learning *hoch Deutsch* or you will give yourself away when we take power here.'

'In Pennsylvania?' One of the isolationists had spoken. Stan Bialik, a thin, timid film editor who seldom bathed, squirmed in his seat. He looked for enlightenment to Edith.

'When the Nazis take over, Stan, they'll make you scrub down every day,' said Edith. 'Cleanliness is next to Godliness.'

'There is no God nonsense in Germany, you know.' Raine leaned against the wall, now holding her canister with some difficulty. 'Religion has no place, and good riddance.'

'Oh, like Stalin?' Burt walked over to her and his burly figure made an enormous shadow. Raine glared at him and he knew she no longer thought him an idiot. She departed.

The lights were still dimmed and Edith hit the switch. Stan shuffled out of his chair and Burt stared into space.

'This is a new breed of folk, Burt,' muttered Stan. 'I hate kikes but these guys mean business, like starting a war over them.'

'Ho-ho! What a turnaround!' Burt slapped Stan on the back. 'I thought you were one of Joe Kennedy's followers—have you fallen in love with a Jewess?'

With that, Edith left. And as she ran down the main corridor, looking for Raine, her face burnt hotter than on the day she had watched the 'Hindenburg' explode. She hated mention of her race and was horrified at the thought of Stan Bialik wanting her when all she craved was the verbal stimulation of the Negro who awaited her tonight. In the distance Raine marched as Edith walked and when the two were side by side they looked identical in silhouette.

Burt came out for fresh air and chuckled as he registered the two figures.

Was it such a crazy thought that a kid from South Philly might be able to convince a Nazi to turn over

29

the most precious film on American soil on the
promise of an ice-cream soda?

6

In Britain, Friedrich Kranz was wishing he had
never set foot in the village of Hunstanton.
Looking at his splendid frame in the full-length
mirror of a tiny Norwich bedsit, he wondered if it
was the new climate that had made him forget
sixteen years of marriage. Crawling naked into the
damp-smelling cot, guilt made him remember his
children, but no force could stop him from the
irrational urgings that had invaded his body since
his visit to the little hut. He was the great-grandson
of a small-time merchant and was carrying on the
family tradition of assimilating: in this case he
represented the newest generation of German
Jewry successfully engaging in commerce, keeping
its ancient rituals as quiet as possible and having a
Christmas tree each December.

Kranz took after his mother, a superb musician
who saw notation as a mathematical equation.
Friedrich was dark and perfectly proportioned like
her, but he had transposed his mother's talent into
the equations necessary to build aeroplanes. Like
his father and grandfather, he progressed in a
Christian world and, in their tradition, seemed to
antagonize a large proportion of his workers, who
resented his facility with numbers, words, historical
information, puzzles, music and literature.

Lying now in his English sanctuary, he winced
remembering his father's horror at the attitude of

one particular worker named Schicklgruber. A young designer fresh out of prison, he had boasted that all progress would be boosted by his Plan for the Working Man scenario involving factories filled with blond-haired boys and girls. Kranz Senior had roared at the words and had made a remark about Jesus having been thought blond in some ancient accounts. Schicklgruber and the Working Man had returned his hilarity with venomous glares, leaving him to laugh alone.

Though enormously popular with the men, Schicklgruber had left the factory soon afterwards. When Kranz Senior was kicked to death some years later by the same men, his last thought was of the blonde women building aeroplanes for Hitler. Inasmuch as the Uniforms dismembered him before he was actually dead, Kranz Senior had a last bizarre vision of those female blondes shaping bent propellers, because they were all really Jews. They could not be checked for circumcision, after all, but they could send the uncircumcized to their deaths in faulty aircraft . . .

Kranz Senior smiled, before he stopped breathing . . .

Friedrich was ashamed that he could not stop thinking about Valerie when he should have been worrying that his mother, wife, son and two daughters were also being kicked by Nazi aeroplane factory workers. He had wanted to have Valerie in the hut—to drive his molten essence into her in a hot-walled tunnel from which she could never exit. Now he dreaded having to return and endure the omnipresent Shirley. Kranz wanted the MP's daughter and bristled at the possibility that even the English might regard his ilk as

31

the depraved animal against whom German womanhood was now being warned daily. His first priority was to set up in business in this supposedly friendly country and to find a way of rescuing his family.

Feeling his loins coming awake for the first time since Austrian politics had frozen them, a wall of dizziness had overtaken his thoughts. He switched off the cold lamp beside the stale mattress and hoped Valerie Cobb's nation had not warned her against his race.

Tomorrow he would make the first step towards including her in his plan. A letter from Tim Haydon MP had arrived at the bedsit that day but he had only glanced at its contents: what was his reason for coming to Britain? He tried to sleep, but could not. Outside, the pub crowd had dispersed and thick Norfolk accents were arguing about the correct route to Marks Tey.

Was it via Sudbury?

No, it's on the road past Blickling . . . That's nonsense—you have to go by way of Bures . . .

Their voices made him yearn for Valerie as if she were every English man and woman, and eventually the voices stopped and tomorrow arrived because Friedrich had not slept.

* * *

At the Air Ministry in London, argument and confusion reverberated in the office of the Director-General for Civil Aviation, Sir Francis Shelmerdine. 1937 was suffering an uncertain twilight and the foresight of those assembled reflected that of Winston Churchill: they were

32

fierce in their belief that war would thunder in, drowning out Chamberlain's bleatings.

Present were Lady Londonderry, dressed in turn-of-the-century layers, Captain Harold Balfour, looking well-connected, and the handsome Commander Gerard d'Erlanger. Top man at British Airways, d'Erlanger was pursuing his pet crusade:

'Women—women, all fifty of them, must be part of this operation. From what I gather, Valerie Cobb has ten close associates qualified to be squadron leaders.'

'Most of them can't drive a car, but have several hundred hours in the air.' Lady L was offering her usual roundabout support for the breathtaking man at her elbow.

Valerie Cobb entered the room noiselessly but all eyes turned. D'Erlanger gasped. He had not seen her for a year and was transfixed. Could none of the others present see it?

'It's what's known as a magnetic field.' Balfour touched d'Erlanger's arm. He knew. 'Magnets ruin concentration, Commander.'

Valerie made her way to the committee's enormous table and sat in the empty space meant for Shelmerdine. No-one objected. The men remained standing, and she smiled.

Lady Londonderry spoke:

'I was talking about the women pilots who can't drive on four wheels,' said her ladyship.

'Both activities are unladylike,' responded Valerie. A door opened, and she looked up to see Shelmerdine enter. She did not offer him his chair, and she continued:

'It follows that anything with a motor should be

33

handled with authority. For this reason, it has come to my attention that most of the instructors at flying clubs around Britain are women—handfuls of men have been trained by them. Obviously we are thought to command great authority.'

From anyone else it would have fallen flat. The committee in this instance was spellbound.

'The top brass cannot accept that females will be competent to fly aircraft.' Shelmerdine was not spellbound. As he watched this woman, whom he saw as manipulative beyond belief, he thought of the idiocy of her notion that women pilots in active service could fly bombers and huge transport planes. At this moment she seemed to have the other men in the room bewitched, and he decided to manipulate her in return. 'We must be overrun with good pilots—let the women make the airplanes, for God's sake.'

'You see the nation's females fading into the factories?' D'Erlanger was furious, having regained his powers of concentration.

'They won't fade, there will be enormous publicity—propaganda campaigns,' Shelmerdine replied.

Now Balfour was enraged:

'So we're marching them into a corner, are we not? The WAAF doesn't want a flying section. So—no place for Miss Cobb's contingent, and you die happy seeing them on a factory poster.'

'Nonsense, Harold—these flying girls are adaptable.'

'Like dogs?' snapped Valerie.

'It was meant as a compliment.' Shelmerdine and Valerie stared at each other for a moment.

D'Erlanger spoke:

'An endless supply of pilots does not exist, and I can confirm that the halls of British Airways are nearly empty. War dreams have begun to dawn on my men and they are disappearing in droves.'

'I will concede, Gerard, that membership of a Civil Air Guard should be open to anyone between eighteen and fifty, of either gender, who can pass the private pilot's A-licence test.'

'Of either sex, did you say, Sir Francis?' asked Lady Londonderry, smiling.

'Don't be vulgar,' murmured Valerie.

'I do beg everyone's pardon. If our gender is to be allowed into CAG, then I move that Miss Cobb have her way. There is no reason why her group of women should not have equal rights, straight down the line, with the RAF.'

D'Erlanger leaned forward in his seat.

'Absolutely! I second Her Ladyship's motion. As I have said, an endless supply of pilots does not exist. We all need these women—God knows how many there are—to transport fifty different types of aircraft.'

'Where does Sir Henry Cobb fit into all this?' Shelmerdine boomed.

Valerie stood, her superb figure dominating the room. 'My father is separate and apart from me, my business and my own personal war effort. As a matter of fact, he hasn't a clue where I am today.'

'How many do you think you could provide?' D'Erlanger asked, as his eyes bored into Valerie.

'There are ten with A, B, C and D licences, including Shirley and myself.'

'How extraordinary,' said Lady Londonderry. 'They would be squadron leaders if only they could change their gender.'

Shelmerdine rose, face-to-face with Valerie Cobb:

'One is astonished to think that a girl of your capabilities can persist in wasting her time, and the time of others, busking, as it were, for women's rights.'

Valerie looked around the table, knew she had the female and all males but one in her pocket, nodded in silence to the Director General for Civil Aviation, and left.

Lady Londonderry was the first to speak:

'Valerie is not one to ask her father for permission, Francis, to lobby the government. I expect she will go to Churchill next, and then the King.'

D'Erlanger, still standing, went to the door, turned for a moment to the others and was gone.

'That woman has overwhelmed him.' Shelmerdine sank into his chair and wondered why that force known as sex, which as a gentleman he could speak of only as gender, crept into a man's life and complicated every situation. His passionless nation would have to go to war. He did not like that girl. She engendered passion.

7

Beautiful Polish ladies in boiler suits were pouring out of transport planes in Bucharest, and the refugees they had carried stopped momentarily to see if these were visions. Hana Bukova, the most striking of the Polish Women's Air Corps, jumped from the wing to the ground, splashing her immaculate coverall with Romanian mud. Though starving and exhausted, the men amongst the party she had rescued looked at her with longing then turned to follow their shouting wives.

In the next aeroplane along, Hana's mother Vera was still in the cockpit, reading a sheaf of papers. A tall, blonde and long-limbed girl, Hana clambered on to the wing and motioned to the small stocky woman to whom she bore not the slightest resemblance. 'They want us in and out quickly,' she said.

Vera looked up and grinned. 'We have an advantage—if we were men, they would shoot us. I'm staying here for the time being.'

Hana had followed in her mother's footsteps from the day she had first set eyes upon a gleaming Fokker DVII in their backyard in Bialystok. Somehow the First World War aircraft had ended up in the county of Grodno and had made its way to her village. All the local boys had climbed all over the magnificent machine, and she had joined the crowd. Her mother was acting as test pilot and the other women in the neighbourhood clucked in admiration. Many young Poles had taken up flying, and it was as common for girls to do heavy factory work as to commandeer a machine that had wings.

Hana's father Libor was influential in the government, administering the Ghetto in which the Jews of Bialystok were allowed to dwell. Every so often, of an afternoon when she had completed a flying lesson, Hana would go with her father on inspection, and she would catch a quick glance of one of the oddities who lived behind the ghetto walls. She had never met a Jew but had heard only terrible things about them, and thought of them as Christ-killers better contained, for the time being, behind those gates.

When Schicklgruber had begun his crusade, the Bukovas had become keenly interested. If large numbers of people were to be transported, large aircraft would be needed, and pilots could have guaranteed work. If war came, things would be even better. Rumour abounded that Chancellor Hitler was to rid Europe of Jews, but that the Reich's intention was to depend on cattle trains to deport Hana's beasts, as she had been wont to call them.

It was not until early 1937 that Hana Bukova met her first beast in the flesh. He was a teenager, a few years her junior, and wildly interested in flying. His father manufactured aircraft in Austria and, to her amazement, the boy was fluent in Polish, Russian and German. He had come to Poland with his father, a well dressed gentleman, to see if his grandmother and cousins would wish to go to England. On arrival in the town, the gentleman was horrified to discover that his relatives had been removed to this filthy slum.

Young Benno kept company with Hana while their fathers exchanged official papers. The two innocents would play maddening word games, quizzing each other in one language and demanding an answer in another. They would sit out on the pavement as a Polish guard looked on with a glazed expression. Hana had begun to notice how alert her playmate seemed in comparison with the guard—who was supposed to be keeper of ten thousand beasts.

When his father emerged from the ghetto visit,

looking much older than when he had entered, it was time for Benno to go, and Libor Buk was kind enough to give the boy a barley sugar sweet in the shape of a reindeer. Everything was polite and friendly, belying the fact that none of these people would ever have had to meet had Christian Poland not been taught for generations that the beasts drank the blood of Polish children at Passover.

Now it was 1937 and the Buk family had had the resourcefulness to think beyond those teachings and to join the small band of Poles dedicated to saving, not slaughtering, the enemies of their national faith. Hana was a highly qualified pilot and the others at her flying club looked on with envy as her lithe figure slithered in and out of aircraft and her thick blonde locks blew in the wind like her own personal banner. She had kept in touch with Benno and had discovered in their correspondence that his father was the famous Friedrich Kranz, Europe's most distinguished aviation entrepreneur.

'The Jews seem to get their fingers into everything!' Libor would exclaim good-naturedly, and Hana had recently adopted the habit of responding to such asides defensively. Benno's photograph, which she kept inside her logbook, was a rich sepia and was signed in the corner:

'Fischtal, Berlin.'

This fascinated Hana. What did the photographer look like? Set inside the deep tones of the picture, Benno's grim, bespectacled likeness seemed of another age, and she wondered if the photographer had been a wizened veteran whose lens had framed images of nineteenth-century wars.

'You will be expected to move on, madam,' grunted a Romanian soldier.

Hana looked up. 'My mother gives the orders. I have to wait.'

'Some of us don't like what you are doing. Why save Jews?'

'We're transporting personnel—their religions are not our concern.'

'Nonsense—every last one of them has a Yid star on his ID. Personally I'd rather fly dogs out of the country.'

Hana kept silent and smiled.

Her mother approached. 'You can't imagine what delights are in store for us, darling,' said Vera, putting her arm around her daughter's waist. 'Sixteen members of top industrialists' families, all smuggled out in a spectacular fashion, are earmarked for our section.'

'Do we know them?' Hana could think only of the bespectacled old man in the portrait of a sepia-toned child.

'Not likely. Most of them are women—they'll all be in fur coats, I expect.'

Hana turned angrily on her mother, noticing that the soldier was not far away from the sound of their conversation, and was laughing.

'You and Father are astounding hypocrites. What about those vulgar women in Warsaw with fur coats for display at Mass?'

'You know damn well it is a common observation that Jewish women love furs, and gold fillings.'

'Their money is shit. I spit on them.' The Romanian warrior had joined in. 'Jewish whores fill up their mouths with gold from their pimps.'

'And how do you know?' Vera looked up at his

40

hulking presence.

He blushed. 'I just know.'

Vera turned to Hana. 'What did I tell you about common knowledge?'

They walked briskly, leaving the soldier smoking and frowning by a dead tree. He wondered about the nature of the relationship between this strange pair of lady pilots. Was the ugly one really her mother?

'What will happen to Benno?' asked Hana.

'That's what we have in our Manifest,' Vera replied. 'One frightened Jewish lady and her three children, amongst others. Your Benno is in the group. This entire operation is being paid for by Kranz, who seems to have turned up in England. Jews travel fast—more common knowledge.'

'I'll collect them. Make it my job.' Hana was shaking with anxiety, and her mother could only smile.

'Last but not least in the unwritten section of our Rulebook is the order never to mix emotion with a mission. You can go on to Warsaw to collect Josef Ratusz—that should give you a thrill. I will take the Jews.'

'Mother, I don't give a damn about Ratusz.'

'Poland's greatest ace? He's better mileage than a bunch of these pathetic Hebrews. And he's single.'

'You fetch Ratusz, Mother, and I'll take your manifest.'

Nearby, the soldier listened.

'I'll bring you the boy Benno on a silver platter. Two Bukovas on a pilot allocation have to obey orders.'

Mother and daughter hugged, and a tear fell

41

down Hana's flushed cheek. It landed on Vera's ample bosom and made a dark stain on her beige flying suit. They looked anxiously at each other, like two fighter pilots about to venture into doom.

Hana handed the papers back and climbed somewhat reluctantly into the cockpit of the large transport aircraft. It looked as if it would never leave the ground, as she taxied at a snail's pace away from the crowd of refugees, now sitting on their bags around the field. She reached the end of the dirt path that served as a runway and as a patch of her blonde hair glistened for an instant through the battered window, her mother and the Romanian soldier watched her while the cumbersome machine lifted into the sky. Neither spoke another word, and, as they walked in opposite directions, Vera to her aircraft and the soldier to his hut, each wondered when next they would see that beautiful girl causing the terrible rumbling above them.

8

Running up and down the corridors of the Houses of Parliament were endless streams of highly-strung men and women who seemed to know tomorrow's history soon enough to be worried. They carried messages, books, newspapers and giant piles of white paper, their feet seemingly noiseless against the polished floors. Clicking sounds disturbed their organized silence as Friedrich Kranz moved up the middle of one large corridor, his heels breaking the hush of soft

English soles. He winced as heads turned, glaring. Were civil servants fitted out with special shoes? he pondered.

He found the door for which he had been searching and announced himself to a secretary with perfect posture, who ticked his name on an otherwise empty tablet. Scrutinized by the soulless female, Kranz took a seat in the cold waiting room of Tim Haydon MP. Elegant furnishings and neatly decorated walls surrounding the Austrian did not allay the brittle atmosphere, the lone visitor keeping his coat buttoned against the damp frigidity of the room. He noticed that Haydon's secretary, in lightweight blouse and skirt, seemed oblivious to the cold, her cheeks flushed by what Kranz called 'British passion mist', the permanent fog that enveloped the Isles. He saw these mists as the cumulative vapours released by bodies constrained by their national culture from expressing passion. Those vapours had to go somewhere, and like young robin-redbreasts experimenting with newly discovered perches, passion mist settled on soft faces. She probably thought the same of Teutons, Kranz theorized, looking at her feet . . . Did this woman have soft soles as well?

Now she was looking at him, sharply. 'Do you wish to hang your coat?' she asked.

'No. If you don't mind, I am feeling rather chilled.' Their eyes met, and he felt deep-frozen. 'Or would you rather have *me* hanged?'

'I beg your pardon?' She placed her hand by her neck and fingered her neat and very old collar. Passion mist had evaporated.

'Is that a blouse handed down from generation to

generation?' Kranz enquired, fascinated by her mannerism.

'Surely that is none of your concern.' Her hands had returned to a resting position.

'Do you have a name?'

'That bears no relevance to your visit, sir, which I will remind you is by the grace of the Honourable Gentleman.'

'You forgot to say "from Suffolk North", my dear,' quipped Kranz.

'Lady Truman. And I am not your dear.'

'Do you have a first name?'

'In this country we refer to it as a Chris-tee-un name.'

'So what if someone is a Muslim? What would you call the Grand Mufti?'

'I beg your pardon?' She observed him carefully and smiled, as if humouring a maniac. Lady Truman did this job to pass the days, otherwise serving society as the wife of a millionaire. It had been unheard of when she became the first woman in her county to take a town job, but if staying healthy in mind meant offending her matronly equals she would enjoy the luxury of offending. Her tall, thin frame was capped by a tight bun of brown hair, and her crystal-blue eyes bordered on the cruel. Taking in Friedrich Kranz, undoubtedly her most unusual guest this year, she left her chair and walked gingerly to the other side of the waiting room, then disappeared into a small passageway.

Kranz noticed that he felt warmer now he was alone.

'Mr Kranz?' She was standing over him and as Haydon opened the door of his inner office at the end of the passageway, another cold blast of air swept by. Kranz journeyed down to the doors, wrapping the coat around himself more snugly. Haydon ushered the Austrian in, but did not offer a handshake.

'Has the approach of war stopped the supply of coffee, sir?' asked Kranz.

Haydon looked at him with contempt. 'Genista?' he shouted.

Lady Truman appeared.

Genista! thought Kranz. What a wonderful name for a Christian—

'White or black?'

'White, please, Genista,' Friedrich crooned, bringing another blast of Arctic air into the room. 'And nice and hot.'

Haydon regretted having to spend time with this man. 'Suffolk—in fact East Anglia, Kranz—could be called the sleeping cradle of England. People have basic loyalties and old traditions—news travels fast if anything unusual happens. You were seen visiting Miss Cobb's air-joyride service, and partaking of her hospitality. Local farmers began to talk. This lady, whatever one may think of her lifestyle, is part of a splendid county family, and one suspects you are seeking a marriage of convenience.'

'That is ridiculous—I am already married.' Kranz found himself distracted by Haydon's comprehensively bitten-down fingernails.

'It has been known. Foreign nationals—Levantines—coming to this country, bewitching wealthy young women and laying claim to their estates, once married. Passing themselves off.'

'What is this expression—passing off?' Kranz knew what it meant.

45

'Men masquerade as eligible bachelors but inevitably sport wives and masses of children back home.' Haydon reached for a box of Havanas.

'You had better cherish those—war will bring rationing,' remarked Kranz.

'Your sort of industrialist could find crates of Havanas even when the Boches are beating down the doors,' Haydon said, clipping the enormous cigar and searching for his lighter. Lady Truman had arrived with the coffee cups.

'Genista, where is my lighter? I seem to have lost it.' Both looked at Kranz.

Haydon turned to his secretary. 'You know how much it means to me. Where could I have put it?'

Kranz rose to his full height and for a moment fear struck the two passion-misted faces. What might the foreigner do next?

'There it is,' Kranz said, leaning over the desk and reaching into the cigar box. He held up the exquisite lighter and one of the Havanas. '*Finders keepers* is the expression, I believe.'

'I should say not!' Lady Truman exclaimed, snatching the lighter.

Kranz's hand was held high, and he still gripped the cigar. 'You British are obsessed with heirlooms and animals. May I keep the Cuban?' he asked Haydon.

Haydon gestured disdainfully, and as his guest went back to the antique chair Lady Truman left.

'That woman astonishes me,' the MP remarked. 'Quite happy to make coffee and type, she goes home to one of the most powerful men in this nation and organizes hunt balls.'

Both men peered at each other. Then the MP examined his minimal fingernails.

46

'You wish to stay in this country and become established as an aircraft manufacturer in Norfolk?' Haydon continued, lighting up and swiftly placing his treasured lighter out of sight.

'It would give work to hundreds of men and women.' Kranz put the cold cigar into his pocket.

'Why Norfolk? Why not Kent or Surrey, Kranz?'

'These are nice people, in East Anglia—very much like home.'

Haydon puffed, smirking. 'Regretfully, I doubt your reasoning.'

Kranz seemed unmoved. 'In a short space of time special friendships have been made, and they happen to be in Norfolk. You should know, having been eavesdropping like a common voyeur.'

'Valerie Cobb and Shirley Bryce have registered a formal complaint with my office about your frequent visits.'

'That is impossible!' Kranz could feel his own passion mist rising.

'Needless to say, Sir Henry is furious. In fact it was he who conveyed their grievance.'

'Naturally, Cobb is upset.'

'Why, Kranz?'

'Could you possibly call me Dr. Kranz?'

'Since when are you a doctor, Kranz?'

'That is what I mean—you make me into a schoolboy you might wish to cane.' Thoughts of Valerie were coming fast, and he could feel his loins raging.

Haydon's colour was fading. 'My summation of your case, Kranz, is that you are free to seek venture finance from one of the London Merchant Houses—they are all run by your brethren, so you will feel at home—but there are absolutely no plots

47

of land in the whole of East Anglia, should you raise that capital. People like yourself are allowed to remain in this country by the grace of His Majesty's government. But, with war looming, German and Austrian nationals may be interned. Please do not say you have not been warned. By the way, do you hear from your family?'

'My intention is to send for them.'

'Good God, man—is there no end to your audacity? What makes you think this country is going to continue accepting refugees?'

'We are not refugees. And how did you know I was Jewish?'

'Instinct. It comes from dealing with refugees.'

'We are *not* refugees!' shouted Kranz.

'Bloody Einstein was! Good riddance, too, I say—he's a madman, if you ask me. Do you know, Kranz, we English took in Marx, and now Freud too. Your tribe does produce some troublemakers.'

'Here sits another Goebbels.'

'Who the devil is Goebbels—that poet?'

'Goethe, I think you mean,' murmured Kranz. 'In any case, Mr Haydon, please be assured that any Austrian businessman who brings his family to England will not become a burden to the State.' *Why am I grovelling so?* Kranz thought to himself.

Haydon stubbed out his cigar and remained seated, satisfied that he had rattled another imperfect immigrant. He loved his job. 'You had better get yourself down to the City, my man,' he said, as Kranz seemed to disappear inside his obscenely expensive coat. *Thank God*, thought the MP for Suffolk North, *that no such man would ever be allowed membership of my club . . .*

Friedrich had departed, the rush of air causing

48

Lady Truman's neatly piled documents to make a noisy whirlwind. She was furious.

Out on the pavement Friedrich regurgitated her coffee into the gutter, and did not notice Tim Haydon leaving the building, and passing behind him—laughing.

9

New York City did not appeal to Raine Fischtal, and after the Hindenburg Disaster she had decided to make Philadelphia her base. There was an excellent assortment of film labs and photographic studios in this seventeenth-century town. Indeed, Europe's greatest female cinematographer had begun to marvel at the architecture engendered by its Germanic founders. She had taken the 23 trolley from 10th and Bigler to Germantown, and had found the houses of which Goering had spoken so fondly one evening when they had sat together in a box at Dresden. He intended establishing a home in this part of America and had fallen in love with the images of Philadelphia. It had been the seat of government of the nation once before—was there any reason why it could not be the North American seat of the thousand-year Reich?

In her small hotel room overlooking the Delaware River at the very spot on which William Penn had landed, she leaned against the old-fashioned window and contemplated the cobblestones below. Had some ancestor of hers walked here? She had been told by her grandmother that an entire branch of the family had sailed here right in the thick of the Continental Congress. Goering had reminded her that every man in his village could boast of an enterprising Yank descended from an uncle's seed. What could people like Edith Allam possibly have in common with such good stock? How could Roosevelt allow people with questionable blood lines to hold powerful positions in post-Depression recovery programs?

Thankfully it was an unwritten credo in the American banking system that only Anglo-Saxons must be hired. Indeed, on a visit to a city-centre money exchange she had been pleased by the personnel, who would have looked equally at home in a cheerful Bavarian banking hall.

She hugged the canister of film close to her, feeling its cold penetrating the warmth of her woollen pullover. Her hands were unbearably tender, but she had made a vow not to let another American doctor near her—why had so many Jews been allowed to practise in Philadelphia? There should be quotas here, as were now being instituted in Berlin and Vienna. Indeed, her father might still be alive today had Mother not been forced to use one of them on Christmas Day a year ago. People always complimented the Jews who would come out to do jobs on the holy days so their Christian colleagues could observe the festival and have a rest. She was quite sure this pig of a doctor had wrongly diagnosed her father with malicious intent—had there been no next of kin he would most likely have drained his blood for use at some unspeakable ritual.

One thing she and Edith Allam had in common

was their want of good looks. Both lacked shape and their faces betrayed the laws of symmetry. She had to confess that her features smacked as much of ancient rapes as did Edith's, and she had a sudden urge to meet the girl once more before departing for the Fatherland. What was the name of that cafe? Heimat? It couldn't be—she probably lived in a ghetto and they had their own food, like the tribes in Warsaw for whom even a Christian chicken was not good enough. Nevertheless she was intrigued to discover the eating place of a typical American photographer, and, locking her canister away in her box-like suitcase, she clenched her teeth against her increasing pain and set out across the cobbles of Head House Square, looking up to admire the relics of the slave market.

*   *   *

Downtown Philadelphia had become dark earlier than usual because of an eerie yellow cloud-cover. Some said it was the souls from the 'Hindenburg' floating over on their way back to German heaven. Walking up Broad Street, Edith thought of the German vision of hell she had witnessed on Raine's footage, and hoped Errol Carnaby would be in a mood to listen to her narrative.

She walked into Fidler's Automat and found her three friends waiting at a front booth for what they always referred to as her 'entrance'. Tonight she did not disappoint them, her face still red from the incongruously combined thoughts of Raine Fischtal and Stan Bialik. Amid the din of a busy city-centre soda fountain, she could hear Errol spouting Blake and explaining to a rapt audience

51

his current obsession, the four Zoas. As she approached through a maze of self-service trays carried by what seemed an endless stream of businessmen in hats, Edith could hear the Negro intoning:

'Let Man's Delight be Love, but Woman's Delight be Pride.'

She put her hand on Errol's shoulder. 'Did you tell them I've met that real Nazi again—the one from Lakehurst?' she murmured.

'In Eden our loves were the same; here they are opposite.' Errol had not heard her, but Molly Santarello had.

'Don't talk about Nazis right now,' murmured the Italian beauty, whose fair hair and light eyes belied a temperament derived from the heat of Calabria.

Edith noticed that the three faces were fearful.

'I'll get you a chocolate soda.' Kelvin Bray went to the counter before Edith could say no. She was hungry and wanted food, not drink. Molly moved along the seat to make room, and she sat, facing Errol.

'That German film-maker is a legend in her own country. She wouldn't let Burt buy her canister.'

'Do you want something to eat?' asked Errol. He shouted to Kelvin, still standing at the counter. The soda-jerk winced at the Negro's voice.

'All my savings are going to go into my flight to Germany.'

Her companions were fearful yet again.

'Are you nuts, Allam?' snapped Errol. 'It's a jungle over there.'

'You can't get chocolate sodas, for one,' said Kelvin, slamming on to the table the heavy glass

52

foaming with Seltzer.

Molly had remained quiet throughout, letting her thoughts wander to her parents' town in Calabria, where Mussolini was making such an impression. What was it that made her American when she thought and when she dreamed? Their home town was like a primitive burial ground, where people were already dead as they began to grow up. Here, there was life.

'If you go to Germany you can't leave until Molly gets her serenade—the Italian bridegroom-to-be sings to his fiancée,' Errol said, reminding her of the primitive rituals connected somehow with life. She turned to Edith:

'Will you come?'

'Do they let outsiders into Catholic weddings?'

'Of course!' she laughed, wishing Edith could be a member of the burial-ground race.

'Raine Fischtal might come here tonight. I told her we would love her to join our crowd.'

Errol and Kelvin exchanged looks.

'She would never stoop so low,' said Errol. 'Besides, she probably carries poison pellets to put into Yankee pop.'

'Get back to Orc, Errol,' crooned Kelvin, and at that moment Raine Fischtal appeared at the door of Fidler's, Philadelphia's only kosher Automat.

*   *   *

Having wandered the streets of this colonial city, Raine had asked herself if it could be possible to like another woman who was earmarked for annihilation. She had made up her mind she would have to acknowledge Edith's courage in following her and wanting to pursue the matter of the canister. Now she was here at the Automat, and without the film and just her burnt hands she felt better able to talk to the strange world around her.

'First Orc was born, then the shadowy female; then all Los's family. At last Enitharmon brought forth Satan. Refusing form in vain!' the coloured man declaimed.

Raine regarded him blankly.

'This is Fräulein Fischtal, everybody,' said a hushed Edith. 'You've already met Errol—in the dark.'

There was laughter as Raine regarded the one Negro face.

'Do I detect a slight contempt emanating from this otherwise lovely lady?' Errol asked, motioning with a flourish for Raine to sit. She squeezed in next to Molly, who was staring at her bandaged hands.

'Did you do that while cooking?'

'Cook? Cook? Why is everyone always talking about cooking in this country?' Raine asked, looking around at the variety of faces.

'Hang around a bunch of greenhorns and you'll get all the recipes!' exclaimed Kelvin, reaching across to dump Edith's dinner of potato latkes on to the table.

'Speak for yourself, sheeny Irish,' grinned Molly. She looked at Raine intently. 'What do you eat for dinner where you come from?'

'I spend most of my time travelling. In hotels it is all the same, wherever you are in the world.'

The table had fallen silent. Edith poured sugar from the metal-spouted jar and pushed it around her plate of latkes.

54

'Raine hurt her hands at Lakehurst. She was very brave, staying there while everybody else ran away. She has some interesting film. We watched it at the studio today.'

Kelvin was mesmerized. 'All this travelling . . . have you met Lindbergh?'

'Amy Johnson, Valerie Cobb, Stella Teague, I know all the women fliers. They come to Germany and we all meet at the clubs. My job is to photograph good relations between the Reich and Great Britain. We are one people, you know. Hitler has said so.'

'British pilots go to Germany?' wondered Errol.

'Why not? As I say, we are one people, the British and the Germans. There are grand meets every six months, when the best of the English girls fly about alongside our top women—Anke Reitsch comes when she can. We had some men along this year—Jim Mollison, and an American, Gordon Selfridge.'

'But what about Lindbergh?' asked Kelvin.

'He's probably a Nazi spy,' said Errol.

Edith kept silent, smiling to herself.

Raine was furious:

'You should be proud of him—he is one rare example of an American not handicapped by his emotions.'

'Exactly,' snapped Errol. 'All the nigger, wop and greenhorn unworthies are to be eliminated to make room for replacement babies.'

'What's wrong with Lindbergh?' whined Kelvin.

'Dad says he's German American Bund,' murmured Molly.

Edith intervened. 'Come on over to my house now,' she said, grasping Raine's arm and dropping a dime on to the table. Errol rose, placing his hand at her elbow. Raine moved away, as if instantly repelled.

'I'll walk you back,' murmured Errol, and he did.

Arriving at the handsome semi-detached house, Raine was astonished to discover that Edith was allowing this man to enter.

'All folks here have gone to Atlantic City, leaving eldest daughter to her photography, her flying lessons and her coloured man,' said Errol.

'He means my parents,' Edith said, smiling at her guest. 'Do you want something to eat?'

'Again? You have just been to eat,' mused Raine, smiling back. 'Do you keep beer?'

'Not only do they keep it, they have a brewery downstairs in the cellar,' joked Errol, motioning with his long, bony hands.

They sat down in the spotless living room, and Raine took in the expensively framed drawings round the walls. She thought of recent moves in Germany to confiscate Jewish property and did some quick calculations on the basis of America's vast acreage. There had even been jokes about future canvases being made from kosher epidermis. Her face tensed as she disturbed herself with that inner paradox: how could she feel tenderness toward a potential lampshade?

Errol was speaking:

'Prohibition never besmirched this house.'

'My father can't live without his schnapps, or his beer,' explained Edith. 'He dabbled in bootleg stuff, but Mom made him give it up.'

'They bought her a piano with the proceeds,' added Errol, and Raine resumed her calculation.

'He never sold the junk, for Christ's sake,'

56

snapped Edith. 'You know perfectly well we needed wine for Seders, and the crooks who brought it charged us ten times normal. Most of them were haters.'

'Haters?' asked Raine.

Edith looked back at her sharply, on her way to the kitchen. 'Basically, the same sort of people who won't let Marion Anderson sing for the Daughters of the American Revolution.' A moment later Edith returned from the kitchen with a bottle of beer and three glasses. 'Are you going to let us have your film?'

But Raine had been distracted:

'Why three glasses?' she asked.

'Oh, you can have most of the bottle—Errol and I will have a sip each.'

'In Germany one person has several,' murmured Raine.

'Films?' Errol grinned.

'Beers, she means,' said Edith. 'Don't you realize we'd pay any amount of money Hitler wants, just to keep that footage? It's great stuff.'

Errol looked at her curiously.

'Money means nothing to us,' Raine asserted. 'Besides, you would twist it around to look ugly and distribute it to schools.'

'What a wonderful idea!' said Errol, pouring the beer into the bottom of the glass, the golden liquid looking like a jigger of whisky.

'It has big propaganda value,' said Edith. 'People would be fascinated and if it got nationwide distribution you could afford a new camera.'

'My equipment belongs to the Reich, my dear. Fly me back to Germany, and we can talk further. In fact, when we get there you can see my studio and perhaps I will make you a copy to take back with you. Frankly I can't believe you can fly, any more than I can believe you can take pictures.'

'Why not?' Edith's throat had gone dry. 'I'd want to meet Anke Reitsch when we get there. What about those other fliers you mentioned?'

'Valerie Cobb and Stella Teague have been avoiding us recently. Anyway, English pilots have inferior capabilities.'

'What about an immigrant's daughter?' asked Errol. 'You'd really trust an enemy of the Reich to do a superwoman's job?'

Raine stood face to face with Edith and her words shot out like pellets.

'I am interested to see you do all the things you say come as second nature. That day at Lakehurst, your boasting went hand-in-hand with our preconceived notions about American racial types.'

'Yeah, well, at least she emerged with her hands intact, honey,' crooned Errol.

'I'd love to do it, Raine, whatever the cost,' Edith said, reaching over to the German and touching her arm before rage had time to surface.

'He doesn't believe me?'

'It's a figure of speech. When do you want to leave?'

Raine rose, having downed the beer.

'I need to get back tomorrow, and I would like to go first thing in the morning. There will be no cost.'

Errol was standing, and the German turned her back on him.

'Tomorrow—Christ,' whispered Edith. She walked to the front door, wondering how many other girls her age were making such absurd rendezvous at this time of night in some corner of the new world.

'I would have assumed your government did all your travel arrangements,' Errol said, still standing in the middle of the living room. 'It's either a great honour for Edith, or this is some kind of crazy trick.'

'You can torment yourself about honour and tricks until she returns.' Raine turned back to Edith. 'At the Philadelphia airfield there will be a small aircraft ready, waiting for you to take the controls. Please have your papers and your licence for inspection.'

'You're the one our guys will want to inspect. Have you forgotten this is our country?' Errol was standing next to her now, his shoulders burning as he sweated.

Edith interceded:

'Fair is fair, Raine. When we leave here, you get inspected, and when we get to Germany I get inspected. Promise me I look Aryan enough to escape a real-life version of one of those beatings advertised in your film.'

'You will be my guest, a kind of untouchable. Thank you for letting me see how they live in this country.'

'Don't take us as examples. We're Shabbas goyim.' She opened the front door as an ice-cream man rattled by in his van, its bell jingling in rhythm with the trolley cobbles underneath.

'Like the German ones,' said Raine with a smile.

They stared at each other as the street outside fell silent. 'Tomorrow, as dawn breaks.' Raine left them.

At once Errol protested:

'You must be nuts, flying some Nazi bitch to Germany.'

'Burt Malone will think it's great. Imagine having to ferry somebody back home just for a piece of film. Tell my parents—tell everybody, will you? I might cross the Channel and join the RAF.'

'They don't take gals.'

'Yes, they do. I've heard Valerie Cobb is recruiting right now.'

'There will be a war and I will lose thee to fortune and men's eyes. I can't bear it.'

'Yes, you can, Errol. You have to—because we're not supposed to think certain thoughts about each other. Maybe our grandchildren will be allowed to think thoughts about each other, but we can't.'

There were no more ice-cream vans and the room went dark as Errol reached out and the one lamp left burning was extinguished.

*　　　*　　　*

Night had never brought excitement to her skin, and Edith knew it was necessary to have the forbidden experience before she undertook her first transatlantic flight. Her father had at one time been an elder in the synagogue and she had experienced the humiliation of orthodoxy, sitting in the upstairs section reserved for the women. Later he stopped serving, and her family stopped praying, and in their home the women prayed with the men. Seder had come and gone each year, and she had remembered the symbolic foods, not so much for the ritual but to provide answers for Christian questions. Girls from her street would be banished for dating gentiles, but now she had acquired a questioning Christian who had a fierce intelligence and was also coloured brown.

Darkness had descended on her house, and that was the way she wanted it to be, as they walked up the old wooden stairs together. One light from the Acme Market pierced the blackness and made red, white and blue streaks on the menorah atop the bookcase, as if its glow sought out the holy object for some future thief. Now Edith worried that her black poet might become the animal against whom women of all white faiths had been warned.

Why did Negroes worship Christ?

At the top of the stairs Errol put his hands on her buttocks and drew her to him, lifting her off the floor. She was transfixed as his hardness throbbed through the clothes that covered them in respectability and which now seemed capable of burning into hot vapour, leaving them on the brink of nakedness.

Now they were on her bed and they were naked, and in a split second she thought of her sister who had shared her bed all those years and then died. It was possible to die now. Errol took her breasts between his hands and squeezed them, his tongue devouring her cleavage as she grasped his head and let her hand slip down his back. He arose and she looked, and as his mouth met her navel she fought to rid her mind's eye of the grim shammas glaring up at her in the women's section of the synagogue. She would have to push the image away because her magnificent lover had begun to kiss her tongue of frenzy which had never before been unclothed. Now she could not control guilt or her heaving thighs or the pleading penis trying to make

61

its way inside her so relentlessly that it seemed to cry out through Errol's head, now raised above her.

Dogs barked in the night.

Errol shivered.

In the Deep South he would be dragged out into the dirt road and beaten until he bled for doing what he had just done, and if her neighbours knew why she had moaned all through this night she would be one of the living dead. Tomorrow she could leave and take her secret with her, and pray never to have to sit in the women's section again.

*   *   *

Philadelphia was seeing the birth of an oil refinery and on its perimeter was an airfield and its first terminal building with lettering on its side:

WELCOME TO PHILADELPHIA
THE CITY OF BROTHERLY LOVE

Edith had been ashamed and had wanted to burn the sheets in the morning. Not having slept, she had wild imaginings of her parents returning and calling in police, their canine corps instantly detecting a black man's scent. She folded one sheet and pushed it to the bottom of her duffel bag. He had gone, and had left her a handsome bit of writing:

O lest the world should task you to recite
What merit liv'd in me, that you should love,
After my death, dear love, forget me quite,
For you in me can nothing worthy prove.

Unless you would devise some virtuous lie,
To do more for mc than mine own desert,
And hang more praise upon deceasèd I
Than niggard truth would willingly impart:
O, lest your true love may seem false in this,
That you for love speak well of me untrue,
My name be buried where my body is,
And live no more to shame nor me nor you.
For I am sham'd by that which I bring forth,
And so should you, to love things nothing worth.

'Niggard truth, niggard truth,' she muttered, and placed the paper in her pocket. She was dressed now, and would walk in her clumsy shoes to the airfield, wishing her religion had provided accommodation for confession.

When she had reached the small brick building that served as air terminal, Edith made her way to the cable room, where she had become a well known and respected visitor. Her *Life* magazine cover had given her access to places Burt Malone envied, including free training by the US Signal Corps at the Customs House. Now she despatched two overseas telegrams, one to Valerie Cobb and one to Press-Shots UK, Malone's British affiliate. She knew that by the time America had breakfasted her news would be travelling, and she expected a well organized reception in London. Walking from the telegraph room to the tarmac, she could see her neatly dressed passengers.

Waiting for her, Raine looked ill at ease. Scrutinizing Edith, she commented:

'Something has happened to you during the night.'

'Raine, are you a witch?'

'You are different—make sure it doesn't affect our mission.'

They entered the aircraft and the man on duty wondered if these two would ever make it as far as the coast, let alone the main ocean crossing.

Inside the cabin, Edith was astonished to discover stowaways: two German males looked at her with disdain as they fiddled with wires.

'You will get to know Hartmut and Zuki as we cross the ocean,' Raine said calmly.

'Where the hell are the fuel tanks, then?'

'This is not a primitive American aeroplane—the tanks are elongated and are directly underneath our two men.'

'If they're elongated how can they deal with altitude and pressure?'

'Our designers have thought of everything,' she replied.

Her two men were strangely silent. Edith suspected they understood English but had remained reticent for a reason.

'I had better not ask too many questions or you will think I am a Yank spy.'

'Our countries are not at war, Edith.'

'Hopefully our Philly ground engineers have copied the layout of this baby, war or no war.'

'Hopefully we will be allies—if there is one.'

'If there is what, Raine?'

'A war.'

'Oh, I thought you meant we might be allies if there were a three-ring circus.' The sarcasm in Edith's voice was palpable.

'Valerie Cobb lives in a circus,' Raine observed, as Edith familiarized herself with the streamlined controls that resembled a Jules Verne prophecy.

Its twin engines purred into life at a touch of the American's hand.

As the little plane, laden with ingeniously injected fuel, made a surprising roar and veered out over a giant new oil drum, an ice-cream man prepared his van and thought he could see a gloved hand waving and a lipsticked mouth smiling from the cockpit soaring out towards Heimat.

10

For years Sir Henry Cobb had had to stave off rude remarks about his daughter's desire to cohabit with another girl. Until 1934 his life had been satisfactory because his wedded union had been perfect—during his wife's life he had often wondered if all men his age, let alone MPs his age, found sex the most exalting of human experiences. Now Julia was dead, and he had become irritable. Other men in the House sought satisfaction in peculiar ways amidst the fog and rain of London's back streets while his needs had disappeared with her ashes. In recent years he had become obsessed with the affairs of the most adventurous of his daughters, principally her business ventures.

From the time she was a small girl Valerie's interests had been far from the norm: her arms became strong in the pursuit of archery, and constant battles with her mother were the result. A sister, Annabel, had remained in the background, thinking her sibling mad and dangerous. When Valerie reached her first teenage year she had wanted to be blooded like the boys and it was no help when other Sirs began to find her figure enticing when she rode to hounds. As Lady Cobb became iller and frailer, so did her husband's cronies increase their imaginings of comfort with his attractive child.

At fourteen Valerie was excelling at lawn tennis and on one afternoon when she had beaten all the village she decided she would go to the most beautiful room in the house and stretch out on the ancient bed. She wondered, some years later, how many previous generations of village fathers had entered that room and ravished other people's girl and boy children on that same bed after the boys had been secretly playing with dolls and the girls had been secretly beating men at their own games.

After Sir Henry's chums had had their way with his daughter she shunned anything to do with tennis and the people in the village lamented the loss of a potential Helen Wills. Valerie decided she would take up a sport in which she would not be wearing enticing gear—a sport which took place out of the reach of her village and her father's hunt warriors . . . She had told her mother about her weird post-match encounters and shortly afterwards the wasted woman died. Valerie tried to recall some things she knew about her mother, but she could not. Having already seen a great deal of life at the age of seventeen she could recall far more about herself. Indeed, she regarded her mother's childbearing an irrelevant achievement if it meant having had to submit to the strange man on the ancient bed who at other times was Sir Henry Cobb MP.

Her father.

Time passed.

On this day in 1937 Cobb was reading a confidential government report on the Hindenburg Disaster and on the build-up of arms and aircraft in Hitler's territories. Valerie was due to arrive at any moment. Tightness in his chest was the symptom he suffered whenever he had to face his unruly daughter. Others saw her as charming and even stunning, but he could see her only as an imagined ex-lover of hordes of huntsmen, a fiendishly attractive goddess to whom he had also given the gift of life. When she was in his presence his imaginings drifted in and out and he wondered if it was any easier for fathers of adopted girls.

His other daughter, Annabel, had fallen in love with an Oxford undergraduate as obsessed with the Spanish conflict as his sister Angelique was with flying aeroplanes. Though Zack Florian's anti-fascist ravings had alarmed the elder Cobb, Annabel had seemed destined for a conventional life. When her man turned his rage into actuality and left for a rebel cell in Zumaya with his brother Paul, she had been inspired to do the same by following them a week after their departure. Unfortunately, she had gone about her mission so clumsily that no-one knew she had left England until one of the Cobbs had been missed at a dinner-party; furthermore the rampaging fiancé had had not an inkling of her unusual travel plans and was not expecting her arrival. He joined others in Spain and they embarked on the road to solidarity, while Annabel Cobb entered the same convulsing country and several hours later disappeared.

Sir Henry could never fathom his odd lot in life: scores of daughters across the British Isles fitted so comfortably into the landscape. Why not his own?

'Haydon has been snooping around again, Henry.' Valerie had arrived. Her libertarian habit of calling him by his Christian name vexed him to an unusual degree today, but he knew he needed to be alert in her energetic presence.

'You had a visitor from Germany. In East Anglia news travels faster than passion, my girl.'

'What's that supposed to mean?'

'Tim has always had his eye on you and Shirley, and now he's pinning his frustration on the presence of a German spy. He knows you're more interested in the spy than in him, so he has got a bit jealous. That's all.'

Valerie bit her lip, something she had done since childhood whenever there was talk of boys. Suddenly she felt a kind of protective affection for her father.

'The man Haydon saw, Dad, was not German. He is an Austrian. How did your dear fellow get his incorrect information?'

'You know jolly well he loves to watch you from afar, as the saying goes.' Sir Henry had become more subdued—it was an occasion on which he had been called Dad.

'I do wish he could get over his infatuation. Anyway, Shirley and I aren't having an unmentionable sort of relationship, if that is what he wants so much to see through a peephole.'

Sir Henry Cobb bristled. It was the one subject which made his orderly brain feel shipwrecked.

'In his position as MP for an adjoining constituency, he is concerned about aliens wanting to do business in this area. What did this Jew ask you?'

'I like to think of him as an Austrian industrialist, rather elegant, who wants to set up an aircraft firm in the county. Hopefully he will not wish to build on the fox's covert.'

'That's no joke, Val—Haydon Senior is Master of the Hounds.'

They both smiled and for a rare moment father and daughter shared the slight contempt that at times they held gleefully for their own class and for its ignorance of catastrophes pending.

'You should meet him, Dad. He needs support. The stories he tells from over there might worry you—if not Churchill.' She went to the old mahogany sideboard and poured herself a small sherry. 'Frankly, we think he's either mad or a prophet.'

'Jews have been known to manufacture such stories on odd occasions. When are you going to stop your nonsense and live like a human being?'

His harshness had started its usual journey into Valerie's gut. She drank.

He continued:

'Everything you two do is under scrutiny, my dear girl. I'm hearing about this Austrian chap because Haydon and his chums have nothing better to do than be voyeurs.'

Valerie downed the liquid in one gulp, with a premonition of worse to come.

'What galls me more than anything, however, is that you think you can go to the Air Ministry *behind my back.*'

For a moment Valerie faltered. Then she said:

'I went like any citizen. They have new information buzzing. I'm a pilot, Dad, for Christ's sake.' For a moment she felt like a baby, defending herself behind the bars of a crib. 'They want people of all ages to fly, and the Ministry is dropping the cost down to practically nothing.'

Furious, Cobb growled:

'Two shillings and sixpence from four pounds—I know that, and I knew it weeks ago.'

'Then why didn't you tell me?' she fumed. 'God, Dad, we work against each other and it's disgusting.' She wanted to smash the fifty-year old glass into the fireplace—but she didn't, knowing it would hurt him more deeply than any confrontation about honesty.

'I didn't tell you because I still have a bizarre dream about you settling into a normal life, even if there is a war. What the devil is wrong with Tim Haydon anyway?'

'He bites his nails.'

'I beg your pardon?'

'Dirty fingernails.'

'Who the devil cares about fingernails?'

'He *smells*, Henry.'

Cobb eyed his daughter oddly, as if she were a priceless yearling gone lame.

Valerie thought of Kranz, and of Shirley, and of a mission she knew she had to pursue—and she felt in the presence of death.

But the dead man was still talking:

'Wherever you go, Valerie, be it the tobacconist's or the Air Ministry, you represent *my name*.'

She looked at him sadly. How many times had she listened to the Tobacconist Speech?

'I represent your name,' she recited, 'therefore how humiliating for you to have a daughter who lives with a female ground engineer in a caravan by a circus tent, and who takes strange men on

70

joyrides.'

'You should stay away from the war business. Please.'

'Dad, if my motive was to go behind your back, it was to prove I can persuade without the mantle of male attire, or an MP's credentials.'

'Your credentials are my name!' he thundered.

'Credentials and names have not got women into the RAF,' she said. 'If they did we would have a Women's Air Force to match the one in Poland. There are a hundred ladies in this country who are qualified to be squadron leaders and the best they can aspire to are instructors' jobs in remote clubs, where the next war heroes will be produced. Who gets the glory?'

'There is nothing wrong with what you seek, Valerie. But you embarrass me by the manner in which it is pursued. Speaking of carrying a name,' he continued, quietly, 'Lord Truman's daughter has disappeared. Scarpered. Flown the coop.'

Valerie bowed her head. 'Tell me,' she murmured.

'Her fiancé was the other Florian boy. He went over to Spain with that anti-Franco mob and left her behind, but she disappeared from Truman's estate soon after. Police in the county haven't dug up one clue. Neither has Scotland Yard. You don't suppose she's run off to join him, do you?'

'Tim Haydon seems to know everyone's whereabouts. Why don't you ask him?'

'It occurred to me, Val, that Angelique Florian might know. You lady pilots have this sort of network of gossip.'

'We keep in touch, like men, if that is what you mean.' She knew he was thinking of her sister.

'Annabel could be there, too, and all we can do is hope that mad bunch are safe.'

Sir Henry's forehead had developed a film of perspiration and he had paled considerably since the beginning of their conversation.

'Please do what you can, my dear,' he said, smiling dimly. 'Truman is a good chap, and he backs your cause. He has the right ear of Churchill. Besides, it's good shooting his way.'

Valerie looked at him with pity and left, aching to see Friedrich Kranz with a physical urgency that cut her off from her father's ghostly presence.

Sir Henry Cobb MP watched her go, and marvelled at how ravishing a woman she was, and how little he could blame the other huntsmen for lusting after this child of his own flesh and blood.

11

Edith Allam had not been Errol Carnaby's first woman. She had, however, been his first pilot. Living in a dream for days after their lovemaking, he had agonized over her mission. It was absurd: could a girl of her minute size fly across the Atlantic at a moment's notice? Had he imagined the visitation by the German madwoman?

Once he had accepted the reality of Edith's tight, begging thighs piercing his last resources of control and making him explode over and over again on that poor suffering bed all through that night, he fought terror at the thought of her parents.

Earlier this day he had met the crowd, and Kelvin and Molly had shown him the newspaper

72

clippings about Edith's successful crossing. Mr and Mrs Allam would come back today, Molly had enthused, and Errol was plagued by images of German Shepherds sniffing him out. Ever since that night he had slept at the airfield, sneaking into the old hangar and bedding down on a giant storage silo. Perhaps, he had theorized, his metallic surroundings could not retain his scent . . . Kelvin had boasted about Edith to the soda jerk at Fidler's and her picture, goggles and all, was destined for the automat's bulletin board. What would destiny bring the rest of them? Errol tormented himself. He would greet the Allams upon their return.

Walking the interminable blocks to Florence Avenue, Errol had brief imaginings of Edith running out of her house and greeting him, and then the pair strolling to the corner for a soda at Weinberg's Drugstore. Now he hovered at the corner of 53rd Street and debated whether he should proceed or march the extra sixteen and take a trolley to nowhere at 69th Street Terminal.

'You lost, sonny?' A gargantuan policeman stood over him. He must be a freak, reflected Errol, whose own considerable size ordinarily intimidated most mortals.

'I was just about to get going, officer,' he replied, terrified for the ten thousandth time in his life. Might this cop have a dog in tow?

'You sure look like you're up to something.'

'No, sir,' Errol murmured. He wanted to recite his favourite Blake but could think only of loathsome spunk and of his penis being gripped in Alsatian gums.

'Where you headed, then?' The giant cop was

perspiring, and Errol could smell him. Had he not washed since his last fuck? This acrid odor offended the black man's nostrils, but his sensibilities did not count, not even in Pennsylvania.

Dare he recite Edith's address, instead of Blake? '5337 Florence.'

'Making a delivery or something?'

'My mother is their cleaning lady, and I take her home every night about this time.'

'I ain't seen you before, and this is my beat.'

You haven't seen me because you've been having a floozy from the taproom, thought Errol, noticing, on the policeman's badge, the name 'Malone'.

'We've got a car, sir, but tonight it's out of order,' he offered, wondering how many different flavours of Malone there are in the City of Brotherly Love. 'I work as a chauffeur and the boss lets me borrow it to pick Momma up.' Errol had kept calm until now, but as he saw the Allams arriving in the distance his heart raced.

'What's the matter, boy—seen a ghost?' Wiping his greasy brow with his shirtsleeve, the Philadelphia policeman grasped Errol's shoulder and with his other hand frisked the well dressed Negro. Did white men get some sort of obscene pleasure from touching a black erection?

'Funny place to keep a gun, boy,' the officer guffawed. 'You people are animals—always ready.'

'I assure you I'm going to that house over there. Walk with me.'

'Don't you fucking tell me what to do,' the still-sweating cop snarled. Errol could have predicted the reaction. For a moment they stared at each other, and the bursting urge inside his trousers

74

subsided as Errol noticed the policeman glancing at his watch. It was time for his own erection, and to the black man's immense relief the giant cop turned tail and headed for the taproom.

*   *   *

Julius and Kitty Allam were carrying luggage from their car when a large black hand offered help.

'Errol!' Kitty smiled broadly. He returned her warmth, taking a suitcase in each hand. 'Have you heard about Edith?'

'Yes, ma'am, I have.'

'We've saved all the newspapers,' Julius remarked, straightening his portly self and shutting the hood of the muddied automobile.

'If you don't mind my asking, weren't you shocked about what she did?' intoned Errol.

'Of course,' replied Julius, facing him. 'Whoever heard of a girl who takes pictures and flies aeroplanes? It was our luck to be blessed with a freak.'

'She was always a little bit crazy, and now all I can do is pray she gets back safely,' Kitty said, moving towards the front door.

Errol felt a certain terror overtaking him as Mrs Allam turned the key, and for a moment he hallucinated thousands of tiny brown babies crawling along the floor and disintegrating into lifeless skeletons. A dog barked, and he jumped.

'That'll be Manon,' Julius shouted. 'One of the German Shepherds next-door. Her brother is called Lescaut.'

Lights were being switched on and Errol stood in the middle of the room, staring at the piano.

'How was your trip, ma'am?' he asked, taking in Mrs Allam's splendidly full figure.

Julius had already made his way to the kitchen, the warm air of an Indian summer filtering through the screen door as it squealed open and snapped shut. On the back porch, the man of the house breathed deeply. Should he have left Kitty alone with a coloured man? Their voices were muffled by the heavy atmosphere.

'Our trip?' murmured Kitty, aware of the young man's energy. 'We argued.' She was tall, and her chestnut hair seemed a bottomless cradle for male yearnings. Errol let out a small cry, feeling Edith rippling through him in one split second. Their ecstasy still hung in the air, but here, now, was her mother . . .

'Let's have some lemonade,' Kitty said, removing her short jacket to reveal amply proportioned shoulders and a smooth, cool bosom seemingly unperturbed by the oppressive Philadelphia humidity.

Errol could feel perspiration dripping down his own chest. Oh, how he hated his inheritance. What a woman. With her freckled whiteness would come coolness and breasts that glowed in the night, their nipples God's one concession to nigger tint . . . again he was hallucinating.

'May I talk to you, Mrs Allam?' he asked, still standing in the middle of the floor. Nipples had replaced skeletons in his hallucination and now as the vision receded, they became the motionless fleurs-de-lys on the carpet.

'Have some lemonade, and we'll talk,' she replied, striding in the direction of the kitchen. He could hear the screen door creaking open once

76

more and the voices of the Allams mixed with a chorus of crickets. Moving to join them, Errol reached the kitchen and the dogs went into a rage. He was afraid to venture any further, retreating back into the living room. Surveying the tasteful art and the dainty nicknacks on dustless shelves, he decided to leave. Now he was at the door, and coolness brushed him.

'Don't go,' said Kitty. Her superb hands offered lemonade.

'You and Mr Allam must be very tired after your long journey.'

'Yes, well—we got tired, as I said, from arguing.' She motioned to him, and he sat.

'One would never know it. You seem a happy couple,' he commented.

'Didn't you have something to say to me? It was in your eyes—they call it a pregnant look, if I'm not mistaken.' Kitty took a seat opposite him.

In the distance dogs continued to bay.

'They sound like hyenas!' Errol exclaimed, smiling. His drink sweated on a small table and the moisture formed a pool around the bottom of the glass.

Kitty Allam leaned over, her cool chest hovering for an instant as she wiped the pool away.

'That crystal belonged to my grandmother. She smuggled it out after the pogroms.' Kitty looked carefully at the handsome coloured boy who was not listening, or perhaps did not understand. 'But why am I talking about pogroms? At a time like this! Let me tell you about our vacation—' She stopped dead, seeing Errol glaring at her.

'Mrs Allam, your daughter and I got awfully close before she went away.'

'In what way?'

Errol was perspiring again, and this time he could barely see through a veil of confusion and the onslaught of tears.

'What's the matter?' she demanded, tensing.

'Edith and I—we had a date, a real date, Mrs Allam.'

Her face had taken on the completeness of terror, circles of white discolouring her splendid cheeks.

Errol was transfixed, and wanted her to lash him. His hard manhood throbbed and he wanted to cry out again, but he could only weep.

'What have you done?' Julius asked in a monotone.

'I'm so sorry, I'm so sorry,' sobbed Errol.

'Did he steal something?'

Kitty could not help laughing at the absurdity: the idea of some petty theft, when in her eyes her daughter's cleanliness, like the Sabbath candlelight, had been stolen forever.

'He's been spending time with Edith,' she said, calmly.

'What kind of time?'

'We're nuts about each other.' Errol moved to the door, and when he turned around the two white parents were staring at him—as if an ancient Pharaoh had come to life out of a museum sarcophagus to enslave the Israelites once more.

'Wait,' said Kitty. 'Do you really care about Edith?' she asked Errol, moving towards him.

'I've died every day she's been gone.' He smiled. 'After all, to whom else can I recite my beloved Blake?'

'Let her stay in England, please God,' Julius

78

muttered to himself.

'I could have predicted you'd say that. She'll be back.' Errol grinned as he spoke and his gleaming, perfect teeth glowed. 'When she does return, none of us—not you, nor I, not the kids downtown—will know her.' He opened the door and, as if his scent had travelled instantly, the dogs awoke and their noise shook the air.

Errol Carnaby slithered down the front steps and into the night.

*   *   *

Kitty watched him strut away and leaned against the bricks of the New World they had made their home. Where would a boy like that live? she thought. Why did we know so little about him? If he were a white kid we'd have met his family, and known what his father did for a living. What kind of food did his mother feed him? Did Negroes sit down to a table like Jews, and gentiles, and Orientals?

'Imagine him coming here to announce such a thing—what chutzpah,' mumbled Julius, standing inside the doorway.

'Their men have different needs, you know,' she said, still staring straight ahead.

Dogs bayed as if on cue.

Kitty moved inside, pushing past her husband as if he were an unsavoury obstacle.

'That boy is refined.'

'You can't refine brown sugar.'

'Why not? Julius, our people are being troubled in Europe. Some people say a war is coming. And if Edith wants to change with the world, we can't stop her.'

Kitty gathered up her jacket and mounted the stairs. Fingering the light dust that had settled on the banister, she stood at the top landing and gazed into Edith's room. Somehow she knew the unthinkable had happened in there, because the room no longer spoke to her in a child's voice.

Young couples strolling down the corner of 53rd Street noticed the din of the dogs drowned out by a disturbance. A coloured boy was being throttled by a drunken cop. When a paddywagon came, just in time, it took the choking Negro youth away, leaving the giant Irish drunkard laughing in the street by the garish taproom light.

12

No sooner had Edith departed Philadelphia Airport than her mishandling of the unfamiliar German equipment began to take its toll on the aircraft. Unnerved by the presence of a glowering radio operator with the unlikely name of Zuki, and another male who looked like a throwback to the Niebelungen, she half-hoped the entire exercise would have to be cancelled: Raine sent back to Germany, with Gotterdämmerung restored to the pilot's seat where he belonged, and Edith on trial in her father's spiritual courtroom.

'Twilight of the Gods,' she murmured to herself as the engine spluttered and the three Germans showed not one ounce of concern. Inside she was panicking but the last thing she wanted was to reveal her terror. Heading due north, she decided to come down in Newfoundland. Knowing the trip was scheduled for a speed of 135 miles per hour, she could not allow her nerves to take over, pressing for a greater velocity. A faster flight would consume more gasoline per hour and could be dangerous. Humming along, and trying to keep to every regulation in the manual she had studied so feverishly before taking off, Edith wanted to reach her emergency destination as soon as the elements would allow.

'Twilight of the Gods,' she repeated.

Raine smiled at her pilot. Their voices were muffled and the air rushing past made conversation tedious, but German craftsmanship had reduced engine noise to a minimum. Edith was impressed, worrying that the Reich might have tricked her into this publicity stunt. She knew Zuki doubled as a secret service agent, a kind of protector for Raine, the film canister and the Reich. On arrival in the Fatherland, she would likely be taken into custody—so when would she ever get home?

Indeed, the whole exercise now seemed an absurd pantomime orchestrated by a regime as insular as the woman who now sat beside her. Fate's map of the world might even have the two men now breathing down her back then raping and killing their American aviatrix for fun, once back in Heimat.

Edith noticed the radio operator behind the pilot's cabin now deeply absorbed in his work. Did German technology extend so far as to allow Zuki to talk to some other country? Inconceivable!

'*Scheiss!*' Gotterdämmerung had spoken, and the lights had gone out.

'It looks like the main fuse,' Edith shouted in German. To her astonishment Raine calmly removed a replacement from the tool box and set to work with the men to remove the faulty one. Did the film-maker know more about flying than she had cared to admit? Edith turned to the small, misted window to her left and gasped at the sight. Heaven looked in at them and the American forced her fears to one side, allowing her soul to experience the exultation she always felt when in command of a flying machine surging through God's domain.

Silence descended on the tiny cabin as they ploughed through a cloud formation. Commerce would not have begun on the ground underneath, and Edith's mind drifted to her empty house and the imminent return of her parents and the resumption of the milkman's visits.

Meanwhile:

'In America, it is the female sex that is loud about its rights, yet nowhere did Anke and I see women so well dressed, or so skilled at showing themselves off in the most flattering way.' Raine was enjoying having a captive audience.

'Where did you and Anke go?'

'Chicago, Washington—those American women were a delight. The men were chivalrous and gorgeous, Edith. I tell you, Anke and I thought the relationships between the sexes in America was one of the most important characteristics of the country.'

Edith could not believe this was the same women talking, who a day previously had held court in Press-Shots and made Malone feel a pig. Her arrogance had disappeared, and the young aviatrix wondered if it was because the air made all souls equals.

For her part, Rainc breathed deeply and had to acknowledge the joy she felt sitting next to the mongrel girl who was possessed of more spirit than a dining room full of Viennese charmers.

Hartmut had come to life. His thick, fair hair curled out from underneath his jaunty cap and his eyes, a deep violet, reached out in want of her friendship. In turn, the aviatrix no longer saw him as a god in twilight. He spoke animatedly to Raine, who twisted her torso around to take it all in, grinning at his chatter. Edith loved the lilt of his German, the soft accent placing him on the Belgian border. She thought of her ancestors, who had been entranced by Crefeld, then stripped of their worldly goods in Antwerp. And of her grandmother, whose candlesticks had miraculously survived the journey to the New World, hidden inside a giant ragdoll.

'When we were at the Cleveland races, one of our top men was thrown off a commercial flight for slapping a stewardess,' Hartmut recalled.

'That will teach you never to slap a woman,' Edith said, her German flowing easily.

'I've never seen anything like it,' he continued.

'Anke Reitsch was sitting next to this man—we were already airborne, and they turned the plane around,' Raine said. 'When we landed his bags were on the tarmac and the pilot threw him off personally.'

There was an ugly jolt, and Edith knew she would have to bring them down quickly. All conversation stopped, and the radio man had an odd, almost leering expression on his face.

'What are you smirking at?' the pilot demanded.
'Can't he speak?' she asked Raine.

'On the ground they are ready to greet America's Amy Johnson,' he said sheepishly.

'God damn! What are you talking about?'

'All the nation's press will be there—Philadelphia has put the story on the wires,' he explained.

'It must be that ice-cream man,' Edith muttered, bringing the aircraft in for a bumpy landing, its tanks still heavy with gasoline. Manoeuvring the unfamiliar monster around the narrow approach path, she could discern crowds of men in hats swarming along the tarmac. Because of the size of the aeroplane she had immense difficulty avoiding the human obstacle course, and came to a complete halt at an ugly angle. Edith did not care—this was Gander and the gasoline had not exploded. Her suit was soaked despite the cold of their journey. Philadelphia seemed still so near, and she wanted to change, to be dry, and to face up to her sin of the night before.

'Is it true you plan to join the Royal Air Force in England, Miss Allam?' asked a hatted reporter.

Raine and the odd couple remained on board, cowering like children.

'Are you transporting foreign nationals?'

Asking the question was a man in black whom she knew to be anything but a reporter, and Edith bristled. She pulled out her papers, shivering.

'They are some friends of mine,' she said.

'We are aware these people arrived last week to work for the German government. There's plenty of folks who think the "Hindenburg" was sabotage. Your three should have been out of the country two days ago,' he muttered, his shiny black shoes glittering against the gravel underneath.

'They wanted to stop and sample Fidler's kasha,' Edith said. Newfoundland's icy gusts tore into her tired frame.

The man in black examined her documentation. By now the reporters had encircled the aircraft. Two ground engineers inspected the machine.

'Those guys are treating that airplane as if it came out of the War of the Worlds,' she quipped.

'It has,' said the man in black, looking up from his reading. 'Know thine enemies, my lady.' He handed her the documentation without another word, and she could feel the damp suit clinging to her aching back.

'Hey, Edith—are you leaving a fellow back home for a Kraut over there?' Reporters crowded around, pushing and shoving.

'I work for a firm called Press-Shots. Yes, I'm AWOL. Raine Fischtal, Hitler's prize cinematographer, is sitting in a German airplane and she wants to get home. We've made a deal: if I can fly her there, I can take back with me a copy of her best new footage. It's stuff our guys haven't got because we're too busy wasting celluloid on Hollywood gossip shots while Europe is sinking into the worst conflict the world may ever know. Did you ever hear of Valerie Cobb? Stella Teague? Val is starting a women's flying corps in England, and Stella's doing airlifts to poor people in the Baltics. I'm coming back home as soon as I get handed that film, then I may go over again. Valerie Cobb needs womanpower.'

'You didn't answer our question, Edie.'

'My beau works for Press-Shots and he doesn't look like any of you.'

85

'What's his name, hon?'

Edith felt a hand on her arm. Raine was standing next to her, and she sensed a strange closeness that had not existed before the two girls had shared the equality of the skies. Now her other arm had been taken by the man in black, and as she was overcome by a sudden rush of exhaustion that stemmed from fear, they led her to warmth and privacy in a tiny shed. Out of nowhere a new flying suit was produced and she suspected it was all a dream: the garment was her size! Inside a hold was a lavish supply of lemons, oranges, cigarettes and chocolate, and a parcel of Canadian bacon snuggled up to a jar of maple syrup. As if drugged, Edith curled into a corner of the shed and forgot about Raine and the man who waited outside . . .

In her dream hungry peasant women in long dresses and British men in rags clung to her and she refused them oranges. Children craved her lemons and she pushed the yellow fruit into velvet bags. Hartmut wore a uniform, and among the people he kicked was a black man in tatters. She wanted to go to the black man but he was filthy. Her belly was swollen with Errol's seed and when it burst forth the infant was filthy and it disappeared under an avalanche of lemons and oranges. Hartmut laughed . . .

When she awoke Edith found that all the goodwill had led to the worst she could possibly have envisaged: the big aircraft had been lovingly repaired by the Canadian ground engineers.

The American Jewess was ready to take off again, and there was no turning back.

13

Edith knew Raine was expected back in Berlin at a specific time, and they were now running six hours late. It would never do, where the Reich was concerned, but the American could not make the aircraft move any faster. Night was falling as they headed out to sea, and then—to Edith's astonishment—the Northern Lights appeared. It was the first time any of the four had witnessed the aurora borealis and from an aeroplane the effect was dazzling. Shooting forth from the distant north the lights seemed a harbinger of sudden dawn. Hartmut had gripped Edith's shoulders, craning to see out of the front of the aircraft, and his touch sent a kind of crackling down her sides.

Voices were hushed as they passed through the phenomenon, and the only sound was the hum of Raine's camera and the rush of air past the magical quiet of the superb German engines. A faultless landing in Greenland brought guilt to the fore, as Edith noticed her heart's urges waning. Even the images of her parents were receding with each air mile achieved. No press besieged her party in this remote stopover, and when they descended on Iceland for another refuel and checkup, she felt her identity had been transformed. No longer was she worried about the neighbours on Florence Avenue, or the ladies in the synagogue, or the money she would be docked from the Press-Shots payroll. Errol had become a gnawing disturbance deep in her womb, as if a knife had cut an open sore in a place she had previously ignored.

Hopefully the sore would heal and nothing else would grow on its scab, because her dream had left her with visions of a hungry black man the size of an infant, who never grew even when he ate lemons and oranges.

Knowing she was expected to head for Prestwick, and knowing her Germans expected a journey straight through to Berlin, Edith forced her mind to thoughts of Valerie Cobb. Dared she apply for inclusion in a women's unit? She had heard that working-class kids from the East End were now being invited to join the RAF and that such rabble included females! Where would a spoilt American girl fit into the British hierarchy? She had better not ask for kasha, at the Cobbs'.

'*Was ist geschehen?!*' shrieked Zuki, the first of her dreaded payload to become aware of a change in course.

'Got a problem?' she asked, calmly.

'Dammit—you are heading off towards *Britain*,' he screamed.

Raine's camera had stopped whirring. 'Is he right?' she demanded, her eyes suddenly cold.

'To be honest, I have a surprise for you,' Edith admitted.

Hartmut's hand reached inside a large jacket pocket.

'What have you got in there, Hartmut?' the American enquired, turning around.

'Nothing. Why are you disobeying our orders?'

'I'm obeying my country's orders. Every American pilot licensed in the USA has to make a stopover in Britain, whatever the registration of the aircraft.'

'Rubbish—*scheiss*,' snarled Zuki.

'I have never heard of such a thing,' said Raine.

Hartmut bowed his head and was strangely silent.

'Listen, crew,' Edith told them. 'Everyone in Britain is dying to meet Raine Fischtal. You yourself said the Britishers and the Germans are racial cousins. Press-Shots UK has arranged for a special reception in your honour, Raine. After all, our countries are not at war, honey.'

'Britain has not forgotten the First War,' Hartmut said, coming out of his trance. 'You cannot tell me Raine is revered in the United Kingdom, of all places.'

'Have they forgotten her Olympic film?' countered Edith. 'Now she's got the best footage in the world of the "Hindenburg", plus some extra goodies they'd all just love to see, and as far as the English authorities are concerned she's hot stuff.'

Raine's radio operator began to argue and she turned, glaring at him. He stopped chattering.

'Do we go on to Germany?' she asked.

'Of course, Raine,' Edith said, quietly, touching the woman's hand.

Raine studied the American for a few moments, agonizing over the decision she would have to make. If the Reich insisted that a guest pilot be shot if any sign of insubordination occurred, this girl would have to go. How stupid of her to have got involved in this ridiculous caper in the first place! Of course, this girl could fly; they should have left her in Gander. The closer they got to Heimat, the more deeply Raine felt the gravity of the wartime threat. Some game between two strong-willed young women seemed fun in the land of ice-cream parlours and Saturday-night dances, but approaching the tormented mainland of Europe, their self-indulgent wager stank of blood.

There was the coast of Ireland looming up ahead, and Edith poured with perspiration. Those emerald isles crept up on her, ever larger and more inviting. Scotland's coast would next be in her sights, one of the most tortuous on the European map. Prestwick came and went, its faraway landing strip unbearably tempting to the aviatrix, now rigid with apprehension. East Anglia would not be far off, and she held her breath. Amazed that Hartmut had not pulled his gun, despite Zuki's whinings, she braced herself for the approach to Mildenhall Field. As they came in for a landing, Zuki fumbled in his bag and began hiding his equipment, then crouching to make himself invisible.

'Don't be an idiot,' hissed Edith, bringing the aircraft in for a perfect touchdown.

'They're frightened,' whispered Raine.

'We are *not* at war, Raine,' she shouted.

'Let's make the best of this situation,' urged Hartmut, smiling at the pilot.

Edith knew he had come close to performing his nation's orders and praised God for the remedy her femaleness had provided in the face of a loaded pistol protruding from his pocket. She smiled back at him.

*   *   *

On the landing strip, wet with mist, a small handful of polite Suffolk mechanics greeted her arrival. There were no reporters scuffling, and no officials demanding papers. Raine and the Germans emerged behind Edith, their faces grim with uncertainty.

'This aircraft is the property of the German government,' Raine announced.

One of the mechanics tipped his hat.

Hartmut did not want to tear himself away from the men, and as he stood over their labours Edith stopped and noticed his hair, which seemed to glow even in the endless grey mist that hung over these Isles.

'With all the fuss Hitler makes about Aryan purity, you're actually the first blond German I've come across!' she exclaimed, grinning at him.

'Don't tell me they've heard about Hitler where you come from, lass,' said a mechanic, straightening up from his examination of the fuselage.

'Roosevelt knows about him,' said Edith. 'And I do too.'

A terrifying roar broke their conversation and the blinding lights of screeching cars swarmed from out of nowhere. Edith watched as Raine Fischtal, Zuki and Hartmut were bundled into the shiny vehicles and she was left alone.

Raine's precious film remained on board the aircraft and Edith climbed back into the cabin to remove the canister. She sat for some moments and felt the chill air leaking into the tiny spaces around the windows and chuckled at the thought of German imperfection. Technically, the two countries were not at war and she was an innocent bystander. Britain could be unpleasant to her three new friends but could not interrogate them like spies. In an odd way she did not want them to be hurt or abused. Confident that all was well with her world, the pilot emerged from the cockpit only to find two well-dressed men looking up at her expectantly.

'Care for some Florida oranges?' she asked, peering down at the pair.

'Would you be Miss Edith Allam?' asked the younger man, his face not dissimilar to that of a ten-year-old schoolboy.

'Only two reporters? Do me a favour!' exclaimed Edith, climbing down over the wing.

The older newcomer offered her an elegantly gloved hand. 'We require two things from you, madam. Your identification, and the Fischtal film,' he said.

Edith had become apprehensive and when she removed her papers from the bag a lemon rolled out.

'I was serious about the orange,' she said, handing him the documents and a lemon.

The younger man wiped it with his handkerchief.

'Don't do that. You'll ruin your hanky!' she exclaimed.

Both men stared at this strange girl.

'Are you Lord Beaverbrook's guys?' she inquired.

'We represent the Parliamentary committee which deals with matters of air readiness and with foreign nationals. You, of course, are our honoured guest. But, as you know, the three Germans will be under surveillance for . . . some time.

'*Some* time?' demanded Edith.

'A day or two,' the young one murmured, smiling weakly.

'Who are you, anyway?'

'I do beg your pardon. I'm Sir Henry Cobb, and this is Tim Haydon MP.'

'Well, you can't have Raine's film. She and I did a deal that if I got her home in one piece, her lab in Berlin would let me take back a copy—it's just some "Hindenburg" footage.'

'We are aware it contains extensive material which might embarrass the Reich,' Cobb asserted, 'and which might strengthen Winston Churchill's position. You know of Churchill, I take it?'

'Yes I know of Winston—how the hell do you know what's on Raine's film?' Shaking with rage, Edith snatched the lemon from Haydon's grasp.

'Press-Shots UK notified the newspapers of your exercise,' Sir Henry explained, 'and in the present atmosphere such information would automatically be passed on to the appropriate government authorities.'

'In America it's the other way around,' Edith mumbled, her thoughts darting from newspapers, to Beaverbrook, and then to Valerie Cobb.

'If I may say so, madam,' Haydon presumed, 'your so-called deal with Fischtal is one of the most childish and foolhardy things I have encountered in my entire career.'

'Considering you look twelve, your career must have been pretty short,' she observed curtly.

'Lady pilots, I must confess, are a law unto themselves,' nodded Sir Henry, smiling with what Edith felt was a kind of conciliatory warmth.

'You can't fool me, mister—your kid is Valerie Cobb.' Edith grinned. 'Okay. Here's another childish deal. You get to keep a copy of Raine's horror movie, if I get a copy from a London lab free of charge, and if Raine gets her original back. In addition, I want to meet your daughter.'

'Of course,' said Sir Henry. 'On my word of

honour.'

Edith had read books about an English gentleman's honour. He just *had* to be honourable—didn't he?

A large car had drawn up beside them and the two MPs fell silent as Edith was ushered into its plush interior. To her relief and amazement, in a day filled with miracles, they had prepared a receipt on official headed paper, in exchange for the canister, which under her fierce grip had by now pressed a ridge into her side.

Haydon remained stony-faced, but Sir Henry smiled and waved as the car drove her away from her now-beloved German flying machine.

Would she ever again embrace its magical powers?

Would Raine ever see her film again?

As they sped away Edith craned to glimpse the main building, eager for signs of her payload—but there were no traces of human activity to be seen.

'Who the hell are you, and where the hell are you taking me?' she demanded of the driver.

'*Daily Record*, madam,' he said.

'Daily *what?*'

'Newspaper.' He steered with one hand and with the other held up a gigantic bouquet of flowers. 'These are for you. From the proprietor, miss.'

'Take me back—I just want to meet Valerie Cobb,' pleaded Edith.

The driver's hand dropped and the flowers disappeared out of sight.

'If I give you a lemon will you take me to Valerie Cobb?'

'What's a lemon to a bloke like me, if you please, madam?'

'I know damn well your government's about to ban everything except turnips and tea,' snapped Edith.

'If you say so, madam.'

She handed him a Hershey bar and a handsome Camel carton, and he accelerated into the Ipswich Road.

'Thank you very much, madam. For your information, His Lordship has already arranged for you to meet Miss Cobb at the *Daily Record*. My job is simply to take you there.'

Edith Allam buried her face in her hands and shook with helpless laughter at the folly of her deeds, and the strangeness of her present situation—as the car raced towards the capital of an England that had long forgotten its childhood, and was now bracing itself for a painful old age that might end in tyranny.

14

Burt Malone seemed to spend his life bailing people out of police cells. On this occasion he was being forced to argue with his own brother, whose severe hangover had made him fractious. Summer had not abated, giving the musty incident room an oppressive airlessness resembling a Mississippi August. Two stylishly dressed young people sat on a bench at the far aide of the room, one a dapper boy sporting a flashy hat, the other a girl too voluptuous to seem real. For a moment Burt pictured them as some weird optical illusion off a carnival display, or fallen off a river steamer, bringing with them that Mississippi oppression.

When Frank Malone emerged his eyes avoided brother Burt's glance as long as neither man spoke. Onc of the youths arose, and both men looked up. Her thick, glowing hair seemed to bring a reflected glow that lit the vomit-green walls.

'Any news on Carnaby?' asked the girl, trying for Frank's attention.

Burt wheeled around to face her, and his brother dashed to the counter.

'Why don't you come back tomorrow, sis?' hissed Frank.

'Do you know the boy?' Burt asked, smiling at the couple.

'He's a friend of a friend,' she said.

'Whose friend?' pressed Burt.

Now the boy was standing too.

'Mine,' replied the girl. 'I'm Molly, this is Kelvin.'

'We wanted to leave him his Blake but this guy won't pass him the book,' Kelvin Bray explained, pointing to Frank.

'No, we just throw the book at him,' the cop guffawed, as Kelvin wielded Blake.

'That's Edith Allam's!' Burt sputtered, reaching for the ancient volume.

'He wouldn't know how to read, son,' Frank said, his breath unbearable in the hanging humidity.

'Listen, officer, Errol Carnaby could tie circles around anybody when it comes to brains,' Kelvin asserted. 'Please just give him the book. This young lady has to get back home—or her fiancé will kill her.'

'I know what the dagos are like, kid,' muttered Frank.

Molly's eyes shot darts at the overweight cop.

96

'Okay, it's time for me to deliver the goods,' said Burt, handing over a wad of bills to his brother.

'Are you nuts?' complained Frank, still leaning on the counter.

'I should be hunting down that goddam Hindenburg film, and my missing photographer—instead I'm wasting a morning over some trumped-up charge.'

'It ain't trumped up, Burt,' Frank said, straightening up. 'This kid gave me trouble first thing last night, and there he was again at the stroke of twelve. Some shitty story about his mother being a cleaning lady.' He turned to Molly. 'Excuse me, miss.'

'You're excused. Now, pass the dough, honey.' Molly grinned at Burt.

'I'm bailing the kid out, little brother. Right now.'

Scowling, Frank took the money, then sauntered off towards the cells.

'By the way, his mother cleans our house—every other Wednesday night,' chirped Kelvin.

'How do you know Errol?' Molly asked Burt.

'He works for me—best projectionist in town. None of the movie houses will hire him, so I take what the others dump. I've got all the eccentrics in Philly—Stan, my editor, who stinks but has a genius talent, and this girl Edith who snaps and flies aeroplanes. I must be crazy.'

'She's become a celebrity—crossing the ocean with that film-maker woman,' Kelvin offered.

'We met her at Fidler's—Fish-stall,' Molly added.

'You met the German broad?!' Burt shouted, nonplussed.

There was a noisy clatter of keys and latches, and

97

Errol emerged, his clothes dishevelled and his eyes streaked with red.

'Who says Jim Crow stops on the Mason-Dixon line?' he joked, smiling at the crowd awaiting him.

'Your mother came to us hysterical today—that's how I knew you were here,' Kelvin said quietly.

'I know why you're here,' Errol murmured, looking at Burt. 'Are you going to dock my pay?'

Frank pushed the coloured man through the narrow passage into freedom, glaring at his brother.

'Down south they'd call you a nigger-lover,' whispered Frank.

'This *isn't* Down South, and I need my projectionist,' bellowed Burt, taking Errol's arm.

'The question is—how has Enitharmon fared in my absence?' Errol grinned as he spoke, loving Frank's expression of horror mixed with fear.

'What's he talking about? We'll take you in again, so watch your language,' he snapped, swinging the keys in front of Errol's weary face.

'Let's get out of here,' said Molly, and the foursome headed for the door. An elderly Hasid stumbled in, limping. Burt started, remembering Raine's footage.

'You all right, old man?' he asked.

'They mean trouble every time,' growled Frank.

'How did you get to be in such a bad way?' Burt was becoming agitated.

Words failed the old man and he tottered to the counter.

Burt wanted to stay, and the others began to look at him oddly.

'Someone given you trouble?' he enquired, his face close to the old man's beard.

'Talk to me,' said Errol.

'You know Yiddish?' the old man exclaimed.

Guffaws reverberated in the police station, and even the Hasid smiled, touching the giant Negro's hand with affection. 'I'm here to announce that for Rosh Hashanah the Messiah is coming.'

'You're two thousand years too late, Isaac.' Frank chortled.

Burt heaved a great sigh, and wondered if this sweet little man knew of the horrors befalling his brethren in places as enlightened as Berlin and Vienna.

'Good Yomtov,' Errol shouted as they left. In the distance they could still hear the cop and the old man arguing about the true Messiah.

'What happened, schwartzer?' Burt asked as they turned the corner into Broad Street. In the light he could see that Errol's dark face had acquired a shiner.

'Malone, your brother by some freak of nature, had had his night of joy on Florence Avenue and decided to pick on me after I'd been to visit Edith's folks.'

'Are they worried about her?' asked Molly.

'Let him finish,' snapped Burt.

'I am finished,' muttered Errol. He stopped. As his body began to shake, tears came. He was ashamed.

Burt looked away, thinking again of Raine's film. Kelvin offered the tattered man an arm, and holding his Blake in one hand helped him continue his journey back to the comforting darkness of Burt's studio. Molly would go home to her fiancé to be serenaded in the name of a religion that had already found its saviour. The gang of four, an

99

Italian dressed for a wedding ritual, an Irishman dressed for its aftermath, a Negro and another kind of Irishman, staggered up Broad Street, oblivious to the raging headlines that presaged their interrupted futures.

15

More flashes popped and reporters shouted as an exhausted and very unwashed Edith Allam emerged from her chauffeured car and was ushered into the luxurious corridors of the Beaverbrook empire.

Pushing past the press men and marching down the halls from which their dangerous words would be printed for mass consumption, the American aviatrix followed her chauffeur, now smoking his new Camel cigarette. Down a flight of stairs, she was led into what appeared to be a hotel suite, its red velvet curtains and pink velvet walls reminiscent of a Philadelphia whorehouse she had infiltrated for Burt Malone's picture library. Turning around to query the chauffeur, she was surprised to see he had been replaced by a genteel curly-haired woman bordering on the elderly, who sported a black dress and an apron and who seemed weighted down with plush bath towels. She moved silently about the room, making her way to a door which opened into a bathroom that took Edith's breath away. Without speaking, the aproned woman leaned over a gleaming bathtub and drew water that created an instant cloud of steam. Was this really happening?

Edith had heard that the British bathed in cold muck and relieved themselves outdoors. Literature had invented Oz, but that was somewhere in America. Had she crashed in the middle of the Atlantic?

Unable to speak, she stared at the aproned matron, who did not seem interested in conversation anyway, and when she was left alone with real bath bubbles and heat and an elaborate wardrobe of designer clothes laid out on the antique sofa, she stripped off slowly, her slim body still smelling fragrant from cologne applied twenty-four hours previously to a scrubbed skin, within earshot of her Negro lover in a house on Florence Avenue. Stepping into this breathtaking bathtub, with its gold taps and pearl facings, its 'B' motif shimmering through the water from the bottom of the tub, and its palatial marble surrounds, she thought of Valerie Cobb and of the rumours that had been spread at her club back home. If the MP's daughter lived with another woman, would it be dangerous to be in a room with her alone?

On the other hand, could her friendship be the most valuable acquisition she might make on the eve of war?

Here in Britain, Edith felt the imminence of a world conflict, and as she soaked in the very hot water, her heart jumped at the thought of an association with Valerie, and it sank just as quickly on thoughts of Errol Carnaby. Running her hand along the insides of her thighs, she shuddered at the memory of his fierce penis breaking through her delicate barriers and expelling its endless contents that had brought her to the brink of ecstasy, and now in this splendid state of immersion she felt she might come with even greater intensity. Lying back and letting the hair on the back of her head become moist, she shut her eyes and thought of nothing, only her nipples hitting the air and becoming erect.

Rustling noises made her sit up, and water splashed over the sides of her marble encampment. Another aproned lady had wandered into this pleasure palace. Did this one talk?

'Excuse me, could you please tell me where I am?' shouted Edith.

As if instructed to flee if spoken to, Apron Number Two scurried away, shutting the door behind her. Craning her dripping neck, Edith noticed the arrival of fruit and cheeses. She laughed, scrubbing herself and rising out of the soiled, lukewarm water. Drying each leg, she rubbed more vigorously as she neared her groin, still wishing Errol's semen away. Towelling her abdomen, she wondered if Valerie's body was identical to hers. She stroked her breasts with the now-soggy towel, remembering Errol's tongue. A stirring in her vagina became a spasm and she yearned to complete its urgings. Terrified another Apron might come in at any moment, she held the towel tightly and crossed her legs, sighing deeply . . .

Walking to the sofa, Edith caressed the smooth nylons—where on earth did Beaverbrook get these things in such times?—and dressed herself in a Chanel. As if timing her every movement, a visitor knocked at the door. Edith turned the doorknob to reveal another female, clad in a suit tailored to hug her most intimate contour.

'Valerie Cobb,' she announced herself.

This was the first voice she had heard since her

lemon chauffeur. Here was a magnificent woman, and Edith took a deep breath. They shook hands, and the American forgot all fear of being alone in the other's company.

'Your legend has preceded you,' said Valerie.

'Same to you. Incidentally, it was nice to meet your father. He arrested my three friends and snitched Raine Fischtal's film.'

'It was Tim Haydon's idea. Daddy is on our side, after a fashion.' Valerie smiled broadly at the weary American.

They sat facing each other on the two sofas. Edith noticed Valerie's skin—it was not the English Rose complexion she had expected, but a tough surface lined with character and framed by dimples on either side of a powerful chin.

'It astonishes me that a world-renowned photographer can also fly aeroplanes.'

'American girls do lots of things.'

'Is your father big on Wall Street?'

'My father is not big anywhere, and my family lives in a little row house in West Philadelphia— that's about it.'

'So much the better. That means you will be able to recruit ordinary working-class girls into an air arm.'

Edith stared at Valerie for a few moments and wondered if she was hearing correctly.

'Are you saying you'd like me to find pilots?'

'Before we go in to see Beaverbrook, who, believe me, we can count on to be on our side, let me fill you in on the latest. There will most likely be a war, and nobody is in the least bit ready. At the beginning, it looks as if male ferry pilots will be moving Magisters from Woodley, and we'll be moving Moth trainers, taking things to places like Perth, Kemble, Lyneham or Llandow, and returning on sleeper trains. Sometimes pilots will report back after a three-day trip and a night train only to be sent off once more without a moment in their own beds. It will be a hell of a responsibilty, and a fiendish life for the duration of a war. If you can find a handful of good people to help us out, so much the better. Balfour and Lady Londonderry are on our side, and so is d'Erlanger, who is the head of BOAC. It is a promising picture. Now let's go to the old man.'

'Before we do, Valerie, can I tell you about America?'

'Please do.' She sat back, smiling.

'We enjoy life, and things have been terrific since the Depression un-depressed. It'll be tough getting boys—let alone girls—to join your squadron. Who the hell wants to go to war when you can spend your life at the movies and down at the corner soda fountain? But I'll try.'

Gazing at each other in the humid room, the fragrance of Edith's bath bubbles still lingering in the air, the two women felt a mutual excitement that came from being blessed with the energy their mothers had lost in bearing them.

'Let's go to the old man,' Valerie said, taking the American's arm. For the time being, Edith had forgotten Errol, and all she wanted was to find an incinerator in which to burn the carry-all containing a meaningless bedsheet.

*   *   *

Beaverbrook greeted her with indifference.

'Who arranged all that luxury?' she asked.

'We treat our guests with generosity—please keep the dresses,' he said brusquely.

'Edith has access to an assortment of healthy people,' Valerie prompted him.

'You have brought the country an invaluable film, a trio of Germans, and a fascinating aircraft,' conceded Beaverbrook.

'Why is it fascinating?'

'It has components never before seen in this country. His Majesty's Government is amazed Germany allowed it to land in America and then be let loose with a foreign pilot.'

'I'm glad you didn't say woman pilot,' Edith murmured.

Valerie winked.

Beaverbrook was pacing the room.

'In any case,' he continued, 'We will be sending your German friends back in their own plane, so as not to provoke Hitler, and we will provide you with anything you choose. All we ask is that you come back with one load of Americans, and then cross over to Australia to bring us some of their lot.'

'Australia!' exclaimed Edith.

'It's a staggering opportunity,' Valerie whispered.

Beaverbrook observed the two females, stopping in his tracks to breathe a great sigh.

'It is my intention to get as many ferry pilots from all over the world as possible,' he asserted. 'Did you know people are still saying that Germany thinks Britain is at the end of its pilot reserve because we are perceived as using women to ferry toy trainers from A to B?'

'What are toy trainers?'

'Tiger Moths,' Valerie replied.

105

Beaverbrook had missed the exchange, and was pacing the chamber once more.

'Maybe there won't even be a war,' suggested Edith.

'By the time you've mobilized this Australian–American exercise, which will be covered by the world's press, there *will* be a war.'

'You're going to organize one especially for me?'

Beaverbrook had finally noticed her. 'Do you have a husband—children?' he demanded.

'Not really,' she responded, remembering Errol and her souvenir sheet.

'You either have a husband, or you don't, woman,' boomed His Lordship.

'I am single,' muttered Edith, snatching a quick glance at Valerie, as if seeking help.

'Then go home, and find us some good pilots. When you return, there will always be a place for you in an air transport auxiliary.'

'I thought Valerie had to test girls before they were allowed to join.'

'I do, and you will,' Valerie murmured tensely.

'The *Daily Record* is paying you for your troubles, and for your photographs. Also for your story—a three-pronged deal.' Beaverbrook turned to Valerie. 'I don't want the girl being tested.' On that note His Lordship departed.

Valerie and Edith were left in the sumptuous room, which seemed to echo even when they breathed.

'Anyone who thinks we will be at peace a year from now is mad,' Valerie remarked, looking up at the ornate ceiling.

'So you think I should do this job?'

'Of course. In any case, I want to meet your

106

lover.'

'Pardon me?'

'He was in your mind's eye when Beaverbrook mentioned husbands. Bring him with you.'

'He wouldn't fit in here.'

'Why not?' Valerie demanded sharply.

'He's a Negro.'

'Good Lord!' Valerie walked to the door and stopped. 'That is rather a calamity.'

'Whatever you want to call it, he's mine and the world will just have to accept him,' Edith paused. 'Do you like men at all?'

'Do you?'

'I just told you I have a lover who isn't my husband.'

'I've one as well,' Valerie said dreamily. 'Can your chap fly?'

'What a question!' giggled Edith, leaning against a large mahogany boardroom table for support.

'It's important,' Valerie said, frowning.

'Errol is a film projectionist who quotes Blake. He can't fly. Maybe he could learn.'

'Maybe he could. Bring him.'

'Do you really think I could make it into your air squad?'

'What I foresee is a group of fifty, clearing new aircraft from the main factories to the RAF installations. You may find it boring, after crossing the Atlantic and photographing the "Hindenburg". But if there is an ugly confrontation with Hitler, we may even reach a point where some of us are eye-to-eye with the Luftwaffe.'

'Honestly?'

'We are so ill-prepared it disturbs my sleep. Most of the women pilots I know are as proficient as the men to hand at this very moment. If it is in a woman to kill, so be it.'

'Women are killing in Germany and Poland!' Edith's intensity took Valerie by surprise.

'How do you know this?' she asked.

'Raine Fischtal's film—it shows women killing.'

Valerie was glad she had followed her father's orders this one time. She had wanted to meet the American girl. Her presence was a revelation—this is what the British woman will begin to be like in fifty years, she thought, smiling to herself. What will the American woman be like then? This girl's species had evolved because it had not been shackled.

Valerie opened the door. 'Now you will meet the press, become an even greater legend, and discover that war can make profits for all concerned.'

They left the chamber and walked back to the luxury suite. Edith folded the dresses into her bag, atop the lemons and the oranges and the nylons and the sheet, thinking of her chauffeur. Had he got through all the chocolate and Camels by now? What day was this?

She turned around and found Valerie had disappeared. Edith's dirty overall was on the floor, and she folded it carefully, placing it on top of the expensive *haute couture*. Stopping to look at herself in the full-length mirror, she reached for the fruit that had been left by the aproned lady, and stuffed it in with her overall. One never knew when one might go hungry again, she thought. At the door, she could hear a commotion outside and her heart thumped. Did she want Errol, or was she missing Valerie's company already? They had hardly spoken. She would want to see her again. If shipping a load of Aussies and Yanks back to this island meant continuing their conversation, she would pursue the task with vigour, starting now.

What about Raine?

Edith went back to her bag and thrust her hand into the folded flying suit. Searching frantically, her fingers rested on the receipt Haydon and Cobb had given her in exchange for the precious film. Burt Malone would crucify her if she did not return with something, after being AWOL so long. She wanted to see Raine and the Germans before nightfall, and she wanted to sleep. Fatigue was overtaking the American, but her urge to find the trio was relentless. That fruit might come in handy, she thought—could British immigration police be bribed with a lemon for their malnourished babies? She hoped they might not, after all, be as honourable as their Movietone image.

16

Warsaw was a bustling city, making it all the more impossible for Hana Bukova to believe that her favourite boy might be starving inside the walls of a man-made ghetto. Animals in the wild marked out their territory by choice, snarling at intruders who sought to destroy a unified existence. Hana had long ceased thinking of her Jews as animals, and, as she waited for Josef Ratusz to gain clearance for special leave from his Polish Air Force detachment, her spirit rumbled inside, wanting to escape the lofty halls of this nineteenth-century building and run to the Ghetto.

Would her mother be successful in her mission?

What if Benno Kranz and his family were found out?

Mother would slope off to a café and wait for another assignment to come along, thinking, 'Too bad for those Jews.'

'Can we get out of the country by sunset?' Josef was beside her, his uniform decorously coloured with his many military honours representing weird skirmishes from an ancient war. He would have to change into a suit before their mission.

'Josef, why all those old coins?' She tapped his chest playfully.

'Dogfights.'

They walked down the corridor of the Air Command Headquarters, and a pair of cadets saluted the ace as they passed.

'You must be old enough to retire—what are you, forty?' she demanded, striding ahead of Ratusz.

'Not quite. Do you think I have a future in England?'

'I can't imagine why everyone is going there. What if there is no war? All the stupid Poles will come back.'

'By that time Poland will be ruled by the Russians—mark my words.' He stopped at the gents' lavatory. 'Wait here.'

Hana Bukova remembered the first time she had met Josef Ratusz, hero of the First War who had helped England win. Her mother had met him at her flying club and had brought him home for dinner. Their housekeeper had been flustered because she had made only enough prohes for three, and Hana's father had been agitated by the

110

presence of a man with exceptional capabilities. Josef's flaming red hair was always too long, offending Libor Buk even further, but little Hana could only marvel at his spectacular looks, wishing he were her father instead. Libor looked so old next to Josef, she thought.

Vera felt her redheaded genius had shown magnanimity in helping the British. He had explained, in turn, that he was distantly related to the Royal Family and could trace his ancestry back to the first Plantagenets, who were, of course, Polish aristocracy masquerading as Englishmen, he asserted . . .

'Father thinks you are mad, you know,' Hana said as he emerged, transformed, from the men's room. They made a swift exit, her hair attracting the usual glances on the sunny courtyard outside the Command building.

'All royal people are a little bit mad,' he said flatly, looking up at the splendid structure. 'This used to be a palace in which the Romanovs stayed when they visited.'

'Rubbish, Josef,' she scoffed, hoisting herself into an old van.

He stared at her oddly, then turned the creaking door handle of the rusting vehicle, and got in beside her. He threw his large bag on to the rear seat, grimacing as he did so.

'What's the matter now,' she spoke as if he were an elder brother, inasmuch as she had recovered from her childhood crush.

'This car is filthy,' he said.

'Wait until you get to England,' retorted Hana. 'I have heard they bath together once a week there, and eat chopped-rat sausages.'

'Hana, what is going to happen to us?' His face had paled, and their eyes met.

She lowered her hand from the ignition at the sight of Joscf's terrified expression. 'Just think of those Jews in the Ghetto, Josef, and be grateful.'

'They don't concern me. Worrying about Jews is tiring. Why don't they all become Catholics?'

Hana started up the engine, and they sped along the main road towards the airfield. She kept silent, and Josef smoked. Out of the corner of her eye she could see that he still gripped his ornate cigarette holder like a woman.

They slowed down.

'Why are we stopping?' asked Josef.

Hana remained silent, peering through the windscreen at the walls of the Ghetto.

'What is this fascination you have with these bloody people?' he complained, waving his cigarette in the air.

'Mother should be here somewhere,' she whispered, glancing from side to side.

'Why, for God's sake? Have you tricked your own mother into saving Jews?'

'She didn't have to be tricked. There are special people in her consignment.'

'If she were to come down over Germany her reward would be worse than that of her cargo, Hana,' he said, looking miserable. 'They are incinerating Jews but torturing Polish Catholics.'

Hana sat up. 'Where did you hear this?' she demanded, starting to shake.

'It is a secret, but now you know it. We will take it with us to the British.'

Hana wanted to run out and stop her mother, but would that mean Benno's fate being sealed? How could she allow anyone to incinerate him? Who could ever torture her adorable Mama? She started the motor again, and they roared away.

At the airfield Hana found her small craft, surrounded by shabby refugees awaiting other pilots. An official approached them, and Hana motioned to Josef to get in. It was too late, and the man in a dark coat tapped the side of her small window. She knew her brief.

'We are travelling to Lvov.'

'What is that in your rear seating?' the man demanded.

'I am under instructions by the Polish government to deliver these confidential papers,' Josef volunteered, uncovering the large lump in the rear section. Hana's heart skipped a beat. Beneath the faded blanket were, indeed, boxes of papers marked with the seal of the Warsaw regime. Their operatives had done their appointed job after all. Josef proffered his own credentials.

'There is an unusually strong smell of fuel in this aeroplane,' the man grumbled, scowling at Hana. 'I will send for one of my technicians. Your papers, madam?'

Hana gave him her documents, and he started.

'Bukova?'

'Hana.'

He was smiling. 'I have met your mother, not an hour ago.'

Hana tried to conceal her elation:

'What was my mother doing?'

'She had a planeload of diplomats—also going to Lvov.' He handed her back the papers, still smiling. 'Please do not go yet—I will bring a technician.' He moved off, the two pilots watching him weave

113

in between the parked machines and the hordes of hopeful escapees. As his image receded, Hana became agitated. There was only one thing to do.

'What the hell—are you insane?!' Josef Ratusz protested.

Refugees unfortunate enough to be close to Hana's aircraft were felled by the sudden explosion of twin propellers, revved with such ferocity as to make the fuselage groan. She knew she would have to be quick, like a squadron leader running to his fighter plane amid a raid, but her small Fokker resisted her urgings.

Above the din Josef shouted:

'They will shoot us—we'll be sent for incineration with those ghetto Jews!'

By now the little aircraft had gained an amazing momentum. Though Hana could not avoid the unspeakable sin of clipping several stationary craft, she was racing along and had cleared the parking patch.

'*Please* don't *stall*,' she muttered to the straining machine.

Ratusz had fallen silent. Outside, sirens began to wail and Hana made for the runway. There was no time for clearance from a groundsman, and as the two extra fuel tanks underneath the diplomatic boxes sloshed menacingly behind the two pilots, two engines agreed not to stall and the aircraft left the ground.

Josef looked down to see the dreaded image of men in Gestapo raincoats firing handguns.

'Stupid pistols!' he hissed.

Roaring upwards, Hana felt the ping of a bullet underneath her feet.

'Not so stupid,' she shouted, grinning at Josef.

'We could still be shot down,' he snarled back. 'That man had our particulars—mark my words he alerts the Germans.'

'Nonsense,' said Hana, still in Polish airspace but already levelling off at an even altitude. It was getting cold.

Ratusz shivered, then turned around to inspect the fuel tanks.

'Leave them be.'

He obeyed, but were she a man there would have been a fight, and that fight would have ended in death. As it was, he could only marvel at her superb flying skills, her control, and the magnificent waves of her hair.

'What are you staring at, Josef? You should be helping me navigate. Stupid man!'

Ratusz reached over and patted the back of her head, snapping the rear band on her goggles.

'Wait until we get to Malmö—everyone will want to know why Ratusz is a passenger and the girl flies,' he said, his hands back on his lap.

Hana remained silent, her concentration now at a dizzy pitch over the dangerous coastline they were fast approaching.

'I am a slave to this airy space,' Josef almost sang, sadly, gazing out of his small window.

Humming its way across the northern extremity of the girl's native land, the Fokker seemed to accelerate of its own accord when the Baltic began to glimmer beneath. Warsaw to Malmö had taken what seemed a few moments, but already the two pilots were sharing an unspoken urge to make use of the extra fuel. They had been travelling for a considerable period, and now it was time to reach a safe haven. Hana did not like the smell of the tanks, which she knew were leaking, and she prayed their re-entry into a warmer atmosphere would not make everything worse. She saw the coastline of Sweden ahead and prepared for her landing approach. Josef Ratusz was nervous and he worried about the landing, but most pressing of all he worried about England and its men. His medals and his royal claims meant nothing when the very idea of chasing a fox revolted him, thus setting him apart as an alien. It had happened in 1918, and, as England never changed, it would happen again.

Hana was bringing the aircraft down through low cloud, and he shut his eyes. In the blackness of his mind's eye he could see men in red coats on horseback.

There was a vicious thud and a scraping of wheels, the fuel tanks now banging against each other as Hana struggled to maintain stability. Josef's eyes were still shut and as he agonized over a woman controlling his destiny a smell of burning rubber permeated the atmosphere. Sweden was upon them, but inside his head were red coats and horses.

He worried about England, and its men.

17

Three days had passed and Raine Fischtal had gained three pounds in weight, her enjoyment of rock cakes, chips and saveloys exceeded only by the fascination she had developed for BBC radio drama. In between bulletins warning of German advances, polite, chirpy voices spent hours at a time mulling over commonplace occurrences, some of those voices belonging to the most notable actors of the day. Raine was in solitary confinement but her humour had been salvaged by the presence of an old wireless in the spacious cell her British hosts had provided for the duration of her stay. For three days she had awaited, with calm resolve, the arrival of Gestapo-style torturers but so far she had met only an assortment of immensely courteous civil servants whose humility had embarrassed her, and who ended up treating her like a celebrity.

With some disgust, she had reflected that the English must either be completely mad or totally incompetent in affairs of national security. As of this hour she had revealed nothing except the nature of her contract as official film-maker to the Third Reich and her knowledge of certain elementary flying techniques. Knowing Hartmut and Zuki, she suspected the British would secure nothing more concrete from that pair.

Lying in her dry and comfortable bed she heard approaching steps and hoped perversely that they might bring some unpleasantness—her figure could use some stress, she mused. Sitting up abruptly, she knocked her plate of cold baked beans to the floor.

'*Scheiss!*'

'Swearing will get you nowhere, Raine!'

Edith Allam, dressed in a stylish zippered flying suit, was led into the luxurious chamber in which her German friend was being held captive.

'Please forgive this mess,' Raine apologized. Then she glared at the uniformed guard. 'You!

Clean this up!'

He obeyed.

'Christ almighty! You've got these Brits eating out of the palm of your hand.'

'Of course,' said Raine, motioning for Edith to sit. 'They know I am someone special.'

'I'm sorry it has ended up this way, Raine.'

'You lied to me.'

'I did not lie. Maybe I'm naive, but I actually thought the British would welcome all four of us. It just shows you how isolated America has become. Apparently my telegrams arrived, were zipped over to Fleet Street and in no time the government top brass were ready to swoop before we had landed. It seems as if the British press and the government are as one. I'm sorry, sorry, *sorry*.'

Raine stared at Edith, unmoved.

'But rest assured your film is safe, and you will get it back,' Edith continued, searching Raine's face for some sign of pleasure.

Creaking open her door and locking it behind him, the guard knelt to clear up the mess.

'No Yank security guard would be seen dead cleaning up for a convict,' Edith remarked.

Observing her in silence, the guard straightened to his full height without making a sound.

'May I see your Leica, Raine?' she asked, eyeing the matchless German camera that rested underneath the bed.

'Of course.'

The guard watched the girls for an instant, then retreated, locking the door again as he disappeared down the corridor of the detention centre.

'They are setting up makeshift places like this all

118

over Britain, I gather,' Edith said, relaxing back into the spacious easy chair filling one corner of the chamber. She reached for the camera.

'It's a waste of time,' Raine asserted. 'Germany will march in to England soon, and that will be the end of it—all the wrong people are incarcerated at the moment, you understand?'

'Sure. Soon the British will come to their senses and start capturing Jewish scientists and lawyers with Germanic names, using this as an excuse to keep Krauts off the streets. In reality, what they will be doing is preparing in advance for the Nazi takeover, showing your guys they can be just as efficient at rounding up undesirables. Think of all the employment Britain will generate, building and maintaining concentration camps. These islands could become the centre of world extermination.'

'How do you know about concentration camps?' Raine asked, her eyes coming alive.

Edith gulped. Her mouth had overstepped her brain once more.

'Oh—it's just a wild theory I developed when I was drunk, that's all.'

Raine scrutinized the American girl. 'Edith, can I entrust you with something?' She knelt on the floor, reaching under the camp bed and pulling out a small, soiled leather bag tied shut with a drawstring. It smelled of petrol.

'How have you managed to hold on to that?' Edith asked, fascinated.

'They have taken nothing from me except my papers. Stupid people!' Raine whispered, as the guard returned to his post. 'They have not even emptied my camera of its film!' Thrusting her hand into the bottom of the little bag, she withdrew a small doll and placed it in Edith's palm.

'Is this something special?'

'If I am interned, or sent away someplace horrible,' Raine instructed her, 'please have this sent on to my family in Germany. It is a precious heirloom that I have always carried with me and I want my mother to have it back. Can I trust you to do this for me?'

'Sure! But what makes you think you'll be interned? This charade is a security stunt—you'll be let go pretty soon.'

'Just take it.'

'Okay,' Edith said, smiling at the woman who should be her enemy, but for whom she was developing an attachment. She held the doll gingerly, as Raine placed the little bag on the bedclothes. 'I'm going to see Hartmut and Zuki, now.'

'What? Where are they?' Raine could not conceal her emotion.

'They've been put in a funny new place on the Isle of Man. I'm being flown over there, then I come back here for my big send-off.'

'Send-off?'

Edith measured her words:

'I am going home and then coming back here.'

'What about Hartmut and Zuki, and the Führer's aircraft?'

'Don't worry. I'm going to see them right now.' Edith rose, stuffing the doll into her deepest pocket. 'Take care of yourself, Raine.' She knew the Führer's aircraft was already well and truly impounded.

'Please tell Hartmut and Zuki,' Raine whispered, her guard dozing, 'I still have the roll of film in my

120

camera—the important roll for the Führer. From my window I can see this whole encampment and I have taken one or two good wide shots with the last remaining exposures. Perhaps I should not be telling you this—I am spying, in so many words, right under their noses.'

'Miss Fischtal?' A polite voice interrupted the two girls. They could see a drably dressed official beyond the steel bars. 'It is time for your interview.'

'They call it an interview!' Raine exclaimed, laughing. 'What a country.' She reached out and touched Edith's arm, squeezing it affectionately. 'You are an amazing girl, little Jewess,' she said, grinning.

Edith had timed her visit to coincide with the interview schedule. As Raine was led away, she lingered in the chamber.

'When you are released, the Hindenburg reels will be returned to you intact. Their word of honour, and mine,' she shouted as Raine was marched down the corridor. 'Rotten Kraut!'

'Go to hell, Jud,' retorted Raine, grinning back. When she had gone the guard was wide awake and was gaping at the American.

'We tease each other,' Edith muttered. 'Have you ever seen these?' She handed him a pack of Winston filter-tips. He became engrossed in the cigarettes as she scooped up Raine's leather pouch and in masterly fashion reached for the Leica, rewound the film and replaced it with a fresh roll, advancing it to the same exposure as before. 'Thank God,' Edith muttered to herself, noticing the American markings on the canister. Had the film been German she could not have replaced it

121

and the mission would have been catastrophic.

Edith walked briskly down the corridor, not looking back and praying she would not be searched upon her departure. At the front gate, to her delight, Tim Haydon had arrived with a gaggle of MPs, to inspect the premises of the hastily organized detention centre. Circumventing the crowd that had gathered, she left by a rear door and thrust her hand back into the pocket containing the doll, adding the film to keep it company. Raine had given her something special and even if destiny said they were racial enemies she wanted to keep one German mother happy. In exchange for her kindness, she had helped herself to what she hoped was a bonus.

Jumping into the car, Edith could see this new Beaverbrook chauffeur looking deprived. He had heard about the riches she had showered on his colleague.

'When I am back from America, Joe, be assured there will be chocolate and Camels for you, too.'

He grunted.

Edith held her breath. His driving was abysmal, and he smelled. She let her mind wander to Hartmut and Zuki. Other American girls, like Molly Santarello, might not have cared, but here she was, a Jewess, worried about the fate of two Nazis. Looking out of the window and trying to ignore the atmosphere of hostility seeming to rise like a cloud from her driver, she watched rural England racing by and fingered the film in her pocket. There was a peace about this countryside that, though flat, somehow reminded her of the rolling hills of Pennsylvania, and she half expected that at any moment a family of Amish farmers would emerge, their black garb set against the yellow of the well-tended fields. Here in a land readying itself for another bloodletting, she watched sheep grazing and could envisage their markings coagulating into swastikas in a year's time, men like Hartmut owning vast tracts of land and women like Raine parading in uniform.

Where would characters with the courage of Valerie Cobb fit in?

Even in the United States, where Roosevelt fought daily with a Congress of appeasement, men on the street knew about the build-up of German air power. While the British took pride in their merchant fleet, chugging in and out of Southampton and New York with grandeur, Hitler Youth of both sexes were learning skills to far outclass the children of the New World, and German factories were producing aircraft by the thousand—dwarfing the meagre supplies of antiquated machines peppering the fields of English flying clubs. Women like Valerie, and her crop of indomitable fliers, could be at the forefront of a sudden conflict: if there were not enough pilots their presence could tip the balance. How odd, Edith thought, that carnage catapulted women into jobs forbidden to them in peacetime— and by those very men who also concocted the war games.

'Is this what you was wanting, miss?' growled Joe, his bull-like neck red, hairy and unwashed.

Edith was gratified that his reckless driving had brought them that much sooner to the airfield from which she would be flown to Hartmut and Zuki. She had consented to being flown, instead of flying herself, because she was still exhausted and dizzy from her transatlantic ordeal.

'Thank you, Joe. When I am back tonight, will you be here to pick me up?'

'Not bloody likely.' He did not look at her when he spoke, and Edith hated the man.

'Then who *is* going to be here?'

'Can't say, miss,' he mumbled. 'It's my night out with the missus.'

'Do you have children, Joe?'

'What's it to you, then?' He scowled at the girl, tapping the steering wheel impatiently.

'I just thought I might bring them some things from home when I come back.'

'I'm not a charity case.' He paused. 'I've a lad that wants to be a pilot—but I'll beat the life out of him before he goes on that lark.'

'Flying is a terrific profession.'

'Is it then, miss?' He had started the motor and was chewing his lip.

'What's his name? Valerie Cobb may want to recruit him.'

'Put my Cal anywhere near that madwoman? You must be joking.'

In the distance Edith could see her aircraft being readied and she backed away from the car.

'Goodbye, Joe,' she said, but he had already reversed, creating a cloud of dust.

Edith walked to the three-seater Spartan and was surprised to see another passenger in the aeroplane. She lifted herself into the tiny cabin and on closer inspection discovered she was in the company of two women in flying suits.

'I'm Barbara Newman, and this is Sally Remington.'

'Edith Allam. You're both dressed for flying.

124

Who's the pilot here?'

'I am,' Barbara replied. 'What do you call that you're wearing?'

Edith looked down at the plethora of zippered pockets across her own suit and she laughed. 'Does one of you know the way to the Isle of Man?'

'Barbara will fly you there, and, as I have just obtained my night-flight licence, I will bring you back.'

Edith settled herself in the rear of the small aircraft and as it soared into the afternoon sky Joe March stopped Lord Beaverbrook's car and spat out of the window. He looked at his watch and headed back toward London, which he would reach by pub opening time. He had not seen his wife or son for a week.

'Bloody pilots. Bunch of perverts,' he mumbled, and drove away, not caring if Edith Allam ever came back—dead or alive.

*   *   *

During that short flight through clear weather Sally and Barbara kept Edith entertained with elaborate anecdotes about their sporting careers. Her dizziness had subsided while airborne, but as soon as the Spartan landed she felt ill yet again. Bracing herself, she climbed out of the aircraft and shook Barbara's hand.

'Thank you so very much,' she said, smiling gratefully. 'I look forward to Chatterbox Number Two flying me back.'

Sally stuck out her tongue playfully, all three women united in the special spirit of friendship that always seemed to blossom amongst pilots. As

125

her ferry team retreated to the tiny terminal building Edith could see the detention centre in the distance. Her energy seemed to return in one great wave, and she walked with vigour to the front entrance.

'I am looking for Hartmut Weiss and Zuki Pilzer.'

She was directed to the back garden of the building, which until recently had been a stately home. Edith chuckled at the sight of Hartmut and Zuki sunning themselves in the company of a uniformed official.

'Edith!' Hartmut exclaimed, jumping from his lounge chair.

'This looks like fun, boys,' she said, as the others rose.

'We are rather new at this, madam,' said the official, making a little bow.

'No need to curtsey—I'm not royalty.'

'Unfortunately, madam, because these two gentlemen are the nation's first—shall we say?— informal detainees, they must not hold conversations with anyone except government officials.' His voice dropped to a whisper. 'We have reason to believe they may be German spies.'

'That's crazy!' asserted Edith.

Hartmut was staring at her.

'Edith is a famous aviatrix,' said Zuki impressively.

'May I give them a message from a friend?' asked Edith.

'No, I'm afraid not,' said the official, still standing.

She knew she could get nowhere, and Hartmut's gaze made her feel uneasy. She sat. To her astonishment he reached over and took her hand in his, holding it loosely but just enough to make her tingle.

'I really must ask you to leave,' the polite English gentleman said, staring at the joined hands.

'They fall in love!' Zuki chuckled.

'God forbid,' Edith said, withdrawing her fingers from the German's grip.

'Please would you come with me,' said the official.

'Why?' she demanded angrily.

'In these times in which we live, one gives obeisance to authority.'

'I'm an American on some puny island, and these are my friends.'

'That is why it would be wise for you to come with me.' He led her away.

'Are you afraid they might run away while you're not looking?'

'They wouldn't. Miss Allam, you should distance yourself from these men.'

'How do you know my last name?'

'We have certain information.'

Edith's heart was banging and she wanted to leave this place. 'Could you please give Hartmut a message?' she asked.

'Of course.'

'Tell him Raine is fine and the film is still in the camera.'

'I shall pass on the message. He did ask me to give you this, if you ever visited.'

Edith saw him remove an unsealed green envelope from his jacket pocket, her name written on the outside in ornate German script.

'Thank you.' She felt another dizzy spell coming

on. 'Mr . . .?'

'Anthony Seifert,' he said, and Edith could have sworn he clicked his heels. 'At your service.' He turned away and marched back to his charges.

Edith waved to the men and made her way to the airfield, where her lady pilots would be surprised to have had so short a break, and where she would board the little Spartan and laugh in their glorious company. There would be no chauffeur to take her back to the Beaverbrook villa, but she would walk, her body numb as she read Hartmut's words by the moonlight, before sinking into bed as dawn was breaking.

18

In a beautifully photographed newsreel, daily life in Naziland was being portrayed by a breathless narrator in a tone of apprehension tinged with a kind of perverse excitement. Hitler's handmaidens smiled out from under Tyrolean headwear, and his footmen kicked in the faces of corner shopkeepers. Frame by frame the natives were proving they were, indeed, the best Germany had to offer— except, of course, for its flagship 'Hindenburg', now aflame in a terrifying finale.

At the conclusion of the newsreel the lights came up on a stage and in front of the screen a troupe of dancers emerged. Pollock's Afternoon Theatre was providing entertainment for an assortment of people who had found themselves in Aldgate East, and on this day Alec Harborne and his fiancée Marion Wickham, in bomber jackets, were laughing their heads off. Scenes of horrors across one Channel and an ocean had left little impression, but the twosome had now come alive watching one of Britain's finest pilots doing what she did to earn a living.

Stella Teague, possessed of all the qualifications for RAF distinction, had trained as a ballerina and her tiny figure gave her a waif-like, almost pathetic appearance. It was therefore a shock, to those who allowed themselves to pity her, when she would rush away from rehearsals to serve a force inside her: aeroplanes had begun to overtake her bloodstream and her body had acquired an ache when compelled to remain grounded. Stella had loved earning a living from an exceptional occupation, but now a dilemma was emerging. Her company had been scheduled to tour the Americas, but rumours of a European war had scotched her greatest chance of New York stardom, as well as the chances her ballet master had had for international acclaim. He was German, his name was Grunberg, and he was classified in Britain as an Alien To Be Watched.

Now Stella had been relegated to movie-house sideshows, because the cancellation of her suspect master's tour had been compounded by her preoccupation with flying. Dance could no longer be her life. To pass her A and B licences, she had had to sit still and study, and to be a Rambert she must keep moving. Her libido had been sequestered, much to the concern of her parents, especially when tutu money had gone into a bomber jacket. Valerie Cobb had visited her flying club and when she had accompanied the MP's daughter to a pilots' gathering in Austria Valerie had warned her that this would be the last of these friendly events.

Upon Stella's return, the senior Teagues expressed their concern that she had no man in her life, but like most girls who had encountered Valerie Cobb her mind had become preoccupied with bettering her flying skills. She would set her sights on C and D licences. Grunberg fretted daily, and Stella got impatient with the ballet master. Why didn't *he* try flying?

'Men aren't allowed in here! Get out!' shrieked an outraged ballerina.

Alec Harborne had marched into the girls' changing room in the cold, damp snake-pit that passed as a theatre.

Transformed into a pilot with the donning of her bomber jacket and trousers, Stella laughed as Alec taunted the other dancing girls, his Scottish accent remarkably out of place amongst the well-spoken females. That they had found themselves in Aldgate East was as incongruous as Stella's tiny figure in flier's garb.

Marion Wickham faced a similar future and was still fighting daily with her parents about her expensive hobby. Flying had been an obsession ever since she had watched her uncle, a World War I ace, putting together a home-made biplane in their meagre back acre. It was not until she met Hana Bukova, the brilliant multilingual Polish pilot, on her trip to Austria, that she realized she was not the only girl to have been inspired by a mad relative. In Hana's case, it had been her own mother and when Marion had related this later to her parents Mr Wickham had taken to his bed and Mrs Wickham had taken to her garden.

All the women who had met at the last friendly fly-in on the Austro-German border were living out a dream beyond the highest hopes of their mundane contemporaries, whose ambitions were to work in a library, or an MP's office, and to marry an affluent barrister. Meeting Alec Harborne, a passionate character never destined to be called to the Bar, had given Marion a semblance of normality in the eyes of her family. Her eagerness to fly still caused arguments, but stocky, red-haired Alec would intervene and shock everyone by declaiming accurate quotations from epic poems.

'Yesterday I took a woman to Elstree and she nearly died when I lit up after take-off,' Alec related chattily, the girl pilots in tow. 'She spent the journey in a state of shock, and when she asked me how long it would take to reach our destination, I shouted, "Four cigarettes." She nearly fainted.'

Now they were on an omnibus and hatted lady shoppers were glaring.

'I'd like to see a few of these dancing girls in the air—out of their tutus and into heavy gear.' Alec was getting louder. 'My dream is to die with them flying right under me.'

'Let's go find Angelique,' Marion said, as more eyes turned. 'She's Romeo when the year ends!'

The Royal Academy of Dramatic Arts had been attractive to young women for many years, and this afternoon the three fliers were eager to collect from its noisy innards the fourth amongst their ranks. Angelique Florian had become the star of her RADA year, but, like Stella, had allowed her concentration to drift to aircraft. Young men had already begun to drift away inside those aircraft, leaving the great roles to be tackled by the girl players. Angelique wanted the roles, *and* the flying machines, and for the time being she was enjoying both rare commodities in a suddenly unusual world.

When the omnibus stopped alongside RADA the conductor gestured as if with contempt and the trio swept on to the pavement. Energy seemed to blast from the open door of the drama school and Angelique emerged, her dark hair framing a face best suited to a Cleopatra she would never portray.

'Next year I'm down for Richard III,' she exulted, slapping Alec on his shoulder. Her height put him at the same level, and momentarily he lost his balance. 'Those boys wanted so to do it—one of them brought his parachute to use for the great toad's hump.'

'They're better off in barracks,' sniffed Alec. 'Now you can make theatrical history.'

'I'm more worried about Zack and Paul,' murmured Angelique, subdued.

All four had stopped walking. Everyone knew that yet another anniversary had passed, marking the absence of Angelique's brothers. Zack and Paul had paid their uninvited visit to Spain but had not yet returned from an anti-Franco colony in France. When she had joined Valerie Cobb's group on the fly-in, Angelique had received echoes of misery from those who had fled Spain, and now she was desperately worried about her brothers. Coming back to the challenge of Perdita and Hermione had seemed a crazy exercise despite its crucial effect on her RADA results. She could see flying, and not *A Winter's Tale*, as her only way to keep sane through a war.

'Do you remember that camerawoman we met at the fly-in?' asked Marion.

Angelique was still thinking about Spain.

'Do you remember, Ange? She filmed the pictures we just saw at Pollock's—the newsreel that goes with Stella's dancing show.'

'Yes, I remember her very well,' said Angelique. 'How do you know it is her footage?'

'Because it ain't her leg-age,' quipped Alec.

'Haven't you heard?' asked Marion. 'She's here, and her film's been smuggled into one of the cinema chains. Apparently she can fly, though it was a big secret.'

'Why have I missed this?' Angelique asked irritably.

'Marion has a private line to Beaverbrook, via my competition,' joked Alec.

'Your competition?' Sheila and Angelique shouted in unison.

'Valerie Cobb,' he replied.

'What a disgusting thought.' Marion grimaced. 'Indeed, I'm told Raine Fischtal may be staying in the country because she knows about some secret German suicide weapon they're developing over there. Anke Reitsch is to be a test pilot—she and Raine are best chums.'

All had gone quiet, and as the four aeroplane pilots reached the corner and turned off Gower Street Marion was determined to press on, having been more captivated by Raine on celluloid than in the flesh. Content was immaterial.

'What did the newsreel show?' asked Angelique.

'They showed old Jews being beaten to death, good books being burned, and educated

133

men delirious because Wagner would not be interrupted at the opera house by the events outside,' Alec related.

A taxi rattled by, and as they walked along the pavement of Goodge Street the girls linked arms. His words had made them want warmth.

'That woman gets around—what was her name? Fish Stall?' Angelique recalled the odd encounter when Raine had extolled the glories of Francisco Franco. 'Do you think she ever took any footage of the Civil War?'

'She might have,' Alec said, as he ushered them into his jeep. Looking at Angelique, he smiled. 'You'll never be able to get to her now—I hear she's getting a top position with the Reich when she gets back.'

Conversation ceased, and as the unsteady vehicle passed buildings that were soon to die, the oddly dressed foursome thought about Spain and the newsreel and Valerie Cobb, wanting more than ever to take on the sky.

19

At Maylands Airfield and Flying Club in Essex, a dark mood had enveloped Alec Harborne. He had begun to dwell on Raine's footage and on the dawn bulletins from the wireless indicating more troubles in Austria. A Jewish youth had been blamed for the murder of a Nazi Party official and had been made a scapegoat. Now there was news of book-burnings and riots.

Alec's group had always come here for fun but

134

now the young flying pupils were disappearing and their female instructors looking envious. Word had got around that Valerie Cobb was searching the country for ten top women pilots. Scores of RAF boys marched away from their final lessons with sparkling qualifications while their instructors— some still in their twenties, some tall, some tiny— stood in their skirts and saw the lads drift down the course runway and achieve what their sex had ordained.

In the common room Alec and his group had assembled for his usual joke prior to flying sessions. His mood had spread a cloud over them today and even the second great passion of his life, Marion Wickham, was causing him irritation.

'Everyone knows when I'm taxiing because of my hair—orange curls keep blowing and I can't control them,' she complained.

'Oh, for God's sake, Wick, the same thing happens to me, and I've got black hair,' snapped Angelique. 'One of these days I'll have to start dyeing it—my nerves are turning it grey.'

'Shut up, shut up,' growled Alec. 'Soon there won't be any hair dye, or any meat, or any celluloid to make films.'

A strangely grim atmosphere descended as Alec continued—it was not the subject-matter so much as the incongruity of this exuberant Glaswegian transmitting gloom that rocked the others.

'Films will always get made,' muttered Stella. 'What about that one by Fischtal?'

'It was only confiscated this week—along with Fish Stall herself,' Alec replied.

'The last time I went to Austria I was stopped from landing and I nearly crashed into a village,'

Marion continued. 'All my friends over there wanted to leave the ground and do nothing else, and now they're Nazis and they want to do everything else but leave the ground.'

Angelique smiled. 'Those friendships are over for good. Maybe we'll get lucky and meet some of them across a gunner's target.'

'What a frightful thing to say, you old witch!' exclaimed Stella.

A commotion stopped their chatter and the group moved en masse to the entrance of the common room. Sunlight blinded them for a moment but they could perceive a crowd of reporters and photographers gathering around what looked like a Fokker.

Alec walked on ahead of the others and plunged into the excitement.

Marion stayed behind and talked to herself:

'It's that bloody Edith Allam again,' she murmured.

Aircraft flying in and out of the field had to take avoiding action to circumvent the huge crowd that had gathered to see the remarkable American girl who had been touted in the news stories as having flown the Atlantic and nearly crashed into the Irish Sea at gunpoint with her priceless cargo of the classified Nazi footage.

Reporters shouted and Edith fizzed with nervous energy.

'What has happened to Miss Fischtal?' demanded a male voice.

'Is it true the American government is after you?'

'Have you decided to remain in England because of a love affair?'

'Yes, she's decided to remain in England because

of me!' Alec Harborne asserted.

'I've never seen this man before in my life.' Edith had spoken for the very first time, her blue eyes boring into Alec.

'Miss Allam, have you a husband at home?'

Edith stared at the woman reporter, and Alec walked alongside.

'You must want to get out of here,' he said gently.

'I can't,' she whispered. 'The *Daily Record* is paying for my trip back, in exchange for a good story.'

'This woman used to be a man, but he ate too much raw coconut,' Alec shouted. He turned to the American. 'Is that a good enough story?' The raincoated, felt-hatted assembly fell silent and Alec, perspiring, took Edith's arm, forcing her to run with him to a Spartan at the far end of the field. The reporters ran after them, and the woman slipped and fell. There was a commotion, and Edith looked back anxiously.

'I can't get into this one,' she protested. 'They have a designated aircraft, just for me,' she pointed to a large Oxford. 'My mission is to cross the world twice and bring my plane back filled with American and Australian pilots ready to fly in the ferry pools if war breaks out.'

'Male or female?'

'Female—it's a publicity stunt of some kind. From ice-cream sodas on a Saturday night to the prospect of talcum-powder eggs over here—those girls won't last a day.' Edith paused and poked Alec with her gloved hand. 'What do you do on a Saturday night?'

'He pours talcum-powder eggs all over me.' Marion was next to the Spartan, humming to herself. Angelique and Stella had left the common room with the others but were observing the proceedings from a distance.

'This is my future in-house paramour,' growled Alec.

Marion's rage made her flush, and as the two women looked at each other Alec became lost in a sea of reporters shouting once more at the little American who had been bred on ice-cream sodas and real eggs.

'Write to me if you don't come back, angel,' Alec urged Edith, meanwhile holding Marion's wrist tightly.

'I have to come back. My own world won't want me any more.'

'What do you mean by that, Miss Allam?' Reporters did sometimes listen, and on this occasion it was the muddied woman.

'Take me to the Oxford,' Edith said, her eyes hollowing like those of Joan of Arc after the rape and before the burning.

They walked, and Alec stopped, looking back at his fiancée. He reached for Marion. His grip was painful and she pulled away.

'I'm not your bloody joystick,' she snapped.

They had reached the gleaming Oxford.

'When will you be back, Miss Allam?' asked a voice.

'You should know—you're from the *Daily Record*,' Edith replied, and with that she lifted herself into the aeroplane, Alec hoisting her bag into the empty seat. Behind her tiny figure were the two extra fuel tanks. Cameras snapped and flashes popped.

'Now I've got spots in front of my eyes,' moaned

138

Edith.

She sat back and made adjustments, her heart racing at the prospect of a solitary Atlantic crossing. Amid the screaming of the gathered press a lone man approached, and as he neared the open hatch Edith's palpitations increased: as airfield supervisor, Sean Vine was not required to carry out a final inspection on the departing aviatrix but she had caught his eye on this brief trip. He circled the aircraft and when his walk was complete he looked up at Edith impassively. Now he was alongside the hatch and the restless reporters still shouted. He said something and she could not hear. Suddenly Alec lurched forward and pushed them back.

A scuffle ensued, and he grinned.

'Are you Miss Allam's beau?' a voice shrilled, grasping the Scotsman's sleeve.

'He's mine,' stated Marion. 'We are all qualified pilots, waiting for Valerie Cobb to find us a place in the ferry pools when the war comes. Alec and I hope to follow in Jim and Amy's footsteps. Print that.'

Alec wanted to add his bit, but his voice was drowned out by the sudden roar of the Oxford. He could see Edith smiling broadly at Sean Vine as she revved, and when she gave Alec a quick wink he felt angrier, knowing she found his passion trivial enough to be left behind. Marion was the love of his life, after aeroplanes, but Edith could easily overtake the excitement of these machines.

As the Oxford roared to its takeoff he noticed Vine walking backwards as if drunk, then turning away, skipping briskly back to his office.

'Do I suspect you're going to miss her?' asked

Angelique.

'He's only just met the girl,' observed Stella.

'She has a secret, a damned juicy one, I reckon,' said Alec, calm again. 'She'll be back because of it.'

'I can't wait,' said Marion. 'Come along, joystick.'

Angelique and Stella commandeered Puss Moths and watched Alec and Marion enter the Spartan. As if swallowed up by the airstream of Edith's departure, the reporters had disappeared.

In the cockpit Marion felt atrocious.

'I have a horrible feeling about the months coming on,' she said, starting up the engine. 'Everybody here is going to be doing something absolutely different from anything they've ever done before.'

'Good,' enthused Alec, strapping himself in.

'Good for the boys, but not for us. Alec, there are hundreds of these girls, and they should be regular RAF.'

'Of course they should, and especially you. First you have to marry me. I'll be an RAF widower.'

Marion taxied and her long, delicate fingers held the joystick gently, as if reflecting the relaxation she always found when about to raise herself up from the earth's gravity. Alec placed his fingertips on her hand and she grimaced. He withdrew and went for his cigarettes. Responding to her lone touch the throttle surged and they were airborne.

It was a calm flight. This was a quiet machine, and they could talk.

'I can't face a war without our being married first, Marion.'

'I wish these engines didn't purr so softly—then I wouldn't have to hear you.'

'Listen, lass, if we are both in a civil air division,

140

we can still be together at night.' Alec drew on the cigarette, and the aircraft lurched as if coughing.

'God, that really is a disgusting habit.' Marion shuddered.

Alec was silent.

'And I'm damned if a three-day assignment for a civil air unit is going to be ruined by my having to troop back to cook for Hubby.'

'Marriage will buffer me against war,' he responded quietly. 'War will buffer me against marriage.'

The aircraft hit a patch of thick cloud and Marion tensed in her seat. When they emerged, blue sky hit them brilliantly and the lady pilot took her fiancé to a higher altitude. Another aeroplane passed to the left and they could make out the distinctive markings of Edith's Oxford.

'Shall I trail her out to sea?' Alec murmured.

'Who?'

'No-one.'

Alec peered out, and the Oxford sped away, its magnificent horsepower seeming to spirit his rage out over the sea.

'Listen—if I am taken into an Air Arm it will mean overnights all across the map,' Marion continued, as if they had never stopped thinking during the clouds and Edith. 'Anyway, how can you sit here considering the implications of marriage and war when you are incapable of self-discipline in any area of your life?'

'You've been spending too much time around unnatural freaks—like the circus twins,' Alec remarked pointedly.

'Valerie and Shirley are vastly superior to any man I've yet to meet,' she said, concentrating as cloud rippled alongside. 'Seriously, Alec. Marriage in this climate could be catastrophic—two fliers competing for top job. It would put us both through a wringer.'

'Unlike the marriage of Valerie Cobb and Shirley Bryce?'

'You know bloody well Valerie has her Austrian for passion and Shirley has her mother for comfort.'

'Have mothers and men ever stopped two women from fancying each other?' Alec stared meaningfully at Marion, and she turned her face away.

'We were talking about marriage, I believe,' she said.

'My belief is that it works, like the Bryce and Cobb show.'

'Like Jim and Amy—look what's happened to them, and there isn't even a war on yet.'

Alec turned to the small window and for the rest of the ride he kept silent as the image of the Mollisons made him feel uneasy and unsexed.

Marion could think only of Valerie, Edith and the German film-maker whose combined images had begun to excite her much more than the prospect of an engagement ring. She brought her aircraft in for a perfect landing as rain pattered on the dirt runway, Sean Vine observing from nearby. He smiled, as if relieved to see Alec close to home.

As the couple walked the slippery road to the common room in silence Marion stooped to pick up a tiny canister. It was marked 'Kodak', and as she pocketed it she laughed at the thought of some distraught press photographer who tonight would be without his pictures.

20

In their home, Jim and Amy Johnson-Mollison were dressing for a small party they were to be hosting. She was a quiet, if not depressive creature, but the prospect of war had made her feel cheerful.

'This could be my big chance to shine,' she said, buttoning her blouse.

'Haven't you shone enough?'

'If there's a war, which more than likely there will be, Valerie will find me something worthwhile to do.' She looked up at Jim, who stood near her with a quizzical expression on his face. Amy knew an anecdote was coming.

'Our genius drew a blower on the blackboard today, and asked the men what they thought it was. Alec Harborne volunteered. He said he thought it looked to him like the cross-section of the inside of a lady pilot.'

Amy remained quiet.

'Please don't humiliate me on this night, of all nights,' she said, her colour gone.

'Are those my instructions, Captain?'

'Yes.'

'They mean nothing.'

The doorbell rang.

Jim was angry. 'Go and answer that.'

Amy went to the door, and the guests poured in. No sooner had Valerie Cobb and her father crossed the threshold than she was bubbling, bringing the circulation back to Amy's veins.

'War is looming, darling,' Valerie hummed.

'Daddy is hoarse from yelling in the Commons. Did I tell you Tim Haydon has been paying us regular calls?'

By now Jim had entered the drawing room, scowling.

'Tim seems fascinated by you two,' said Amy.

'He's fascinated by deviation—new word,' Jim growled. 'Not even in the dictionary.'

'I see you are in regular form, Mollison,' retorted Sir Henry. 'Valerie is abnormal, you say?'

'Oh, let's not go sour,' begged Amy.

'He's not sour, he's pickled,' laughed Valerie, good-naturedly squeezing Jim's arm. 'May an unnatural woman touch you?'

The doorbell rang again and Amy was gratified to see Gerard d'Erlanger and Hamilton Slade, a fine pilot too old for the RAF but still a vibrant figure, his strong frame topped by a warmly handsome face and thick blond curls, now greying at the temples. He had a sadness about him that matched Amy's melancholy. She walked towards him and the others stood aside.

'God, Ham, I was thinking tonight, while Jim was ranting on about something, that my world is coming to an end.'

'I'm surprised you can think about anything when he rants.'

'You'd be amazed at the ground I cover inside my head when he starts,' she whispered, knowing the guests were close by. A hand reached over and offered her a drink. It was Valerie, and she was grinning.

'Don't let me interrupt you two,' she said.

'That's all right, Val,' Amy smiled back. 'I was just saying to Ham that my world is over.'

'That's what the American girl was saying this morning—you know, Edith Allam?'

'Oh, God, that one,' groaned Jim, now leaning against Amy's small frame.

'She took off today, but before she left, Alec says she told the reporters her world had changed.'

D'Erlanger had joined them, and Amy perked up.

Valerie continued.

'What a story—that girl sold a cover photo to *Life*, flew the Atlantic, and helped us pinch Fischtal and her film all in the space of a fortnight.'

'Could we use her?' asked d'Erlanger.

'Allam? She's coming back with a load of Americans and then doing another load from Australia—all female,' said Valerie.

'Ho-ho! I like the sound of that!' exclaimed Jim.

'You would,' murmured Amy. 'Has anyone thought of me?'

'Essential for the war effort—publicity,' enthused Slade. 'We could use you to get support for anything.'

'Amy gets support even when she's flying with her entourage of admirers,' snapped Jim, downing another vodka. 'She uses her fame and freedom to flirt around the globe,' he continued. 'I stay at home and brew, Slade.'

'No woman ever has freedom,' muttered Valerie.

'Are you really going to take on the Air Ministry, Val?' asked Amy, her voice shaky.

'I may,' Valerie replied.

Sir Henry looked sharply at his daughter, but knew it was not his moment for contention.

'I'll come along as an accomplice. Would that be all right?' asked Amy, more nervous than a minute before.

'It might backfire, Amy,' said d'Erlanger. She could sense his gravitational pull, and knew her world was receding. He wanted good things for Valerie Cobb.

'This is monstrous!' exploded Sir Henry. 'Enough is enough. Women will be needed in the canteens, and lesser ladies will be sent to staff the factories.'

'Nonsense, Henry,' said Jim, suddenly subdued. 'There are loads of stunning young women flying at our club.'

'That's what's worrying all the suits in the House,' said Slade.

Sir Henry was cornered.

'Dad, women like Edith are coming back to fly for Britain, and the rest are already here.'

Jim sniggered unpleasantly. 'One of our girls at the Club exercises by standing on her head,' he mused. 'I can think of one lady pilot who ought to do that—it might improve her . . . performance.' Having delivered his punch line, Jim Mollison collapsed in a heap on the floor.

Another evening at the Mollisons had turned into a disaster, and to divert everyone's embarrassed attention the pale and trembling hostess pointed to her newest trophy. No-one looked, and her husband remained prostrate. One by one the guests dispersed, and only Hamilton Slade remained as a blast of cold air blew past after a slam of the door.

Amy was sitting on the floor and Hamilton crouched next to her. They would leave Jim to sleep.

'I'm joining the Civil Air Guard,' said Hamilton.

Amy looked up at him, bemused.

'You should join too, Amy.'

'What? Why?'

'Ten choice women are to be picked for front-line service. Valerie will do it—mark my words. Everything she does is marked by perfection. You and I could ferry from the same pool when she gets started.'

By now he was holding her and his majestic size sent a rush of rage and want surging through her. Then she became miserable. Like clockwork.

'Please leave,' she asked Slade quietly, without conviction.

Moments later he was touching her and she was more miserable, Jim's snoring drowning out her moans as Hamilton erupted inside her and another Amy came.

When he had left her alone with her trophies she sat on the floor, looking through a scrapbook of clippings and holding her blouse tightly against her damp flesh. These were well organized clippings, and the other Amy wallowed in feeling miserable as the night ticked away in rhythm with the imperfect man's noisy dreams of women standing on their heads.

21

Smithfield Market at dawn was a rough, noisy hodgepodge and on this particular morning the men were huddling in groups. Talk was of mobilization, and each worker was already a soldier in his private fantasy. Chatter became a

147

roar as boys and men speculated on their days to come.

Inside a small warehouse office, Nora Flint was sorting market files and Cal March, the energetic sixteen-year-old runner, had stopped to make tea. Their boss, Sam Hardwick, tumbled into the office, his overweight frame breathless.

'I can't get any discipline this morning,' he gasped. 'Those men have decided they're already serving another master.'

'Perhaps they are,' said Nora.

'What? How can you say that? This is one of the busiest times of the year—it will destroy me if things go wrong.'

Cal handed him a cup of tea and his hand was unsteady. The hot liquid reached his mouth too soon and he spluttered.

'All the papers are full of war,' murmured Nora. 'Surely you're absorbing it, Mr H?'

'Of course I am,' he boasted, and Cal cowered, moving towards the door.

'Stay where you are, boy.'

Cal sat, and Nora put her hand on his arm. He was always apt to run when a voice rose in volume. Hardwick stared at the boy and wondered if he would flee someday when he was upon his first woman and had made her cry out in the night.

'If there is anyone who is taking this war business on board, it's me,' the boss continued. 'We have a world crisis looming and if it brings rationing my life is over.'

'That won't be nothing new for me,' said Cal, squirming at Nora's touch. 'My Dad's been rationing our table ever since I can remember.'

Nora and her employer were quiet.

148

'My mum and I are like sticks,' Cal continued, 'and the old man just gets fatter and fatter—funny, in't it?'

All had gone silent within their small surroundings, and the roar of men outside gained momentum. Hardwick looked up from his tea and took in the two children he had added to the workplace.

'Why would a young woman of your class find satisfaction working in a place like this?' he asked.

Nora thought for a moment and her colour began to fade. 'I suppose I ought to tell you the truth, as this seems to be crisis morning.'

'Go on,' said Hardwick.

'I rise at three a.m., to be here at four o'clock start, and in the afternoon when the Market has finished I dash to Maylands.'

'The airfield!' the boy exclaimed.

'People there work in any kind of toil to raise the three guineas an hour for a lesson,' Nora went on. 'My friends are in theatre, the ballet, mechanical engineering—all girls, all pilots.'

'Their dads know?' demanded Cal, wide-eyed.

'Mine does,' said Nora. 'It doesn't make him happy.'

'He beats you?' asked Cal, quietly.

'I've yet to see any bruises on her,' said Hardwick, rising from his chair.

'You might say I am a daring young woman in a Puss Moth,' Nora asserted, her voice animated.

'This is amazing.' Cal had calmed down. Nora's raised voice charmed him and for a few moments he was devoid of terror.

'I have accumulated nearly three hundred flying hours,' she continued. 'Every penny has been paid

149

for from this—by you, Mr Hardwick. My parents have always refused to contribute, where my lessons are concerned. They're frightened, I think.'

'Frightened?' asked Cal.

'They would be. *I* would be,' mused Sam Hardwick. 'Children make one fearful. Everything they undertake scares a parent.'

Nora felt a warmth towards her boss that transcended her class.

'I suppose they haven't thought as far as a war,' she said. 'They fear for my life because I boast that the flying is not a hobby.'

'But what does your Dad think?' asked Cal anxiously, as if her entire future rested on patriarchal judgement.

'They've both resigned themselves to my long days.'

Hardwick could not fight the paternal emotion rising with the warm tea in his belly.

'When do you sleep?' he asked, aching for the daughter his spawn had never hatched.

'Every spare minute is spent in the air, like all the other girls in my group. I sleep when I'm not here in the middle of the night or flying at teatime.'

'Will you be flying if there's a war?' Cal asked.

'A hunch tells me I'll soon be airborne for the country. Whether I'll survive is up to the factory workers. If they make a faulty plane, I'm the one who dies.'

Hardwick scooped up a pile of messages and handed them to the boy.

'Take these to Liverpool Street,' he commanded, and Cal returned to his cowering stance. He took the papers and as he moved to leave, turned to Nora:

'When next you fly at teatime, look out for me. I'll find a way to be there.' Then he ran off as if pursued.

Sam Hardwick smiled and watched him run down the busy corridors, his reed-like legs circumventing tables of carcasses and animated men—many of whom would soon be butchered too. This boss was a warm character deeply entrenched in his comfortable routine, and terrified of change. How could these men think of soldiering? Like so many in that limbo between working-class and middle-class, his love of family was compounded by that terror of a return to poverty.

'Be careful,' he murmured, turning back to Nora.

'God, I'm more worried about you here on the ground, than about myself up in the air.'

'I've spent a lifetime building up this corner of someone else's monumental profit and now I've a legacy of three sons.'

'You won't lose both,' she said. He had touched her—she could not remember when last her own father had moved her so.

'Soon I may be left alone,' he pondered. 'How could you be part of a war machine?'

His sharpness had come abruptly and Nora felt lost, wanting to justify her peculiar goal but having no passion to express herself.

'What about your family?' he shouted.

'They can cope. It's in their blood.' She wanted to cry. 'For you, I'll make an extra effort to keep alive.'

Clatter and conversation from the maelstrom of men was beginning to drown out their voices, and Nora returned to her typewriter, wondering whether she could keep to her promise. Hardwick went back to his desk and at the end of the day had convinced himself that if three sons and the meat market were doomed, and this girl had to be lost to a Spitfire, then he too would need to make an extra effort to stay alive.

At midday when the market shut and Nora left for the airfield, Sam Hardwick departed from his lifelong routine and did not return home to his wife on the dot of noon. Instead, he followed Nora at a distance, and at the airfield he stood on the outskirts, watching young men and women pursuing their unnatural obsession. As the sun began to set and he began to fall asleep standing up, Sam was approached by a pilot in smart flying gear. He was bespectacled and his age indeterminate, but Noel Slater had the gift of acquisitive charm. This he now used to acquire Sam Hardwick.

Mrs Hardwick would have a long wait that afternoon, and for the rest of her married afternoons to come.

*   *   *

In the cold-water misery that was his home, Cal March sat with his parents over a meagre lunch. One half of a dry biscuit in his mouth seemed to stay there forever. Terrified of the thoughts surging through his head, he could not swallow. His mother glanced sideways at him and pushed a mug down the table towards his tightly clenched fist. Without looking at her, he opened his fist and grasped the drink, slurped it, and wondered if he dared broach a dreaded subject.

'Slopping like swine again, are you?' grunted his father.

'That new airbase is opening up to lads—only two and sixpence to learn to fly!' Cal blurted, the cold tea running down his chin.

March glowered, and sneered:

'RAF types are there to teach little lads just one thing—queer habits picked up at fancy schools. If I ever hear that you've gone anywhere near them, you'll rue the day.'

'What would you be wanting with the RAF, then?' asked Mrs Bridie March.

'It was four guineas to learn for an hour, and now the Air Ministry is dropping it down to two and six, Mum. Anyone can join up.'

'That's just what I'm saying,' groaned March. 'It's white slavery—these top boys bring in poor lads and use them for evil carryings-on.'

'Like what, Dad?'

'Don't go on like that, Joe,' Cal's mother cautioned her husband.

Dry biscuits had never before curdled in Cal's stomach. 'I've already been and I'm on to lesson three,' he rasped.

'Been where?' Joe March inquired menacingly.

'To the airfield—' A back-handed blow came down on Cal's ear before he could expand on his achievement.

'You bloody young swine—I'll belt you like never before,' March raged. He drew his belt and pulled Cal to the floor, on his knees.

Bridie March gasped.

'I'm listed for Air Cadets—the youngest ever!' screamed Cal, but he was overcome by the blows raining down from his father's raging fists. Was this

153

the fear of which Nora and Hardwick had spoken?

When March had finished and gone, and the boy had vomited, his mother treated his bruises.

'Give up this craziness, please,' she begged.

Brightly he sat up and his eyes sparkled again. 'I see myself as Stepney's first Air Commodore.'

'Dad is right, Cal,' said Bridie, her rough, work-swollen fingers stroking his soft face. 'RAF means Background, and you'll always be trod on.'

'War means there's no more class, Mum.'

'Class comes back with peace,' she said, smiling sadly.

'As long as the war lasts, no one can tread on me.'

'You'd be surprised. For God's sake, Cal, don't do this.'

He was unmoved. As if left alone for the first time in his life, he felt a coldness creeping into his psyche. Staring at his mother, Cal remembered that his flesh was half hers and half that of the creature who feared him, and he welcomed the freezing sensation.

Could it be much different from death?

'I must reach the sky,' Cal said, his mother now at the far end of the room, her eyes full of that fear. 'Home is hell, and if flying means heaven, I'm ready to die now.'

Bridie March turned away. As she mopped the floor, Cal left—wondering why in one afternoon he had lost the ability to cry. After every previous beating he had ended up in tears. This time he had been sick and he had been able to argue. He walked down the road and passed the local costermonger, who did not recognize him when he said the usual hello.

That pleased the boy.

154

22

At Maylands, Angelique Florian was dramatizing excerpts from the latest news cuttings. Recently it had become a ritual for her flying group to listen together, entranced, as the wild brunette read the grim bulletins. On this day their sombre session was interrupted by the arrival of Noel Slater, the young flight engineer who could also pilot fifty different types of aircraft. His irritating boastfulness had made him intensely unpopular, compounded by a loud ambition to form his own airline.

Girls mocked him.

His poor eyesight and slight lameness had kept him out of the RAF, and every girl he dated reminded him that he would still be a flight engineer while they were transporting giant bombers. His contempt for them, in turn, would blaze in his tormenting criticisms when airborne with a lady pilot, often leading to near-catastrophes.

'Which one of you was responsible for that dented Anson? It was spiffing new,' he shouted, stopping Angelique's magic.

'It would have to be one of the boys, Noel—you know bloody well we're not yet allowed near those things,' Stella replied.

He slammed his gloves down on the table and grabbed a printed news-sheet from the actress.

'There is something obscene about you people making a show out of horror,' he said, and he began pacing the room.

'Have you got something new to offer us today, Noel?' asked Angelique, rising from her chair. She moved to the door, and all ears were alert. 'Come with me,' she said. 'I recommend we go out, right now, in a training aircraft, which I will pilot, and that you show me all the latest developments in flying technique to have come about in the past twenty-four hours.'

There were some giggles, and Slater followed her to the field. She went for a new Oxford, and the man flinched.

'We can't afford to ruin one of these,' he muttered.

'I've flown three hundred hours and haven't ruined anything yet,' she said. 'You know I have authorization, which is more than you get around here. Get in,' she said, glaring at his thick lenses. His body did not respond to her splendid shape, which now hung so close to his, and which made other men on this field drool. His own sex did not make him drool, so what could he call himself? Little wonder, he reflected as he boarded, that he had been dubbed Tin Man by his one or two friends.

When they were airborne, Noel put the trainer into a sharp spin. Angelique was livid—she was designated pilot and his hands were forbidden anywhere near the controls. Every time he went up with a lady pilot, he meddled. She had heard the stories from every quarter.

With an effort, Angelique righted the plane.

'Feel sick?' he asked, grinning.

'No!'

'No, sir!' he snapped, attacking the instruments again and putting the machine into a reverse

156

spin. It was a horrible sensation and extremely dangerous in this type of aircraft. He loved the effect this was having on the woman, without thought for his own life. In the face of death, he might see and be whole.

Somehow Angelique managed to right the Oxford before disaster. 'Now, do YOU feel sick?' she shouted.

'I'll have you up for insubordination when we are back on base,' he yelled back.

'On base? What do you think this is, the RAF?' They were cruising now.

'I'm your superior, fatty,' he snorted.

'That's a new one—I've been called buxom, and juicy, but you can only see fat, eh? Just remember, Slater, you'll never make the RAF, so we're in our own war together.'

At the airfield, a crowd had gathered as Angelique, senior pilot, came in to land after the unexpected show of aerobatics. It was not a smooth approach, and all breath was held as she did an extra circuit before wobbling and bouncing in. The craft was at a standstill and Angelique scrambled out of the cockpit as if pursued. Running to the main airfield building, she headed straight for the club supervisor.

Sean Vine was not sympathetic. As operations head of a civilian field he was long accustomed to female pilots making complaints about Noel Slater. With new faces invading the pitch and footage of jackboots being shown in Soho screening rooms, things were changing.

'You had better get lost, Florian,' he said, and Angelique was dumbfounded.

Voices could be heard nearby, and Vine

stiffened.

'Sean, Noel Slater is filth.'

'Shall I file that as a formal complaint?' Vine was tense, and his voice had reached a high pitch. 'Did you know we have guests about to visit the club?'

'War folk?' asked Angelique

'Perhaps. One of them is your lady idol, Miss Cobb. The lesbian.'

'And I'm Armenian royalty.'

'There's royalty, and there's royalty.'

'Listen—Noel Slater is a lunatic and there's a new word being touted by Freudians to describe him: *misogynist*. Please file that.'

Turning into their path was the VIP brigade. Lord Brabazon, Gerard d'Erlanger, Captain Balfour and Valerie Cobb were touring the premises, and all indications were that the lady was in charge. She showed them the main building with a sweep of her hand and the men appeared fascinated, as if they had never before seen bricks and mortar in their lives. Sean Vine joined in and they talked amongst themselves.

Angelique grabbed the moment, taking Valerie aside:

'I can't get anywhere with Vine about banning Slater. He should be locked up, Val. He put me into a reverse spin—any beginner would have been killed. Why should his deathwish kill one of our girls?'

Brabazon had come over to the two women.

'Who was responsible for that shaky landing just witnessed by all?' he asked.

Angelique was ready to speak but Valerie put her hand up, resting it on the other girl's abdomen and silencing her.

158

'That was a student pilot on his third flight,' Valerie asserted with a steely smile. 'Shall we inspect the main building? It has an assortment of functions.'

She let the men wander on ahead, then said:

'It serves you right, Ange, if you're stupid enough to get airborne with Slater. If this bunch had known it was a woman bouncing in at the controls of that damned new Oxford, our cause would have been reversed, with great tut-tuts all round.'

'How was I to know you were on your way here with the gods?'

'Every time we do something that looks wrong, whether living under the same roof with another lady or skidding on the landing strip, we are ten times guilty. That is the way the world works. Stay away from Slater. There are men and there are men, and he belongs to the fiend category.'

'I know a few female fiends, Val.'

'Introduce him, then—get him mated.'

Valerie marched off, and Angelique, suddenly exhausted, walked slowly to the common room and winced at the sound of aircraft engines. She wanted to be in another place. Not stopping for her usual mug of muddy coffee made with her own Armenian brew, the actress headed for the changing room. Gone was any desire for further flying this day. As she removed her flying suit and donned skirt and bomber jacket, she could hear voices again.

Captain Balfour turned the corner of the corridor and stopped at the changing-room door. Angelique looked up as she fastened her suspenders. He blushed.

'This is one of our top lady pilots—three-

159

hundred-plus hours and total instrument proficiency,' Valerie announced.

'I can see a uniformed women's unit arising from the report I'll be submitting,' Balfour enthused, eyeing the garter and the Florian legs.

Would he remember her legs tomorrow? If a women's unit could come from a wild memory of stockings, so much the better.

Valerie and Angelique exchanged meaningful looks.

23

A week had passed since VIP day at Maylands, and in Hunstanton Shirley and Valerie were clearing out their hut. A pounding on their door made them share the same thought: that it could be either Kranz or Tim Haydon, and neither would be a welcome sight. Shirley was becoming wary of the Austrian, and the degree to which Haydon snooped redoubled her wariness. Anyone being trailed by an MP had to be dangerous. Kranz might take Valerie away from her, and that would destroy her life.

Did Valerie know that?

The pounding became more persistent, and Valerie went to the door. A member of the circus troupe stood at the entrance, soaked by the heavy rain.

'Please come to our office, miss,' he said, terrified of the two females who lived without men.

They followed him out and made their way to the small room in which primitive bookkeeping

160

recorded the transactions of their art. Taking in their surroundings, the girls found a silent collection of odd characters and freaks, crowded solemnly in a corner by a wireless. Discussing, in slow, laborious tones, news of Hitler's annexation of the Sudetenland, the BBC voice could have been broadcasting a state funeral.

'Why are these discussions of such importance to this sordid lot?' Shirley hissed.

'They're Czech and Polish—for them the catastrophe has already arrived. They can't go home now.'

Shirley looked at the faces of the performers but none had eyes that could see. Their vision was taking in not the dusty floor of a hovel in Norfolk but mind's-eye pictures of homelands annexed by a new master.

'Are they safe here, I wonder?' Shirley asked, gazing at her partner.

'Probably not—Tim Haydon will be after them, and it will be nasty.'

For a brief moment one set of eyes came back from Prague and bored into the two female figures. Before the Pole could speak they left in a hurry. As they rushed across the field they thought they could hear shouting, and they wished their door had bolts.

Inside, they resumed their housework, unable to stop shaking.

Valerie found their precious whisky bottle, rationed from the Cobb collection. 'I've been giving Kranz advanced flying lessons.'

Shirley faced her, the tremors gone. 'Am I hearing correctly?'

'We've met many times since that first occasion

when you were reading poetry. He even jokes now about being a Hitler operative.'

'This makes no sense—what about all that testiness when you first met?' Shirley pushed her partner's hand away as it proffered a chipped whisky glass. 'Why do you always give me this one, and you get the perfect crystal?'

Valerie downed both measures, one in each hand, and slammed the glasses down on the wooden table.

'I'm going out to the Spartan.' Shirley opened the door and driving rain poured in.

Valerie followed her out.

'Friedrich has a special mission, and I am trying to help him,' the pilot shouted to her ground engineer.

Shirley came out from the muddy underside of the plane. 'Has he told you, Val, that his mission is to rescue a wife and two daughters?'

Valerie stood up and let the rain soak through her clothes. In the distance a Czech circus freak leaned against a shack and smoked a cigarette, puffing more frequently as she became wetter. He was far away but as her eyes cleared and tears ran into her mouth she was aware that he stared at her nipples, exposed by the relentless wetness. She drew her hands up to her chest and thought of a recurrent dream in which she stood before the Air Ministry naked and Lady Londonderry handed her a handkerchief . . .

She had made her way to the hut and Shirley was standing over her.

'That circus manager has had many chats with Friedrich, you'll be pleased to know, Val.'

'Why?' Valerie looked up at her partner with

swollen eyes.

'These people, whatever their national allegiance, should not be trusted. Obviously Friedrich never told you he was married. So, beware his motives.'

The hut was unbearably silent as the lady pilot, white and powerless against a force greater than the Air Ministry, curled up in a corner and let her clothes drip in unison with their ancient tap.

Shirley felt ashamed of herself because for the first time in weeks, since the advent of Kranz, she was explosively happy.

*   *   *

'The menace is the female who thinks she ought to be pilot of a bomber when she really has barely enough skill to polish the floor . . . too much self-assurance, an overload of arrogance, a disdain for orders, and nil experience: the combination causes crashes . . . this whole affair of engaging women fliers when there are so many men fully qualified to do the work, is disgusting . . .!'

At Maylands the common room was hushed as the women pilots took turns reading aloud from the latest issue of the widely-circulated and highly respected *Air* magazine. Cigarette smoke and the smell of stale coffee did not deter an assortment of voices from projecting the well-researched words into every surrounding corridor.

'The ladies in question are only doing it as a pastime and should be ashamed . . . When will the RAF wake up to the fact that the good they are doing is being ruined by this abominable lot of women?'

Angelique Florian's mesmeric reading was

163

interrupted by the arrival of Alec Harborne.

As if electrified, all present froze.

'There will be no more flying at this club. The Air Ministry is confiscating all civil aircraft and grounding non-RAF pilots. I'm as devastated as the rest of you,' added Alec.

Several other men had wandered into the common room and were beginning to look neglected.

'Our only hope', Alec continued, 'is that an air auxiliary will be formed, so we'll not all go to waste. It's what we've all been hoping for.'

One by one the girls rose from the table and soon Alec was alone with the magazine. He picked it up and read the page left open. Nothing in the text made him laugh, and he lit up a cigarette. Noel Slater and Sam Hardwick sat down at the table and took the *Air* from his limp hand.

They read.

Noel laughed, and Sam frowned.

Alec stubbed out the fag end, stared at Slater and murmured, 'Blind eunuch,' moving slowly to the door.

He could not expect Slater to challenge his abuse and he wandered on to the field. The girls had gathered a few yards on, and they watched busy RAF personnel scurrying amongst the manifold types of little planes.

'They had all better start learning how to rivet,' Noel shouted from the doorway.

'So had you,' Alec shouted back.

Angelique turned around.

'That would be national suicide,' she said, approaching the two men. 'Every machine he'd touch would be faulty.'

164

Slater was not perturbed.

Angelique glanced at him again. 'Richard III will be mine for sure now,' she said to herself. 'My model stands before me.'

Alec, who had overheard her, went off roaring with bitter laughter.

24

At Smithfield, Nora Flint found the place a ghost town. Even a few hanging carcasses would have been a welcome sight but there was no meat, and there were no men. She heard talking: in the office, Hardwick was being harangued.

'Your section will be terminated for the duration of what looks to be a wartime future, Sam.' It was the big man.

'It may all blow over,' Hardwick whispered.

Hardwick's boss was immense, his shoulders like a bull's. Smithfield knew him for his permanent bow tie and handmade shirts that never seemed to stain when a carcass was inspected. His tongue was prime beef, and Hardwick cowered instinctively in the company of class.

Truman.

'People will still want meat—what about children?' Hardwick sounded weak and finished.

Nora entered the room and his face lit up. 'Nora Flint is my assistant—the only girl allowed on the floor, as you know, sir,' he said excitedly.

Truman gave her his carcass look.

'How do you do, young lady?' he said, eyeing her provocatively.

'You haven't any meat to inspect today, Lord Truman,' she chirped.

'Nora plans to fly for His Majesty, should war come,' said Hardwick obsequiously.

'Is that what the Master of the Hunt would have his little girl doing?' Truman asked sweetly.

'My father hates my flying,' said Nora matter-of-factly.

Hardwick watched her with envy, wondering how her class acquired the ability to talk down to one another and yet stay within one world.

'You, Hardwick, ought to find something useful to do, too, if you have any sense,' said the Master of the other Hunt.

'Isn't Nora remarkable, sir?' said Hardwick desperately. Anything to postpone the inevitable. 'She has accumulated three hundred hours in the air and hopes to ferry aircraft across the country. She may even cross the Channel.'

Truman was unmoved. Nodding grimly, he said:

'Make sure this place is spotless before closing down. I'll see to your creature comforts, Sam. Those sons of yours should be support enough for the future, but if you need anything, for God's sake . . .'

For a moment Nora thought she saw a tear in His Lordship's eye. He had been known for his extraordinary generosity in the past. Again he looked at Nora, only this time with a glint of menace that made her want to be near Hardwick and his East End terraced cottage.

*   *   *

When Truman had gone Nora shut the office door

166

to keep her thoughts from wandering. Those men who toiled outside were still alive, but she could already feel a roll call of ghosts assembling. She did not want them to listen, just yet.

'You can't imagine what has been going on at Maylands!' she exclaimed to Hardwick, thinking to cheer him. 'RAF men have swarmed in and all the gorgeous planes we flew have been requisitioned. No-one can fly for pleasure, and they say Hitler is about to invade.'

Hardwick sat up. 'Invade where?'

'Us!'

'He won't get any meat here if he does.'

'Valerie Cobb is going to the Air Ministry yet again, because she's heard the RAF is planning to use fighter pilots to ferry things into France if there's a war. If we can get permission to do it, the combat fliers will be released and the women can ferry.'

'Overnight we have become the equivalent of vagrants,' muttered Hardwick.

'How do you mean?' asked Nora, taking a chair.

'You will never ferry to France and I will never do anything from this day forward.'

'You must train for something.' Her worry was intense.

'My every last penny goes into the household. It is a horrible prospect to be useless and unskilled for anything else. I'll tell you a secret: I have followed you several times to Maylands and have met Slater. He wants to set up in business with me—running his own airline.'

'You and Noel Slater? Unbelievable!' she exclaimed. 'He's a maniac.'

'Not to me he isn't. My boys take no notice of

me—never have—but this lad looks up to me. None of my boys would give me the time of day— it's all contempt—nor would they think of me running a business. They claim I can't even run the household.' Hardwick sat forward in his chair and noticed Nora fumbling in her bag. She reached out and put a handful of notes on the table:

'Take it.'

Hardwick was flabbergasted. 'That's a year's wages,' he protested.

'Today I will pack up my London lodgings and go home to the country—as if these last twenty-four hours had never happened.'

'Please don't make me take that money.'

'You can use the cash for flying lessons—they'll be wanting old men before young girls.'

Hardwick stood and picked up the bills. He folded them carefully then pushed them into Nora's small bag. Flashing through his mind was an image of Neville Chamberlain, whom he knew to have no comprehension of Hitler's awesome evil. His back straightened as he said:

'When we meet on the airfield, as I think we shall, I'll be Sam to you, and Hitler will have made us companions. If Slater succeeds, I'll be rich. If Hitler invades, he'll be our boss. You'll still have your aging heirlooms and your young bloodstock, and maybe I'll still have my boys.'

'That sounds like treason.'

'When you have a child of your own, you'll understand why I'd rather be a traitor.' Hardwick hugged the girl, and for the first time she noticed the smell of his worn clothes and faded necktie.

Nora went to the door and her footsteps echoed on the empty cavern that had once been a living

Smithfield. Had this not been a place for martyrs once? Ghosts already booking space echoed as she sped out of the market, and they whispered prophetic words to her that she could not yet comprehend: Burma, Singapore; Dunkirk; Hertgen Forest . . . more places for martyrs?

Nora headed home to the bloodstock.

25

In a room at the Air Ministry Sir Henry Cobb sat at the back of the chamber as Balfour, Brabazon, Lady Londonderry and a new committee member, Lord Beaverbrook, heard d'Erlanger and Valerie stating the case for female pilots' active service—a women's RAF. Cobb was not taking part, and he had chosen this back seat to be invisible. He could take it all in as a bystander, mute as one of the birds carved into the top of the pillar that partially obstructed his view of the proceedings. Perhaps, he thought, he could change places with a curiously macabre stuffed fox, which had somehow found its way to a table in this otherwise characterless room in the halls of occasional power.

Cobb turned his attention to his daughter, who at this moment was confirming that she had access to ten highly qualified women pilots who could replace the men sorely needed by the RAF for combat duty. They would be available for ferrying all types of craft, she reported, as opposed to your average RAF man who would have spent a career knowing just one type of plane . . .

Where had she got this audacity?

Cobb switched his gaze from the stuffed fox to his dazzling daughter and nearly spoke aloud. His ancestors had been clergymen and naturalists, always taking time to do a bit of missionary work for the Church of England but never stepping out of the prescribed middle-class mould—certainly not the women! Had his wife been of exceptional stock? He racked his brain. So much they had shared, so intimately, and now she was dead and he hardly knew anything about her forebears.

Brabazon was shouting. All this talk was well and good, he scoffed, but for every woman there were a hundred good men, Hitler was manufacturing aircraft at a hundred times the capability of any other country, and here in England Winston Churchill was coming up against a brick wall.

Why does Winston get all the attention? Cobb crossed his legs and folded his arms across his tightening chest. *I've been browbeating the House but only Churchill leaves an impression. Why . . .*

Brabazon was still shouting: Winston was trying to generate enthusiasm for war mobilization, and side issues about women's rights were a damned nuisance.

Now there was Lady Londonderry raising her voice.

God, thought Cobb, *how war brings out the amazon . . .*

Her Ladyship was astonished, she confessed. And if the reason for convening could be regarded as a side issue, well, then she would simply have to step down.

Voices overlapped and Sir Henry cast a glum look at his daughter. For once she was keeping quiet.

170

Cobb sat forward in his seat. What an absurdity! Here were some of the most powerful people in the country, debating whether ten girls should be allowed to hop in and out of aeroplanes in between love affairs ending as marriage, pregnancy and ultimate uselessness. What a waste of national funds. Fancy Lady L becoming militant! Would he were a reporter—her home county might never recover from the disturbance.

Beaverbrook had restored order, and Cobb chuckled. The committee wrestled with the proposal that the female air force should not be wasted, particularly if a full-scale war meant the ferrying of thousands of combat-ready aircraft from factory to base. Combat-ready! Some would never leave the ground, and parents would grieve twice as hard for lost daughters as for sons. Women as test pilots? His constituency barely tolerated female show-jumping and it surely deplored his daughter's single-sex cohabitation.

Now Valerie was speaking.

Had he missed anything?

Valerie talked of having as many flying credentials as an RAF squadron leader. He knew little of his dead wife, and less of his living child. The committee seemed bewildered. To emphasise her point, Valerie reeled off the names of other remarkable characters in her circle who had similar credits in their airborne records. All she asked of the committee, she explained winningly, was that her squadron not be left behind . . .

What an astonishing thought! *Here is my girl, of all the spinsters in Norfolk, being recorded for all time in committee records as having a squadron to her name.* Cobb sank down in his chair and was glad of the pillar.

Valerie looked up for him but he was obscured from her view. Where was that fox? He searched the room and focused on its glass eye. It brought him comfort. Had pride confused him? He wanted to hug the girl but felt better behind the pillar.

Next there was some talk of Amy Johnson, and Cobb half-listened. Valerie was keen to have her in a first ferry squadron. There was noise. Sir Henry moved to a seat away from his pillar. Suddenly he would see and be seen. He murmured an objection, as if he were still in the House.

Some eyes looked up.

Balfour met his gaze.

Pride had made Sir Henry Cobb want to go down to the floor, and now he was enraged. This girl had come from his loins and others dared discuss her like a publicity poster. Perhaps he should not have come at all.

Suddenly Lady Londonderry stopped the din and sat up like a schoolmistress. She let her eye catch Cobb's for a moment and he smiled.

Her Ladyship asserted that a decision must now be made, and she recommended that ten girls from diverse backgrounds, each with no less than two hundred and fifty flying hours, be sent to Hatfield to be tested for uniformed service in an Air Transport Auxiliary—Johnson to be tested along with everyone else.

For once, Valerie Cobb was speechless.

Simultaneously her father, shaking with desire to hold her, was for once puffed up with pride.

D'Erlanger continued:

Perhaps Valerie's father might be able to speak in the Commons about equal wartime pay for men

172

and women . . .

All was well, and the two women in the room had no more to say.

Outside, Sir Henry Cobb MP showed a rare fatherly smile. A hug came as well. Valerie had got nearly everything she had wished for, and he could pursue equal pay in the Commons whilst she went out and lured her ten aces in.

In the taxi she was silent, and Sir Henry waved to the Three Big Bs, now standing outside the majestic building. He liked Beaverbrook—but why was Valerie grieving?

She turned her face away and was relieved when they finally drove off, never noticing the fiendishly handsome presence of d'Erlanger lingering by the gutter. Images of her with Kranz made his body throb all over and his brain go numb.

Could Haydon be pressured to intern these Austrians?

D'Erlanger would make enquiries.

26

Summer was lingering, and in Shirley Bryce's house preparations for a midday lunch party were under way. In the background the wireless played Sophie Tucker. Humming to the music, Mrs Bryce bore a close resemblance to the lady on the radio, and her large but handsome figure moved swiftly about the kitchen, the white apron bulging over her opulent bosom.

'Another party filled with couples, and you the odd character,' she said, half to herself.

'Talking about me, Mum?' Shirley shouted from the small drawing room.

'I'm singing along with Sophie.'

Shirley came through to the kitchen and her underweight frame contrasted starkly with her mother's cheerful aproned figure.

Looking at her critically, Mrs Bryce said:

'There is something about . . . your disinterest in men.'

'There's no point in losing oneself to someone who will soon be gone?'

'*You*'ll soon be gone if you don't start eating normally.'

'Mum, I'm talking about war—men should be ignored for the immediate future.'

'What does Valerie feed you in that caravan?' Mrs Bryce looked with puzzlement at the girl. How sad that she had never known her father. Had he not died, would destiny still have fixated her on the person of Valerie Cobb?

'*I* feed *Valerie*. We eat well, but I never stop working.'

'I never stop working, either. When I had your father, sex kept me thin.'

'What are you saying, Mum?'

Mrs Bryce was perspiring. She wiped her face with a corner of her apron.

'Please don't do that when Valerie is here.'

'My sweat is as good as hers, my girl.'

Mother and daughter faced each other, as they had done countless times before.

The doorbell rang.

Shirley did an about-face but her mother grabbed her by the arm, its bony wrist looking fragile enough to crack.

174

'Remember,' said the older woman darkly. 'Hitler would have a field day with you and your woman friend.'

'She's a friend, Mum, and just that,' Shirley muttered. 'She loves men, and I don't.'

At the door, Valerie Cobb and Friedrich Kranz made a glamorous couple, his cashmere coat and extravagant shoes making Mrs Bryce gasp as she emerged from the hot kitchen. Valerie's skin seemed to glow from under a grey suit, and as Shirley kissed her lightly, her mother wiped her fingers on her apron and shook Friedrich's outstretched hand.

Shirley's emotions were confused, and she let her mother gush while her own stomach churned. Why did he make her shake? Her uneasiness in his presence, of late, had given her the urge to go to Haydon—if it could only mean Kranz's disappearance . . .

The bell rang again and the rest arrived. Nora Flint had brought her daredevil pilot friend Gordon Selfridge. Marion was with Alec, and Amy was accompanied by Jim and Hamilton on either side.

'You three look like clothes on a hanger!' Shirley quipped at the sight of the trio.

'What sort of hangar?' punned Hamilton, kissing Shirley. Her mother was overwhelmed, as always, by the abundance of males.

'Friedrich and Valerie are lovers,' Shirley lied, whispering in her mother's ear.

'That's sinful, too,' she whispered back, and her daughter gave her a playful slap. 'So why couldn't you have found him first?'

At table, Valerie took in her surroundings more

closely. She could never understand what attraction Selfridge held for Nora, whom she saw as a prospective Commanding Officer. Was it his money? And Amy? She seemed to fade into a shadow when Jim was present. What could her future be when she was torn between two men and hounded by a clamouring press? One day she would let it all cave in on her and go down . . . Shirley's mother was the sanest person here.

'Friedrich is a refugee,' remarked Marion. 'He has lots to tell and he's training to fly the new machines.'

Shirley reacted sharply:

'Of course we all know that my house is marked as a haven for German spies,' she snapped, glaring at Valerie.

'Austrian,' Kranz said sweetly.

'An Austrian must be like a Scot,' mused Alec, wanting to defuse Shirley's aggression. 'May I lighten the atmosphere by commiserating with an outcast?'

'What atmosphere?' Shirley asked sarcastically.

Her mother glared at her and there was an embarrassed silence.

'If anything has a bad atmosphere it's Smithfield,' Nora commented lightly. 'It's a ghost town, and I'll not be going back.'

Mrs Bryce brought in a meal of dumplings in soup, potato pancakes and chicken stew.

'This is like home for me,' Kranz observed.

'Do you live in a little place like this?' asked Selfridge good-naturedly, provoking another scowl from Bryce junior.

'Gott, no! My home is a mansion. But a few peasant delicacies creep in every so often—

176

kreplach, latkes . . .'

'My impression is that German Jews don't stoop to Yiddish,' joked Mrs Bryce, smiling at Friedrich.

'We stoop.' He smiled back.

'You lot always seem to make good wherever you turn up in the world,' Marion said.

'Beauty', Kranz continued, 'has gone out of the lives of Germans because a disease of the mind is becoming a compulsory state of being. Joseph Goebbels is perpetrating it—news of Jews taking over the world and robbing good Christian folk like yourselves of your homes, your children's sweat and blood, and your code of moral honour. Even here in England you've had your blood libel massacres.'

'Implying?' glowered Selfridge.

'It's the reason why we may have a war, Gordon.' Valerie's resonant tones broke in. 'You may not comprehend it over ice cream in Manhattan, but the rest of the world is sinking fast into the Dark Ages.'

'Can we please talk about something else?' urged Shirley.

'I have something to tell everyone.' Valerie pulled a letter from her purse. 'From the Air Council, a message to us all:

'"We do not want a flying section in the WAAF—I still have to be convinced that the Civil Air Guard as a class, will be competent to ferry RAF aircraft . . . If any women CAGs are competent to ferry Moths, they should be employed on this, but as civilians . . . Otherwise they should undertake some alternative form of useful work."' Valerie folded the paper and lit a cigarette.

177

All present watched her as if she were performing a rare conjuring act.

'Undertake useful work,' she echoed to herself.

'We should all train to be undertakers,' groaned Shirley.

'There was no doubt in my mind at that last meeting,' Valerie said, her bitterness brimming over. 'I'd been so sure, as had my father, for God's sake. No one dreamed the committee would change its mind.'

'Britain is backward,' Kranz asserted. 'Does Chamberlain really think Hitler is just going to tip his hat to that valuable outpost across the Channel?'

'Keep your criticisms to your own country.' Jim had spoken for the first time, after wolfing his meal. 'Is there no official drink in this household?'

'My husband kept wine.' Mrs Bryce seemed frightened of Mollison.

'Then kindly get some,' he snarled.

Amy looked at Valerie as if help could be secured from a female quarter. Hamilton had kept his mouth shut throughout the meal, and he knew if he spoke now Mollison would destroy the peace of this good lady's table. He watched as Mrs Bryce, not greatly different from the Jews depicted on the footage coming in from Germany, moved under Jim's verbal boot and headed submissively for her cellar.

'Do you have to disrupt a dry house?' Amy whispered to Jim.

'That is not the issue here—I have tolerated a foreign cuisine in my own country this afternoon, and now I demand the very least—native alcohol.'

Overhearing him, in the cellar, Mrs Bryce turned

ashen.

'My mother's people have been cooking like this for two thousand years, by necessity,' said Shirley.

'Here goes—another history lesson,' moaned Jim.

Mrs Bryce emerged from the cellar breathless, holding a dusty bottle of Kiddush wine.

'This is all we keep,' she said weakly.

'Hand it over!' burbled Jim, an alcoholic smile breaking through his troubled features. He examined the bottle like a fascinated child and removed the seal, covered in Hebrew script.

Mrs Bryce thrust a large glass under his hand.

Mollison drank, then spat. 'What is this?' he asked, grimacing at the unfamiliar taste of Kiddush wine.

'What you might call sacramental wine,' Shirley said in a monotone which masked her fury.

'Rat's piss,' sputtered Jim, slamming the glass down and rising from his chair. 'I suggest we retire to the friendly local for a real pint,' he announced.

Amy rose, and pushed Jim away from the table. At times like this she had an astonishing power over him, and her small figure seemed suddenly like a bulldozer as he moved sideways from the little dining room, now cloudy with Valerie's cigarette smoke. Mrs Bryce sat in Jim's vacated place and heaved a sigh of great relief. When Amy returned, Valerie stubbed out her cigarette and held up the offending letter.

'I intend fighting this Air Council decision, chums,' she asserted.

'Anything I can do—please,' Amy pleaded, lowering herself as if exhausted into her chair.

'Oddly enough,' Valerie continued, 'My father

179

was overjoyed when the Committee said yes, and now he'll fight with us.'

Conversation burgeoned from all corners, but Shirley's mother seemed in another world. She retired to her kitchen and began to think about her life and her adopted country's future. Piling the plates and bowls alongside her basin, made immaculate for the impending Sabbath, she wondered how her daughter could embrace the values and customs of her partner so quickly; abandoning tradition, to eat sausage in a hut. People like Jim terrified one—could he not become a thug, like the Polish gentlemen who got drunk on Passover and threw bricks into her grandparents' home, and on Monday morning were back at their offices administering municipal law?

Her heart leapt at the sound of her guests, and before filling the basin she wiped her hands, reached forward and increased the volume on the wireless, which had been playing softly during the restless lunch. She noticed the music had stopped. From the other room Valerie's voice stood out from all the rest.

'Wouldn't you men be insulted if you were relegated to ferrying Moths and forced to be classified as civilians?' she asked.

'Surely you told the committee about all the qualified squadron leaders floating around in skirts?' queried Hamilton.

'They've had it stuffed down their throats,' Valerie replied, lighting up yet again. 'Navigator's licences, A and B licences, and two thousand hours in the air—all fallen on deaf ears.'

'Balfour wants a separate corps of women pilots,'

Alec remarked.

'Balfour wants Angelique, full stop,' said Valerie, grinning, and puffing.

'Really?!' Marion and Shirley exulted in unison.

Voices overlapped and a great deal of laughter stopped abruptly because Mrs Bryce stood ashen-faced at the kitchen door. Over their silence the grave BBC voice continued . . .

Germany had invaded Poland.

'Trust Adolf to ruin everything,' mumbled Shirley.

'It's a kind of good news,' Amy said. 'Of course, we'll now be at war, and the Air Ministry will see how desperately they'll need every pilot who is still breathing.'

'Foreigners again—always the source of England's troubles,' Marion muttered, looking sidelong at Kranz.

'To foreigners!' toasted Alec, holding up the bottle of kosher wine.

In the background was the restless voice on the wireless, a faceless man trying to keep his aplomb as paper harbingers of death were passed in front of him in a radio studio built for the light entertainment of peacetime.

The ethnic luncheon at Mrs Bryce's was over. The guests dispersed, and outside, in Valerie's car, Freidrich grasped her arm.

'There will be a declaration of war, and sooner than anyone would expect, Valerie. It means I have to disappear. Perhaps tomorrow.'

Her thoughts were of odd things at that moment—of her dead mother and of the squires on the Hunt who had tried to rape her. Who was this man?

'What do you want from me, Friedrich?'

'Can you get me an aircraft? I need to get out.' He was distraught, and felt sexless.

'Has Tim Haydon frightened you into this? Has he threatened you with deportation again?' She wanted him now, but he could only tremble like a child.

'I'd rather die than face internment, Val.'

Was he about to cry as well? Valerie turned away, frightened by her own desire and by his impotence. Was this the Jew in him? It disgusted her.

'Why do you people always jump to conclusions?' she snapped. 'War hasn't even been declared. Tea and scones are still being served at Claridge's.'

'And I'm not yet good enough to join a Gentleman's Club,' Kranz countered, more composed. 'One has been jumping to conclusions for generations. That's how we have survived.' His trembling had ceased and his manhood was returning. Family duty urged him to return to Hell but Austria seemed another planet as Valerie's irresistible figure, provocative even through tweeds, stirred his loins. She knew, and could feel them coming together at some future moment. Near future? She throbbed inside and as Friedrich's hand came to rest on her own she gripped the cold machinery and the car's ignition exploded into power. At once she felt shame and ecstasy, with the eyes of her friends boring into her as they stood on the pavement in the still-bright afternoon light of the first of September 1939, but more potent than her shame was her urgency to envelop this man in her own country. And never let him get away.

They drove off.

Shirley and Amy, having seen and heard all, stood by the side of the road.

'That Austrian will be my chum's downfall,' Shirley said quietly, kicking the pebbles gently under her heavy-duty shoes.

Amy looked on and kept silent for a moment. 'I know what Valerie is going through, Shirley,' she remarked flatly, before walking off, leaving the ground engineer alone in miserable descending fog.

Shirley watched Amy Johnson, celebrated aviatrix, wander hesitantly down the street, heading for the local which would spew out its malingering patron for her to take home. Somehow, she thought, Jim and Amy had managed to stay together. Had sex endured, she wondered? They had a terrible, relentless energy about them which suggested as much—did she put up with even more in bed than at the feet of his drinking chair?

Why does Mum think I am a lesbian?

Hamilton Slade said they were ancient witches who came from Lesbos and inhabited this dim little island by flying in on their own aeroplanes. She had cheered herself up, and as Amy disappeared into the fog Shirley felt an urge to attend to her loved one.

Back in the house, Mrs Bryce initiated her ritual: after every party, she became infuriatingly inquisitive about all the guests. This time, however, Shirley was uncooperative.

'Is Hamilton Amy's lover?' asked her mother.

'Does it matter, Mum?' she raged, now storming about the kitchen.

'I wouldn't blame her. Jim is destroying her, and

183

she must have been pathetic even before he came along,' Mrs Bryce observed, ignoring her daughter's rage. 'Will Gordon take Nora to America?'

'Mum, I am fiendishly worried about Valerie— the others don't matter.'

'You can't ever get her off your mind, can you?'

'She might go off with that Jew.'

Mrs Bryce had stopped her work and stood to her full height.

'May I remind you of your own heritage?' she murmured, her matronly figure dwarfing the girl. 'It might be worthwhile finding a man for yourself who will take your thoughts away from Valerie Cobb. I'm going to bed.'

Shirley did not give or take a goodnight kiss, and she stood in the empty kitchen in the dark, staring intently at the freshly polished carving knives her mother had kept so proudly since her wedding day. She did not want a wedding day, nor did she want knives or tablecloths or the excruciating birthing of a lust-engendered babe. Through years of distorted thoughts in a fatherless existence, Shirley had come to think of marriage as a form of rape, and if that was her future she might consider walking down the road into the fog, with one of those wedding knives in her pocket.

Would her absence mean anything to Valerie Cobb?

Upstairs, her troubled mother could not sleep.

27

Hatfield in Hertfordshire had a main airfield
which was being converted for use as a ferry
training pool. War would happen now, and men
were everywhere. The older ones were to be tested
for Air Transport Auxiliary and the younger ones
eagerly awaited cadet training.

In the cockpit of a Tiger Moth trainer, Nora Flint
reviewed procedure with a jovial American too old
for the Air Force but still a crack pilot. Bill Howes
had been one of the first to sail over through
U-Boat Alley to do what he could while the
American Congress dithered in isolationist folly.
Grey-haired but sturdily built, he brought an
endless fund of mirth into Nora's otherwise
routine job of familiarization: each plane had its
own characteristics and the new ATA pilots had to
be quick learners.

'Ever meet an Idaho potato?' he bubbled, as
Nora held her manual open.

Nora looked up. 'What?' she asked, nonplussed.

Manically he continued:

'Ever hear the story of the lady whose favourite
cat turned into a handsome prince?'

She shut the manual and glared at the American,
his neatly combed silver mane glistening in the sun.
'No,' she said coldly, 'but I have a feeling you're
about to tell me.'

'The Prince stood over her bed and said, "*Now*
aren't you sorry you had me altered?"'

'Altered? What on earth does that mean?'

'Shit—goddam, miss, you missed the whole joke.'

Now Bill looked depressed, and it was Nora's turn to laugh:

'You're not really interested in winning this war, are you, Bill?'

'To tell you the truth,' he said, suddenly sober, 'I haven't yet gotten over the shock of passing through the U-Boats alive.'

'You're not married?' she asked, not particularly moved by his story.

'I was. She died—a haemorrhage nine days after giving birth to my daughter,' he explained, his voice quiet. 'People said I deserved it for not marrying a Polish girl. Goddam Polish Catholics are so superstitious, you know?'

'Catholicism isn't so popular here,' she said, lost.

'That girl was brilliant—half Italian, half Negro. Thank God our baby is blonde—the family accepts her, just about.' He reached over and took the manual from Nora's lap. 'Lets go on.'

'What happened to her Negro blood?' Nora asked, now fascinated by the colourful mental scenario.

'It got diluted.' He buried himself in the book.

'Bill, while you are in England, who is taking care of your daughter?'

'Oh, she's here!' he said brightly. 'I've got her tucked away in my lodgings. She's all I've got in the whole wide world.'

Nora was amazed. 'How old is she?'

'Old enough to enrol for ATA, if they ever let girls fly,' he said, grinning. 'Jo's her name. Her mother was called J'phine because when she was born the local witchdoctor couldn't spell Josephine so he abbreviated it. Now her living daughter is a regular Josephine, spelled right.'

186

'New ATA pilots have to be quick learners, or so we are told,' Nora said, starting up the engine. 'No more talking, Bill. But when she's ready I want to meet your girl. Just remember that in this country she will always be a second-class citizen, a half-caste mongrel.'

Bill looked back at her as if she had spoken in another language, but his voice was drowned by the fully revved aeroplane, which taxied along the field's edge as a young blonde child watched from a battered jalopy.

* * *

In the common room at Hatfield, Valerie Cobb was surrounded by a huddle of angry women.

'I've heard nothing so far,' she asserted. 'As far as I am concerned, we will all sit out the war, and you should be jolly pleased to have jobs as instructors. Some of you are weather officers—a damned sight better than hole-punching.'

Stella and Angelique had been joined in the huddle by an oddly dressed teenager, and all eyes turned. Those lady pilots present were in flying suits, and her brightly spotted summer dress made them blink.

'Did you fall off the banana boat?' teased Angelique.

The girl blushed. 'My Dad is a pilot out there. He's just taken off.'

Valerie walked over to her and put an arm around her shoulders. 'You're a long way from home.'

'I want to train and I want to start today.' Her strong American twang seemed to bounce of the walls.

'Train as what?' asked Marion Wickham sharply.

'She wants to be one of us.' Valerie had read her and was intrigued.

'My father is Bill Howes. He was decorated in the last war and now he's too old for medals or for making love,' she said, her eyes a blank.

'What an extraordinary thing for a child to say,' Amy exclaimed. 'Are you alone with him?'

'I've never been alone in my life,' she replied, and at that moved to the door and wandered off on to the field.

Noel Slater had arrived. 'Who is the waif?' he asked, scowling.

'She seems to have materialized out of Bill Howes,' Angelique replied.

'I thought he was a bachelor,' Noel said, placing his goggles on the table, disrupting a pile of neatly stacked playing cards.

Valerie experienced an instant desire for the child to be kept away from Slater. Could she persuade the naive American to sequester the brightly clad daughter? Her thoughts were jolted by shouting.

It was Noel again.

'Your Jerry boyfriend is on the premises,' he hissed.

Valerie's heart began its involuntary pounding. She excused herself as the girls bickered amongst themselves. Crossing to a secluded spot on the airfield, she found Friedrich.

'You shouldn't have let yourself be seen here today,' she murmured.

'I need to organize this aeroplane—can you do it? Can you fly with me?' He was immaculate and magnificently dressed: Valerie imagined submerging beneath the power of his loins—how many times might they make love till ripe old age would part them?

'It is impossible for me to accompany you—you know that,' she said.

'Make believe I'm one of your father's hunting partners—Tim Haydon, or one of the others from the acceptable breed.'

She frowned at him. Did he see all of life as a pogrom?

'I have too many problems to surmount on the ground, Friedrich,' she said.

His hand was limp as she took it, the dampness and cold shocking her own palm. 'You know how many times they have done an about-face on me,' she continued. 'My girls are going out of their heads. They need to be in the air.'

'You will do nothing?' Kranz looked poor and shabby now.

'Please don't leave—I'm taking a cottage, Friedrich. I'll look after you.'

Kranz walked off—leaving Valerie alone, as a thin mist descended on Hatfield. Noises from ceaseless activity gradually seeped back through her deadened ears, and she turned away, heading back to the common room and her angry women. For a moment, outside, she stopped and listened. In the common room the radio voice droned on:

Britain was at war.

Part II

Battling for Freedom

28

At the Air Ministry, Beaverbrook was fuming. As he fumed, Valerie smoked and d'Erlanger looked on, wondering when he could stop burning inside. Outside, the factories were beginning to churn out aeroplanes and their chimneys spewed clouds of industrial waste, while from many other European chimneys belched clouds of human ash.

'I'll turn to the coalfaces—to anything, for men to ferry these aircraft from the factories to the battlefield bases,' thundered Beaverbrook.

'British Airways has a few elderly ghosts creaking round the runways,' said d'Erlanger. 'We can let you have them, if they're still standing. Remember Valerie still has all these good women waiting for an opening.'

'Then get them mobilized!' shouted Beaverbrook.

'My women have been put on hold too many times,' retorted Valerie. 'I cannot keep their hopes rising and falling like this for ever.'

'All that was *before* the war!'

'Why should that matter?' she asked. 'It is outrageous enough that before war was declared, the committee changed its mind, but this time I am not about to go back to my girls empty-handed.'

'You won't,' stressed Beaverbrook. 'I promise you.'

D'Erlanger smiled, and as the other man rose, Valerie continued to smoke, determined to finish this cigarette before leaving the room. It was unspeakable that at this moment of her greatest triumph her body churned uncontrollably as she allowed thoughts of Friedrich Kranz to intrude. When she had ventured into this chamber her mind had been in neutral, a facility she had acquired at puberty when being pursued by huntsmen.

She rose at last, keeping her mouth shut, thinking she might bring a curse over her girls once more if she uttered another word. Beaverbrook's arm was outstretched, and as his palm and hers touched, she looked at d'Erlanger and recalled her last handshake, which had brought so little. They left Beaverbrook's office and Valerie remained silent. If only intimations of Friedrich would leave her flesh! It was a sensation embedded more deeply as each day passed. Meanwhile d'Erlanger, so close, seemed far away.

What did he want?

Outside, as dusk descended in a sudden rainstorm, Valerie and d'Erlanger stood drenched, oblivious to the weather as people rushed past.

'I suggest we celebrate,' he said, gripping her arm so hard that it hurt and she awoke.

'I have an errand to run, Gerard.'

Letting go of her arm, he looked down at the wet pavement, smiling to himself.

'Are you mobilizing the girls?' he asked.

'No. Something else. An errand.'

This time when d'Erlanger had grabbed Valerie's arm she was awake when it hurt.

'Friedrich Kranz wants something?' he asked accusingly, his eyes wild. People turned as they walked past. Gentlemen did not usually behave this way in front of government buildings. Gerard d'Erlanger did.

'Gerard, you are breaking my arm for the war

effort—that's treason.' Her taunt struck home and he let go abruptly, causing her to lose her balance. Gracefully she righted herself.

'Kranz is an unwelcome visitor in this country,' he growled. 'We are not interested in his business acumen, nor in his manufacturing wizardry. Aside from that he is an arrogant sod who is out of his depth in this country and who would never be allowed into my London club. You've allowed him intimacy. That disgusts me.'

'By intimacy, what do you mean?' Valerie's hair was soaked and she could smell the dank odour of wet wool rising from her sodden jacket.

'You have welcomed him into your own private club—your body.'

'How interesting—women aren't allowed into men's private clubs, yet we welcome men into ours, you say?' she said, smiling.

'It enrages me that you could be prejudicing the monumental task ahead because of some Austrian.'

Valerie's height brought her face to face with d'Erlanger and he moved to wipe the rain from her mouth with his lips. She backed away and ran to her car. Inside, the smell of wet wool seemed worse and she wanted to strip off. What would happen if she drove naked through Whitehall? She rolled down the window.

Gerard bent down to speak:

'The Ministry is earmarking you for Head of ATA and they know your every move, Valerie,' he said.

Valerie sighed with weary relief as the car left Whitehall. Beaverbrook had brought her the best news of her flying life and she would mobilize her girls. Ten aces would be brought to an appointed place where they would master fifteen different types of aircraft. Driving down the Mall she noticed sandbags being hauled on to the pavements. Women in overcoats, carrying shopping and pushing prams, hovered alongside the hauliers.

What separated her girls from these females?

Lighting a cigarette, she accelerated and raced towards home. Her visceral churning had begun again. She would mobilize Friedrich Kranz.

29

Like Biggin Hill, Hatfield Airbase had acquired a wartime atmosphere without much alteration to its buildings. Evening patrols changed over from the daytime lads who headed for their pint, and on this evening Friedrich Kranz slithered amongst the aircraft parked in a far corner. Looking splendid in a city suit, he avoided guard posts but was unlucky near a cluster of old Moths requisitioned from a nearby club. He was amazed to discern a mere boy approaching him through the mist and as he fumbled for his papers Cal March's uniform confronted him.

'I am on an urgent diplomatic visit on behalf of the Polish ambassador,' Kranz explained smoothly, sounding more Polish than a Pole.

Cal was charmed by the tall, distinguished foreigner and marvelled at the elegance of the script on the diplomatic papers. He let Kranz move on, excitedly contemplating how he would tell the others at his lodgings about this encounter.

Entering the main building, now no longer decorated with the flying-club banner but adorned with RAF colours, Kranz saw danger approaching yet again. Stopped once more, he knew he would have to impress these older uniforms.

The uniforms examined his documents and were unmoved.

Should he try the Polish ambassador line again?

'My mission is confidential but I can tell you it is on behalf of the Polish Ambassador.'

'Who's he, then?' asked a uniform.

Kranz mumbled and it worked. He had succeeded, and was being directed towards the new CO's office.

'May I use the men's room first?' he asked.

They nodded. The two who had challenged him had succumbed to the persona.

Once in the latrine, nerves returned and Kranz fumbled furiously with a set of keys.

A figure loomed. Bill Howes. 'You a new recruit, Bud?' he asked officiously.

'Not exactly,' Kranz stuttered.

'Where do you hail from?'

'Poland.'

'I've got a Polish sister-in-law back home.' Howes' voice was a bellow and Kranz felt seasick when he slapped him on the shoulder.

'How delightful to meet you.'

'Howes, call me Bill. I can fly anything. These RAF guys don't know a thing. Put 'em in an Anson and they're sunk.'

'Could you please tell me how to get to the locker room?'

'Sure thing. You are a new recruit, aren't you?

Secret mission?'

'You could say that.' Kranz smiled. Would the gods allow him to enlist the American's help? He fought seasickness and held on to the persona. Howes pointed to the door and as they left Kranz felt the eyes of the two uniforms, now joined by Uniform One, hovering at the entrance to the latrine. Cal March was babbling but three stern faces silenced him and he followed Howes down the corridor.

'See you later,' yelled the Yank, leaving him alone, back at the reception area. When the coast was clear Kranz strode through the large chamber and detoured into the dingy storage section which housed endless rows of lockers. All were locked, and he fumbled again with his keys. Tampering nervously in a corner, he dislodged a padlock and to his delight was rewarded with a treasure trove. Donning a uniform that the gods had sent down in a perfect fit, he stuffed his suit into his empty kitbag. Why had the Uniforms never searched it?

Leaving through a rear door—*unpatrolled!* he gasped to himself—he found he could blend in with the others. That adorable little boy who had been his first obstacle leaned against a gate and smoked. What would Benno be like by now? Did he still have a son?

'Howdy, Bud!' Kranz jumped. Bill Howes was tinkering with a Fulmar. Darkness engulfed them but their uniforms seemed to glow.

'What is that you are doing?' asked Kranz.

Howes looked sharply at him and inquired:

'How come you turned up at night to sign on?'

'In truth, I am on secret intelligence work as a night flier.' Kranz grappled for charm.

198

'My line of work gets me pretty close to intelligence and I've never heard of night fliers from this dump yet.' Howes was suspicious: that accent?

'Actually this Fulmar has been designated for me,' Kranz asserted, the American no match for his cunning. 'Don't ask me for a chit—as you know, anything printed must not be on my person.'

Now a pawn in the thrall of charm, the American handed over the keys.

'Good luck, Bud.'

Friedrich had already shut the door and was starting the motor when Howes turned around.

'Hey, I don't even know your name!' Bill toyed with his tools. 'Shit.'

Watching as Kranz taxied, Cal March was envious of the man who could take to the skies at night. Had he ever been beaten by his father? he wondered.

Airborne, Friedrich made a sharp turn due east. The weather was dismal and the light virtually non-existent. He fumbled with the controls and cursed the plane. Pulling out his map he had a moment of panic, and his seasickness turned to terror. The engine was juddering and the aircraft faltered. What had Howes not finished doing? He shook and the machine made almighty convulsions but underneath he could see nothing. His persona had long gone and he prayed to his gods that the nothing beneath was not humanity practising its first blackout . . .

30

Through the steamy windscreen of her motorcar the chaos of Piccadilly Circus was upon Valerie Cobb and she drove up a side street. Parking, she pulled herself out of the wet seat and into a warm cinema. It had been two days since Beaverbrook, and she had not slept. Entering the small theatre, she settled into a chair and noticed she was the only female in the audience. Her thoughts turned to Friedrich, as they had for two consecutive sleepless nights, and she ignored the old man gaping at her from the end of her row.

A newsreel flickered on the fraying screen.

In blaring tones it announced the formation of the new Air Transport Auxiliary and the appointment of Beaverbrook as head of 'ATA', vociferously backed by Winston Churchill. Valerie sat forward and contemplated whether this film had been put together before her meeting with his Lordship. Animatedly, the voice on the soundtrack blared on:

Ten young ladies will be allowed to fly for their country...

Valerie sat back, and as the main feature unfolded sleep came to her at last. She dreamed of ten young ladies, all in trousers, and of their passions, and of smoke funneling up from factories that once had belonged to Kranz and which now were frying human flesh in the land of Raine Fischtal and Richard Wagner...

*   *   *

Valerie had made her new cottage into a warm home in a very short time. She had felt war might bring changes unprecedented since the Norman Conquest, and she wanted to own a small space before it was taken away.

On this evening in late October a large gathering of men and women filled her study. There was no food or drink. She would have volumes to say, and primitive urges would have to be suppressed. Hunger and thirst would creep in, she theorized, but her group would have to get used to self-denial now that the Wagnerians were dominating the world's thoughts.

'We have had to assemble here,' she said, 'because ATA has yet to be allocated a base of its own.'

Listening on the floor, between a uniformed Alec and Hamilton, was Delia Seifert, her boyish good looks crowning a tall, athletic body in a boiler suit. Her father had been a brigadier and her mother a dogged slave to his demands, which now constituted regular trips to stock his liquor cabinet. His vicious dependency had by now so depleted her household that generations-worth of money and valuables had disappeared. Other daughters might have brought in a rich young husband to combat the degradation, but Delia had chosen a job. Now, working alongside Shirley Bryce she had learned everything about aircraft types and had passed her A, B and C pilot's licences. As she heard Valerie Cobb delineating ATA responsibilities she contemplated a future in which her father could be sent away somewhere and her mother supported by a pilot's wages.

'Nora here has achieved much by earning lesson

money at Smithfield Market,' Valerie went on. 'Angelique has been contemplating leaving RADA to fly for us on a regular basis, and Stella has given up her beloved ballet to be amongst our first ten aces.'

Delia's smile had not faded as she thought of these girls with charmed lives who had not been stung by a parent's creeping madness.

'Delia Seifert has risen to the top of pilot ranks through the Civil Air Guard's government subsidies.' Valerie meant well by revealing her financial dependency but Delia's smile vanished nonetheless, and she wished she could disappear.

'Didn't Beaverbrook say he'd go to the Seifert-faces if he had to?' punned Alec, grinning at Delia. She knew he was being his usual boisterous self but still she hated his loudness.

'Amy Johnson and Jim Mollison we all know,' Valerie continued.

'Famous and infamous all rolled into one bed,' Alec interjected, reaching over to light Valerie's cigarette. 'This woman—Miss Cobb—is larger than life, I want you all to know, and she will go down as a legend, mark my words. There is no person in this Kingdom more capable of convincing Lords with colic and Ministers with gout that females should be allowed on to RAF bases.'

Valerie bowed her head. It was her moment of triumph. Bill Howes, curled up in a corner with Jo, clapped enthusiastically, Angelique and Amy adding to the applause. Valerie looked up, her face a deep red. She would have to continue, or the events of the past year might swamp her in a split second and her voice would be sabotaged by thoughts of Friedrich. She cleared her throat and focused again on her notebook:

'Most pressing, everyone, is my need to brief you on the main points of the net ATA charter. His Majesty's Treasury insists on a percentage of the basic salaries paid to women for the same job as men.'

'Oh, Christ,' muttered Delia.

'We mustn't grouse,' Valerie continued, casting a quick glance at the brigadier's daughter. 'Everyone will come in as Second Officers. Women will receive £230 a year—with, I'm afraid, no billeting allowance.'

'Why ever not?' complained Delia.

Alec seized her hand and kissed it with a great cheery slurp. 'Because they'd all rush to billet with me, and the RAF cannot support unwanted offspring!' he gloated.

'Alec, pack it in,' snapped Jim, lighting a cigarette and blowing smoke in the Scotsman's face.

Through it all, Valerie remained unperturbed. 'RAF men will get a billetting allowance,' she resumed, 'but we must make our own arrangements for lodgings. The first women's ferry pool is expected to be based at Hatfield, with a mixed pool at White Waltham—each of us will be expected to fly every type of aircraft—if you do not know the procedure, you had better be a quick learner.'

'What does that mean?' asked Marion.

'Pilots in the regular RAF need only know one type of aircraft,' she replied. 'We will need to know how to fly a new monster straight off the assembly line. There could be one hundred permutations of war machine, and you the first pilot to read any given manual. By the time you have taxied, those notes will be engraved on your memory.' Valerie looked at the rapt faces and realized some, like Bill, had seen atrocities before she was born, and others, like Angelique, had watched brothers go off to do courageous things in places like Spain while on the home front men chased foxes for pleasure.

'Churchill is playing Hamlet,' she continued, 'and no-one seems to have awakened to the fact that Germany could swamp the British mainland. But we must think in those terms. This is war, and even if some are calling it a phoney war, we've got to be prepared—even if others are not. There will be no maps, hence my emphasis on memory. You will have to exercise a capability to retain flight data at short notice, in all conditions. Drinking is discouraged at all times and forbidden when ferrying.' Valerie felt at once the squadron leader, the schoolmistress and the mother. 'Hamilton will speak now,' she announced, sitting down and lighting another cigarette. Shirley leaned over and patted her hand. She withdrew it, feeling ten pairs of eyes watching a moment of intimacy the partners had shared countless times in the privacy of their hut. It meant nothing, but to others it spoke volumes.

Hamilton had risen from his chair.

'Each morning', he began, 'you will collect your chit and the Operations Officer will allocate you a plane to ferry. Flying boats, bombers . . . could be anything. God knows what the Ministry will have in store for us—rumour has it the Germans are manufacturing suicide bombers and killer rockets. Their pilots are testing them off the factory floor.

204

Anke Reitsch, our old friend from happy club days, is starring in the top job. Meanwhile, over here, factory production is well under par. You'll need every ounce of energy to ferry machines off the assembly line to Location A and then over to C to ferry another plane to D, and so on. A month's work for a junior ferry pilot could involve flying several dozen aircraft to and from places like White Waltham, Hamble and Worthy Down. Some weeks you'll be sleeping in eight different spots.'

His audience was rapt and even Alec remained solemn.

Hamilton looked first at Amy and then at Valerie, who knew all breath was held over the main question. Tense faces awaited her words and she rose again.

'I have called you together here in one place knowing that some will be chosen for the first ten, and some will not. There were hundreds of names submitted, and do not turn instant bitch if yours is not one of those selected. Not all have been able to attend here tonight but amongst those present Stella Teague, Marion Wickham and Delia Seifert will be on my list of premiere aces to be tested.'

Inevitably eyes moved to Amy, who smiled and applauded. Was she pleased for the others, or relieved that she had been excluded from the next piece of history? Jim rose, dropped his cigarette on to Valerie's Persian rug and stomped the fag-end into the ancient weave.

'Too bad, isn't it?' he snarled. 'I'm off to the local.'

Valerie's gaze was drawn to the large dark blemish on the Oriental pattern, but her mind remained on the present-day passion of her ladies.

'Each pilot will carry a book called Pilot's Notes,' she continued. 'Eventually, Class II pilots, boys and girls, will be transporting single-engined fighters—they will, in other words, be Spitworthy. Class IIIs may go on to twin-engined. Some of us may even go on to four-engined craft ...'

Valerie's lecture continued for some time, as on this pin-sharp night the stars and moon over her neighbouring East Anglia shone down on the lonely sight of smouldering aeroplane wreckage ...

31

Kay Pelham had heard about Amy Johnson when the aviatrix had landed in Australia and been feted as a heroine. Life along the Great Barrier Reef meant long days and sunshine, and everything that mattered—movies, fads, wars—came from Europe or Hollywood, even if some of those wars were manufactured on a studio sound stage.

Ever since Amy's achievement Kay had become obsessed with flying and had spent every spare moment away from her acting jobs inside an obsolete Airspeed Courier. Now that news of Edith Allam's mission to recruit lady pilots for the British Civil Air Guard had reached North Queensland, Kay was determined to make her way into the American's team, even if it meant abandoning a career in the theatre. She could always go back to it, and after all, she told herself, if she settled in England she could end up in a national repertory company.

Kay's sharp good looks and thick red hair were

coupled with a tall, sturdy frame: her youth had been spent barefoot on the Reef, swimming and breathing the good air of a country not yet cursed with the waste products of industrial achievement. Somewhere in her background, Kay knew there had been an unconventional incursion and though she had been sent to a Baptist girls' boarding school she had been told by her mother that she was not descended from a convict, and that 'Pelham' had evolved from a ghetto in Lithuania.

In recent days Kay had been reading reports of terrible atrocities in Germany. Her father, a civil engineer, had seen a film at work about the European troubles, its footage so chilling that he could hardly believe a woman, Raine Fischtal, had had the stomach to shoot the hideous frames. All of this gave Kay a secret glee: it meant there was a real war brewing after all, and that Edith Allam's visit was serious business. In the Townsville Central Library Kay had managed to get her hands on every available periodical on aviation, and had devoured stories of Anke Reitsch and of Valerie Cobb. She had laughed at the most recent issue of an aviation magazine and while the librarian wasn't looking she had torn away a prize editorial suggesting that British tax-payers were subsidizing well paid American lady pilots.

'Look at this! Maybe the Poms'll pay us even more,' shouted Kay, causing every face in the library to turn and ogle the throaty redhead. She read on.

'The arrival of Americans is a propaganda exercise perpetrated by the present Minister of Aircraft Production, well known for his outlandish capers. We hold no brief against American aviators. But to despatch them across the Atlantic and then have to send them back, some because they could not even handle a trainer, is a waste of time, money and tempers and does not help relations with our American cousins.'

'Lousy arrogance,' snorted Kay.

Armed with the cutting she ran all the way to her mother's office at the primary school—to beg for the fare to Sydney. Edith Allam would be arriving in twenty-four hours and she simply had to be there to be tested for ATA.

Summer was just beginning, the heat not yet unbearable. Kay knew her mother would be in a good mood with Christmas approaching, and she mounted the steps of the new school building with powerful strides. The lunchtime bell had sounded, and as the children poured out into the glorious sunlight, Kay wished fleetingly that she had been allowed such freedom instead of the rigours of a damp Baptist boarding establishment, its cold walls making girls feel unnatural. Phyllis Pelham was emerging from the teachers' smoking room and when they walked down the corridor together the athletic daughter towered over the articulate, learned woman whom the pupils revered, year after year.

'Mum, I can't even stop to have lunch with you. I've got to go to Brisbane for a job interview.'

'What job is this then?'

'Something to do with a movie company—Australia's first,' she lied. 'I could be in on the big time, and I don't even have to go to Hollywood.'

'How long will you be away?'

Kay paused. It could be forever—what would her father do if he lost his only daughter?

'A week, perhaps.'

'Where would you stay? Terrible things happen in places like Brisbane, to girls on their own. Let your Dad come along.'

'No!' exclaimed Kay decisively. 'I'll be all right. I'll get a room somewhere.'

'Promise us you will send a cable when you've arrived.'

'I will, Mum. Will you lend me the money?'

'For the cable? Of course.'

'For the trip.'

'Where did all your savings go?'

Kay had never revealed to her parents her true destination when she had walked the seven miles to the tiny airfield and flying club outside Townsville, making up a story about tennis lessons.

'Those lessons—you know, the tennis.'

'Nearly one hundred dollars—that's a year's allowance!'

Kay could see her mother's face softening, as it always did on these occasions, and she reached into her handbag.

'This was meant to be for your Christmas present, so take the cash instead.'

'Brilliant!' With no further thank-you, Kay had bounded down the steps of the school and disappeared before Phyllis Pelham had snapped shut the metal clasps on her handbag.

Leaping into the house and racing up the stairs to her room, Kay grabbed the bag she had already packed and stopped only to wipe the perspiration from her deeply tanned brow. In the mirror she could see why people said she looked far older than her twenty-four years, the lines around her mouth and eyes giving her a sensuous expression that inflamed more and more men with each passing season. She wanted to see her father one last time, but knew the wrench would be unbearable and, even worse, he might talk her out of her latest madness. Life would be less complicated without the constant attentions of young cowboys, the majority of whom she detested but whose physical prowess fulfilled a need that had tormented her since late childhood. Unable to control urges that overtook her in unpredictable waves that struck by day or by night, Kay had risked acquiring the reputation of neighbourhood tart. England, with its rain and fog and its odd people, whom she regarded as sexually stagnant, might help her to temper the insatiable appetites that seemed to burn into her with the rays of the Tropic of Capricorn.

Now changed into a crisp white suit, Kay made her way to the dirt courtyard that served as a mainline bus station, trying not to think about her father in his hot office overlooking Townsville City Hall. When she did not think about him visions of her last encounter with a cowboy surged into her brain and triggered an instant throbbing down her torso. Why did other women get on with their lives while all she could ever think about was the sensation her next liaison would create between her thighs?

Other girls she knew, who had married, talked of love and contentment but the idea of having just one man for life was to Kay a massive waste, like eating porridge for breakfast every morning from cradle to grave. Two nights earlier she had crept away from home at thirty minutes past twelve to meet Buck—appropriately named, with immediate urges like her own—their hands digging into each other and his hardness thrusting so brutally she felt he would rupture her and she would break in two. Those married girls who told her of wedded unions would have struggled and called his sex rape, but if she was the rapist more often than not, how could these lust-crazed men be blamed?

So far, however, ultimate ecstasy had eluded her. And as she was violently mounted and her rampant victims grunted, she wondered what it was like to come like a total woman.

'Been waiting long?'

A female voice pulled Kay out of her thoughts and as she looked up from the bench a droplet of perspiration fell from the tip of her nose.

'Oops! What a mess I am!' Kay exclaimed, reaching for a handkerchief. 'I don't honestly remember when I got here.'

'They tell me it could be another hour—roos crossing the roads or something.'

'Is that so?' Kay responded, as the girl, dressed in a dainty frock and hat, sat down next to her. She smelled of soap and expensive cologne, making Kay feel unwashed.

'Oh, well—I can't say I'll miss all this wildlife. You going a long way?' She looked at Kay with great interest.

'It depends,' Kay replied cagily. 'If things work out this trip may take me to Pommyland.'

'Me too,' the girl murmured.

'No shit!'

Her eyes widening in awe, the girl seemed to shift a few inches away from Kay to the edge of the bench.

'What's the matter? Don't I smell as pretty as

you, darling?' There was a silence. 'What's your name? Mine's Kay—Kay Pelham. I'm local.'

'Lillian—Lili for short—Villiers.'

'Christ Almighty! Are you one of that rich Villiers mob?'

'My father is one of *the* Villiers family, if that's what you mean. Yes.'

'No wonder I've never come across you in my crowd.'

'Did you say your name was Pelham? My Dad has been working with an engineer called Pelham. He's thinking of building an aircraft factory right here outside Townsville—maybe I shouldn't be telling you all this, but surely you must already know.'

'It's news to me. How do you catch on to what goes on in your father's office, then?'

'I'm a partner.'

'Jesus Christ.'

'Wherever it is you're going, will they let you swear like that?'

'Of course! They're always swearing in the RAF.'

'RAF?'

'I'm auditioning for ATA.'

'So am I!'

They looked at each other, and for the first time Kay broke into a grin, her magnificent dimpled smile framing perfect, gleaming teeth. Grunting in the distance like one of Kay's Bucks, the bus approached the platform.

'We'll have to stick together then, won't we, mate?' Kay asked.

'If you like.'

Swinging their bags on to the bus, the pair of girls could have been mistaken for lifelong friends, or

212

sisters, from the ease of manner with which they chatted and laughed.

Settling into their seats for the lengthy journey south, Kay and Lili ignored the elderly couples who seemed to regard them as noisy intruders—the one reeking of perfume and the other dressed like a prostitute.

'How many flying hours have you managed, then?' Kay asked her companion, reaching into one of her large bags for a banana. An old man seated across the aisle stared as her long fingers stripped the yellow skin down with slow caressing movements. Her mouth enveloped the ripe fruit and as her piercing, taunting brown eyes focused on the old man, he retreated back to his newspaper and pulled the rim of his cap down over his face. She could see feeble veins pumping the blood of his twilight along a scraggy neck, and for several unsuccessful moments she tried to picture him young and virile.

'Are you listening?' shouted Lili, as the bus pulled away from Townsville.

Kay grinned at her provocatively, munching the banana.

'You asked me about flying hours.'

'Tell me, then.'

'Nineteen hundred and fourteen,' Lili declared.

'Your year of birth, you mean?' Kay heaved the banana peel out of the coach window.

'Those are my hours!'

'Two thousand—my God, that's as many as Valerie Cobb's flown, and she's old enough to be our mum.'

'I've been taking lessons since I was fourteen, and I qualified to *A* before my seventeenth birthday. Now I have *B* and *C* too. What about you?'

Kay gazed out of the window. 'Let's hope there are some hunky men out there,' she murmured distantly.

'Who cares?' Lili hissed. 'Well?'

'Well what?'

'Hours up there.' Lili pointed skyward.

'Several hundred. Not quite two thousand.'

'What can you fly?'

'Sopwith Grasshopper. Westland Wigeon. Comper Swift. You name it, I've flown it.'

'I've never seen any of those in Queensland.'

'You wouldn't have. They belong to one of my fellahs who's a collector. I've done hundreds of hours in them.'

'Why have we never met at a fly-in?'

'I hate fly-ins. They're a stupid waste of time, if you ask me.' Kay shut her eyes and feigned sleep as the bus rattled through Woodstock. As the hours passed, the heat became unbearable and the girls drifted between sleep and nausea. Coolness arrived with dusk, Lili now deep in slumber. Their driver had pulled over at Claredale but Kay did not want to disturb her companion, whose blouse had fallen away to a pink chest and breasts as white as snow. Did this girl never sunbathe? Kay pondered, staring intently. One elderly couple had ended their journey here and now they were the only females remaining on the bus. When the driver returned it was dark and when Kay removed her gaze from the other girl's large, perfectly formed bosom her neck was stiff and she let out a small cry.

Lili awoke. 'What's happened?' she asked, her

hand reaching up to cover herself.

'Nothing. I hope you don't have to pee because you won't have another chance until midnight.'

'I do, as a matter of fact.'

'Too late.'

Lili looked fearful and Kay took her hand.

'You'll survive. Just think of Amy Johnson.'

'How did she pee, anyway?' Now Lili was staring at her.

'I've never worked it out.'

'Will we meet her over there?'

'Probably, if we get through our auditions.' She smiled at Lili, still holding her hand. 'You said *pee*. I bet you've never said that before in your life.'

'I'm learning some bad habits from you already.'

In the darkness overtaking the coastal glory of North Queensland, desert mice and bearded dragons watched as the ugly bus trundled from Gumlu to Guthalungra, its female passengers tense in anticipation of their approaching ordeal and terrified of the loneliness they might inherit from the future.

32

No young man of good family and education could have resisted the attraction of the excitement in Spain, and when Zack and Paul Florian had turned down their sister's offer of flying lessons in favour of a trip to the Civil War she had burst into tears. Angelique had never understood their propensity for causes at a time when the world was at peace and England could be enjoyed.

215

Their parents had been the cream of Armenian aristocracy but were still struggling to be accepted into British high society. Angelique had voiced great protestation when they had threatened to make her a debutante, giving as her excuse the obligations of a RADA production. Her real motive had been to protect her father and mother from the ultimate humiliation of being scorned by the old moneyed set. Ironically, many of the girls with whom she had shared air instruction had made their debuts and had taken up flying as a kind of rebellion against the female roles foisted upon them by tradition-bound families. Angelique, the youngest of the Florian children, had excelled as an aviatrix and had shown genius in her comprehension of aircraft engineering. Her brothers, dark and well built, had studied in the humanities and were drawn to the anti-Franco expedition despite serious love affairs with well connected ladies. Angelique had flown the boys to their folly in a rickety Airspeed Courier, and had managed to leave the Spanish airfield in one piece despite flak from a freshly arrived loyalist unit.

That had been in 1936, when she had found it all a great adventure.

*　　*　　*

In order to forget excruciating pain Zack and Paul focused their thoughts on their sister. This morning's torture session had been exceptionally harsh because a group of French freedom-fighters had tried to escape from the prison in which the two British scholars had been held for eight months. Early the night before, a rumour had got around that Germany had invaded Poland.

'Wimbledon will surely be cancelled next year,' Zack muttered, his mouth swollen and bruised. Virtually all his teeth were missing, his gums a pale reflection of the handsome smile in the Oxford graduation photograph at which someone in England might still be gazing. His thick black hair had begun to fall away, leaving weird patches across a head that had not yet reached its twenty-fifth year.

'Who was the last men's champion?' Paul asked, his battered body clothed only in ragged, soiled shorts.

'I can't remember.'

Zack shut his eyes and folded his legs, grimacing at the bite of the manacles that tore into his bony wrists. He noticed that his brother, whose beard was still ginger, had gone grey on top—and he speculated on the reception their scalps would attract should the pair ever again dine at the Florian table, or make love in secret with Annabel Cobb and Sarah Truman.

Every morning at seven, both boys were taken into an interrogation room that stank unbearably of sweat, the smell emanating from the captors as well as from the victims. From what they could interpret when the guards chattered in dialect, sex was in generous supply at the moment, provided by terrified female detainees who had arrived in Spain with ideals and virginity intact. Now, as the reeking interrogators compared notes, Zack and Paul exchanged sickened looks while a cascade of dialect described chained shadows of women near suffocation as queues of penises filled their ulcer-ridden mouths and bleeding caverns that had once

217

been vaginas. Cramped with diarrhoea the Anglo-Saxon females were rewarded for their efforts with a finale of torture performed by one or two men still energetic enough to wield blunt sticks.

After every session one girl always died, and when Zack and Paul heard about the men's daily depravities they felt relieved only to be men on the receiving end of simple, uncomplicated brutal beatings. In the back of their minds they assumed that when all the women had died off the Spaniards would discover buggery. One night Paul had dreamed that all nine of his torturers had turned up at Ascot, dressed impeccably and welcomed into the Royal Enclosure on Derby Day, their English perfect and their political views being praised by all around them. On awakening, Paul felt as if his brain had committed a form of high treason, and for some days afterwards he had been plagued by the depression of guilt. Zack had cheered him up by reminding him that neither Chamberlain nor Churchill had acted to achieve the unfastening of their Spanish manacles.

'Florian—Stupid,' intoned Virgilio, chief torturer for the fascists.

Paul stepped forward mechanically, having by now become accustomed to his new Christian name. One of the guards pulled his shorts down, and he stumbled out of them.

'Florian—Ugly.'

Zack was already naked, his hairless genitals clotted with diseased sores. As on every morning, he tried to hide them with his hands.

'No woman would ever want you, so why do you care what happens to your puny marbles?' Virgilio's speech never departed from this pattern.

'At least you are not an imbecile like your brother, so please dig into your memory and give us some names. It is nearly Christmas and you will be rewarded.' As usual, silence prevailed, but Zack could sense an urgency about the fascists that made him uneasy.

Neither Oxford graduate had ever been given much opportunity to speak on any of these monotonous mornings—the ferocity of their reeking attackers never ceased to amaze them. Spanish spunk had soiled their female counterparts for hours the night previous to this nervous morning, eventually having driven the scarred and breastless girls insane, and yet these men had reserves of energy for further violence after little sleep. Once again, blows rained down and Paul hoped his hearing would not disappear completely, his left ear already permanently deafened by one of Virgilio's cruel techniques.

Taking a breather, the torturer lit a cigarette and smiled. 'You are interested in the reward?' he asked, lifting a prostrate Paul's chin with his boot.

'Not really,' Zack replied for his nearly deaf brother.

'I didn't ask you, shit,' Virgilio snapped, moving over to crouch next to him. Cigarette dangling from his mouth, he reached out and took Zack's lifeless manhood in his palm and caressed the pathetic testicles with his other hand. For the first time in fourteen months the Briton was overcome by terror because his torturer had never before touched his organ—but now Virgilio was grasping his penis.

'We will give you some nourishment and this will come to life. Then you will be given some women

219

who need finishing off.' He stroked Zack's pale appendage. 'We have three remaining who have survived longer than we had expected.'

'British?' Zack gasped, wanting desperately to push him away.

'Who knows?'

Virgilio stubbed out his cigarette, the Briton's screams causing even Paul to hear as small puffs of smoke rose from Zack's penile flesh.

One of the guards was cringing but Virgilio had not seen. Paul had been thinking deeply of Angelique and as he watched his writhing brother's tears stream over the surface of boils that had once been his face, the deaf man spoke.

'Vera Bukova,' he mumbled, hoping Zack would not hear.

At once the Spaniards scrambled around him, lifting him like a crouching chimpanzee on to the table. Virgilio motioned for his deputy to write, and Zack moaned.

'Give him water,' one of the guards barked, pointing towards the moaning.

'Kranz—Friedrich Kranz—he helped finance the airlifts,' Paul continued, his voice a tiny whisper. 'Polish women pilots—they go from Romania to England.' He paused, and because Zack had fainted he provided his torturers with what he thought could be a final gift. 'Our cell was based in Zumaya.'

An assortment of guards removed the deaf man from the room, and for a moment Paul reached out to touch his brother but he was dragged down a corridor into a cellar where his chains were undone. Here, in a clean room that to Paul was a palace, a clean bed and immaculate furniture were arranged on a spotless floor, where his bony torso now sat. One of the guards lifted him on to the bed with a gentleness he would not have believed possible. Out of nowhere, food appeared, the aroma of fresh fish and sweet potato making Paul's head reel, his fingers probing the offerings like those of an infant before its first solid meal. His chest constricted as he downed a morsel of fish, guilt that he had forgotten his brother, and for a moment he wanted to regurgitate this glorious banquet, for which he had just betrayed that multitude of terrified comrades of Zumaya.

But now Paul wolfed the food, and a guard presented him with good wine, which he sipped in a stupor of remorse and ecstasy. When he looked up again another gift had been presented to him, in a wrapping of white sheets. Lifting his hand to push away its mangled grey hair that was matted with knots, he felt only bone under his fingertips, the creature crawling on its knees to the bed and banging, banging, banging its body against the frame, grunting in a voice so ugly as to chill the soul, but which Paul could not hear. Cries that would never reach his ears were echoing down the corridor and permeating his new palace, their agony making the creature curl into a little ball whose head rested against the spotless mattress.

As Paul sipped the exquisite liquid, he thought he might inspire the female torture victim to look up for the first time, but she had died. This made him panic. He jumped up, and realizing he was alone with the corpse paced the room but accepted the fact that he had been left for an indeterminate time. When would he next see Zack? He shouted in Spanish but no-one came.

He languished with the decomposing body and was now being attacked by vermin himself. His misery was so acute he had stopped wondering who the girl had been, only hating her for stinking so badly and for becoming so grotesque. At the end of that day his captors returned.

'Why haven't you fucked her?' asked a guard.

Paul saw lips moving.

'Idiot! Why aren't you fucking her?'

He could see the guard's rage and noticed the others covering their faces. One turned away and disappeared.

'Fuck her now.' He grabbed Paul and pushed him down next to the terrible mess of death on the floor.

'Leave me be,' Paul screamed, thinking he could hear his own voice inside his head.

His tormentor tore off his rags and took his buttocks in both hands, forcing Paul to thrust his groin into the mound of infestation that once had been a woman. He stood up and kicked the emaciated Briton, and Paul shut his eyes. A maggot crawled up his nostril as another blow landed on his torso. Then the man was bending down again, his breath close to Paul's face. Eyes still tightly shut, he felt strong, supple hands reaching around his wasted frame and settling on his genitals. His eyes wide open now, he looked up to see faces laughing as he was pulled by his most vulnerable extremity in supreme agony around the room. Then he was thrown to the floor, and pathetically he asked for Zack.

The men went.

She was still there.

What were other young men doing at home at

this very moment? he thought to himself. What was Britain doing?

His loins were suffering searing pain and that night his urine came in excruciating minuscule spurts. More bugs arrived in the night and he dreamed of the woman the Spaniard had wanted him to assault in death. When he awoke the next morning she was gone. The room was clean and he was given a washbasin filled with hot water. He asked for Zack and saw lips moving again. They were saying he would be brought back to him today. Later another white-haired young woman came, with good food, and he had to fuck her. Her lips moved incessantly and he was beaten when he could no longer function. He wondered what her name was as she too was beaten, but much harder than he, so that she broke open and oozed.

At least, he told himself, he could not hear anything.

Then she died.

33

Never had a woman been so desolate and disoriented as Edith Allam on this solo flight across the Atlantic. During her dazed episode at the hands of Beaverbrook, she had agreed to participate in the publicity exercise and had not thought beyond the excitement and the money during the preparations for the trip. Now, horrified at the prospect of an interminable journey without company, at regular intervals she recited her name, address and occupation out loud because her mind had begun to panic. She would have to endure hours airborne in a state of terror, not out of fear of the ocean below but of the frigid void inside the cabin, which refused to talk back to the aviatrix.

'How could Amelia and Amy have done these journeys?' Edith said aloud, her voice distorted within her headgear. 'How will I ever do the Australian leg? If I refuse, will it cause an international incident?'

Forcing her brain to concentrate on peripheral subjects she let her mind wander to Errol: when she returned to Britain, Valerie's suggestion would be put to him. He could come back to England and be part of ATA—their sole Negro! thought Edith, grinning to herself. Looking down at nothingness, she was grateful for a smooth flight, the aircraft functioning magnificently and the air currents in her favour. Now she was dropping altitude in the approach to her first stopover in Iceland.

'My name is Edith and I live on Florence Avenue in Philadelphia,' she repeated to herself, as the aeroplane coasted on to the runway, a thin mist obscuring Edith's vision.

Her papers cleared, the aircraft checked and refuelled, the young American woman was ready for the next leg of her crossing. Having made human contact for an hour she felt more confident, and had shut herself back inside the cabin when a noise made her freeze. Already taxiing, Edith guided the Oxford past the ground crew and drew to a halt. Turning around, she could feel the blood rushing to her head as Hartmut Weiss, blue and nearly frozen, emerged, almost crushed, from underneath the extra fuel tank that had been lagged with heavy blankets. He was whimpering and his watery blue eyes were expressionless. Without a sound, Edith put the aircraft into full throttle and they were airborne.

'Christ Almighty, Hartmut,' she shouted as they achieved cruising altitude.

He sat up slowly, moaning.

'It's hours before we land again. Don't you dare pee on the floor.'

'That's unlikely—I am frozen and will never pee again.'

His lady pilot glanced around and saw a face coming to life, a dead man miraculously revived, and she was dazzled. 'You goddam Kraut—why are you here?'

'I got away from that crazy Isle of Man by giving my watch to a security guard, stole a ride from a pair of Austrians on the run in East Anglia, and got under this back seat while you were flirting with Sean Vine and Alec Harborne.'

'So you didn't miss a trick.' Edith felt tense—did he still have his gun as well?

'I was jealous. You read my letter?'

'It was silly. I've never read anything so stupid.'

'A great deal of effort went into it. Passion is a pig on paper.' He was trembling, but Edith did not care. 'How many letters must I write to make you begin to feel?'

'Feel what?'

'Feel—like a woman.'

'A woman lives right here.' She pointed to her chest.

'I love you.'

'For God's sake, we still have six hours to go on this trip. Can't you freeze up again?'

He had struggled to climb out from beneath his

impossibly placed hideout, and now he sat next to the American. A brief pocket of turbulence shook the Oxford and Edith bit her lip. It bled, red droplets falling on to her jacket.

Hartmut removed his handkerchief, emblazoned with a swastika, and wiped her chin. 'We share common blood,' he said, shivering.

'That'll be the day.' Edith stared straight ahead, thinking of Errol and of her crowd on a hot July night drinking ice-cream sodas in South Philly. 'Do you want to share the flying, Hartmut?'

He was not listening, his foot tapping nervously. 'You must know I am Jewish,' he murmured, reaching for her hand.

'And I'm a heavyweight pugilist,' she snapped, pulling away from his icy grasp.

'When we get to Greenland I will show you.'

'Not on your life! Anyway, I thought you said it had frozen.'

'Not when I am with you.'

'Oh, God, Hartmut. Shut up.' She turned to her right and he was grinning, holding in his hand a tiny mezuzah on a delicate chain. Looking down into the majestic space in which her aircraft sailed she had to admit to herself that his presence had turned this ordeal into a dizzying dance in the sky.

'How did you get into the Luftwaffe?' she demanded coolly.

'I have no living family, and very few friends who could accuse me of having Jewish connections. Besides, just look at me.'

'Don't they give you a medical? Surely that would show.'

'It showed, but in those days, Jews still had jobs in high places, including inspection doctor to the

226

German air force.'

'Okay, just try that on Burt Malone or Eddie Cuomo, or on some hardnosed reporter when we get back to Philly.'

Hartmut took Edith's hand once more and placed the mezuzah in her gloved palm. She was glad of his company and of his beautiful face and thick blonde hair. He would need her from now on and though his presence would complicate everything wherever she went, for ever, Edith believed he was one of her own. She vowed to make room for him in a future that looked more agonizing as each hour brought her closer to Florence Avenue and to the City of Brotherly Love.

*   *   *

'This would be a great time for us all to go out for a soda.'

Philadelphia Airport had never received a gleaming Oxford and the crowds awaiting the city's best-known daughter were as interested in her aircraft as in Edith Allam's latest achievements.

Eddie Cuomo had been fired for his Hindenburg histrionics, then rehired by the local radio news station, his first job this transatlantic spectacular starring the Philly girl herself. A war was brewing overseas, but here was another reason for a fun day out alongside the oil refinery.

Edith seemed ill at ease, wanting the crowds to disperse as quickly as possible.

'What about a soda, honey?' Eddie persisted.

'No, thank you. Have you seen Burt Malone, Eddie?' she asked, ignoring the other reporters thrusting and shouting at her as she walked behind the aircraft.

His face fell. It was obvious Burt would not be there to greet her. Nor would her parents, and nor would Errol Carnaby.

Facing the huddled press, Edith smiled and waved for their accompanying photographers. She noticed there was no-one from Malone's firm, which seemed odd, because Beaverbrook had gone to such pains to liaise with the US affiliate. Everyone must be angry at me, she thought, smiling again for a popping flashgun. Her heart leapt when the reporters dispersed and she was able to extricate her German from the bowels of the Oxford.

'You've peed in your pants, stupid Kraut,' she muttered, helping Hartmut out of the aircraft. They had been left alone, the ground crew—consisting of two World War I veterans and a black cleaner—chattering away to the reporters alongside the small terminal building.

'Aren't you going to take me to your house?' Hartmut asked.

'My father would think the coastal invasion had started,' she said, looking over her shoulder. Unzipping one of her pockets she withdrew a small handful of dollar bills and thrust them into the top of his undergarment. He reached inside and salvaged the money, which had fallen down along his hairless chest.

'Listen, Hartmut. By now my parents will know I have been having a romance with a Negro, because he can never keep his mouth shut. Burt Malone will be steaming because Britain has beaten us to it in distributing Raine's film. It's all my fault. Now

228

Beaverbrook expects me to recruit Americans, then I have to go to Australia. He's paying for it, and Valerie Cobb is waiting for me to succeed. On top of all that, I'm goddamned if Jacqui Cochran is going to overtake us.'

'What does this mean?' Hartmut was grinning, and Edith was becoming irritable.

'Jacqui is only the best woman pilot in America, and she knows everybody, including the President. I want to beat her at getting an American contingent for Valerie Cobb's gang.'

'Instead, why don't you marry me?'

Edith pushed Hartmut out of the aircraft, on to the wing. A small ladder had been provided, down which he climbed.

Edith could see Eddie Cuomo approaching. 'Get moving, Hartmut,' she hissed, pointing towards the swampland at the edge of the airfield.

'Who's your friend, Allam?' Cuomo shouted, running towards the Oxford.

Hartmut froze, his back to the radio man.

'He's a maintenance man, Eddie,' Edith replied, slapping him on the shoulder and trying to manoeuvre him away from the scene.

'Hey, boys,' he yelled, motioning to the others in the distance, 'We've got a real-live stowaway down here!'

Edith was shaking, and Hartmut shut his eyes, slumping over where he stood, the orange flame of the oil refinery jets as bright against the sky as his rich head of hair.

'Weren't you here a little while ago, sonny?' Eddie persisted.

Hartmut was speechless.

'They're saying your pal Zuki spoke to the

German American Bund—is that right?'

'Listen, Cuomo, leave him to me, okay?' sighed Edith.

'I need a story, baby,' he said, casting an avuncular look at the tired aviatrix. 'You should feel lucky to have one friend left in this town.'

'What are you talking about?'

'They made that coloured boy talk—and you're a scarlet lady.'

'Who did?'

'Malone's brother—the cop.'

The reporters had gathered around Hartmut, and Edith's fury grew: why had the German not made a run for it, to be absorbed into a place like Tinicum Island or Atlantic City? Hartmut was enjoying the attention, his stunning looks a dream for the press photographers. Edith focused on one of the figures fumbling with a large camera, his skinny arms and legs grotesque inside a baggy suit.

'Stan Bialik,' she said, approaching him. 'Why haven't you said hello?'

He ignored her, his face reddening and his fingers unable to organize the photographic plate.

'Here—let me do it,' she offered, taking the camera from his grasp.

Bialik moved off, but with her free hand Edith pulled at his sleeve, forcing him to remain by her side.

'Don't go anyplace, Stan,' she murmured.

'You two know each other?' Eddie asked, as Hartmut continued chattering.

'Stan is our projectionist at the famous agency,' she replied, aiming the camera and shooting.

'You'll have to pay her big bucks for that picture, Stan,' Eddie taunted. One of the other

230

photographers aimed and shot Edith at work.

'Will you please excuse us? Britain's Lord Beaverbrook has arranged a special meeting downtown with his American agents, and we're late,' she lied, ploughing through the sea of reporters and taking Hartmut by the arm, the feel of his steel flesh comforting against her fingers. With amazing speed she was able to scoop up her bags and scramble amongst stationary aircraft, winding a path to the rear of the terminal building. The reporters chased after the pair, but came to a halt when Edith found her favourite secret dirt passageway leading to the main street.

'Believe it or not, we are going to have to hike all the way to West Philly,' she said, hurrying the German along. Now stripped down to his white long johns, he looked thoroughly comical.

'What the hell did you tell those guys?'

'I said I was a pilot and that I had come as your chaperone from Lord Beaverbrook.'

'Gott in Himmel—wait until that appears in his own newspapers.'

* * *

That day Edith and Hartmut traversed the outskirts of Philadelphia, not wishing to accept offers of transport from curious drivers, and by evening she was in a daze. It was with dread that she turned the final corner into Florence Avenue, having forgotten the magnificent Oxford the British had allowed her to fly, and from which its native girls were still banned. She had forgotten the remarkable transatlantic crossings and the meeting with Valerie Cobb. In Florence Avenue

231

she was just a worried girl coming home to people who could no longer comprehend her, the eccentricity of her life more an embarrassment than a source of pride within the ethnic ghettos. She had become an uncontrollable leviathan growing bigger all the time, and Edith hoped her German guest would defuse hostilities and make her appear more containable. Guilt had begun to creep in once more, but she knew that debilitating sensation would have to be fought, or she would never again leave the Avenue, let alone play Queen of the Skies.

*   *   *

Lights were burning in her parents' living room.

Edith and Hartmut were cold and hungry, her stiffened fingers tapping on the front door. They could hear voices within.

'It's open,' Kitty Allam shouted.

When Edith walked into her house she was greeted by bewildered looks and by a huge hug from her mother. Sitting uncomfortably in the corner chair was Burt Malone. In a fleeting instant Edith recalled her last encounter in this room.

'Has anyone heard from Errol?' she asked boldly, Hartmut hiding behind her.

'We don't discuss him here,' her father growled. 'Who's your friend?'

'This is Hartmut Weiss—he's a German Jew.'

The men exchanged handshakes in silence.

'Where the hell is that film?'

Edith fumbled in her huge bag and handed Burt a British-made copy of Raine's film.

'It's old hat by now, of course,' he said, laying it

232

on the floor.

'Isn't anybody going to congratulate me on crossing the ocean safely?'

Unmoved, Burt demanded:

'What about the camera film you said you'd snitched from Fischtal?'

Bending over, she reached into a pocket of her bag and withdrew the leather pouch she had acquired what seemed an eternity ago. She searched, thrusting her fingers into the bag and then going back to the larger one, her breathing becoming heavier.

'It's not here—Christ.'

'Don't tell me you lost it.'

'Let the girl have some rest, Mr Malone, and then she can bring it in to work tomorrow.'

'I wrote to Burt and told him I was bringing hot camera film, and I keep promises,' gasped Edith, wanting to cry because she knew the film had disappeared.

'Perhaps it fell out inside the Oxford,' offered Hartmut.

'We'll search you in a minute, buddy,' Burt said, taking in the long johns.

'Your friend needs a shower,' Kitty whispered, bending down to a crouching Edith.

'I know. He peed in his pants and he stinks,' she shot back.

'Hartmut, come with me,' cooed Kitty, leading him up the stairs.

Edith straightened up, facing the two men she feared most in her ghetto.

'I'll find it, Burt. I promise.'

'When you do, you'll have your job back.'

'What do you mean, Mr Malone?' Julius Allam

demanded, suddenly animated.

'I've spent the past week handling nothing but aggravation caused by you, young lady. You have an exclusive contract with us. Now you're carrying on with Beaverbrook and that Cobb lady, while I'm left here without any help. Why have you double-crossed me? That's all I want to know.'

'Raine and I met up and decided I'd fly her home—if I hadn't done so, you wouldn't have even had that copy. No film at all. Nothing. Don't kid yourself, Burt—she knows it's explosive. If it pleases you, she's still in England, under what they call house arrest.'

'Speaking of that,' Burt said calmly, 'I bailed Carnaby out of jail—he's a good kid.'

'Errol?' she blurted. 'What has he done?'

'He's tried to join up, is what he's done,' said her father, smirking.

'Joined up—what?' She fought the tears that were sure to come.

'For some reason,' Burt explained, suddenly gentle, 'he thought you were gone for ever, so he tried to join up. They'll give him a civvy job and send him to a fleapit outfit down south, I bet. Imagine the rednecks listening to Blake.'

Edith was already halfway up the stairs, the horror of her task growing with each minute. The smell of her mother's excellent cooking made the thought of ATA and an American wing and the Australians seem unbearable. Her stomach fluttered as if she had stolen something valuable and was now about to confess to a judge. Here on Florence Avenue, in the house smelling of prohes and lockshen, she could have been awakening from a dream, like the wizard's Dorothy—except that

Edith still had to journey to Oz, and in a remote world caught up in war she knew the mission she had to fulfil might lead not to an emerald city but to atrocities no Coke-swigging young American could imagine.

But tonight she herself would take Hartmut for an ice-cream soda, while her homeland still drifted in cosy isolationist peace.

34

Travelling the roads of Norfolk and Suffolk like a tramp, Friedrich Kranz had become fascinated by the geographical schizophrenia of this island kingdom, and by the variety of plant and animal life growing wild in perpetual damp. Nothing had changed since Elizabethan times in certain villages, whose people wore modern clothing but whose slowness of uptake was mediaeval. Was it possible Germans were sharper, not necessarily intellectually, but in their grasp of reality? Might this strange island race someday grab hold of a Schicklgruber culled from their foggy fens and make him—or her—their human clamp on reality?

It had occurred to Kranz that most of the hysteria in the land of the Third Reich had been engendered by a reluctance on the part of the masses to take control of their individual destinies. No wonder America did not wish to enter such a war: every racial group had congregated within its shores, trying to assert one thousand different visions of reality, none of which was perfect, but each of which cried out 'I am!' like kittens in a multicoloured litter. A land nurturing the spirit of the individual might endure and flourish, Kranz thought, more triumphantly than one overrun with eccentricity, or one commandeered by a failed artist.

Spending what seemed like his hundredth day on the road, Kranz was becoming aware of his appalling lack of cleanliness. Stealing into the abandoned bread van that had become his home, he could feel the comforting warmth of late summer being sabotaged by the onslaught of his first English autumn.

Today, moreover, he had been beset, since awakening, with a feeling of disquiet. Thoughts of Valerie had been exceptionally vivid but he had tried to distract himself with the section of comic he had re-read so often since embarking on tramphood. In it the hero, Sir Sagramore, battled with First World War German soldiers and at the end of the comic the publisher had inserted a choice morsel of propaganda:

'Don't trust that nice German family next door— they could be here to destroy our green and pleasant land!' There was no date on the cartoon sheet but Kranz imagined it had been sitting in the bread van for many years. Or was it recent? How he longed to read a newspaper.

Debating whether or not to spend another day incarcerated in his makeshift abode, he was jolted by another wave of thoughts: Valerie was doing something extraordinary today, and he would have to find out. If there were such things as brain waves, he was receiving them now from the woman he craved. Counting the money remaining in his wallet, and stroking his long thick beard, it dawned on Kranz that he could by now pass for a poor Hasidic Jew.

Had they ever seen such things in twentieth-century East Anglia?

Eight hundred years before, Jews were thriving in Norwich and were the proud possessions of the King, who had ordered his people to emulate this industrious sect. They had redeemed themselves, the King proclaimed, through centuries of virtuous work and should therefore be known no longer as Christ-killers.

Then the first Blood Libel had taken place.

Kranz chuckled at the thought of being the first Jew to walk the road to Norwich since those prosperous men, women and children, supposedly protected by the King, had been massacred, and their culture wiped out, by a raging mob in the capital of Norfolk. He remembered reading in a religious-history book that anywhere in Britain, a road named King Street would have been inhabited by that town's Jews because of the protection provided by the monarch. In this autumn of 1939 he would walk to Norwich and find a doctor to treat his rash, his sores and his painful throat, and he would also read a newspaper. After so many weeks he doubted whether anyone would think him alive. War was about to explode, and the uniformed services would have more important things on their minds than unwelcome aliens with false papers who quoted an unsuspecting MP as his sponsor and who stole aeroplanes from RAF installations.

Kranz began his walk, wrapping a thinning body in the long, torn coat he had taken from a lorry two dawns ago while its driver had stopped to relieve himself.

Thrusting his hands into the deep, frayed openings on each side of the garment that fateful morning, he had been dismayed to discover holes for pockets. Wrapping his hands around his torso, he felt a lump in the upper portion of the coat. Stopping, he had reached inside and found an elegant wallet, filled with an array of illustrious calling cards, neatly sorted papers, and a wad of cash that had made even Kranz draw breath. Retreating into the bushes, a habit to which he had become accustomed in the past weeks, he had rifled through the papers and in the deepest recess of the fragrant leather he had found the name *Truman* inscribed. Tucking his treasure back into the breast pocket, Kranz thought he might go back to his abode and bury the find. Hazy sunshine was poking through, its hopeful appearance such a rarity in this dreary county that Kranz had decided to carry on, marching his way back to the road to Norwich. Every time he stopped on subsequent days, he had occupied himself with the thick collection of calling cards, trying to construct a mental picture of this man Truman who would carry on his person enough money to buy a twin-engined aircraft.

On this particular day he had walked for three hours when the pain that had begun to wrack his body gradually overtook the wandering Austrian. In the distance he could see a stately home situated at the end of a vast clearing and surrounded by hundreds of ancient trees. Had they been saplings when the Blood Libels were born? he pondered. Kranz had never before been really interested in the history of his faith—why was it that his new existence had made him feel such a reverent Jew?

*   *   *

Weston Longville had never come across a bearded character like this before. Kranz had reached the entrance to the baronial estate, and he marched along the drive with great dignity.

'You there. Stop!'

Charles, gardener to His Lordship, was frightened.

'My name is Truman,' Kranz explained, holding up the wallet as if it were a set of identity papers assembled to satisfy the Reich.

'Like hell it is. There be only one Truman and that's what lives here,' the gardener shouted.

Kranz felt his heart skip a beat as the reality of his folly dawned.

The gardener kept his distance from the smelly, bearded tramp.

'Indeed,' continued Kranz in a polished English drawl. 'I am recently returned from safari in Tanganyika. You remember me, don't you, from the Hunt Ball?'

Charles eyed him, leaning on his rake. 'Can't say as I do,' he murmured, the spaces his mouth once offered for teeth making his face resemble a jack-o'-lantern.

'Alexander Truman, distantly connected to the Greek royal family.'

'Why you so shabby, then?'

'Dreadful story. Set upon by thieves who stole my motor and all my belongings. Took three thousand photographs of animals in the wild, and the wretched men went off with them. Have had to walk all the way from Bungay.'

'Bungay, then? How'd you get from Africa to Bungay?'

'Flew my own aeroplane.' Kranz stopped. Had he opened up too much? 'In any case, kindly take me to my cousin.'

Charles leaned for an instant more then dropped his rake, his gnarled hands a legacy of the care with which he had tended his master's garden for nearly half a century.

They stood at the massive, russet-coloured front door and, as quickly as the butler appeared, Charles disappeared.

Kranz heaved a momentary sigh of relief. 'Could his lordship spare some food and a bed for the night for a once-rich man?'

'I should say not! How dare you!' Butler moved to shut the door, but Kranz stopped him, more with his eyes than with his still powerful arms.

'He and I used to know each other, in better days,' drawled Kranz, mesmerizing the butler. 'Please forgive my appearance—in fact . . . might the lowliest servants' quarters afford a poor fellow a bath?'

'Who are you?'

'Actually ashamed to give my name. Fear of disgracing the family.' Kranz held his hand close to his heart, praying the butler would not frisk him. Obviously Truman had been robbed, his wallet and small fortune believed to be in the grasp of a thief for whom the whole county would now be searching.

Without another word, the butler led his tramp along a narrow corridor lined with miniatures

Kranz knew were priceless. Truman had good taste, so far. Down a flight of stairs, he found himself in an empty scullery.

'Cook and the maids are out for the day. Wash quickly.'

Kranz had to be satisfied with filling a large steel tub with water from a noisy Ascot. Butler stood and watched, and his guest was gleeful when the drawing-room bell tinkled in the scullery, and Butler was forced to leave.

Kranz laughed as Truman's servant stumbled and missed a step, nearly falling down as he headed towards the Lord of the Manor.

Entering the drawing room, the butler was surprised to see Truman pacing about, agitated.

'Gardener says there is some sort of eccentric on the premises,' he snapped.

'Indeed, your lordship, a man claiming to be a failed entrepreneur.'

'Bring him in.'

'I am afraid that this moment, sir, he is naked.'

'Why?'

'We have offered him a bath.'

'Have we? I haven't. He might have lice.'

'With all due respect, sir, it is not like you to be uncharitable.'

Truman went to the window and looked out at Charles, the trusted family retainer he would soon have to lose. His family had never recovered from the Great War and the Slump, and to him it seemed there loomed ahead the end of Empire as well. Now, Smithfield was his last remaining enterprise and a new war could mean an end to everything. He had been known for his philanthropic deeds and loathed the prospect of

241

having to lose his standing in the charitable sector. Crippling tremors had begun to limit his mobility, and in recent months he had laughed at the concept, engendered by his wife, of a charity being set up to benefit Truman himself. Now he had a visitor: perhaps this eccentric was his Guardian Angel.

Truman faced his butler, as if they had reversed roles and he was the servile fixture. 'Perhaps you are right—it is out of character for me to carp. When he's had his bath and whatever, bring him up.'

Butler grimaced ritual obsequiousness and headed for the scullery. He dreaded having to go down to that ghastly place: it was bad enough when cook was chattering away and chopping onions, but now there would be a filthy tramp stinking up the room. Cook would have his head if he did not fumigate her domain before teatime.

*　　*　　*

Scrubbing himself down in the now-blackened water, Kranz knew he would have to be quick about his ablutions. Butler might take fright over the physical attribute that set him apart from the male natives of Weston Longville. He wanted to leave this dirty bath and be clean again for Valerie; dared he don the crumpled suit he had worn the day he had begun his wanderings, and which he had carried in a bag ever since? Would anyone recognize him if he kept his beard? With Truman's cache of money he could walk into any flying club and buy a small craft to take him back to Austria, and he could arrange for a Polish pilot to transport

242

the rest of his family out of the Warsaw Ghetto.

Did flying clubs still exist?

Perhaps England was already at war?

Oh, how he yearned for a newspaper.

'His Lordship will see you presently.' Butler had slipped into the scullery and was gazing disdainfully at the murky bathwater.

Kranz never ceased to be amused by the mechanical inhumanity of this breed of servant. He decided to rise from the tub with majestic confidence. Butler could only stare with disdain, handing him a large, fresh-smelling towel which he tucked around his bony waist.

When Kranz had dressed, his suit hanging grotesquely over his emaciated torso, they made their way up the stairs, Kranz carrying his frayed coat and praying the stolen wallet would not tumble on to the superbly polished floors to falsify his story.

In the drawing room, sunlight bathed the lid of a magnificent grand piano tucked into a corner. Kranz thought he could discern a photograph of Truman with Furtwängler.

'Tibbs says you lay claim to being an entrepreneur,' Truman said, his silver suit stripes gleaming in the sun.

'I am indeed an entrepreneur,' Kranz asserted, acutely aware of Butler's stare.

'Tibbs, you may leave,' Truman murmured, never looking at his servant. 'What sort of business do you do, my man?'

Kranz yearned for Valerie, and in his racing mind he grappled with the terror of betraying his true identity, and then his freedom, in exchange for a pathway back to his passion. Surely Truman knew

243

Cobb—landed gentry knew everyone, in Weston Longville just as in Austria.

'Aircraft manufacturing is my business. May I sit down?'

Truman motioned for him to sit. 'Then how did you get to look like something out of the Old Testament?'

'As I mentioned to your gardener, I have just returned from Africa.'

'According to my gardener, you were also laying claim to being a family member, which is a load of old rot because I have never seen you before in my life. Besides, we are all fair-haired in this family— both sides.' Truman was calm, his voice soft and comforting. His weatherbeaten face twitched slightly, as did his right hand, which he tried to conceal by repeatedly tucking it under his thigh.

'In actual fact,' Kranz said, bracing himself, 'I am on a confidential mission for the Polish government and have been travelling non-stop for three months.'

'What sort of mission?' Truman smiled, fascinated by his heavily bearded intruder, who was gradually becoming a guest.

'Unfortunately, it is highly confidential. You should know I was attacked last week and had all my papers stolen.'

'Good Lord! So was I—attacked, I mean! What did the chaps look like?'

'I . . . did not get a good look at them. My impression was they were short. Anyway they hit me on the head, and when I came to I found myself in the forest.'

Truman looked Kranz up and down. 'You are in want of money, then?'

'No!' Kranz exclaimed.

'Those robbers took a huge sum from me—I'd had it earmarked for something crucial.'

'Indeed?' Kranz trembled.

'Perhaps I should not be telling you all this, but my daughter disappeared about the same time as Cobb's.'

'Cobb's?!' Friedrich fought to maintain his composure.

'Do you know him?'

'Hardly at all.'

'His daughter Annabel and our girl Sarah—it has devastated my wife. Thank God she has work which keeps her distracted. Anyway, the money was for a chap who thought he had a lead. The police have been useless. I miss her terribly.'

'Was this chap a friend of yours?'

'It's too complicated. Please forget I mentioned it, will you?' Truman looked pleadingly at Kranz, his power spent and the loss of a child overshadowing all else in his life.

Friedrich spoke:

'Thank you for letting me bathe—that was all I wanted.'

'Do you never eat?'

Kranz caught his breath.

'That suit is falling off you. What the devil's your name, anyway?'

'Wojtek—Pavel Wojtek.'

'I've never heard of a Wojtek aeroplane, that's for sure. Do you want something to eat?'

It must have been the earnest look that Kranz could not hide that communicated itself to Truman, who smiled warmly and rose from his chair. Kranz stood, leaving the coat on the rosewood piano stool. They retired to the dining room and as Charles peered in through the window, Friedrich Kranz was determined that, in the absence of a newspaper, he would extract as much information from this man as possible. He already possessed Truman's wallet and had learned so much from those cards. Now he could complete the picture of this person and perhaps find refuge in his midst.

Butler had arrived in the room and his lordship gestured. With Cook away, this manservant would have to find them a meal.

Meanwhile:

'What sort of aircraft business does Poland have these days?'

'None of its own,' Kranz replied. 'Our factories build Fokkers.'

'Then what is your connection?'

Kranz had to think fast. 'I am the only competition to Fokker—we have one small plant but we are growing rapidly.'

'So you are the only native Polish aeroplane manufacturer—I like that,' Truman smiled broadly at the Austrian.

'Do you know of Valerie Cobb's achievements?' Kranz could feel his heart beginning an uncontrollable gallop.

'Henry's daughter? We've known her since she was a tiny thing. Beautiful child, she was. Something about young girls, don't you think?'

Truman had begun to drink the wine Tibbs had brought, and Kranz was fascinated that once again his host had made reference to 'we'.

'Your wife lives here?' asked the bearded guest.

'She is what is known as a working woman—goes

246

up to town each day and back—madness.'

'What does she do—in town?'

'Works for Haydon. She loves the hustle and bustle of Whitehall. Not that Whitehall has been able to locate our daughter.'

Kranz wanted to change the subject:

'If I may say so, your lordship, it is pleasantly un-British of you to invite me to dine in your house on first meeting.'

'I love eccentrics—I'm one myself. Do you know—' He broke off as the butler returned, and said to him:

'Tibbs! Bring Mr Wojtek my papers.'

What papers? Was this a dream? Kranz was reeling from the savoury smells and now his host wanted to produce papers. This could be a trick, in which Truman would compare British identity papers with Polish ones. Dear God, thought Kranz, what could I show him other than his own stolen wallet and my circumcision?

Tibbs seemed to slither rather than walk from chamber to chamber, and when he returned from the drawing room Kranz nearly shouted with elation as the butler sidled up to his master carrying a pile of newspapers.

'There's a piece today about that American aviatrix,' said Truman, 'and a little item about Henry's girl.'

Kranz reached out, perhaps too eagerly, and Truman seemed startled.

'Shall I read it to you?'

'Could I look at the newspapers myself?' Kranz pleaded.

'Yes, of course.' Truman handed them to his guest, eyeing him cautiously as Tibbs looked on impassively.

14 November 1939, Kranz read silently, relishing the odour of newsprint and wishing the small photograph of Valerie would come alive in his hands. *Miss Valerie Cobb has been attending meetings in Whitehall yet again, leading to speculation about an important appointment for the top aviatrix.*

'They're thinking of letting these women fly, you know!' Truman said, all the while observing Kranz closely.

'Yes, I do know,' he muttered, still staring at the picture. 'Russian women have been flying for some years—now the Polish women are ferrying refugees into Romania.' He placed the newspapers on the table and rummaged for a handkerchief to wipe his moist brow.

'Get Mr Wojtek a handkerchief,' Truman ordered, and Tibbs slithered away once more.

Truman turned to Kranz. 'What do you think of this American woman, Edith Allam?'

Kranz was trapped. He would have to improvise.

'America has large numbers of superb lady pilots—none so attractive as she,' he replied.

'What? She's short, fat and plain.'

'Perhaps I am thinking of Jacqui Cochrane.'

'This girl has far outdone anyone, including Cochrane.'

'Yes, I suppose she has.'

Tibbs had arrived with the handkerchief, a rough beige-coloured cloth with frayed edges.

'What is that?' Truman snarled.

'There were no fresh ones available from your store, sir, so I have brought a clean one from my own drawer.' He handed it to Kranz with disdain.

'There is no need to return it.'

Kranz took the handkerchief and smiled. 'I must get on with my journey—thank you for helping me back to life,' he said. 'Hopefully the police will find our attackers.'

Truman stood up, as if to deliver a speech, and Kranz felt a wave of relief, like a prisoner nearing release.

'Do come and visit us one weekend—I'm not sure if the Poles enjoy huntin' and shootin', but we do do a bit of that. I shall see that some money goes to help your refugees.'

Kranz was amazed at the generosity of this man. He gathered his belongings, feeling for the wallet as he donned the coat, the butler's eyes boring into him as he made his way urgently to the door.

'I never asked if you have a wife,' Truman remarked. standing at the entrance to his vast domain. A few yards away, Charles was taking in the proceedings.

'In Warsaw—I have a wife and two children— one boy and one girl. My mother lives there as well.'

'Perhaps we could use you in this war effort. Bring your know-how to England and help us make aeroplanes. You should meet Beaverbrook, you know.' Truman reached inside a jacket pocket, paused, then laughed. 'I wanted to give you a calling card, but my wallet is somewhere out there in the wild.'

'I know where you are,' Kranz said, shaking Truman's hand and feeling for the leather treasure with the other.

'How the devil are you travelling?' Truman asked suddenly.

'I am being met at the next town by a driver,' Kranz replied smoothly.

'Let me take you there in my motor.'

'Thank you, but no!' Kranz protested warmly. 'I must walk—my doctor says it is necessary for my heart. I had rheumatic fever as a child and I must take long walks.'

'You must have been a strong lad to have survived that. Both of my brothers died in 1918—flu epidemic.'

'I have to go,' said Kranz.

'Do come again, won't you?' Truman smiled, a wave of sadness enveloping him, as his new friend departed.

*   *   *

Walking down the long pathway that would lead Kranz to what he welcomed as a sort of freedom, he sensed he was being followed. At the exit leading to the main road, he looked behind and saw Charles a few feet away, staring. Kranz was startled when the gardener broke into a broad smile and tipped his hat, his one remaining tooth like a gleaming fossil. Just as rapidly he turned away and marched off, still carrying his clippers.

God help me determine the parameters of eccentricity, thought Kranz, as he marched out of sight of Truman House.

Now he needed to reach a large town and blend into the surroundings, as he charted his next move. Surely the money in Truman's wallet would not buy an aircraft. How could he leave the British Isles? Walking towards a main junction, he was jolted from his reverie by the sight of a telephone kiosk. Thrusting his hands into the depths of his baggy trouser pockets, he found a coin and wracked his brain for Valerie's telephone number. Dared he ring her father's residence? If he appeared at the MP's door Sir Henry could not even know who he was, beard or no beard! There might be the possibility of a repeat performance of his Truman encounter; if he spread the word in the county of Pavel Wojtek's presence, he could start a whole new life . . .

He had dialled and the phone rang perhaps twenty times as raindrops began to plop on the kiosk roof.

Friedrich Kranz continued his long walk and by evening he had reached the outskirts of Cambridge. Twenty-five years had passed since his days here, a time Englishmen never forgot as long as they lived, but for him a period in his life as dark as the one he now endured. Indeed, his stay in the University had been cut short when he had been reminded of his origins by a handful of cruel, educated and otherwise civilized men. It had been a time of complete despair for the Jew from Vienna, and though he had yearned to be included in the sacred music and in the rituals of one of Christ's monarchies he had been harassed in the subtlest ways until anti-Semitic Vienna had seemed a gateway back to twentieth-century enlightenment and he had sped home.

But now he needed England and its rituals.

Entering All Saints' Passage he fingered his beard and headed for the chapel he had so loved in his youth but whose congregation had spurned his affections. Perhaps as a tramp, rather than as the brilliant physics scholar of a quarter century before, he might be more welcome. As he walked into the damp interior, memories of that chapter in his life rushed back in tandem with the smells that had not changed in so many years. He sat down in one of the empty pews and listened to the music of the famous organ, drifting off to sleep while his stomach agonized over its first good meal in two months. Too much food on an empty belly brought dreams of coins too big for the slots in telephone kiosks, and of Valerie Cobb being taken by another man.

35

Marion Wickham had become Mrs Alec Harborne unceremoniously, both pilots having been called to ATA flights immediately they left the tiny church in her home village of Gillingham. None of the other girls had been able to attend the simple wedding service, and young Cal March—who, during his apprenticeship, had come to idolize Alec—was the only member of the flying fraternity to occupy a pew. Marion's parents were frosty to their new son-in-law even after the long courtship: it was a marriage well beneath their standards and Alec had no land save his primitive cottage in the hills beyond Forfar, his parents having died penniless.

Outside the church, good wishes were given all around with polite detachment, and the newlyweds, with Cal tagging along, jumped into Marion's car, their destination Hatfield. As he started the engine, Alec noticed Sir Guy Wickham glowering at the daughter he had lost.

Sir Guy strode to Alec's open window and bent down.

'Is it customary to take someone else's child on one's honeymoon?' he whispered.

'Honeymoon!' Alec guffawed.

Good Gillingham heads turned.

'We're going straight back to work—all three of us. Wee Cal here has just qualified as full Air Cadet, and he reports with me to White Waltham. My lady love, if you will pardon the expression, is spending her wedding night with a lady—Shirley Bryce. Satisfied?'

Marion leaned across Alec and blew her father a kiss through the open window. He straightened up, and as the car crunched over the ancient churchyard pebbles, the couple could see her parents standing motionless, not even waving.

'Some lively event!' Alec exclaimed, accelerating along the open roads of Kent.

'Alec, don't take offence,' she murmured, running her hand across his head and tousling his thick hair.

'I wish I could see my mum,' Cal said, curling up in the corner of the seat.

'We could drop you off in London, but then you'd have to forget the RAF,' Marion said, turning around to face him.

'No!' the boy exclaimed. 'But I do miss her.'

They travelled on in silence, the green and pleasant land of England cold and calm as Italy prepared to declare war on the Allies, Paris and Norway sensed imminent doom, and Hitler prepared to occupy the Channel Islands. All three passengers sat quietly as the car rolled along, each

253

engrossed in thoughts of war.

As they began the long, punishing journey to Scotland via Hatfield, their route carefully mapped to allow the most out of their petrol supply, Alec reflected on his good fortune at being excluded from the regular armed services. Although, unbeknown to Marion, he had been earmarked for sudden and urgent ATA missions to help the RAF master Hurricane fighters, in an attempt to halt the German advance, he knew his chances of survival were good. His air combat days were over, and though at times he felt a deep nostalgia when he saw the pilots dashing off to a skirmish, he knew age had overtaken his reflexes and that his best technique now flourished in bed. Marion's parents had browbeaten her into retaining her virtue until her wedding night. Had it been known the pair had explored every imaginable permutation of copulation during the past year their only daughter's name would have been wiped from the parish register as if she had never been born.

Passing one beautiful village after another, Marion's thoughts drifted to their most recent intimate encounter, which had happened on a Tuesday afternoon when VIPs had taken over Hatfield . . .

*   *   *

Marion had arrived unexpectedly from Perth, having been afforded the rare luxury of a taxi Anson flight rather than the dreaded train ride. They had scurried to Alec's lodgings, and the house was empty. He remembered that on Tuesdays and Thursdays the landlady was now occupied with a wartime sewing club in the next village along. Hamilton and Sean, who shared the accommodation, had decided that instead of VIP-watching they would go to the pictures that afternoon.

Alec and Marion locked the door of his tiny bedroom. Every time they were alone like this, he in the handsome ATA uniform and she in a tightly-fitting suit, Marion always felt awkward and ashamed. Rain had begun to pelt against the window, and for some reason the cold of the room and the presence of war made her bold and she tore at Alec's collar, wanting his tie to come undone, her other hand forcing away his buttoned shirt and digging into his chest. Alec felt invigorated by her furious urgency. He threw her on to the small bed, and as her arms still begged for his nakedness his loins became his master, raging at him to enter her devouring lusciousness *now* . . .

'Men are animals,' Shirley Bryce had screamed at her one night not long ago, and now as her wet, throbbing skin clung to Alec's Marion smiled to herself. She was grasping Alec's thighs, his legs hanging over the end of the bed while her burning vagina felt the soothing touch of his tongue. She stopped, crying out and lifting herself above him as she came, her breasts silhouetted above his awakening groin. Her clitoris afire with delight, she fell back on to him, her hands sending charges like electric current through his testicles as he moaned again when her mouth enveloped his member. As the hot seed she craved exploded he cried like a child and then in a matter of moments it seemed they found themselves out of the bed and

255

somewhere on the floor, her nipples pressing through his hands as they hardened against the heat of his palms, his revitalized penis demanding entry. Her buttocks raised, Alec raged into her and she roared as they anchored themselves against a corner wall. He thrust and thrust, urging the rivers of fire inside to break their banks and fill her until like a volcano she would erupt. Still he thrust, his penis seeming to swell so huge inside her she thought she would die. Never had she known anything like this, her blood and her mind and her flesh all fused in lust so fierce that when he came he could see her nails had gouged rills into the wallpaper but as the house was still empty they knew they were far from finished.

Now Marion lay on her back, with her eyes half shut, and when she lifted her knees, her raw wetness stared back at him angrily like an irritable bearded man. He wanted to sleep—he would have to sleep—and he pulled himself to her gently, resting his head against her abdomen. She placed his hand on her vagina and allowed him twenty minutes of slumber before slapping him playfully: he awoke and she gripped his hand and made him stroke her until a wave of exquisite orgasm passed through the very depths of her being. She moved to the bed and sat on the edge. Alec stood, and as she tried to cling to his erection between her blushing breasts, he made his way down, the tip of his penis leaving a moist droplet on her navel. Now he felt he would be driven to distraction as never before in his life, his hunger rampant and his organs committing an ecstatic violence he had never yet allowed to ignite. As the house remained mercifully empty the sounds that reverberated

256

could have been those of death but their source was a human furnace creating life, its insatiable interior knowing ever greater levels of ecstasy as afternoon turned to night.

*   *   *

'There's my Dad's garage!'

Marion jumped at Cal's sudden shout.

'Do you want to stop, then?' Alec asked, pulling over to the pavement.

'No, don't.'

'He ran away from home, in case you'd forgotten,' Marion murmured under her breath. The car had stalled.

'Noel Slater says you're to be flying things to France, sir,' piped Cal.

'Nonsense,' Alec said, struggling with the ignition.

'When did you hear this, Cal?' Marion asked.

'Noel talks rubbish—we all know that,' scoffed Alec.

Still the car would not start.

'Let the boy speak.'

'He said you would be allocated Hurricanes to be flown to France, and that you would return in unserviceable aircraft to be sent for repairs back home.'

With a loud cough and bang, the engine came to life, and Alec stamped on the accelerator. They lurched into the line of traffic and a Post Office van honked its horn.

'I'll drop you off at Shirley's,' Alec muttered.

'Is what Cal says true?'

'We're all in on this exercise. D'Erlanger can't

pull pilots out of the air, and the brass need fighters. I have to do it.'

They had arrived on Shirley Bryce's doorstep. Marion could not move. She had thought ATA would mean Alec's constant presence. Apprehensive at the prospect of these missions, which she knew were perilous even for a seasoned RAF officer, let alone for rusty, boisterous part-timers like her husband. Already, on this trip up from Kent, she had begun imagining their next union, when they would be locked together in a passion she was sure no other creatures had ever experienced on God's earth. Even as they had trundled along in this aging automobile, with the boy in the back, she had envisaged Alec's return from his next ferry trip to Perth, when they might spend the following twelve hours making exquisite love and drifting in and out of sleep and feeling guilty the next day when Noel Slater or Gordon Selfridge might show quicker reflexes in a Magister fitted with racks to carry eight twenty-pound bombs . . .

'Come on, then!' urged Cal, holding open her door.

'Cal, you're going on with Alec,' she said wearily.

'This is my neighbourhood, you know,' he persisted, grinning at the bride. She looked up at the boy, and pulled herself out of the car. Alec sat in silence, his smart uniform so attractive to her at this moment that she dared not allow her eyes to linger.

'I thought you were terrified of stopping around here,' she said, glaring at Cal.

'Not really,' he said, bowing his head. 'My Dad's at work, or maybe he's drunk down the pub. It's my mum I'd really like to see.'

'After we leave here, I'll take you to her, but just for a few minutes, mate,' Alec said, leaping from the car and walking over to Marion.

'That's awfully generous of you, my baby,' she whispered.

'It may be the last time the lad sees his family—he'll be RAF before Christmas, mark my words,' he said quietly, holding her and kissing the soft curls that fell across her forehead.

'Congratulations!'

All three turned around: Mrs Bryce had come out on to her small patio and seemed to have grown even fatter since that day not long ago when war had been declared.

'Come in,' she said, waddling towards the couple.

Cal leaned against the car, scowling at Shirley's mother.

'It's nice to see you, Mrs B,' Alec intoned, hugging her with one arm and holding on to Marion with the other.

'You two should be spending tonight together—it's almost sacrilegious not to in these times.'

'Never mind, Mrs B—Alec will be back soon.'

Both women were close to tears and Alec knew this was his cue.

'Make sure you lock her bedroom door tomorrow morning so she doesn't give her virtue away to the milkman,' he teased, letting his hand slip down to Mrs Bryce's bottom.

She squealed.

They had reached the door and Marion felt a sudden terror, her fear of tomorrow's ATA test amalgamated in her shaky psyche with the burden of Alec's true occupation, and the seed growing inside her still-smouldering womb. Could she be so base as to desire him right at this moment? Was it fear that brought her to these primitive states?

'I've got to go,' Alec said sharply, for the first time his mirth gone and his twinkling grin evaporated into a worried, faraway frown.

Mrs Bryce went into the house and outside Alec held Marion to him so firmly she thought his hands might become embedded in her flesh, and when he had released her she prayed the sensation they had left behind might linger until his return. He wanted a long lovers' kiss but Marion could only brush his lips with a tearful smile. He went to the car and as she struggled for breath the motor coughed—if only it would stall! she thought—but then her majestic lover was gone and there was nothing left for her to do but to go inside.

36

The 'phoney war' was over, but while everyone had been keyed up for massive bombing the only operational flying for the RAF had been the dropping of leaflets over Germany.

Valerie was burdened with the fact that the girls she had taken on would have to be satisfied in the interim with ferrying the Tiger Moths from Hatfield for storage at Kinloss and Lossiemouth and returning in those Godforsaken trainers. Her first task had been to flight-test these women at Whitchurch. Many of the pilots were close personal friends of long standing. The Director-General for Civil Aviation had been adamant that only eight British women pilots could be included for the initial pool at Hatfield, though Valerie had lists a yard long of females, including Amy Johnson, qualified far beyond the requirements of male ferry-pilot criteria. Now, however, events were taking place across the Channel that made quotas look absurd. Much anger had been aroused when news of American pilot recruitment had reached the frustrated ranks of immensely qualified home talent, but secretly Valerie hoped Edith's crop might bring an infusion of excitement into ATA.

Christmas had come and gone, the first festive season to have been overshadowed by the imminence of death since the days of Sopwith Camels and airborne chivalry. Valerie knew this conflict would be different, and from what Friedrich had told her—so many months ago as to seem an eternity—chivalry was the last thing on the minds of Hitler's warriors.

She was bitterly disappointed that the Ministry would not allow her to recruit the entire abundant crop of British women pilots, augmented by the foreign support. However, having been kicked so often she elected to take her orders with aplomb. Shortly before Christmas she had attracted yet more publicity by managing to gather together all in one place twelve girls who were at the top of her list. She had taken them all out to lunch before they were tested, and whether or not they had failed each had been presented with a signed copy of her first published volume of 'aviation poetry', as she called the book. Later her father had said this was an unspeakably vulgar thing to do, and that obviously she had been spending too much time around Americans and Lord Beaverbrook.

D'Erlanger was now known as the Commodore. He had some forty good men, and in a short time the ferry-pilot pool at White Waltham had rapidly acquired the lively atmosphere of a flying club. In its first three weeks of operation over two dozen aircraft had been shifted and by spring 1940 its men were in great demand. Meetings at British Overseas Airways were held with great urgency, and soon White Waltham had been split, pilots and Ansons going to Whitchurch to service the West Country factories, and more pilots and Ansons to Hawarden near Chester to deal with the northern plants. In the space of a few months Air Transport Auxiliary had metamorphosed from a tiny collection of civilian ferry pilots to a major undertaking consisting of four ferry-pilot pools.

Within the all-women's unit at Hatfield the minute male presence remaining would consist of Sean Vine, Hamilton Slade, and Alec Harborne, along with an assortment of air cadets soon to be moved to White Waltham. Hatfield's Commanding Officer was a woman, Valerie Cobb.

On this summer's day in 1940, the Germans were busy invading Holland and Belgium, Marion Wickham was marrying Alec, and Valerie was watching Nora Flint come in to land an Airspeed Courier at Hatfield in deteriorating weather conditions. She knew Nora's brief had been to collect from far off Perth two male ferry pilots who were destined for White Waltham. She was astonished to see Nora in this aircraft which was forbidden to women's ATA.

'Are you mad?' Valerie demanded as Nora stepped from the cockpit.

'Look inside,' she said grimly.

Valerie peered into the rear seats where two heavily bandaged men were bundled, half-conscious, with their kit bags.

'What's happened to you, or are you corpses?'

One opened a swollen eye for a split second, then closed it tightly, letting out a brief groan.

'They had a nasty mishap,' Nora explained. 'Can you guess who very nearly made them our first fatalities?'

'Noel Slater,' Valerie said, smiling.

'I was coming in to Perth in a Moth, as you know, and I could see these two being chased by Slater, who was showing off. They had appalling landings, badly damaging two brand-new Lizzies. They were meant to report back immediately to White Waltham, with me as a passenger in this thing, but that rather wet CO at Perth gave me a special clearance to take them. I was the only reliable pilot available before the real weather set in.'

Valerie knew it was folly for the Ministry to suppose her girls were incapable of flying things other than Moths and she burned inside at the thought of Slater being ATA and free to fly anything. Were he a woman, he would have been banned. What infuriated her even more was the inefficiency of Perth in not taking these men to a local infirmary, and keeping them up there to await the Accidents Committee inquiry.

'Who are they?' she demanded, her aggressive tone startling Nora.

'I'm told they are a pair of American brothers. Parsons, I believe someone said.'

'Parsons! Well I never!' Valerie laughed, putting her arm around Nora. 'Let's see if we can't save them.'

Oscar and Martin Toland, ordained Baptist preachers of Lynchburg, Virginia, were carried from the Courier by air cadets. Valerie chortled when the rescuers looked Nora up and down in disbelief, as if a physical miracle had been wrought in the ferrying of this forbidden craft, which had neared the end of its useful life and was unserviceable.

In the main building, the Americans were brought in and Angelique Florian, just returned from a hair-raising ferry trip to a near-snowbound Kinloss, rushed over to help. Nora busied herself with paperwork and, to her immense glee, so much commotion ensued over the arrival of the brothers that Nora's exceptional assignment was overlooked.

'Who the devil mangled this lot?' demanded Angelique, tampering with the bandages.

'Your favourite person,' frowned Nora, as the small population of Hatfield ferry pool gathered around her cargo.

Angelique had gone quiet, her sensitive hands revealing the appalling wounds of the two men.

'They need hospitalization. What did you say caused the damage?'

'Noel Slater,' Nora replied, still gripping her goggles and kit. 'He harassed them on their approach to Perth and they nearly lost everything.'

An ambulance had arrived and as the men were loaded into the rickety vehicle Angelique turned to Valerie:

'I think we're all finished for the day—may I go with them?'

'Whatever for?' Valerie frowned.

264

'Someone from ATA should be there when they are admitted to hospital.'

Nora and Valerie exchanged looks.

'In the CO's opinion, who are we to stop you?' Valerie remarked, and as the ambulance men shut all doors Angelique made for the van, turning the metal handle and swinging her shapely form into the rear compartment where the two pilots lay. As the siren screamed its way through the torrential downpour, the skeleton staff that manned Hatfield packed bags for an early night. Weather fronts had stopped everything.

'We are going to need a full-time weather spotter, Valerie,' Nora said as they walked through mud to the First Officer's car.

'It will happen,' she said. 'Nora, what would you say if I told you the Ministry might consider appointing a woman like you Commanding Officer of another small pool, working alongside the RAF?'

Nora climbed into the car and waited for Valerie to sit down at the wheel before she replied.

'This sounds like a Beaverbrook stunt,' she said, grinning.

'Sometimes stunts are worth performing, if they further our cause.' Valerie started the motor.

'So it *is* Beaverbrook?'

'No, it's Cobb. Copyright 1940.' Valerie's mouth was grimly set, her mind shooting fleetingly to the task she most dreaded.

'It is tomorrow, is it not, Val?' Nora's voice was soft with caution.

'Yes. I wish it could be you testing them.'

*　　　*　　　*

265

Shirley, Amy and newlywed Marion arrived for their day of judgment. Fleetingly Valerie wished they had taken up factory work. Amy was the least of her worries—she would attract the press, but her kind, calm warmth was a huge compensation for the aggravation. Marion would be mad to join Alec's pool. But Shirley? Their eight years of closeness and the ground engineer's obsessive devotion to her made the routine administration of a test some form of torture. She would cover her uncomfortable feelings with harshness, and if Shirley failed it might stifle her obsession once and for all. Since Friedrich, ironically foisted upon Valerie by her partner, she could no longer compassionately concern herself with another woman's imperfection.

With Nora, Valerie drove out of Hatfield.

A young girl pilot-hopeful saluted.

Valerie stopped, and rolled down her window.

'I'm not RAF, you know,' she said, recognizing Jo Howes.

'Yes, ma'am. I saw you land that Courier—my pa says it's a collector's item!' she shouted above the din of the motor and the pouring rain.

'That wasn't a Courier, Jo,' Nora yelled back, smiling weakly.

'It sure was.' She was staring at Valerie. 'Have you seen this? You're famous, miss!' she gushed.

'Since when?' the Commanding Officer snapped.

Jo held up an evening newspaper, one of the London editions.

On its front page was a picture of Friedrich Kranz, and a larger one of Valerie and her father in the country on a hunt outing.

266

'Let me see that.' Valerie grasped at the damp paper.

All over Britain a story had broken about an alien calling himself Pavel Wojtek who had committed crime after crime and was now in custody, his only plea that he might see Sir Henry Cobb's daughter before the English locked him away. Friedrich in prison? Valerie handed the newspaper back to the American and shut the window, her hair now soaked and the steering wheel dripping.

'So he's alive,' Nora murmured, touching Valerie's cold, shivering hand.

They sat in a state of frozen quiet.

'Dear God,' gasped Valerie, starting up the motor once more. 'More ferry pools, more women, Amy and Shirley on the verge of joining, more promotions, and now it will all end with me in disgrace.'

'Aren't you pleased he's alive?'

'Of course I am,' she said, biting her lip and handling the steering wheel so tensely that the car swerved alarmingly along the slippery road. Terror had overtaken Valerie, and Nora's offers of comfort seemed to come as murmurings from a distance as she drove mechanically and tried to grasp the enormity of the crisis her lover had engendered.

37

Marion had excused herself when Mrs Bryce had begun to chatter. Carrying her own luggage up the narrow flight of stairs, her first task on her wedding day was to empty her head of the guilt she had accumulated on the journey up from Kent. In her mind's eye was her father's sour expression. If only she could expel the image! There was a washbasin in the corner of the bedroom and she splashed cold water on her wrists and on her forehead, moving to look out of the old, dirt-encrusted window.

How could Alec have accepted such an assignment?

ATA could easily have used men fresh from BOAC. Here, in the spare room Shirley always kept for visiting flying chums, Marion would lie down and try to think of a way in which she could disentangle her energetic lover from his unnecessary diversion to France. Hopefully Hitler would overrun the whole bloody place, and they would just have to forget the Hurricanes.

Smells of food were drifting up from Mrs Bryce's magic kitchen, but Marion was dizzy. She closed the door and lay down on the sagging, musty bed. Closing her eyes, she could taste and smell Alec, the dank chill of the room and the mattress depressing her as she contemplated the next twenty-four hours. It was crucial that each member of Valerie Cobb's hand-picked shortlist passed her test with merit, not only for the image of women pilots but also for Churchill: now it was said that he had a staunch ally in Lord Truman, who raged against the Nazi threat in the House of Lords.

Poor Valerie—she had a lot on her plate at the moment, Marion reflected, letting her shoes drop to the floor and curling up under the woollen blanket. No-one dared mention Kranz in her presence—it would have been bad taste—but everyone knew he had used her name to steal a valuable Fulmar earmarked for d'Erlanger and that the registration letters on the wrecked fuselage had been confirmed as matching those of the doomed aircraft. Could Valerie face being CO and testing a bunch of chattering girls, as well as handling Beaverbrook, the Air Ministry, and that prat of a father?

Not that my dad is much better, thought Marion, snuggling down to escape the creeping damp. What folly . . . to think that the Germans had amassed a giant air force, and that in Poland before the occupation women had long been employed as combat pilots, but that here at home the Air Marshal had only succeeded so far in supplying ATA with a precious handful of Ansons, Airspeed Couriers and Stinsons. Pushing her face into the pillow, Marion imagined Alec's warmth insulating her against the damp and the fears but all she could think of when she opened her eyes was poor Valerie, the Fulmar wreckage and that dear Austrian Jew their tomboyish CO had loved so passionately.

'Making love to that teddy bear you carry around?'

Shirley stood over Marion, her wedding day now well into the darkness of a London twilight.

'You should be congratulating me!' She sat up and Shirley reached for the small bedside light, its faded lampshade casting variegated shadows on to the ceiling.

'Let me see.' Marion held out her hand, her gleaming wedding band tight against the engagement ring for which Alec had sold the bulk of his supply of Harborne's Original Forfar Malt

Brew.

'Tomorrow's the big day, mate,' Shirley said, dropping Marion's hand and moving to the window where she drew the curtains with a force bordering on disgust.

'Today was mine.'

'I know, Marion. My mother hasn't stopped going on about it.'

'Aren't you going to be just a little bit happy for me?'

Shirley jumped on to the small bed and hugged Marion. 'Congratulations, and I wish you well, but right now we should be closing ranks to support Valerie, so don't start telling me long stories about Alec.'

Marion pushed her away, but gripped her arms. 'That's a bit hard, and hurtful, Shirl,' she said, looking into the other woman's troubled face.

'Have you ever tried to take your own life?'

Marion abandoned her hold on Shirley. 'What are you asking me?'

'Certain things upset me, and this business with Valerie and Friedrich has nearly driven me mad.'

Rising from the bed, Marion felt even more chilled than before, and she hugged her arms to herself, wanting the dizzy feeling to recede. Food smells were getting stronger in the house, and she fought sickness. What solace could she offer this fiercely independent creature, who, like her soul-mate Valerie, did not need a man to help her greet each new day? Still sitting on the bed, Shirley looked up earnestly but the cold and the smells had left the newlywed speechless.

'I am sorry to depress you on your wedding day, Mrs Harborne, but there is no-one else to whom I can talk. Angelique is now ATA premiere ace and never spends more than two minutes on the ground. Stella is so wrapped up with Selfridge that it sickens me.'

Marion went to the window, releasing the catch to allow a reviving breeze to enter the dreary bedroom.

'Has marriage made thee so meek thy tongue now hath another master?'

'Shirley, I'm not too well myself.' She turned and faced the bed, where the ground engineer had retreated into a corner against a pillow. 'It may be exhaustion but I have these spells. In answer to your question, I have never contemplated topping myself.'

'I have,' Shirley said quietly. 'My mother doesn't know, but I nearly cut my wrists that day you all came over for lunch. For one thing, all I have to do is *look* at Amy and I am depressed, but then Jim behaved badly, and Valerie went off with her Kraut Yiddle and it all just overwhelmed me.'

'Obviously you are almost still alive!' quipped Marion, moving to the side of the bed and leaning against its sagging innards.

'Aren't you concerned? Haven't I shocked you?'

'One could say I am bewildered by the idea of your best friend's happiness making you want to slit your wrists. Are you fond of Valerie?'

'Of course I'm fond of Valerie—what is this conversation all about?' Shirley leaped off the bed angrily, her strong stocky frame filling the flying suit amply.

'You been overeating, chum?' Marion touched her abdomen playfully.

Shirley smiled. 'Every time I think about Valerie

271

I eat—which is often.'

'There isn't that much to go around these days.'

'Marion, listen to me. You have no idea how much I miss our caravan. For eight years we lived, ate and slept under the same roof, in horrible conditions but with such laughter that we never cared about Tim Haydon snooping, or Val's Dad carping. We were a perfect partnership. Flying was our life's blood.'

'Flying is life's blood to a lot of women, Shirl, but it doesn't mean you have to hate men.'

'What are you suggesting?'

'Perhaps you have an illness.'

'Unthinkable.'

'You asked for an audience, and I have listened.'

'If you imagine I have some mortal illness you had better not be in the same room with me, or you might catch it, Marion.'

'One doesn't catch being fond of someone.' Marion was feeling better, and the room seemed to take on a warmth despite the moist breeze struggling through the inch-open window.

'Marion, I have this horrible feeling Kranz is still alive, and that's what's driving me mad.'

'Nonsense! No-one could have survived a crash like that. The Fulmar was demolished and nobody has found parachute remnants.'

'Precisely!' Shirley was standing close by Marion, her intensity almost amusing in its childishness. 'Kranz got away by bailing out, and as we know, it was a clear night. He's probably tramping the roads even now, looking for Valerie. Honestly, Marion, if a criminal were lurking I couldn't feel more threatened.'

'Threatened? For whom?'

272

'For Valerie!'

Marion went to the window and shut it forcefully, her energy restored alongside her equilibrium.

'Shirl, you must put any unusual thoughts about Valerie out of your mind. She is a Commanding Officer, and after tomorrow she may be our CO— if we get in. Some months ago she was lucky enough—or unfortunate enough, in your eyes—to meet and fall madly in love with a rich industrialist.'

'Ever heard of a poor industrialist?' sniffed Shirley.

'Let me finish. He happened to be married, and it also transpires that you have become too fond of Valerie. Forget her.'

Mrs Bryce was shouting and when they opened the door the glorious smells wafted up with her sing-song dinner call.

In silence the two women, one still wearing her modest bridal attire, and one in dirty flying gear, went down to the waiting feast.

'What's all this?' Marion marvelled, as she took in the challah and the candles.

'It's a custom in this house to observe the Sabbath on Friday night and Saturday.'

'Surely the Sabbath Day is Sunday,' protested Marion.

Shirley grinned, motioning for her to sit down. 'If the Jews should ever take over the world, watch out!' she warned. 'You and Alec will have to work on Sundays.'

'Shame on you, Shirley,' tutted Mrs Bryce, dishing out the chicken soup with kneidlach.

Before spoons reached any mouths Shirley's mother chanted a prayer in Hebrew, and then

273

waved her hands over the candles, lighting them with another sung verse, followed by 'Amen'.

'Valerie and I never did any of these things—she never prayed to Jesus,' grumbled Shirley.

Both Mrs Bryce and Marion glared at Shirley, who had already embarked on the soup.

'What about the prayer over the bread?'

'Oh, Mum!'

'Could you do it? I'm intrigued,' murmured Marion.

Over the challah another chant was performed and Marion tore into the plaited bread with the eagerness of a starving vagrant.

'This is a celebration of a nice girl's wedding, in not-nice times,' Mrs Bryce remarked.

They attacked the food, forgetting war and rationing and the ATA test looming. Shirley's mother watched the young people devouring her Sabbath fare and sighed with a mixture of pride and contentment.

'Has everyone seen the newspapers tonight?' she asked, folding her arms along the edge of the table.

'I haven't read a paper in weeks, Mum—we lady pilot candidates are too busy being part of the war they're reporting.'

'I must confess I've not caught up with the news,' said Marion. 'Has Hitler arrived?'

'You shouldn't joke,' Mrs Bryce said, realizing that neither girl knew what had happened. Both faces rose from their soup bowls and stared.

'Oh, it's nothing, girls, nothing—just some gossip.'

'We love gossip, Mum.'

Mrs Bryce took a mouthful of soup and chewed forlornly on a dumpling.

274

'You've got a secret, Mrs B!'

'Someone called Pavel Wojtek has been arrested and is claiming he visited you and Valerie at Hunstanton. Some mad butler at a country house says the man bathed in their scullery and was circumcized. I thought it might be that Friedrich chap who ate at this table, please God.'

'Kranz is dead,' said Marion, her soup bowl empty.

'Why please God, Mum?'

'He was a wonderful man, Shirley.'

'He was married and I hope he's dead.'

'Don't say such things on Shabbos!' Mrs Bryce gave her daughter a rough push, knocking her arm off the table.

'I'm sure it is nothing to do with Friedrich,' Marion murmured, stacking the empty soup bowls. 'He would have contacted Valerie, not the press.' But as she rose to help her ample hostess, Marion felt nearly overcome by a strange and terrifying roaring in her ears. Weakly she sank back on her seat.

Mrs Bryce, having arranged the spread of Sabbath fare on the table, drew a newspaper from the spacious pocket in her apron.

'God, that *is* Friedrich,' murmured Marion, sitting upright and peering at the press photograph.

'Why is he calling himself by a false name?' Mrs Bryce inquired, patting her brow with a large cloth.

'Everything about that man is false,' chimed Shirley. 'He never told Valerie he was married, and I expect he knows nothing about aircraft manufacturing.'

Marion pushed the newspaper away.

All three women sat, the fluttering candlelight creating a kind of warmth that made the damp little house seem a cosy refuge.

Mrs Bryce cast a fleeting glance at Marion. Did these other girls suspect anything unnatural about her daughter?

'Let's just eat, then if you're too tired to get into your flight manuals you had better sleep,' she said, wanting them to fail because deep down inside she yearned for her daughter to be a girl.

Later that evening Marion and Shirley retired to their rooms where they battled fiercely against tiredness, while the fine print of the rulebooks hammered its way into their aching heads. Fishballs, kneidlach, cholent and kugel lay heavily on their stomachs, an overwhelming malaise overtaking both pilots. Near midnight, Shirley's mind wandered to Valerie and Friedrich . . .

*　　　*　　　*

Not long before they had packed up Hunstanton and the joyride service, Valerie had told her about the glorious perfection she and the Austrian had shared in his tiny bedsit. Over eight years of partnership the two aviation geniuses had demolished any barriers that might have existed between friends of the same sex. On that night in 1939, when the worried circus performers had chattered away into the small hours in their impossible, restless language, Shirley had listened to the voice of the woman she loved most in the world with stony detachment, staring at the ceiling like a blood donor at the moment of the needle's prick.

'When I came to his lodgings there was a well-dressed man leaving the building,' Valerie had recounted. 'What an awful place, Shirley! Friedrich was standing at the top of three flights of stairs and I was terrified that someone I knew might suddenly jump out from one of the closed doors. It was an absurd thought, out of a nightmare. Inside his tiny room he had a battered old kettle like ours, and a little Belling cooker. He offered me tea, but as soon as we realized we were actually alone in the same room, and that no-one would interrupt us, everything happened. Do you mind my telling you this?'

'Go on.' Shirley had drawn her blankets up tightly around her ears. 'That woman will be Prime Minister one day,' she muttered to herself, creeping down into the bedclothes.

Valerie talked and the night wore on, Shirley drifting in and out of sleep in rhythm with descriptions she half-heard . . . Friedrich being so clean, and so gentle . . . if only Val would shut UP . . .

She knew Shirley was not listening, but she would continue remembering anyway . . . she had been terrified of undressing, but his hands, which smelled of soap and were so meticulously manicured, seemed to drift from one garment to another and soon he had carried her to his bed. How ridiculously small it was, and yet when he had settled gently on to her, space seemed as unimportant as time, his kisses deliberate and full of the affection that everyone had warned her would be lust. Valerie had never before been touched like this, nor had she wanted so much to touch, each meeting of their flesh bringing her to

277

the edge of a gravity that convulsed her and made him weep. Through that night he held her, and every inch of her he stroked with a fascination that amazed her. When he did not hold her she clung to his delicate frame, but then he would come into her and she would forget fear and the aeroplanes and duty and the men of the Hunt . . .

Friedrich had teased her about the boyish figure and small breasts that were dwarfed by her broad shoulders, but she kept silent, only wanting to feel his presence inside her again and again and to taste every inch of his trembling carnality. Had any woman of her mother's genteel county circles ever known the passion that could travel from the tip of her being through him and back through the eager, waiting womb that had opened for his firestorm? She had heard the grotesque village fiction about Jewish men. This man could only be called beautiful, and Valerie marvelled at his sinewy arms, perfectly proportioned torso and soft, sparse hair that made her tingle and laugh.

Her experience of men had been a virtual abyss and Friedrich knew this. Though his raging desire for this woman was tempered, minute by minute, by waves of guilt, he knew his love was a bottomless pit and urged her quiet Englishness to burst forth with identical desperation. Now he took every part of her, and when the power of her own passion began to fight its way out of her polite, hesitant sexual self he felt a sense of achievement that shamed him to the core of his being. Never had he been able to release the pent-up frenzy that he suspected dwelt within his own wife, but now as he gripped Valerie and tried to control their rapture and prolong their moment on the brink of

278

climax, he wanted to turn this English girl into a wild creature who would rage within his grasp for all eternity . . .

*   *   *

'How much do you want to wager Amy Johnson gets in and we don't?'

Marion was hovering over Shirley's bed, the ground engineer perspiring and pale.

'What? What are you talking about?'

'Those Air Ministry people are publicity-hunting at the moment, or so Alec says.' She sat on the bed, her hand outlining the pattern on the knitted quilt Mrs Bryce had made for her only daughter.

'Valerie would never fail us, unless we made a colossal error.'

'Perhaps someone else should test us.'

'Do you think she is too close to her girls?'

'Perhaps.' Marion moved closer to Shirley. 'You're all in a lather—it must be nerves.'

'I was deep in thought about the futility of it all, and the fact that we are going through all this aggravation just to ferry Tiger Moths. It must be so humiliating for Amy!'

'Would you rather be working in a factory? At least here we're alongside the RAF and we're up in the air. No girl I know who has got the flying disease can bear the idea of being earthbound in peacetime, let alone in war. Maybe if Valerie can keep her mind away from all this Kranz business, she'll fight to get us on to bigger things.'

'I remember her saying something about us being Spitworthy!' joked Shirley, grinning at Marion and propping herself up in bed.

'Spits are starting to come out of the factories and if this country isn't careful the beauties won't go anywhere—Valerie will have to put up a good battle.'

'I'm worried about this Friedrich affair.'

'I'm worried about Amy Johnson.'

'Why?'

'Shirley, she has such unhappiness with Jim—she might find ATA unbearable—the last straw.'

Shirley burrowed under the covers.

'Marion, go to bed. Happy wedding night. Don't sleep in here or my mother will think I've stolen you from Alec. Just remember one thing: HTTMPFGG.'

'Hot-tempered MP fancies girls,' Marion mumbled mechanically.

Both girls looked at each other solemnly, and as the residue of the erotic narrative Marion had interrupted still made Shirley sweat, the bride retreated to her bedroom and spent the rest of the night awake and on fire with visions of what might have been. Alec had been out of her grasp for only a few hours but her body ached and she wondered, with a degree of shame, whether her own mother had ever lain awake like this, craving Daddy. Tomorrow's test did not loom like an important, dark cloud—it took a remote place in a throbbing tapestry that kept her hunger in the forefront and her man's offerings a delicacy that had suddenly escaped her grasp.

'Think about the test—think about the test!' she told herself as she forced her mind to Moths and **Hydraulics, Trim, Tension, Mixture, Pitch, Patrol, Flaps, Gills, Gauges** and MPs who fancied girls . . .

38

'You're a no-good bitch and there's nothing so boring as you in the bed department.'

Amy wanted a good night's sleep before she was tested, but Jim had chosen this evening for an analysis of her abilities. Lately he had turned it into a game which he called 'Department Store', and when he was rampantly drunk the game got rough.

'Why aren't you pleased we are near to being in a flying group together, Jim?' she asked, her eyes half shut from concentrated studying.

'That is not the issue here, my dear—you should not be allowed anywhere near a ferry pool. As I say, one of these days you will be among lost and found—you lost, baggage found. Or I should say, baggage lost, valuables found.'

Amy's head was now swelling inside. It was a sensation that, thankfully, only Jim induced—had her monumental headaches intruded when she was airborne her career would have had to be jettisoned. As it was, the crucial nature of tomorrow's events made her heart pound and the thumping between her temples intensify.

'I've changed my mind, Amy. You're not worth defending.'

'Thank you.'

She watched as Jim undressed, his youthful body still undeniably enticing, and his smart uniform an enhancement to his rough masculinity. In the low light of one lamp, Amy admired the élan with which he removed his wristwatch.

'Do me a favour and answer a question,' he rasped, standing over the bed and staring at her.

'What question?'

'How many times have you held Hamilton Slade in your little hands?'

Amy felt a rush of blood to her pounding head. For a moment she felt she would go blind. Jim's acrid breath stung her to clarity. He crouched next to her like a lion about to pounce.

'Hamilton has a woman, and it isn't me. I'm sorry to disappoint you.'

Jim gripped her shoulder as on so many previous occasions but tonight the pain was worse and she was frightened.

'Just tell me where he's fucked you—here?' He was hurting her now, his knuckles bruising her with the force she had so wanted from his manhood, but which he had rarely been able to give.

'Jim—stop, please,' but his cruelty worsened and she had to submit. Amazingly, he was erect and though his only outlet was loveless, Amy chuckled bitterly to herself. The possibility of her having further success in the outside world had enraged him to a degree so unprecedented as to make him potent.

Some hours later, when he had disappeared downstairs to commune with his dwindling wartime supply of Forfar malt whisky bought from newlywed Alec Harborne's personal still, Jim had lost interest in Amy and was talking to himself in the study. She ached in every crevice of her body, and knew she had to seek sleep as soon as possible for the crucial event of tomorrow. If she lingered over her discomfort he would become enraged, and her rest would never come.

By the time she had drifted off to sleep, feeling dirty and diminished, light was coming up and the birds were singing. In two hours Amy Johnson would have to report to Hatfield, where the newly appointed Commanding Officer, Valerie Cobb, would treat her as nobody special and take her on a gruelling expedition to certain failure. As sleep overtook her, Amy's last thought was of those other girls who would also test tomorrow. Shirley Bryce and Marion Wickham led normal lives and were unknown but would take the same expedition with Valerie Cobb to certain triumph. Marion had just got married, Amy recalled with inexplicable unease, and as she fell into dreams she saw Hamilton before her, his glorious face attached to a female form that Jim fondled tenderly, as he had never fondled her. Amy's weird dream went on and when she had watched her husband take her lover she awoke, so keeping her terrified confusion at bay. She wanted to get to Hatfield as soon as possible to be near Hamilton, because he was the only man she had ever known who could be as gentle as a woman.

* * *

Newsmen had gathered before first light and were impressed when Amy Johnson arrived at dawn. They put her eagerness down to her legendary enthusiasm but as she drove past their prying trench coats her mind still recalled Jim's rancour. Indeed, her grip on sanity had come to depend upon the encounters with Hamilton, and now she wanted the test to transpire and disappear so she might be enslaved. Dreams were evil. Her mind was caressing Hamilton and she was driving much too fast around Hatfield when Valerie appeared in her line of vision and she screeched to a halt.

'Being harassed, Mrs Mollison?'

'Sorry, Val,' Amy smiled warmly at the trim, vigorous figure in ATA uniform.

'You can be first to be tested, if you like,' Valerie said, peering into the car.

Amy was aware the interior reeked of alcohol. 'I'm sober, in case you were wondering,' she said forlornly.

'I know.' Valerie's face was even and confident, like Hamilton's.

Amy looked away, confused.

'If you park here, we can go on the monster over there, and kill two birds by avoiding the press.' They could see the gleaming Moth in the morning mist and the ace who had circled the world in aviation feats could not help giggling at the absurdity of this humiliation.

'Must I?' she asked.

'You know what the brass are like,' said Valerie apologetically. She did not want to lose this valuable pilot, who at the age of thirty-seven would be a crucial addition to the unit that was growing every time Hitler invaded another territory.

'Do you know, Val, the French are letting women into the air force over there?'

'Let's get moving.' Valerie walked away, and Amy parked the car, leaving the windows open to relieve the air's drunkenness.

As Amy Johnson and Valerie Cobb entered the aircraft that either could have flown blindfolded, Shirley Bryce and Marion Harborne arrived at the field and watched the graceful takeoff.

'Hydraulics, Trim, Tension, Mixture, Pitch, Petrol, Flaps, Gills, Gauges,' Amy shouted to Valerie as they gained altitude.

On the ground the two upcoming contestants mirrored her ordeal.

'Hot-tempered MP fancies girls,' Shirley murmured, watching Amy Johnson's test as if she were a paying customer at an airshow. Marion laughed as the pressmen gathered around and took down Shirley's words.

'Would that be Lord Balfour, madam?' one of them asked earnestly.

'No,' Shirley said, her gaze still fixed on Amy's spiralling aerobatics.

'Is it a code?' another demanded.

'It is indeed,' Marion said solemnly.

'What are you telling them?' Shirley snapped, turning on Marion.

'HTTMPFGG' Marion continued, unperturbed. 'Something to baffle Hitler, invented by the women of ATA.'

'Careless talk costs lives,' one lady reporter muttered.

'So does careless journalism,' Marion countered.

'Do you have any comment, Miss Bryce, on your partner's alleged liaison with the man in custody?'

'What man in custody?' Shirley's nerves vibrated.

'Pavel Wojtek. It's all over the front pages, miss.'

'Never heard of him. HTTMPFGG—much more important.'

Shirley could not refrain from smiling as the newsmen slunk off, stymied. 'They are quick, you know—obviously they've twigged that Balfour fancies Angelique. Next thing, they'll be off to the House to stop the war meetings and unravel the code.'

Marion was laughing so hard she cried, and when she reached inside her flying suit pocket for a handkerchief a film canister rolled out on to the ground. She bent to pick it up and remembered that day before war had been declared—the last day on which she had worn her flying gear as Marion Wickham.

'What the devil is that?' Shirley demanded.

'I found it the day Edith left in such grand style,' she replied, examining the small canister closely.

'Silly fool. It could be crucial intelligence material, dropped by a pilot.'

'Nonsense—Maylands was teeming with reporters that day, and the war hadn't even started.'

'You can still have intelligence without a war,' Shirley observed.

'What a provocative image,' Marion muttered.

'Pardon?'

'Could you have war without intelligence?'

'Wars are always made by men, and you know what I think about their lack of intelligence.' Shirley reached for the film.

'Oh, no, you don't,' Marion snapped, pulling away.

Amy was coming in to land, and despite a heavy mist her approach was perfect and she hit the mark with absolute precision.

'Imagine someone like that having to be tested,' Shirley said, still eyeing the film.

'Valerie wanted total democracy,' said Marion, 'and I think Amy was bending over backwards not to be given preferential treatment.'

Marion stuffed the Kodak roll back into her

pocket as Valerie and Amy jumped from the aircraft and approached. Both looked exhilarated.

'All set for the day of judgement, ladies?' the Commanding Officer asked brightly.

Shirley resented Valerie's patronizing tone, which she seemed to adopt whenever there was a third person present.

'Amy will be in, you'll be pleased to know, provided she passes the oral,' Valerie continued, and Marion offered Amy a congratulatory handshake. 'Shirley, you will go next.' She stared icily at the ground engineer with whom she had once shared giggling, sleepless nights under the Hunstanton starlight.

'Don't you dare lose that film, Marion,' snapped Shirley.

'What film is this?' Valerie asked.

'Oh, nothing,' Marion replied, glowering.

'Keep Amy company until I come back for you,' the CO ordered, and with that instruction the partners marched towards the waiting aircraft to embark on the crucial test, an examination that would turn a ground engineer into a pilot if she kept her nerve.

'Do you mind if I relieve myself, Amy?' Marion asked as soon as the aircraft engine came to life.

'If you don't think you'll be disobeying the CO's orders.'

'She isn't my CO yet.'

'I'll come with you.'

Amy meant well, but Marion had an urgent mission to perform and she did not want company, not even the famous aviatrix.

'Oh, Amy, do you really want to have to contend with all those reporters? Stay here where you're

287

safe.'

Amy had turned pale and seemed to sicken.

'I'd rather not be alone this morning,' she said, her pleading look piercing Marion with an awful suddenness.

'Is something wrong? It's not Jim again, is it?'

'Right at this very moment I am my own worst problem.'

'Come with me, then.' Marion had a terrible urge to take Amy's hand, as if she were a small child on her first trip to school. They walked together and Amy's colour returned to her aging face.

'Haven't you just got married?'

'Yes, and someday I can tell my grandchildren I spent my honeymoon with Amy Johnson.'

'Where is Alec?' asked Amy.

'He's had to report,' Marion replied. 'The Ministry is going mad trying to clear Hurricanes from Brooklands and Langley, and he's been lucky enough to be detailed little trips to France. They're making them bring back unserviceable things.'

Amy gasped, and had stopped walking.

'I wasn't supposed to know that,' Marion continued, 'but Cal March, that Cadet who's latched on to Alec, spilled it all in the car after the wedding. Why couldn't he be clearing Oxfords from here, in Hatfield, or Masters from Woodley?'

'Because those jobs are going to be left to us, Marion. For most of the girls, that's news from heaven.'

They walked on for a bit in silence.

'Have you heard about those two Americans who had an accident at Perth?' Amy asked.

'Two girls?'

'No, ATA men—the two vicars from Virginia.

288

Noel Slater harassed them on an approach and they had a bad one, but somehow they've ended up here.'

'That sounds like Slater, too.'

'The only reason why I am telling you is because Alec may be in just as much danger within our shores as he might be going to France.'

'With all due respect, Amy,' Marion said, 'it's the working-class boys who are getting the rotten work. I'll wager Delia Seifert will get the plum jobs while that poor illiterate American girl Jo will probably be sent out on faulty equipment.'

'We're all at risk, Marion. A barrage balloon has no way of differentiating class when it decides to collide with a ferry pilot.'

They had reached the main building, and a grim Marion rushed on ahead.

'Will you forgive me? I'm expecting a message from Alec.'

Marion evaporated around a corner, and Amy made her way timidly into the common room where Barbara Newman and Stella Teague were playing cards. They ignored her, which was just as well—she so wanted to be invisible.

Marion watched from a distance as Amy settled into a chair where the card game was progressing, then marched into Sean Vine's office without knocking.

He looked up, surprised. 'You should be airborne, Marion,' he said, frowning. 'Have you failed already?'

'Sean, listen carefully. When that American woman was here Alec and I were on the airfield for her send-off, do you remember?'

He nodded.

'When all the reporters had gone I found this Kodak on the tarmac. I completely forgot all about it, what with getting married and all that, but here it is. You've got a darkroom, haven't you?'

'What's in it for me?'

'We'll strike an agreement: if you can pull strings to get Alec off the Hurricanes and on to a job that keeps him on home soil, you can have the film, whatever's on it.'

'Do you have reason to believe it's sensitive?'

'That's what Shirley said—intelligence.'

'How does she know about it?'

'The bloody thing dropped out of my pocket just now—and she saw it.'

He reached out. 'Let me have it.'

'Do we have an agreement, my sweet?'

'Let me see.'

Marion dug into her pocket and removed the canister. Still holding it, she showed it to Vine. He opened a drawer and drew out a magnifying glass, peering with great interest at the printing on the side of the roll.

'Okay, Mrs Harborne. Agreed.'

'Why?'

Sean dropped the magnifier and glared at her stonily.

'What do you mean, why? I thought you wanted your beloved husband back.'

'Just out of curiosity, what is it on the side of that film that has made you say yes so quickly?'

Now Marion was standing over Sean, straining to see the tiny print without the aid of a glass.

'Nothing special, really,' he said, dropping the canister into the pristine crystal ashtray.

'Mind if I smoke, Sean?' she quipped.

290

'Yes, I do.'

'Make sure the cleaners don't pinch it,' she said, picking up the film canister for one last look and then dropping it back with a loud 'plink' into the crystal.

'I'll see what I can do for Alec. I promise.' He took her hand, and she was reminded of the brief coupling they had known, just over a year before, when she was still pure. Alec had done a transatlantic ferry job for huge money on behalf of a Canadian, and she had got it into her head that he might never return. Sean had been kind, his long, feminine fingers introducing her to sensations to which she had thought only loose women were privy, and when his fingers had made way for his robust appendage she had become terrified and had tried to push him from her taut body. Only then had she comprehended the unearthly strength that could charge a man's loins when he was driven by a relentless boiling that sent his substance into her bloodstream and made her cry out as if held against her will inside a maelstrom. Marion had never understood Alec's lack of shock and surprise when they had made love for the first time and he had discovered her impurity. Perhaps, she had thought at the time, he had grown accustomed to disappointment, from the first realisations of the limitations of class, to the poverty his parents had left him as their legacy.

'Please let me know what is on the film, Sean,' Marion said. 'I had better get back, now—I'm childminding.'

'Really?' Sean looked alarmed.

'Amy Johnson, silly.'

'When do you test?'

'Now.'

Marion grinned at her former lover as he pocketed the film canister, which under his glass had revealed its German markings. He could not wait to get to the darkroom. When the aviatrix had been gone a few moments he grabbed the telephone, and there seemed nothing he could do to stop his hands from shaking.

* * *

Shirley Bryce was furious with Valerie for having made her ATA flight test such misery. It was not so much the technical aspect that enraged her as Valerie's businesslike manner, which seemed to negate everything that had happened during the past eight years. Shirley had no trouble taking the Tiger Moth trainer up and doing a few turns, medium and steep, when Valerie suddenly closed the throttle.

'Your engine's cut,' she snapped. 'Now make a forced landing.'

Shirley felt panic rising, and searching frantically for smoke to check wind direction, thought she might land in the nearest field. Somehow she managed to make it back to Hatfield and to perform a near-perfect touchdown within feet of Amy and Marion.

'Now you will wait until Marion has had her flight test, then there will be an oral interview.' She turned away, taking Marion by the arm and leading her to the Moth.

Amy stood alongside Shirley.

'What a nightmare,' Shirley groaned.

'I thought Valerie was very polite, as test

292

administrators go,' said Amy.

'Hot-tempered MP fancies girls—don't forget, Marion,' she murmured, looking up as the Moth soared.

Marion's test seemed to last a far shorter time than Shirley's and the Tiger Moth slid in to Hatfield to deposit back its valuable cargo. Valerie and Marion approached, smiling.

'Believe it or not, my nerves are jangling,' Amy said.

'Too bad, Mrs M,' Valerie chirped, smiling at her celebrated candidate.

The foursome walked briskly to the main building, and for the rest of that day three of the nation's most supremely talented pilots were subjected to a gruelling examination that tested them twice as rigorously as any RAF cadet— because in the eyes of society they were just girls, and in the eyes of the Air Ministry they were an inferior species of pilot known as women.

39

Alec had promised Cal he would make a detour to the ugly terraced house in Shoreditch after leaving Hatfield. It had not troubled him to double back on a limited petrol supply—he could tell the boy ached to see his mother and that he had put aside fears of fatherly animosity. Journeying through the streets that had already felt the pain of enemy bombs, they came upon the March family home and Cal jumped from the car to bang vigorously on the front door. Time passed and he banged again, this time to be greeted by the appearance of his mother, hesitantly opening the peeling wood a fraction. Inside it was dark, and Cal pushed his way past Bridie. She peered out at Alec, who stared back from his seat in the car as if she were stealing his most precious personal property.

There was an acrid smell in the usually tidy house, and Cal's face screwed up into a wince that stopped Bridie from hugging him. They had not seen each other for months, but the putrid smells and the darkness and unhappiness that hit out at the boy from these walls made him shun affection.

'Where's Dad, then?'

'Got some sort of driving job—down by the coast,' she said.

'Loads of money for you, Mum?'

'He comes home on the odd occasion—I don't see much of it.'

'What's that horrible pong?'

'Neighbour's cat, love—you do ask a lot of questions.'

He moved to her, and let her hold him while he rummaged in a pocket for the pile of coins he had accumulated from his small wages.

'Here's enough for a few months.'

She ogled the money, and for a moment Cal pictured her as a child receiving her first allowance.

'You don't look old at all, Mum,' he said, smiling. 'We could be brother and sister.'

'Yes, well, when he isn't here . . .' she murmured, pulling up a chair and sitting.

'You mean Dad?'

'He does terrible things—you're old enough to know now.'

294

'Has he murdered somebody? Is that where the stink is coming from?'

Bridle laughed an unearthly cackle, and for the first time Cal noticed his mother had developed a wildness in her eyes that emanated from beyond their wet twinkle, as if her brain were generating two tiny picture houses running high-speed reels of horror.

'There was an air raid and the people across the road got it,' she said. 'The pong you're smelling is the cat and her new kittens.'

'You took in their cat to look after?'

'Well, after all, Cal, that was all that was left of them, wasn't it? After the raid I said I'd go and see to those poor devils and I kept saying I wished our Cal was here, then I saw and that was it—the cat in her basket looking a stupid fool, the rest of everything flattened. All clear, all clear, they call it all clear for a few bodies, a few families and a few truckloads of corpses. Clear them all away ready for the next time.'

'Mum—this war's making you crazy.'

'I'm not crazy—it's you who are.'

'What's crazy about the RAF?'

'Wanting to die before your time.'

'We need to stop Hitler.'

Bridie's head was bowed and she kept silent. Mewing noises in a corner moved Cal to inspect the rescued animals, their colourful markings like a merry-go-round of painted horses on a summer's day. They looked remarkably healthy, their fur already lustrous and their narrow eyes just beginning to open.

'How can you afford to feed them?' he asked.

'Don't even think of destroying those babies,' she

snapped, sitting up in the chair.

'I never said I would, Mum.' He stood motionless in the middle of the dreary kitchen.

'About your father, Cal—he's taken to all sorts of peculiar things.' She motioned for him to sit. 'Your friend is waiting and I want to tell you before you leave me.'

Cal was close to her now, the fresh smell of his uniform and boots a disturbing contrast amid the aftermath of bombs.

'What he does—he goes off on these trips, and drives tarts about in fancy cars. He comes home and smells of them. You aren't too young to know about this, Cal. Your father had all his faults, you know, but at my age—to have to put up with the scent of fancy ladies.'

'How do you know—their perfume?'

'No, my love—a wife knows, like that mother cat over there. Instinct, or some such thing. They're not the sort who'd wear perfume—more mannish like.'

'What are you saying?'

'It hurts, Cal—these girls are pilots.'

'Rubbish, Mum!' He was shouting and felt as if she were a stranger casting aspersions on his proudest loyalties. Had he not felt that ATA people belonged to each other, pledged to protect one another and do a job no human had done before at the expense of home, lover and child?

'Our girls aren't tarts—not any of them! Besides, they're all too busy working. Just last week, a few days before her wedding, Marion Wickham did three major ferry trips in ten hours. Delia and Stella were flying all over the place and Angelique was dropping with fatigue. There aren't enough of them to go around—and I can tell you, Mum, there's none of the new recruits are cheap slags. Not one—'

A smack as hard as anything he had ever felt from his father's belt stung into his face and he thought he would lose his sight. His hands shot up as if to press eyeballs back into place and he rose to his full stature.

'What was that in aid of?' he asked, staring stonily at Bridie.

'Someday you'll understand what a woman goes through. I curse your flying ladies every day. They are no-good, drunken slatterns without a fibre of morality in their thick skins. Edith Allam, Sally Remington, Barbara Newman—I've heard about them all.'

'Sally Met!' Cal exclaimed, laughing.

'Is that what they call her? How many men call her by funny names then?'

'She's our Met Officer,' he said, wiping his face with a perfume-laden handkerchief he had taken from Marion's car after her wedding.

Bridie looked her son up and down with a suspicion she had never held for him before.

'You had better go before your father returns.' As she spoke voices could be heard. In strode Joe, his face animated as Alec followed on his heels looking enraged yet nervous.

'Bloody ignoramus,' Joe snarled, oblivious to Cal's presence.

'Your boy's here, Joe,' Bridie said, her eyes now a blank screen between features.

Joe did an about-face, his gaze meeting Cal's.

'Here's a pretty sight, then,' he said, leaning against the sink drainer.

'I'm not staying, Dad.'

'So your friend said.'

Alec had composed himself, and stood to attention as if before a tribunal.

'Mum, Dad, this is Alec Harborne, real RAF Retired—now ATA, and my tutor.'

'Tutor in what, I ask you?' Joe moved across the room and pressed against Alec's torso.

'As I tried to tell you on our way in, the wee lad has impressed my wife with his prowess in the air.'

'What other prowess?' Joe demanded, his voice grinding against the thick, putrid atmosphere.

'He's a good boy, Joe,' Bridie whispered.

'I'll tell you precisely, if you really want to know,' said Alec evenly. 'Unlike the ferry pilot, who seldom flies enough hours on any one type either to reach the sublime state of being in unity with his mount or to know its dials and knobs blindfolded, this boy will have one wedded mate, an aircraft he will come to read like a spouse.'

'I've never heard of a man leaving his bride on his wedding day to go off somewhere with a young lad.' Joe was becoming agitated, and he was shouting into Alec's face.

'War has that effect, sir,' Alec said, smiling.

'I've a mind to keep my boy here,' Joe snapped.

'Dad!' Cal screamed, moving to the door. His father was fast upon him, gripping his arm with a twisting, burning cruelty that made the boy cry out. Alec pounced on Joe, pushing him away and wresting Cal from his grasp. In the corner, the kittens squealed and Cal broke away from Alec, darting to the box and overturning its contents, the mother cat's howl reverberating against the four ugly walls.

'Bloody devil himself, you are,' cried Bridie, crawling on her knees on the filthy, greasy floor to gather up the frail newborns, thrusting them against their mother's agitated breast. Red, swollen teats on the cat's upturned underbelly seemed to glare at Cal. He ran from the room and raced for the car, locking himself inside and hiding on its warm floor. He dreaded the sight of his father tearing out of the house to pursue him with the usual beating, but as his heart pounded and guilt at the memory of the distressed animals rose in his overworked heart he wanted to cry at the sound of the car door opening.

Alec was there, and Cal no longer wanted his mother.

He wanted to travel, and to meet other people's mothers. He wanted to leave this horrible legacy behind. He wanted to love, and he agonized to imagine the girl who was his own private picture as some loose woman turning tricks in the back of Lord Beaverbrook's car. Jo Howes had been left in peace by the men on the base and if she were not pure, as Cal thought, then could it be everything was the opposite of what it seemed, and Hitler not so bad?

40

This pilot was overjoyed when handed a Heinkel Transport, knowing it would be one less aircraft destined for conversion from passenger to bomber class. Her cargo had been paid for and was causing no problems so far, but she dreaded the turbulent entry into airspace over the English Channel. Once an ace, Vera Bukova had flown thousands of hours in her lifetime and had trained fighter pilots whose medals were a legacy of her teachings, but now she had to be doubly vigilant as the years eroded her brilliance. Soon she would have to retire, but not before transporting the Kranz family to be reunited with Friedrich in England.

There had been innumerable delays in this mission, and for some weeks she had doubted the Jewish cargo could ever be collected from the ghetto and herded to the airfield. By the time they had managed to escape she had made another sixteen trips ferrying refugees to Romania. Her inebriate husband hated her, after a while, and in recent days had become alcoholically violent. She was pleased to be airborne virtually all her waking hours. Every time she arrived at Bucharest the same Romanian soldier, Ludo, harassed her about the cargo and spat out racial obscenities, but always waved at her and smiled as she taxied.

When she had brought the Kranz cargo in to Bucharest, Ludo had asked about Hana—he remembered hearing something about a boy called Benno who had appropriated the golden girl's affections and he wanted to know of her again. Vera made cheery excuses, saying Hana was on holiday, for she dared not reveal the truth about her daughter's perilous journey to Allied shores. Ludo seemed exceptionally anguished and she wanted to tell him something more concrete about Hana—could he write to her? a postcard?—but her cargo needed transporting and her secrets needed preserving. Her tired, aging brain felt an enormous strain and she very nearly invited Ludo to come along for the ride to Britain, her exhaustion bringing momentary madness to a terrifying scenario. Everywhere around them refugees—some once rich and brilliant and now with nothing, some poor but becoming brilliant in adversity—begged for a place on air transports, but her package of people was paid for . . .

'These are my special Jews.'

'I'm impressed,' said Ludo, circling the aircraft.

'If they were my own family I wouldn't let them all travel on one flight,' she said. 'The father's instructions were specific: they must go together.'

'You will wear your own parachute, and if something happens, bail out.'

Vera looked into the soldier's dull eyes. 'What about them?' she asked.

'If on land, they will perish. But if on sea, like flotsam they will rise to the top.'

'You're a poet, Ludo.' Vera checked inside her holdall to see if her belongings were in order, and she ran her hands along the sides of her flying suit as if frisking herself.

He smiled. 'When will I be seeing Hana again?'

'I hope to bring her here on my next trip, Ludo,' she replied, studying his face more closely.

Ludo scratched his head, poking his finger underneath a soiled cap. He looked at the aircraft, which rested in the small, muddy field unnoticed amid the usual din of confused refugees and even more bewildered officials, all of whom, deep down inside, yearned for safe refuge too.

'Anyone who helps these worthless people without being asked will be a traitor,' he said. 'Everywhere in the world, Hitler will be the owner and the citizens his guests. Doing something out of

301

the ordinary will be treason.'

She gazed at him with thoughts of Hana surging through her mind, and could not control an urge to squeeze his burly arm before turning towards her aeroplane and joining the cargo.

Vera shut her eyes and thanked the Guardian Angel of Aviators for the commotion that had distracted all the officials present on this day, allowing her to leave Bucharest without a proper inspection of papers. There was an atmosphere of excitement inside the Heinkel, but she was irritated that the cargo insisted on speaking German, with which she had always had tremendous difficulty. Vera concentrated on the controls of her aircraft; the Heinkel had been lovingly designed by the race she hated, and she had to admit the specifications created a machine unlike any other she had ever piloted. When she landed in Britain, there would be joy all around: here was a technical masterpiece their geniuses could dissect.

She allowed the engines to roar with pride, skirted the runway and made a dangerous ascent, barely missing the tops of cottages peppering the village. Benno Kranz was sitting next to her now, as she manoeuvred the magnificent aircraft well out of Romanian airspace and on a course for the rain and the pallid men of England.

Were there any real men left there? Or anywhere?

Vera convinced herself that this mission had been performed for Hana. During Friedrich's visits to the ghetto, the well-dressed boy had practised his Polish with her daughter and developed a bond: he had told her about the *Dybbuk* and afterwards his father had berated him for scaring the girl. Hana had laughed—she was a woman and a pilot, and she was never scared—and on Benno's next visit she had told him the story of Our Lady of Czestochowa. It was not meant to frighten, but he had been terrified.

Listening now to the women talking, she glanced around and noticed their fair hair and small features: they could easily have stayed in Austria or in Poland, blending in with the Aryan population. Was it their intensity that made them different? Suddenly she recognized a few words: Kranz's mother was drifting into Polish, and she wanted to talk to them all.

'How long is it since you saw Dr Kranz?' Vera shouted, mouthing her words slowly.

'Ages!' his wife replied, her Polish perfect.

'All this time I thought you spoke only hoch Deutsch!' Vera yelled, as the engines gained a happy momentum.

'My mother speaks five languages fluently, and she once played a violin concerto and a piano concerto all in one symphonic concert!' Benno announced, staring straight ahead.

'You people seem to undertake ruthless goals,' the pilot responded. 'There is never a sense of fun. Have you ever thought of getting drunk and being ridiculous?'

There was a silence as all four Kranzes exchanged guarded looks.

'How could we allow ourselves to get drunk?' Frau Kranz asked testily. 'What do you think would happen to us?'

'When you get drunk, you get drunk,' Vera said.

'Does your husband?' asked the old lady.

'My husband? Yes, he does.'

'When?'

'When he comes back from your ghetto.'

'My husband could never get airborne,' murmured Vera, 'so he hates, and therefore he drinks.' Then she noticed the permanent pout on the face of the younger Kranz daughter. 'Do you miss your father?' she asked the girl.

'He didn't have to leave,' she replied lifelessly.

'I'm not quite sure why he did,' Vera said, pleased to be as relaxed as a passenger in this aircraft.

'England had an attraction for my handsome man,' said the younger Frau Kranz. 'He thought the British might want his aeroplanes, but I suspect it has turned out to be a wasteland for him.'

'All I know is that his money has reached me and I have been able to bribe half of Poland to get this aircraft. You are aware of what contortions I have had to endure to smuggle you out of bondage and into the air.'

'Our life was not bondage,' snapped Friedrich's wife.

'Are you suggesting it will be so in England?'

'Inside her head is bondage,' Benno whispered, his face darting a swift look at Vera and then returning its intent gaze towards the heavens.

'You have an old man's head,' she whispered back, her hand reaching sideways and taking his. It was icy cold. Did he fear his own bondage in the hours to come? Was every country another potential prison to these Jews, these people who rejected Christ and worshipped the dismal solitude of scholarship?

'Fires ahead!'

Vera's heart jumped. The boy was shouting in Polish and she understood.

'Don't worry,' she said, astonished that the flames had come up on the horizon so quickly and that the smoke could so completely block her vision. She took an immediate course away from the conflagration but at once realized the nightmare was everywhere. In the back of the aeroplane the four women—Kranz's wife, his daughters . . . his mother—had gone strangely silent, and as the smoke began to seep into the massively insulated fuselage of the most advanced aircraft in Europe, Vera pondered the absurdity that after thirty years of perilous flights she might suffer the indignity of being asphyxiated. Why had she not brought masks for her cargo? She remembered the huge book that accompanied the Heinkel had mentioned something about it being equipped with its own ultra-modern oxygen goggles that were supposed to drop from the ceiling. She reached behind her, straining to touch the fuselage above, but there were only gaping crevices.

'Please see if there are masks anywhere above you—hanging from the ceiling!' she shouted, all the while trying to steer out of the hellish blackness. Any moment she knew she would strike another aircraft or career into the hard, life-ending ground. She had lost her bearings and the sheer power of the enormous Heinkel Transport seemed to be driving her, its propellers still healthy as if defying the smoke like an infant defying exhaustion and crying long into the night. One of the women was crying, but now Vera could only hold on to every second, stiffly contemplating the inevitable impact and feeling gratified she had not had time to acquire an affection for her cargo. Everywhere was blackness and now the engines were spluttering. Unbelievably, in a few short moments both had cut out. She was gliding, and the immense grace of the aircraft enabled Vera to guide it through its last moments without noise or tremors or terrible somersaults. There was no noise: she turned to the boy in the seat alongside, and he was looking at sepia-toned photographs. He handed one to her, and as they spun faster towards earth, she saw in the corner of one the celebrated signature:

Fischtal.

Suddenly the engines came back to life, and they were climbing, but when the blackness cleared Vera's heart sank and the horror of what lay ahead made her spine harden and her thoughts of Hana and of picture albums stop with this vision of calamity. This was not Switzerland, nor was it Scandinavia or any other gateway to Vera's own special brand of treason . . .

Friedrich Kranz's wife gasped as the aircraft landed on a beautiful stretch of green, its wheels skidding and Vera praying that she could pull the machine back under control and be airborne again. Her cargo of women gathered up their belongings as if they knew they were not meant to leave the earth again and as Vera struggled to steer the giant transport into a takeoff position a loud banging made the boy cry out, and he reached for the pilot whom at this moment he saw only as a soft, round woman. Banging was reverberating within and Vera could no longer think, the awful sounds from every angle outside now penetrating their stifling

306

cabin. Benno stood up. He imagined he could see the tops of helmets. There had been banging in the Ghetto, and he remembered the tops of helmets that had tumbled from pickup trucks and herded old ladies out of houses. Now Vera was working the engines to fever pitch, but there was an even louder, more terrible bang and the aircraft lurched, only to sink down into the mire.

41

One element of Noel Slater's personality had caught Sam Hardwick's attention, so much so that he had begun to suffer sleepless nights in its wake. He had never before encountered an aggressive young man whose background had been as deprived as his own, defying the rules of lower-class obedience. Lying alongside the woman who had borne him three neutral characters of the male sex, Sam had speculated that Slater awoke aggressive, ate his first meal with aggression, lived out each day as the total aggressor, and did not ever love. That was the aspect which fascinated Sam the most—had Noel sacrificed his heart for an ambition that by the end of every twenty-four-hour period was replete? In the mornings Noel would most certainly be an empty shell needing replenishment, other humans being the bollards he had to knock over to achieve it.

Neither Sam Hardwick, nor his sons, nor any man he had met in his limited life, had resembled this mere boy, who had taken an adult twice his age under his tutelage and begun to mould him into a fresh creation. Had Sam taken a mistress, the patchwork symmetry of his home could not have gone more askew.

War meant that men of his age would be allowed to learn to fly for a few shillings an hour and to ferry simple craft; when the RAF needed every pilot in the country, men like Sam would be allowed to fly more dangerous machines into the war zone and across the Atlantic. Noel wanted Sam to learn everything. They had lived through 31 August 1939, the last day on which civil aircraft had been allowed to fly, a day on which Maylands had been full of youngsters eager to join Air Cadets. But Noel took no notice of the Cal Marches of this world when he could have malleable antiquity in the person of Sam Hardwick, and be father to the man.

For many months Sam had been accumulating skills that would enable him to become a taxi pilot, and with dramatic intonations Noel had explained that on his shoulders would rest the outcome of war. On any given day, a taxi pilot would set out in the morning with a list of the aerodromes he had to visit, against which would be written the names of pilots to be collected or delivered. In hushed tones Noel explained to Sam that when an RAF squadron moved, Ferry Control would ring up, ordering ten new fighters to be delivered that day; priority telephone calls would stop everything and a pilot would find himself being taxied to a factory that manufactured one very special fighter.

Noel trained Sam well and soon he was flying Fairchilds, but as country after country fell to Schicklgruber he graduated to Ansons, the first low-wing monoplane to be taken into RAF service.

'One of the most beautiful aeroplanes ever built,' Sam wrote in the diary he had begun to keep ever since he had outlived his usefulness at the meat market.

'When all this is finished I think I will buy myself an Anson and spend the peace flying around in it,' he wrote another time, having marvelled all day at the magic machine's ease of maintenance and supreme economy, its unbelievable reliability and the spectacular loads it could carry.

Dawn was arriving on this summer's day, and Sam was waiting for Noel to join the group who ate breakfast every morning in the makeshift Mess that had once been a club dining room. For weeks everyone had been waiting for a massive invasion but the Germans had remained quiet. Nonetheless, in the darkness of the bedroom he shared with a quietly breathing woman who once had been his lover, Sam had experienced a giddiness as he had dressed for another new day at Maylands. Something extraordinary was about to happen.

'Lot of money to be made from it,' his wife would scold, in a voice suggesting his livelihood paled next to her special soothsaying talents. Now that he had given up meat for aeroplanes, she had stopped predicting the future and had developed a penchant for collecting: newspaper cuttings, magazine pictures and empty cigarette packets filled an old knitting bag to overflowing. She never allowed Sam to look inside, but he conjectured she had lost her mind when he left Smithfield and that newspapers took her mind off a future that could hold nothing now but death. All his life he had been surrounded by carcasses and she had never cared. Now he was transporting men who could be downed by one balloon while his wife cut, cut, cut like the workers who had once inhabited the gory corridors of the market.

Here in the canteen men gathered and joked, a corner of the room occupied by a tiny handful of women on a stopover. They had no lavatory or mess of their own, but these rare visitors, whose numbers occasionally included Amy Johnson, seemed cheerful amid the men's tension. On this day every male available had been assembled, including Jim and Hamilton Slade, and the boy Cal. Gordon Selfridge had received a cable as he prepared to sail to the United States and they had heard he was on his way from Liverpool. His ship was to have left twenty-four hours before, and Gordon was lucky because it had been attacked as he had stood, bags in hand, reading the telegram. Everyone missed him when he was away, his Anglicized American charm as attractive as the voluptuous victuals he poached from the store on Oxford Street for the benefit of this privileged ferry mob. He would be here presently, with Sam and Noel and Alec and the Yank Bill, to be taxied to a place where their collective dreams would be realized and their boyhood passions renewed, because they were to spend this entire working day, from now until dusk, doing something they had never done before. They were to be moved to a permanent home at White Waltham.

It was time to prepare for the Spitfires.

*   *   *

Rumours had been circulating that there were to be twenty-three different versions of Spitfires.

310

Everyone knew that a full-scale battle for the survival of Britain was just months away, and though the women had to accept their exclusion from fighter deliveries, their instincts told them Spits would soon be within their grasp.

Now Delia Seifert and Angelique Florian were munching on toast and groaning at the sight of Sam and Noel, dressed in flying boots, fur-lined leather trousers and jackets, huge scarves, helmets and goggles, their ration bags hanging around their necks and jotting pads strapped to each knee. They were talking, Noel's gravelly voice carrying as far as the girls' table where they could detect words about drift angles. Here were two men whose odd coupling had alienated them from the rest of the pools and towards whom Hamilton had a particular animosity. Delia had told him she thought the men were friends, but Hamilton detested Noel and now loathed the older figure he called 'the bedfellow'.

'But he's married!' Angelique shouted at Hamilton, who was sharing his breakfast with the slender females.

'I'm sorry to keep dwelling on the subject, but that March boy ought to be sent elsewhere,' he hissed, as Delia removed a sliver of Selfridge's smuggled bacon from his plate. 'Lads are being moved to White Waltham and I think he should go.'

'Sam has three sons,' Angelique said, smiling at Delia. 'He's strong and normal. Not that one could say the same of Noel.'

'Cal March needs to get away from rotters,' Hamilton muttered, his fingers tapping restlessly against the empty coffee cup.

'Alec Harborne looks after him,' Delia asserted.

'Which reminds me that I am supposed to be looking after the Toland brothers, who would not be in hospital were it not for Slater,' Angelique blurted in hopes that her voice might carry.

Sam and Noel were to be separated for the first time and that was what made this day so crucial.

'Why are you wearing that foolish suit?' snapped Angelique, following Noel out to the main field.

'Why not, actress?' he said, walking on.

'You aren't allowed to fly, Slater.'

'Someone I know has bent the rules, and I shall now be on Spits,' he muttered, stopping and letting the others proceed. 'Did you know that until recently actresses were regarded as synonymous with harlots?'

'Flight engineers with deficiencies are synonymous with accidents. The women's pool knows all concerning the Toland brothers.'

'Are you proposing to report me to d'Erlanger?'

Angelique smirked, wanting to demolish this man and triumph on a Spitfire at the other end of the Anson's journey.

'Harold Balfour would love to learn more about your behaviour,' she said calmly.

'He couldn't care a fig about a bloke like me. There are a thousand men, at this very moment, being trained to fly all kinds of things. He has them on his mind, not Noel Slater.'

'You have Sam Hardwick on your mind all the time, and that can't be very good for your record, big man.'

Slater took hold of his kit bag and, with a movement swift as any gazelle, pushed past Angelique. She walked to the edge of the field, the

312

taxi Anson now filled with the best of her circle but joined by a man whose menace made her ache with dread. Determined to pursue a personal mission she had been formulating in her head during the night, she watched as the lovely aircraft left Maylands.

Noel's unchivalrous behaviour had moved her mind to images of disturbed acts in European ruins. As the Anson soared into the early morning sky she thought of Zack and Paul with terror. They were in a place unknown, but she knew she could not stay here much longer . . .

42

Sitting in the back of the Anson, Noel talked softly to his older pupil:

'Why don't you leave that woman?'

'In the middle of a war?' Sam looked incredulous.

'Who cares?' Noel grinned.

They stopped talking as the Anson struggled through thick cloud, but even when the view had cleared the other men remained silent.

'What a glum bunch,' Noel chimed, eyeing the congregation of pilots seated in the taxi aircraft. Not one of the men responded, but Sam whispered in his ear:

'They're all still wary of us after the accident. I expect they think of themselves as perhaps the next Oscar and Martin Tolands in your list of intended victims.'

Noel smiled.

'Are you having a romance with that gal?' Bill Howes broke in.

'Which girl?' Noel demanded sharply.

'The gorgeous Florian dame,' he replied.

'Perhaps I am, perhaps I'm not.'

'You either is, or you isn't,' Bill quipped.

'What difference does it make, Howes?' Noel peered out of the small window on his side of the aircraft.

'You been pushing her around?'

Only the engine could be heard as breathing stopped.

'Nonsense.'

Four pairs of eyes stared at Noel as if he were about to reveal a terrible secret.

'In public.' The American was relentless.

'Howes, she's a tart,' hissed Noel.

'Whom are we talking about?' asked Hamilton, who had leaned back in his seat next to the pilot, wanting to defuse a dangerous situation that would be one hundred times worse airborne than on the ground.

'He means Angelique Florian,' Sam offered, smiling meekly.

'Angelique is to play Richard III at RADA next term, war or not,' Hamilton said. 'She is known as their best leading man. Not that she isn't all female. Harold Balfour is pursuing her, and she is not a tart.'

Guffaws exploded spontaneously from the men on board, and Hamilton let out a long breath. Noel stared out of his window but the other men cackled and joked and that was the way Hamilton wanted it until God saw them back down to earth.

Noel turned again to Sam as the others made

314

what to him was a ridiculous noise. 'You're special to me, Sam.'

'Be quiet.' Sam looked at his colleagues with fear but Noel was still talking:

'We could have a business partnership. It was meant to be, mate.'

Sam moved closer to him, his paraphernalia getting in the way and his pockets jangling.

'What have you got in there, old man?' Alec shouted, winking.

'Chronometer, stopwatch, protractor,' Sam replied colourlessly, while the men resumed their laughter.

Noel was glad; the din drowned his words:

'If we get together I can start on something I haven't told you about. It will make you drool, Sam.'

The Anson had begun a sudden descent and soon with a tentative juddering it came to a halt.

Conversation ceased.

'Ancient and Tattered Aviators,' shouted Alec as the door opened and the cool air drifted into the fuggy cabin full of pilots.

They had expected to see gleaming new Spitfires peppering the landscape, one for each man, but at Hamble airfield all that greeted them now was a small collection of ragged machines, one battered Airspeed Courier resembling a museum piece rather than a wartime defence offering and a spattering of Moths that seemed perfect targets for German bombing raids. Jim strolled a full circle around the Courier and smiled.

'It's a good way of getting rid of trash,' Bill volunteered, looking up at the bright sky and brushing his hand against an aged Fox Moth's fuselage.

Sam and Noel walked away, heading for the main road leading to the Vickers factory.

'Disgusting,' Alec mumbled as he watched the pair vanish around a distant corner.

Never in his life had Sam Hardwick ever contemplated a close partnership with another man, and he knew the ferry group resented their relationship. Noel hated women and Sam was miserable, but neither wanted the other; both men knew there was, indeed, a smouldering volcano within.

'Did you hear Harborne just now?' Noel asked, as they walked briskly along the sandbagged road.

'We ought to have women friends, Noel,' he said. 'They're good for show.'

'Punching bags are good for show, too,' snapped Noel, striding on ahead of Sam.

'How can you hate them so?'

'You've asked me that a hundred times before.'

Sam had caught up with him, but his breath was coming in fits.

'Hardwick, prepare yourself for a monumental surprise.'

Turning into the entrance drive to the Vickers plant they were stopped by a guard.

'First of the ATA Spitfire pilots,' Noel snarled, arrogantly waving his log book.

'You have no authority to enter the premises as yet. Only the CO can.'

'I *am* the new CO,' declared Noel.

Sam was astounded. The flight engineer's audacity was as boundless as were his flying ambitions.

'If you do not leave the grounds you will be

'arrested,' the guard said calmly, surveying Noel as if he were a giant leek.

'This is my Adjutant, Hardwick, and I must insist you allow us entry to the works,' Slater asserted, his voice grating on Sam's ears.

'Come this way,' the guard instructed, pointing to the front entrance.

They walked, Sam wanting to run away and never be seen again. It was the first time Noel had got him involved in a situation as embarrassing as this, and in one split second he regretted every direction in which he had allowed his life to go this year.

'Watch this,' Noel whispered to him as they followed the guard.

In the main reception area, sitting beneath a new painting of King George, another guard perused the outlandishly-dressed aviators and smiled at them: Sam could not help thinking of a zoo-keeper cooing at the deadly lion who had escaped her cage.

'First Officer Noel Slater reporting with taxi pilot Hardwick for Spitfire deliveries.'

'Your CO would find this most amusing, gentlemen,' said the guard, still seated under his sovereign.

'I am the CO,' said Noel, this time whipping out an impressive, leatherbound document book and waving it in front of the incredulous pair of guards.

'As you know, Mr Slater, the Ministry of Supply has laid down quite specific rules about the organization of ferry trips from this factory. In the first instance, we have test pilots who take Spits out on a test run and it could be one further day before we are ready to release them from

Maintenance Units for this particular operation to take place.'

'I thought the RAF was screaming for them!' sneered Noel.

Sam nodded sheepishly—standing, as always, two steps behind Noel.

'In any case, Slater, Miss Flint is to have overall charge of this procedure.'

'Miss Flint?' howled Noel.

Sam retreated another two steps.

'Indeed, sir. The new Commanding Officer, Hamble. Nora Flint.'

'This is an outrage,' spluttered Noel with a look of helplessness.

'She is an awfully nice girl,' Sam croaked.

'A woman CO—this is the ruination of the Services,' Slater ranted, perspiring through his heavy flying gear. 'This will get into the press just as we are about to receive Germans landing in parachutes in our own back yards—literally—and all the Ministry can do is appoint a girl CO.'

The reception guard was still seated, and he gazed with disdain at the flight engineer. 'May I assume you wish to retract your original contention that you are in fact CO Hamble?'

'How do you mean?' Noel was incoherent, his hand pressing into a creased forehead, his receding hairline glistening under the bright lights of the famous manufacturing establishment.

'I thought perhaps you would not wish to be mistaken for a woman, having previously made claims to being Hamble CO.'

Noel grabbed Sam by the arm and marched him out of the building, nearly knocking their first escort off his feet. Walking at a fierce pace he soon reached the main road —but with Sam lagging behind, his irritation grew.

'Move, for God's sake!' he bellowed, and the older man sped to his side, panting.

'What an achievement for little Nora,' gasped Sam, stopping by the roadside.

Noel would not speak again that day or that evening, his mortification addling his thoughts and curdling the small breakfast in his stomach.

Gordon had arrived with glorious delicacies from his secret cache, and the men celebrated Nora's promotion to Commanding Officer by crowding into the single ladies' lavatory cubicle and toasting her with Selfridge's own Lloyd George Vintage.

Noel experienced a vague awareness of the festivities, his mind clouded by visions of a beautiful, unobtainable woman who had given birth to him, bathed and dressed him and pushed him out into a world where he had hoped females would be extinct. His torment, however, could not cloud Sam's delight in Nora's achievement, and as the men gave generous obeisance to the prospect of her command, Noel's mind drifted to the words the Vickers guard had spoken: test pilots must take new aircraft out on a trial run . . .

This was of great interest to him.

43

Angelique had forgotten religion since war and the ATA.

Having been one of the choice eight selected for Valerie Cobb's first ferry pool, she had been in great demand, with rarely a day off between flights. She could still remember her very first assignment, which had taken all of twenty-five minutes: she had delivered a T1176 from the factory at Cowley to Wroughton. Anson-loads of ATA pilots were being dumped in Cowley for trips to Scotland. Stella Teague would drop the girls off and they would scramble, often getting only as far as Carlisle where a night-stop would be necessary. Back in their respective cockpits the next dawn, the girls would fly on and refuel at Ternhill, grabbing tea in the Mess.

'You never eat!' was the one complaint every ATA girl's mother would shriek on the now-rare visits home, but on occasions like these time was of an absurd essence, the nation still ill-prepared for onslaught, and the barrage balloons a daily nightmare. Indeed, when Angelique, Nora and Delia managed to get through the barrage in their Moths they could barely see one another but pressed on past Liverpool and on a northerly course to Lancaster. Angelique recalled vividly one journey in which the cloud base had started to drop, and the girls were sandwiched between the hills and the cloud, with the light fading all the time. They caught sight of a lone railway line and followed it until, to their relief, they could see a major town materializing on the horizon. Having to spend the night at an ancient inn, the three pilots spotted Sam Hardwick and Bill Howes, who were ferrying Lysanders to Belfast, though both men were officially listed as taxi pilots . . .

All three women vowed they would be flying 'Lizzies' before the year was out. On that long journey, Angelique remembered her exhaustion as they flew up the Dumfries Valley in good weather, using this as a short cut to Prestwick. The trio knew this route was perilous and would eventually cost the lives of some ATA pilots, and should only be attempted in fine conditions.

'How do you say West F-r-e-u-g-h?'

Oscar Toland had awakened from a painful slumber and Angelique was thrilled to see the colour returning to his cheeks.

'You must have been reading my mind,' she exclaimed.

'Why's that?'

'I was just thinking about all those trips up to Prestwick, and the Dumfries route. You know—the short cut around West Freugh.'

Oscar smiled, the bandages covering most of his face and his extremities. Hatfield General Hospital had been host to the Toland brothers for two days and their horrific injuries had been a new experience for the young doctors and nurses accustomed to the occasional push-bike casualty. Now that the airfield was fast becoming a centre for multi-level operations, hospital staff knew they would have to gear themselves for wartime horrors.

It was afternoon, and Angelique was grateful for the arrival of a humid summer storm front. She had become fascinated by this American clergyman, whose brother Martin was a withdrawn, timid shadow of Oscar's vibrant personality. Both boys had been reared in a well-to-do, fiercely evangelical background, in which affluence was tempered by their father's obsessive zeal for New Testament rantings and moral speechmaking. Over the dinner table Ezra Toland had lectured his boys

321

about the evils of temptation, and while Martin had gone out into the world and resisted the burning that had arrived with the first hairs of puberty, his brother Oscar had gone out into the world and taken on every temptation.

Much to the indignation of old man Toland, his boys had developed two unspeakable fascinations: one for flying, and the other for European history. Though they had missed out on the Spanish Civil War they were drooling at the possibility of helping fight Hitler from a base in England. 'Europe is the home of Satan,' their father had cried as they had argued bitterly for paternal permission to board a steamer bound for Canada and the United Kingdom. They had been ordained Baptist ministers less than four years, and neither had reached thirty. Even their mother, who never spoke except in church, opened her mouth to protest and for a brief moment both lads were moved, but when Ezra went for his Bible to proclaim them almighty sinners they decided they would make a pact: one weak, and one strong, they would travel together to help Europe, birthplace of the Shakespeare, da Vinci and Euripides that they loved in secret, and home of the remarkable Valerie Cobb, who was breaking the barriers of traditional womanhood.

Jesus, they both agreed, would have liked that.

Indeed, their congregations commended the boys to the Lord for safekeeping and in spring 1940 Oscar and Martin braved the growing threat of U-Boat approaches and boarded a ship sailing to England with magnanimous volunteers from the land of isolationist politics.

Arriving at Liverpool while Whitehall was

322

digesting breakfasts of German advances, the Americans and Canadians expected late nights and jolly pub crawls as they disembarked. Grim faces confronting them on the dock shocked the new immigrants to their souls. Nowhere would they find rich foods or fun, and the Toland brothers made their way with solemnity to Norwich, where they had been promised a place to stay at one of its plethora of churches. Soon these American preachers had become immersed in English traditions and ritual, and in time, though Baptists, were enjoying services at the Cathedral. Their days, however, were taken up with flying, and when their turn had come to test for ATA they put their first calling on the back burner and asked the Lord's forgiveness for leaving Him unattended for the sake of something called war.

'My brothers are stuck out there somewhere, and as soon as they get us off Tigers I'm flying over to find them.' Angelique spoke softly to Oscar, not wanting to disturb the dozing Martin in the next bed.

'Where are they?'

'Spain, I think.'

'You aren't sure?' Oscar peered into her eyes, straining to catch their true colour.

'Their last letter came from Zumaya.' She caught his glance and blushed. 'Zumaya is a cell in Northern Spain for anti-Franco forces.'

'You mustn't go out there! It's insane, honey!' He was straining, and his colour faded.

'It was only jest,' Angelique said, moving closer to his ashen face.

'You Italian?'

'No, I'm British.'

'Let me rephrase that—are you of Italian extraction?'

'My family could be called deposed Armenian royalty.' She smirked at him. 'Do people ever call you Oz?'

'All the time. Father Oz, in fact.'

'Then I shall call you Ozzie.' She took his hand, and for a few seconds he gripped it and then let go, wincing.

'Are you in great pain?'

'Not as bad as Martin's.' He smiled and let one of his fingers touch the back of her hand, which still lay on the bed. 'What was that you were saying about getting off Tigers?'

'ATA will not allow women to ferry anything but Tiger Moths, as you know, Ozzie. We are starved for pilots and every last man is being siphoned off to the RAF. There must be two hundred girls in this country qualified to fly anything operational, but the answer is No.'

Angelique felt a tap on her shoulder and she turned around to find Matron sporting an uncharacteristically worried expression.

'Could I see you privately, miss?' she asked, her frightened eyes now devoid of the sparkle that had given her the nickname 'Dame Dazzle' amongst the male patients.

Oscar waved weakly, and the aviatrix felt a terrible urge to kiss his forehead, but Matron had already reached the end of the corridor. Angelique hurried on, following her into an area ordinarily off-limits for visitors. Seated around a wireless were doctors, nursing sisters and a handful of cleaners.

'France has fallen,' Dame Dazzle whispered in

324

Angelique's ear.

'I must go,' she murmured, hugging Matron, on whose cheek she thought she could see a tear.

Rushing back down the corridor she walked up to Oscar's bed.

'You had better recover soon, mate,' she said. 'Adolf will be parachuting in to London this coming weekend.'

'Is that so?' Martin was awake, and he had heard.

'I'm sorry, Martin. You should go back to sleep.'

Other male patients were sitting up, anxious to know why the staff had disappeared, and straining for the lady pilot's words.

'France has fallen, chaps,' she said, her gaze taking in a sea of faces born in the last century and which had already witnessed one obscene world conflict. Somehow she knew this obscenity would be worse. 'It will mean a battle for Britain.'

Oscar leaned towards her and took her hand. She felt tears welling up but she fought them, wanting to prove she was worthy of the stripe she bore so proudly on the blue ATA uniform.

'Whatever you do, Angelique, please promise me you will not fly into the war zone to rescue your brothers.'

She withdrew her hand. 'I can't promise you things like that, First Officer Toland.'

He sat back, exhausted. Now she noticed a tear pushing its way to the corner of his swollen eye.

'If you go, promise me you will come back in time for Christmas Mass. Norwich Cathedral. I'll be useless for flying. They'll probably ship me back.'

'Rubbish—ATA keeps all sorts of characters in work.' She could fight the tears no longer, and as they poured down her cheeks she could barely discern through the mist Matron and the nursing sisters bustling in to attend to the men who had also worn uniforms in past wars and who had not been allowed to weep. She left the hospital and was gratified to see a clear sky, for it might mean one last ferry job before nightfall. Wiping her face with the pale blue handkerchief that accompanied ATA uniform issue, she walked at a feverish pace to the airfield and as she approached the main building a feeling of overwhelming excitement enveloped her youthful spirit.

'We've been taken off Moths,' shrieked Stella Teague, jumping up and down like a tiny puppy and running to Angelique. They hugged, nearly falling over in the rough gravel that was drying in the warm teatime sun. Stella stared at her colleague. 'Why are your eyes swollen?'

'Old age, Stella,' she replied, her arm flung around the little ballerina's shoulders. 'After all, you're eighteen, and I'm twenty-three.'

'It's so exciting, Ange—Nora has just got the news. What a pity Valerie has had to miss it all.'

'Where is she?' Angelique felt her chest constricting.

'Didn't you hear?' Stella halted, her shoulders drooping.

'Stella, has something happened to Val?' Tears were on their way again.

'She was called away to London. When she left her face was white as a sheet. By the way, how are those two Yanks?'

'They could be better.' Angelique craved more information about her Commanding Officer. 'Do you think Val has been put on to a secret assignment, now that we're off Moths? Perhaps she will be flying into the war zone.'

Stella fell silent as they reached the lounge to discover a great commotion. In one room had assembled many of the nation's most outstanding fliers, now on the verge of an achievement no woman had ever attained before.

'Magisters are waiting to be ferried from Phillips & Powis at Woodley to Burtonwood,' Nora read from a large sheet of paper, hardly able to contain her excitement. 'Those of you who have done the Central Flying School Course will be on Oxfords and Masters, and you will be expected to taxi groups in Ansons. Our more junior pilots should be reminded you will not be full members of Air Transport Auxiliary until you have passed the official acceptance test at Whitchurch. Tomorrow Amy will take any newcomers still to pass the test down to Bristol. You can all bundle into the Airspeed Courier that appeared at this field some days ago. Everyone will be fitted up with a proper uniform.'

'Where does Valerie Cobb figure in all this?' asked Delia Seifert.

'For the moment she is not available to ATA,' Nora said noncommittally, moving to the notice board and posting her paper.

There was a strange silence, as though the excitement of their new status had been dashed by the sight of an accident in which a loved one had been struck down. Angelique and Stella moved to the notice board, and the others wandered off to the common room with a nonchalance that suggested their work plan had not changed.

44

Alone in what had been Valerie's office, Nora walked hesitantly to her desk. Slowly she lifted a document from its otherwise uncluttered surface. She moved to the light by the cracked old windowpane and read the page for the third time that day. Looking up, her gaze fixed upon two girls examining the parked Airspeed Courier, their eagerness to fly the no-longer-forbidden craft expressed by their animated gestures. Feeling the need for male company amid the torrent of news with which she had been inundated in one short afternoon, Nora wished Hamilton and Sean had not left for the day. Although they would arrive back at some odd hour when darkness had fallen over the airfield, their inebriation might somehow cheer her up, but by that hour Nora would have had to return home to her lacklustre mother and father. Her parents had been bewildered by her occupation and she had never been able to share calamities with them. Now that an earthshaking bit of good news had fallen into her lap, she wondered if their reaction would be equally phlegmatic.

'Commanding Officer Flint, may I speak?'

Nora whirled around to find Delia Seifert standing in the middle of Valerie's office.

'Dear God—how did you know?'

'Everyone knows.'

'How on earth—?' Nora stared wildly at Delia.

'It's in the latest editions, for all the nation to see,' Delia explained, a rare glow illumining her face. 'Beaverbrook seems to want the whole world to know about it—principally Adolf. Did you hear he reads the London papers?'

Nora folded her document and placed it inside the breast pocket of her trimly-fitting uniform.

'Beaverbrook! Beaverbrook! Oh, God—if anything, Delia, it will set the war effort back—does that man really think Hitler will feel threatened by a press release announcing that a girl is being made CO of a ferry legion?'

'*You* will become famous overnight, my friend.'

Bowing her head, Nora did a tour of the office and tapped her fingers on the desk. 'What is the use of confidentiality, I ask you? I went to such trouble keeping these documents hidden, and after all that? The newspapers tell my family and our girls before I am given clearance to do so.'

Neither woman spoke, but outside a gaggle of pilots had gathered, snippets of their chatter wafting into the office, with words like 'bombers', 'dogfights' and 'rear gunners' standing out amid the banter.

'What's to become of Valerie, Nora?' asked Delia.

Nora faced her as if standing to attention. 'Why do you ask?'

'I'm speaking on behalf of the other girls. Things are escalating faster than anyone had expected. Out of the blue Val disappears, and no-one in the Ministry cares to tell us what has happened.'

'Why are you so worried, Delia?'

'Her talent is magical, and without her, we stagnate.'

'Pilots never stagnate!' Nora stopped for a moment and hovered over Valerie's desk. 'She has been sent on a secret mission, and that is all I am prepared to tell you, which is already far too much.'

'It doesn't matter, Nora, because I know it is a giant fib.'

Nora moved to the door, forcing Delia to walk across the room as the newly appointed Commanding Officer switched off the lights.

'Delia, there may come a time—very soon, in fact—when you are a CO and there will be twenty ferry pilots of both sexes under your charge.'

'What nonsense!' Delia hooted, standing in the corridor. 'Imagine the Air Ministry appointing the impoverished daughter of a drunkard a CO—Cal March will reach that rank, but not Delia Seifert.'

They had emerged from the administration building into a brilliant afternoon sun, and to her delight Nora saw Hamilton Slade on the Hatfield runway, talking animatedly to Amy alongside the Airspeed Courier. By the end of the week most of these girls would be entitled to fly a whole range of aircraft they had been denied until today, but Nora knew Valerie would not be there to enjoy the sight.

'Have the newspapers told the general public where I am to be posted?' Nora asked Delia.

'Good Lord, yes—Hamble,' she replied. 'To be precise, you will be heading a women's pool with immediate effect. *We* all know the purpose of the exercise is to clear Spitfires from the Vickers Supermarine factory at Southampton.'

It was nearing twilight and though everyone knew the Battle for Britain would take up every waking moment from this day to a possible eternity, a searing urge to celebrate spurred Hatfield's ferry contingent to converge on the Stone House Hotel. Six of the girls were staying there, and proprietress Mrs Bennell developed a sentimental attachment to her unusual clientele. On this quiet, sunny afternoon Mrs Bennell had read in the newspaper that one of the other pilot girls was to be made a Commanding Officer. She had an ominous feeling that changes would ensue with the Southampton appointment of Nora Flint, ex-Smithfield office girl, and that the lodgers she had come to love as daughters might disappear as rapidly as Battle of Britain air warriors.

'When are you going to find me that Ouija Board, Mrs B?' asked Stella Teague, bounding on to the small covered porch at the entrance to the Stone House.

'You may not be here when I find one,' she replied, her face expressionless as the shape of the boarding house she had run for twenty-six years.

Stella hovered on the porch, her mirth evaporating as she met the landlady's gaze. 'Why would I not be here, Mrs Bennell?'

'Your Nora Flint is being made Commanding Officer of a base in Southampton, one that is filled with regular RAF men.'

'Lucky Nora!' Stella exclaimed. 'You must have read it in one of the papers.'

Mrs Bennell stood rigid, watching the others approaching. Folding her arms across her chest, she could feel an almost primeval urge to strike out at the nearest human being, keeping her back to Stella.

'It means you girls will be leaving me,' she said.

'Nonsense,' Stella pouted, thinking only of the RAF men and of the luck Nora took with her wherever she travelled. 'We all stay at Hatfield— it's Valerie's HQ.'

331

'People are saying Valerie has been arrested,' Mrs Bennell said, turning around to face Stella.

'Arrested? Whatever for?'

'It has got about that she was harbouring a German spy. Think of how it will damage her poor father's career. Frankly, I do not trust any lady pilots who take their own lodgings.'

'You have said this before, Mrs B,' Stella said, grinning.

'Fliers should all live together, eat together and cry together under one roof. You are very special people, Stella, especially if you are women.'

Noise and shouting had overwhelmed their words as the other girls, accompanied by Hamilton and Sean, had gathered in the porch.

'Will you be letting us in, Mrs Bennell?' Angelique asked, squeezing her landlady's arm affectionately.

There was a pause as the older woman surveyed the crowd assembled in her immaculate porch, their faces flushed and expectant. Her words came sluggishly as she fought back emotion.

'You may all be leaving me soon, and please—' she raised a hand to stop a startled Sean from speaking, 'don't argue with me. I remember in the last war, when one or two little announcements were made, and we were told our lives would not change, but in the passing of a day whole villages were being emptied of their men. Only in war does this happen. You are all naive and I want you to believe me.'

'We are going nowhere,' Delia asserted, her makeshift ATA uniform blowing in a warm breeze that cut across the porch and sent leaves scattering among their booted feet.

'Of course we aren't,' Amy added. 'Hatfield is our base, and I much prefer rural Hertfordshire to Southampton.'

'Let's go in,' Hamilton murmured, putting his hand on Amy's shoulder for all to see. 'When is Jim due back from White Waltham?' he asked quietly, as the rest of the group entered the spacious hotel bar.

'I've not enquired,' she said, sitting on a corner stool with her back to the rest of the group. 'Ham, when I fly that Courier tomorrow, I want you to come with us.'

'Impossible!' he snorted, loudly enough for heads to turn.

'Why?' Her sad eyes pleaded.

'This Valerie business—Sean and I are working on it full-time, and the press will be on our doorstep in the morning.'

'What press?' A voice pierced their concentration, and Hamilton and Amy whirled around to find Angelique at the next table.

'Press about Valerie,' Hamilton replied, biting his lip.

'How are your two Yanks, Angelique?' Amy asked, smiling generously.

'I've just come from seeing them in hospital,' she replied, her expression glum. 'They'll be back to flying soon.'

Angelique surveyed the room impatiently, as if one of her American aces might walk in at any moment, unhindered by injury. She took a deep breath, wishing Valerie were there with her endless supply of cigarettes. Amy and Hamilton looked down into their glasses, pondering the calming liquid.

Angelique was speaking:

'When we go to Bristol, Amy, I am not coming back with the rest.' She made her announcement with such matter-of-factness that Amy wondered if the world had gone mad.

'Have you had clearance from Valerie on this?' Hamilton asked.

'Yes—she cleared it last week before she went into hiding.'

'Do you believe she is in hiding?' Amy asked, fascinated.

'Lord, yes!' Angelique replied, downing a large gulp of beer. 'It has something to do with intelligence, and some photographs, but that's all I can say.'

Hamilton mused at this girl. How could she think for one moment that he was not privy to the most sensitive information coming in from the Ministry? It made him laugh, and he slammed his glass on the table.

'Why are you laughing?' Angelique asked, always feeling uncomfortable and out of place in the presence of Mrs Mollison.

'No reason,' he replied, his face set once more.

'I'm worried about your not coming back with us,' Amy continued.

'Again, Amy, all I can say is that it has something to do with Intelligence. There will be no ferry chit.'

Amy knew that masses of new aircraft would be requiring transport as soon as her Courier-load of girls had passed the new test, and she also knew exact numbers and allocations, her squadron being due to fly back in formation when their new fighter aircraft had been rolled off the assembly line. Angelique could be strong-willed, but Amy had a feeling of horror about the plan she was concocting; as she sipped her pale ale she resolved to use her influence to establish the whereabouts of Valerie Cobb.

Amy's world was continuing to disintegrate around her, and as she watched Mrs Bennell scowling in the opposite corner over a well-worn newspaper, she wished she had stayed in Australia so many years ago and become a happy bride to the splendid Mr Vickers. Pale ale went to Amy's head and made it ache on every occasion it met her stomach, and while Hamilton and Angelique sat in awkward silence, the Battle of Britain began its agonizing birth within earshot of the Stone House Hotel, a rumbling making all the drinkers smile and then, for the first time, think seriously of death.

45

Several days had passed, Kay Pelham and Lili Villiers having had to spend considerable portions of their travel money on extra nights in lodgings. Edith Allam had been delayed on her flight to Australia, despite rumours that the Beaverbrook empire had laid on a large passenger aircraft—the most advanced available—which the American girl would be flying from her home town of Philadelphia.

'They say Philadelphia is just like Townsville,' Kay announced, bright day pouring in through the window of the room they were sharing on the outskirts of Brisbane. She lounged on the small bed, her splendid shape exuding a seductive air.

'How would you know?' Lili asked, grinning.

'I know a lot about the world,' Kay replied, noticing Lili's neatly arranged make-up kit and her compact figure. This was the longest respite Kay had had from the amorous demands of her latest partner, and she felt refreshed and lightheaded. Forcing herself to ignore the pulsating libido that was trying to distract the attractive actress from present business—the prospect of a career in aviation—she contemplated Edith Allam's arrival: would the American be like the Yanks who had come backstage to pester her every night during the short run of *Pygmalion* in a tiny Townsville theatre house?

Perhaps Edith would be glamorous, wanting only ugly girls to travel with her to England, so as not to outshine her.

Kay looked again at Lili, who dozed on the battered chair in their room, the hot sun beating down and raising a musty smell from its cheap, ancient cushions. She was one of the most attractive people Kay had ever met, male or female, and she wondered if it was the staggering wealth of the Villiers name that gave her such allure. Some people had said that she, Kay Pelham, had a stunning aura that drew both men and women to her and made them become obsessed, and one thing she knew was that she was terrified of being seduced by another girl, or even worse, by an older female. She could never imagine life without the love of a man, and she hoped Edith might be quick in her assessment of the lady pilots so Kay Pelham could get back to doing what she craved most.

'My Dad had an affair with Amy Johnson,' Lili recounted, her head leaning against the back of the old chair.

'Is that a big secret?' Kay asked, her mind conjuring up instant visions of a handsome man and a lithe female in wild contortions of passion on a hot coastal shoal.

'It got around,' she replied, raising her neck and grimacing, its stiffness making a small cracking noise in the blissfully quiet room.

'What did your mom say?'

'She walloped him, when he came back to her.' Lili grinned at Kay, whose eyes were widening at each piece of news.

'How did she find out?' Kay was leaning forward, hanging on to every word and letting Lili's pleasant fragrance hover around her head.

'You must be joking—news travels like wildfire in Queensland, and of all people, Amy Johnson . . . do me a favour.'

'How come I never heard about it?'

'You probably couldn't read yet—that was in 1930.'

'Ten years ago,' Kay mused, sitting back on the bad. 'My first fellah made me want to die in 1930.'

Lili sat up, her face flushed. 'Kay! You've been with men?'

'Holy shit, girl, of course I have.' Kay's eyebrows arched and she frowned, wishing Edith Allam would arrive at this precise second and redeem her.

'Where do you do it?' Lili asked, watching Kay carefully, like a child peering down at the lion's den in a zoo.

'Around town. Different places.'

'You're a whore.'

'Don't say that, Lil.' Kay had turned pale, and as the sun disappeared behind a rare cloud their room darkened, turning cool in the shadowy dimness. 'There's a big war on, now, so let's forget who's immoral and who's moral, if you don't mind.'

Lili walked to the door and opened it, the silent corridor brightening suddenly as the sun emerged again, and Kay jumped off the bed, moving towards the other girl and touching her arm. Lili pulled away in a fear that communicated itself to Kay as disgust, prompting her to run down the stairs of the rooming house and find in Brisbane what had eluded her for so many agonizing days. Lili would spend that night alone, lying awake for hours and thinking about Kay, tormenting herself about morality and about the misery of her own fantasies.

*   *   *

When more days had passed and the girls had run out of funds, Lili telegraphed her father and instant cash appeared in the hands of an effusive bank manager in central Brisbane. Kay had decided they should give Edith Allam another day's grace but in the meantime have an extravagant meal and a late night out on the town. During their long wait for Edith and her entourage, the two Australian pilots had languished in the city, drinking too much and eating too little but keeping to an otherwise harmless routine ending in early bedtimes—with the exception of Kay's only sojourn on their first evening in Brisbane.

Her night out alone had been a disaster, the partner she had found a droll little man who had undressed and taken her with great tenderness, his hesitant, careful touch interspersed with words that made Kay laugh. Soon, however, she had become bored, yearning for the businessman with whom she had fornicated before her journey, and whose humourless fucking had been punctuated by barked demands for acts which the law would have regarded as grossly indecent. On this first night in Brisbane she had left Lili alone to think innocent thoughts of aeroplanes and England, but now Kay was dizzy with boredom.

Still, it was she who had had the hunger that had driven her to this man's cheerfully tidy town flat that seemed a haven custom-made for the commonplace. She had been surprised when he murmured, 'You reminded me of a boy, and that's what I wanted—sometimes I do so love having boys,' holding her face so tightly she thought he would crush her skull. After a while Kay had more pain, and as the night wore on he began inflicting perversions she had not known existed, and for which he would afterwards apologize, always kissing her tenderly. At daybreak he coaxed her into submitting to a final humiliation . . .

*   *   *

Dining in Brisbane's most expensive restaurant, Kay and Lili were looking ravishing twelve hours after the former's all-night adventure.

'He could have murdered you!' gasped Lili, wide-eyed as Kay described the culminating episode.

'I've never been so disappointed in my life,' Kay

339

said, waiting for the white-gloved boy to finish pouring wine into elegant glasses.

'Why do you do it, Kay?' Lili asked, smiling at the thin, handsome waiter as he departed silently.

'It's not what I do, mate. It's what *they* do. Some girls pick them, as they say. As it turns out, he really wanted a bloke, not a sheila. And as men go, he was awfully sweet.'

Lili scrutinized her new friend's face, the flawless skin and deep-set, intelligent eyes setting off a restless energy that transmitted itself to admirers as a kind of sexual want.

'How could this guy get any pleasure from you if he likes playing with little boys?' demanded Lili.

At the next table a pair of young men cast a flickering glance at them.

'Keep your voice down, for Christ's sake,' Kay said, giggling. 'That wasn't the end of it—he was making the most pathetic noises, and I think he did me permanent damage. As I say, he was a real sweetie, but God, it hurt.'

'Did he pay you?' asked Lili.

'What is this, the police station?' snapped Kay.

'I'm just concerned, that's all—when we get back to the room you should let me look at your wounds,' Lili murmured. 'They might get infected.'

'You're a nurse, then, as well as a millionaire's daughter?' asked Kay, still uneasy.

'I'm a pilot, actually,' Lili responded. 'Let's not forget why we are here. By now our families must be dead worried about us, you know.'

'That's unlikely,' Kay remarked. 'If you say your father works with mine, they've probably figured out between them our real reason for coming to town. By the time they get into a blind panic Edith will be here and we'll either end up being sent back home or off to Pommyland.' Kay was feeling ill, and the food on her plate had become cold and unappetizing.

'What did your queer gentleman look like?' asked Lili.

'Youngish, a bit lame, bless his heart, and sort of overweight. At least he was clean and affectionate—you'd have liked him.'

'Thank you very much! Kindly credit me with some intelligence.' Lili gulped at her wine. 'You ought to report him to the police,' she continued in a whisper, leaning across the table. Suddenly she was aware of the physicality of Kay's allure, dwelling momentarily on the perfectly shaped breasts that seemed to peer at her from behind the provocatively revealing blouse. Lili tried to imagine this woman amid the awkward embraces of the night before, her clean scent and delicate skin incongruous against a panorama of sexual perversion.

'Let me explain something to you,' Kay said, the girls' faces now an inch apart. 'This fellah did give me money—lots of it—and he'd classify me as a whore if he met me on the street again tomorrow.'

'Couldn't he expose you as a prostitute if you become famous?' asked Lili, at once fascinated and horrified.

'By the time I'm famous I'll be in England and I'll be doing Shakespeare. Who the hell is he, anyway? He's just nobody, baby.'

Later that evening, after the largest meal Lili had eaten since the grand summer ball at Villiers Industries, the two girls went to their room to recover from the feast.

'Let me see your bruises, then,' Lili said quietly.

There was no response from Kay.

'Are you asleep?'

'If I am asleep, why ask?' croaked Kay, turning on to her stomach.

Lili moved to her bed and gently pulled down the loose-fitting blouse to reveal a muscular back with shoulders powerful as a man's. Gently probing Kay's tense neck muscles with her inexperienced fingers, Lili felt as if a new and unknown power had overtaken her as if, with the excess of wine, the spirit of a a prowling jungle beast had invaded her soul.

Kneading Kay's muscles, Lili felt an overwhelming excitement beginning to churn within herself, and she shut her eyes, fighting back an impulse to settle on to Kay's magnificent flesh and envelop her whole. She knew Kay was not asleep, but she could feel relaxation in the worn muscles, and it was only when a hand began to stroke her thigh, so slowly, that Lili knew her explosion could no longer be contained.

Her mouth met the back of Kay's neck and with an ungodly strength Lili held her and tore away the blouse, covering Kay's back with wild movements of a tongue that wanted to sweep across her fragrant beauty without end. Still Lili held Kay down, but opening her eyes realized there would be no resistance to her relentless passion, and soon they were as one, flesh to flesh, their complicated, fruity wetness joining in a fiery throbbing that held them both at the brink of a precipice . . .

Sobbing, moaning, crying out and begging for more of this ecstasy, Kay could not recall ever having known such terrible urgency with any man, each touch of Lili's skin and fingertips and adoring mouth bringing her to almost unbearable rapture. Having come completely after what had seemed hours of electrifying awakenings down her hardened nipples into the depths of her womanhood, Kay took Lili in her arms and held her in silence. Slowly, her fingertips outlined Lili's form, falling gently along the soft skin of her young thighs and moving into the shy, untouched garden that Kay now probed with tenderness, its virginal treasure wanting and pleading . . .

Every night thereafter the two girls slept as one and though Lili's moaning voice declared true love, Kay would only revel in the newfound form of sublime orgasm and over nine sleepless nights of insatiable, devouring, never-once-mentioned love.

46

No sooner had Hana Bukova and Josef Ratusz arrived in Britain than their lives were being commandeered by an assortment of Polish agents and military eccentrics who appeared more menacing than the Nazis they had just left behind. Hana had landed with crisp precision at Prestwick, spending the first night on friendly soil at the Orangefields Hotel, where the wizened, bow-legged proprietor had been convinced his new guests were German spies.

Little sleep was had by either flying ace, and by six o'clock the next morning a hearse had arrived to whisk the pair away, its darkened windows leaving the hotelier bemused. When they had gone his bobbing bald head pleaded with his assortment of long-term resident ferry pilots to do something about this calamity, but these residents were Americans and on this morning they were setting out on their busiest day yet. The Battle of Britain was raging, their President could do nothing, but they had survived U-Boat alley to be where they most wanted their talents to be used.

Departing in a cold dawn mist, the car carrying Hana and Josef had an odd identity plate, the letters of which were recorded by the vigilant proprietor. By the time he had lumbered back to the breakfast room, where smells of black pudding and toast entranced the last of the pilots remaining at the table, his wife was bustling at the washing-up and mumbling about the absence of eggs. He wanted to tell someone about the car and the spies and their bizarre uniforms, but she could only wail while the American pilot scraping his plate laughed and took his leave.

Arriving in the centre of London at what seemed an eternity later, Hana and Josef laboured to extract their stiff bodies from the automobile, hunger and thirst pushing them to the brink of collapse. Being allowed no respite, their sullen driver, and in turn his tall, colourless companion, ordered the pair in Polish to mount a fiendish pyramid of steps. At the top Hana felt she would faint but Josef seized her by the arm and when she had recovered her breath they could see these were the headquarters of Poles in exile. Not one word had been exchanged during the seemingly interminable car journey, but now Josef wanted a response.

'How did you know we were arriving?' he

demanded, grasping his driver's richly-woven coat lapels.

No reply was forthcoming, and Hana grinned.

They walked.

'They knew we were on our way—amazing!' Hana whispered, hopping on to her toes to make Josef hear.

'This is an impressive edifice,' he said, choosing to ignore her as if at any moment a gunman might jump out from behind a pillar and cut him down for speaking out of turn. He peered up at the ornate ceiling as they marched along a wide, echoing corridor.

'It has been occupied since 1908 by some English oddity called the Automobile Association,' the accomplice explained. 'They have kindly given us the seventh floor, which has a clock on each corner. My office is underneath the clock of Leicester Square.'

'Kind?—I would go insane!' Hana exclaimed, her step overtaking the others. 'Are you sure this gesture was not some sort of joke?'

The two British agents for the Polish government in exile walked on in silence. When they reached the end of the corridor, their guests were escorted through a heavy, windowless door, into a debriefing area. This also served as a storage cellar for the AA but the Poles had been allowed to set up an assortment of makeshift, windowless offices that had a sinister ambience out of context with the Englishness of the dank, mediaeval odour emitted by its walls.

Josef and Hana sat down and were relieved that food and drink had been laid before them and that the two men, now facing them across a wooden table, were smiling. Hana grabbed at the food, gulping down a sausage roll and a cup of lukewarm tea.

'Can you give me my mother's address, please?' she asked, her speech interrupted by a hiccup.

Her escorts exchanged glances, and Josef, deeply involved with a sandwich, seemed uninterested in the proceedings.

There was another long silence, and Hana hiccupped again. 'My mother brought the Kranz family to England and she was to stay a while before going back to my father.'

One of the men, clad in wool, came to life:

'Our concern is for your comfort and safety. As you know, the Air Transport Auxiliary is keenly in need of expert pilots, and we have been instructed to engage your services for them immediately.'

Josef choked on his food. 'God Almighty! I am not a ferry pilot—I am a fighter. Surely they could use me. I would not have risked my life, or Hana's, to come here and ferry Queen Bees.'

'Indeed,' said the giant of the two, 'Queen Bees are your first assignment. A pair will be needed for delivery to St Athan as soon as possible. Can you start now?'

'No!' screamed Hana, rising from her chair. She was dirty and she hated the way she smelled, wanting to be clean to greet her meticulous mother.

'There is nothing more to say,' said the small man, his expression pained. 'We were expecting you, and the British government needs your expert services for special missions ferrying across perilous routes.'

Josef had now risen to his feet. 'Hana and I must

346

bathe and rest. Then we must see her mother, who is the great ace Vera Bukova.'

One of the men produced a sheaf of papers. 'Please sign these and we will find Madame Bukova for you.'

Josef and Hana were feeling strangely lethargic and as they sat once more and perused the documents they realized they might never again see daylight if they did not agree to the absurdly simple terms on offer. Josef felt an urge to assault these characters for using Hana's mother as a bargaining tool. Their dungeon had an unspeakable stillness about it and the damp smell had begun to permeate their clothes. Reading the print, which covered several sheets of impressively headed paper, the two pilots learned that they were each to take a short test, and that Hana would be restricted to single- and twin-engined aircraft, should she pass. Josef would be inducted as a senior ATA man, on a handsome salary with room and food provided. It was attractive, and they were sick with tiredness.

They signed.

*   *   *

That evening Hana waited in a hotel room overlooking Maida Vale, her expectations rising with each passing hour as the prospect of news intensified. She had been promised a personal visit by the Polish Consul at nine o'clock precisely, and from the lively tone of his voice she assumed her mother would be found within the plush confines of his limousine, fueled for all contingencies even while Royalty volunteered for rationing. At this moment Hana did not care about the British, or the smouldering, bombed-out ruins of Northwick Terrace she had seen in a dream as she slept in her chauffeured car; the disgorged skeletons of Northwick Mews, the flattened entrance to which until that day had been a church. She was not moved by the fact that in Lisson Grove an orphanage was now in a state of carnage. She did not care that the electrical generating station on Aberdeen Place had been the target the Luftwaffe had missed, nor did she care now whether the light in her room violated the blackout. This was the longest gap she had ever known away from her parents and the prospect of ferrying Spitfires made no impact as she awaited the arrival of familiarity in a sun-baked but worried country full of brave strangers.

Her wristwatch, a gift from her great-grandfather, ticked loudly and she smiled at the thought that she had been the first female to wear it in the history of the Bukova family. Now its delicate hands showed nine and she moved from the small bed, her leg tingling as the circulation returned after having been tensely tucked under the other in a corner of the bedding. Walking to the door, she turned the icy-cold brass handle gingerly and moved across the corridor, listening for the slightest sound from Josef's lodging. Her hand moved to tap at his door and then stopped, Hana realizing two minutes had passed and that the hotel was silent . . .

At midnight Hana, her hands frozen and her mind nearing distraction, went again to Josef's door, there to hesitate once more before returning to her room and curling up on the cold mattress.

No-one had come, not the Consul nor her mother, and she watched from the window as a light show in the eastern sky seemed a laughing reminder of the war she thought she had escaped. Hana resolved that in the morning she would go to the Consulate in person and demand to see the highest in command. Her mother was Poland's greatest female ace, she would shout, and surely they would let the two women meet at last. Secretly Hana had always wanted her parents to split their union, and now there was a chance to enrol her mother in ATA, where the two could serve as a team.

She had it all mapped out, and with that Hana slept.

47

'While we are here we can write a history of the Blood Libel.' André Grunberg had not envisaged spending his war within the confines of a British internment camp on the lovely Isle of Man. He could have blamed his plight on Friedrich Kranz, but the two needed each other in these unspeakable circumstances and the past would have to be filed away in a mental cavern.

'I imagine there is no scholarly account available in this country,' Grunberg continued, pushing a wedge of white bread into a pool of gravy that swilled on a green plate. 'We would be doing the Ur work by delving into mediaeval manuscripts. It would raise a few eyebrows up in East Anglia, don't you think?'

'How would we do research, Grunberg? Here in

this ridiculous camp? You're mad.' To adjust to this sudden detour in his life, Friedrich Kranz had had to set aside debilitating worries. His family, whom Vera Bukova had been paid to evacuate, and the Englishwoman he craved, seemed to have evaporated into this island's foggy air. For months he had heard nothing, nor had the occasional newspaper allowed into the camp revealed the latest achievements of Valerie Cobb; she had disappeared from the headlines as the grim war news brought 1940 to its cold conclusion.

'There is a library nearby, and these officials here are quite civilized. They'll let us go there, under escort.' Grunberg leaned forward in his bunk and placed the plate on the concrete floor.

'Believe me,' Kranz said, 'at this point the Blood Libel is not the focus of my life.'

'What *is* the focus of your life, may I ask?'

'My children! My wife, for God's sake, you idiot,' Kranz shouted, leaping off his bunk and towering over the ballet master. He paused. 'My mistress.'

André Grunberg looked up at his brilliant compatriot, amused at the afterthought. 'Your fantasy?'

'She's not a fantasy,' snapped Kranz, moving back to his bed and sitting down again. 'This woman is very real—she writes poetry and lives in a caravan with another female—a young girl who idolizes her.'

Leaning back against the barracks wall, André Grunberg wondered how he, distinguished choreographer and senior ballet master, had arrived in such a state so late in life. In Vienna, he reflected, he would have been removed by the Gestapo, probably in the middle of a class, and

350

sent to a death camp. At least the British, with greatly apologetic gestures, had sent him to what he had come to call a 'Life Camp'. Still, it was a form of imprisonment and he had been flabbergasted when the authorities had arrived at his studio—having been tipped off by his landlady of twenty years standing—to whisk him away from his young dancers and the plinking piano. Here he had met Friedrich Kranz, who had rescued his sanity with a breathtaking knowledge of music and of history, and whose family, like Grunberg's, was spread across the ghettoes of Eastern Europe as well as being assimilated within the enlightened walls of Vienna.

Nonetheless, that same assimilation had brought the same result for his relatives as the Warsaw Ghetto had brought for those in Poland. He wondered if Kranz knew the full extent of the horrors now taking place; the businessman seemed never to receive any post, his cursory perusal of the infrequent newspapers leaving him indifferent.

'Why haven't you told me about your caravan lady before?' he asked, smiling back at Kranz, whose colour had returned to his sunken cheeks.

'Something about the Blood Libel,' he mused, his long fingers rubbing the side of his face, as if to extinguish a searing pain. 'Since you mention it— her friend, Shirley, found the subject fascinating. Listen, Friedrich,' he continued, relentless in his quest, and now curious about the other man's liaison. 'If you can get permission to contact this girl Shirley, we could say it is with reference to a useful historical research project. Then we could enlist her help in explaining to the authorities that we are harmless Jews, not Nazi spies, and at the

351

same time we could find your lady.'

'What makes you think I am trying to find her?' Kranz demanded, his voice strained as he felt an odd onslaught of tears approaching.

'Don't think I haven't noticed you receive no post, but that you pine for a woman who isn't your wife.'

'For a man with no wife, you receive a hell of a stack of communications—perhaps you are a spy of some sort.'

'Those letters are from my students. They claim to love me, but none has lifted a finger to protest at this curious incarceration.' Grunberg leaned back against the wall and curled up into his cool, damp corner. No heat ever reached these barracks, and the sanitary facilities were a shock to the elegant, meticulous folk the British had seen fit to intern regardless of their religion. It was the height of absurdity, Grunberg reflected, that a bunch of assimilated Jews, each an expert in his field, should be cooped up in this makeshift concentration camp just because His Majesty's government thought all German-speaking people were followers of Hitler.

Grunberg laughed to himself.

'What is so funny, old man?' Kranz leaned over, poking his head into André's corner.

'We are brought here, forced to neglect our work, and left to languish while the British, in their great Christian wisdom, think they are guarding society against Nazis.'

'I suspect you were a lapsed Jew before this happened.'

Grunberg smiled:

'Friedrich, I never even thought about being one of the tribe until the British authorities chose to remind me. I'm sure it was the same for you.'

Kranz rested his head against the side of the bunk and listened as other men chatted, mostly in their native German, while some played chess and others listened to music on the old phonograph provided by a sympathetic guard. Closing his eyes, he thought of Valerie, and the smell of her skin was as fresh in his nostrils as if she had been sitting beside him on this atrocious concrete. Grunberg knew nothing of his torment, nor of the horrible consequences his actions must surely by now have had on Valerie's life. Reflecting back on the past months, he wished everything could be reversed: there was not one occurrence of which he was not now ashamed.

Only his passionate joining with Valerie was worth preserving, and even that would most definitely never happen again. Could he continue to live this way? Why did he not think of his wife, or of his mother and children? He closed his eyes and recalled the string of events that had culminated in his present imprisonment.

*   *   *

When Friedrich Kranz had left Truman's estate and found himself at Cambridge, it had been a stroke of luck to meet André Grunberg, whose organ virtuosity captivated him and forced him to linger in the chapel far longer than he had intended. He drifted off to sleep, and when his eyes opened again the music was still playing but night had fallen and Truman's wallet still pressed against his clean, scrubbed chest.

The two men had made friends instantly,

Grunberg a legend in the ballet world but now unemployed and on the run from the authorities. They remained in Cambridge, André playing daily in the chapel and Friedrich spending his days discovering that war was in full swing and that anyone wishing to purchase a private aircraft would be regarded as either a madman or a visitor from another planet. All civil air activities had been halted months before, and when a suspicious manufacturing executive from Australia had listened nonplussed to Kranz's calm request, he alerted the authorities.

Why would Kranz want an aircraft?

How had he found access to so much cash?

After leaving the inquisitive, unhelpful Australian millionaire, Kranz comandeered a small car and with a full petrol tank the pair moved on. The boarding-house landlord eyed them quizzically as they departed, half wondering if Grunberg's story about an organ virtuoso festival had been rot.

Traversing a series of villages, and blissfully unaware of petrol rationing Kranz reflected on his confrontation with the Vickers magnate. Something about the man had struck him. He wanted to see him again, but would officials in suits be at the factory gates in Southampton next time he visited the premises? Thoughts of Southampton brought back sensations he wanted to bury—Valerie might be at Hamble, the new ATA pool he had just read about in the national press. If he went back, this time by car instead of by train—a train filled with rows of hostile eyes— he could find her and relieve her uncertainty about his fate.

Surely she must think him dead.

'What am I looking at?' cried Grunberg, pointing straight ahead. Kranz had flicked from his reverie to the sight ahead, bringing the car to a swerving halt.

A carload of men in uniform, all sporting wings on their shoulders, had stopped and were blocking the road.

Friedrich felt a wild urge to turn back, but one of the men was already approaching their vehicle.

'You look young enough to serve,' Noel Slater declared, his face so close to Kranz's he could feel the hot alcoholic breath sweeping past his left cheek. Soon Slater had been joined by a curious Jim Mollison and Sean Vine, tailed by a timid character hovering in the background. Sam Hardwick seemed to be studying the automobile.

The three men had been rude and sarcastic, while quiet Sam circled the car several times and smiled at the two Austrians.

'What are your wings—?' Kranz had asked, his voice weak and croaky.

'ATA,' Vine replied, folding his arms across his chest. 'Saving Britain, without glory.'

Kranz had been genuinely terrified, but Grunberg could only smile back at the circling Sam, seemingly unperturbed by Noel and his taunting band.

'So healthy and not in uniform,' Noel continued, his face now brushing against Friedrich's. 'In the next town along it will all catch up with you.'

'What will catch up with us?' Grunberg challenged him, speaking for the first time.

'The fact that dogs will growl at your scent,' Slater said, winking.

355

Indeed, when they were allowed to pass and the Austrians could no longer see the bevy of pilots as they sped along the road, the next town offered up its local MP, who had been called to a public presentation in the main square. As he laid a small wreath on the war memorial, his Labradors growled at the two onlookers, and soon the crowd's attention had been drawn to the men eating a meagre lunch in their muddied automobile. The dogs had become agitated. Their owner finally left the podium and shouted to the animals, and when he did this Friedrich dropped his stale roll, and when Tim Haydon came closer to pull his dogs away from the scent of foreigners Kranz knew his chances of seeing Valerie had been obliterated.

'It occurs to me that your lot shouldn't be eating pig,' Haydon said, calmly observing the bedraggled travellers, their food now being devoured by the dogs.

'Pig?' Kranz asked.

'Is it not some form of primitive blasphemy?' the MP asked, peering at Grunberg. 'My friend Captain Slater makes a habit of setting up roadblocks to capture wanted criminals, when he is not ferrying for ATA. Who is your cohort?'

'André Grunberg, ballet master,' he offered, outstretching his hand.

Haydon looked at them both, a small crowd gathering around the car.

'Valerie has married me,' Tim said quietly.

Kranz felt his chest tightening, the roll burning in his gullet as his heart thudded unsteadily. He wanted it to stop, but its fibrillation made his head reel.

Grunberg was talking:

'Congratulations,' he said, grinning at Tim.

'I shan't invite you to tea, Mr Kranz, but I will be taking you into custody.'

The dogs were whining at Kranz's feet, their slobbering making him dizzier as he thought of this horrible man violating Valerie—his pallid, clammy skin against hers, its unkempt odour permeating her cells and making them both dirty and faded like old torn vests. He did not care, now, what Haydon did with him, but he lamented Grunberg's victimization. In a distant haze he could feel strong hands and unloving arms lifting him from his seat as his head knocked loudly against the roof of the car.

Grunberg had been taken and the pair were pushed into another vehicle while Haydon resumed his war memorial presentation.

Voices talked of Kranz's theft of the Fulmar, and of his visit to Lord Truman, as the car in which they were prisoners moved away from the town square.

Grunberg was astonished by the bizarre nature of their afternoon: did Haydon carry thugs with him at all times, seconded from nearby boxing clubs to capture renegade German Jews from the roadsides of rural England? Why had Kranz told him so little in the time they had been lodging together? Was he in fact a common criminal?

'Beaverbrook is making a big killing out of your friendship with Mrs Haydon,' one of the boxers muttered, his hulking body causing Kranz pain as he struggled to breathe in the cramped conditions. 'Everyone has heard about your visit to His Lordship, and your Hebrew feature revealed to the

357

butler in the bathtub.'

'The butler in the bathtub,' Kranz murmured, his mind still glued to the image of Valerie's sinewy thighs being forced apart by Haydon in the clumsy messiness of his attempts to penetrate her: spewing nowhere and leading him on to painful gropings that left her cold. He could imagine her hair greying and her face becoming lined with discomfort, as Haydon lost interest in the boyish figure and firm breasts, drifting into perversions with real boys whose mouths kissed his own nipples. Kranz could envisage the whole scenario and imagined Truman's butler being present, urging the boy on and partaking of the anal splendour offered both men in turn as they demanded blood and degradation within their worlds of psychotic penis-fixation.

* * *

Here in a place that would soon become an official internment camp Kranz had stopped imagining Haydon's couplings with Valerie, and now he worried that the marriage had put an end to her mastery of aeroplanes and her authority in ATA.

How could she have given it all up so quickly?

A voice inside his head suggested Haydon was blackmailing Valerie in some way—the MP would protect her forever if she would come into his clammy, acrid bed, not ever revealing her immoral associations with Jews and with other women. Though she would hotly deny the latter, Haydon would taunt and in the end triumph.

And now war was upon the world.

From what he could grasp from the often stale barracks newspapers, places as far-flung as Africa and the Philippine Islands could soon come into the appalling maelstrom. Kranz worried periodically about his family, and Grunberg wondered if his favourite student, Stella Teague, might stage a spectacular parachute jump into the camp from an ATA aircraft, and rescue the two men from this ridiculous humiliation.

In the next bunk along was a small man called Zuki who kept pictures of Hitler on the wall and who shunned their overtures. He had a friend in the women's camp who was 'illustrious', as he described her, and who in his eyes had been wronged by the British to such an extent as to cause a secondary war front. Her camera had snapped his shots of the Führer, and for a while she had been based in Poland near the Warsaw Ghetto, making topical films for the Reich. Kranz wanted to meet this woman—he ached at the thought of her: his earthly senses, which had become more acute in his incarceration, told him she had been in the presence of his flesh and blood, but he knew not how. His life might be lived to its conclusion in this place, should the war go on for a generation, and by that time they would be of one species, like convicted murderers condemned to death and united in the simple pursuits associated with the slow demise of those who become anonymous.

Kranz could foresee a communal existence, inmates tolerant of each other's needs because boredom would eradicate any form of fervour. Was this not what happened in factories, and in offices? He looked forward to meeting the illustrious woman, who might assuage his boredom with tales from the Ghetto.

48

Mrs Bennell had been determined to find a Ouija Board for the girls. They were now flying aircraft that terrified the landlady in her dreams and laid waste any preconceived images she might have retained about post-Edwardian womanhood. Word had been circulated that in Battle of Britain missions there had been a number of close calls in which ATA pilots had come under direct enemy fire. Debates were raging about the arming of ferry personnel, and she could see no reason why an Anson-load of young women should not be defended. She had been told by Cal March that the arming of civilians was against the rules and that if ATA were to fully arm they would be in violation of international convention.

The boy, now sporting a handsome moustache and the uniform of a senior air cadet, kept her abreast of things he should not have revealed, but she swore secrecy and prayed nightly for his safety. His closest friend, Alec Harborne, had been ferrying incessantly and now that Cal had developed an acquaintance with Jo Howes, her American slang had provided an endearing counterpoint to his throwaway cockney phrases. She had come out of her awkward, sullen girlhood and emerged a confident, talkative character in keeping with the exceptional qualities of ATA ladies, qualities which aeroplanes seemed to bring out in all manner of humanity.

Jo was now flying trainer Moths and though the Battle of Britain had left her the youngest, and therefore the least experienced, amongst new ATA arrivals, she utilized her time on the ground assisting the 'Met' who provided weather updates. ATA's latest addition, Sally Remington, had shown a keen proficiency for meteorology and had become known as 'Sally Met'. She was flying less frequently than the others, and that made her landlady very happy. Mrs Bennell had to find a Ouija Board and if Sally had a few hours off, they could search the town together.

'It's my turn to go to Upavon,' Jo Howes announced, arriving back at the lodgings.

Mrs Bennell awoke from her daydream, half expecting to see Cal at the door, but just as gratified to see one of her girls, post-flight, all in one piece. She ushered the American child-pilot into the warm lounge. Then, as she placed the kettle on the gas ring, she could feel her heart racing at the whole scenario: barrage balloons, girls, Ansons, fear and munitions . . .

'You'll still be stuck with us this Christmas,' Jo said. 'I'm going to have my tests for Oxfords and Masters. Now I can fly what Edith Allam took across the Atlantic. Fourteen other girls have passed, and I'm going to be the fifteenth. Sally Met and Barbara Newman are coming along. That'll make seventeen. Just think, Mrs B, seventeen gals on their way to the next step—bombers.'

'I hope this country takes proper pride,' said Mrs B, pouring out the tea, her thin hands showed

361

signs of arthritic bumps where her joints glowed white. 'Who would have thought it—young females stepping into giant air machines,' she marvelled.

'It wouldn't surprise me if people didn't know what we've been doing.' Jo blew on the tea and stared into the cup as if another, more peaceful world, existed at its bottom. 'Shirley Bryce has been keeping a diary, and hiding it when she's at work. Someone told her the Air Ministry could confiscate it if she wrote about operations, so her mom puts it away somewhere when she's out during the day. The brass are supremely embarrassed that girls are being used in an RAF-associated location. Embarrassed! Can you believe it, Mrs B?'

Mrs Bennell sat down facing the American:

'You're all children,' she said solemnly.

'Cal says we are the first of many, or something like that.' Jo sipped the tea and winced. 'Gosh, what I wouldn't give for a chocolate soda with seltzer.'

'This will have to do for the time being,' the landlady said, smiling. 'Why does Cal think you are the first of many?'

'He says hundreds of girls are going to end up flying every type: even flying boats and four-engined advanced bombers. Valerie Cobb said he was right—before she disappeared into never-never land.'

Mrs Bennell let her cup fall back into the saucer, its angle causing liquid to spill along the side and on to the table. She wiped the spot with a rag.

'Surely you know the truth, Jo,' she said, her face pale. 'Did Valerie die on some secret sort of mission for ATA?'

'Nobody knows. Now they're saying Jacqui Cochrane is coming over with her ladies and will be taking over ATA. That'll make the English flyers puke. Daddy hates her. He thinks she's going to start a new front—Britain against the USA—forget Hitler. Personally I'd feel real bad if Edith Allam didn't get her chance to come back in humble style.' She had downed the tea and was tugging at the waistband of her flying suit. 'Did you know Jacqui goes around in a Rolls Royce and wears fur coats while she flies?'

'I'm sure she'll come down to earth when she sees how we are struggling over here,' Mrs Bennell said, not really caring about Jacqui Cochrane, and still wondering if Valerie Cobb had met a fiery, excruciating death amid a tangle of balloon cables. 'I must get Stella Teague her Ouija Board.'

Jo had begun to let her mind travel. She thought of Upavon, where since 1912 the Central Flying School had functioned at the joint expense of the Admiralty and the War Office. Little had the men who founded the place foreseen the day when females would troop in for an air war as frenzied as this 1940s conflict. Jo hoped her conversion to Oxfords and Masters would be quick—she wanted to return to work before Cal was called up by the RAF. He was adorable, and unlike any little boy she had met at home, often behaving as if she were another lad destined for airborne glory.

'Did you hear me, lass?'

'I'm thinking, Mrs B.'

'Would you help me find this Ouija Board? I'm told one has to go to pubs or to gypsy camps to get a nice one.'

'I've been to pubs,' Jo said, rising and removing

363

both cups and saucers from the white-clothed table. 'They should sell chocolate seltzer.'

'Not now, darling. Not even for twenty years, I should imagine.' She buttoned her faded coat.

'I'll go with you.' Jo stared at Mrs Bennell, who seemed lost. 'Are you scared or something?'

'I am a bit.' Her eyes pleaded with the teenager for a kind of protection. 'Just thinking of you lot getting into monsters and flying into the clouds.'

'Come on, old lady.' Firmly Jo took Mrs Bennell's by the arm.

Soon they were walking along the road and when they entered Hatfield town centre the sight of the aged locals made Mrs Bennell bristle. Standing in front of the pub, for a fleeting instant she remembered her late husband's expression for the place: 'Obliteration oasis,' he would say, and now she dreaded entering its innards. Leaving Jo Howes standing in the middle of the road, she ambled to its weather-beaten oak door and pushed hesitantly. Although it was creeping past closing time, clouds of smoke and a blast of hot air confronted her as she moved forward amongst the men too old for service but too young to forget the previous conflagration started by the death of an unwitting Archduke. She recognized some of their faces from the yearly sojourn to the War Memorial, and her frame, cloaked in a thick overcoat, thrust its path away from the men and into a back room where the landlord kept his small office. Neatly stacked piles of receipts rested in a corner of an open roll-top desk and the smell of disinfectant gave an incongruous atmosphere to the otherwise bustling public house. Emerging from a corner of the heavily-beamed room, as if on cue, a slight, scowling man in spectacles looked intently at Mrs Bennell.

'Would you be the landlord, then?' she demanded, suspicious of this man, a new face in her familiar village midst.

'Indeed,' he said, his eyes reduced to slits as he seemed to grimace at the sight of a female. 'Are you the new cleaner?'

'I should say not—the impertinence!' she snapped. 'To be specific I am in want of a Ouija Board.'

He peered at her doubtfully and pointed towards the room she had just left. 'Come into the lounge,' he said.

She followed, and as the smoke seemed to burn into her lungs and hair she could discern Jo Howes hovering in a corner with a crowd of old men.

'Funny you should ask about an oddity like this,' the landlord was saying. 'Our two Polish arrivals have brought one.'

Mrs B craned to see through the haze. When her eyes had focused she saw a shiny Ouija Board, covered with esoteric symbols.

'Do you think they would sell it to me, for the war effort?' she asked the landlord.

'They *are* the war effort, my dear,' he retorted, crossing his arms and scowling. 'Apparently the chap is a Great War ace and the girl is one of Poland's top pilots in active service. This country seems to have some sort of soft spot for Poles at the moment. Barbarians, if you ask me. And you: what's your business?'

'My business is keeping this Pole-mad country's native pilot population happily bedded. I run the Stone House and my clientele is mostly female.'

'WAAF?'

'ATA.'

'I see.' The landlord looked puzzled. 'Valerie Cobb's organization?'

'Exactly. Good girls.' Mrs Bennell studied him for a moment. 'Yours is a new face.'

'I was a butler in one of the best Norfolk houses until my retirement last month. It has always been my dream to run a pub.'

'As a former butler you should know a cleaning lady when you see one.' Mrs Bennell moved towards Jo and tapped the girl's arm.

'That Ouija Board—they're not supposed to bring it out during the day,' Jo said excitedly, 'but these old guys made them do it. It's really bad luck.'

'Can you speak Polish?' Mrs Bennell asked.

'Yep—but both of them have some English.'

'Ask them if they would sell the Ouija Board.' She was shouting above the din of male voices.

'I get no pleasants from this game!' Hana Bukova whined, waving her arms as if to disperse her elderly admirers.

'Would you sell us your board?' Jo shouted.

'Why?' Josef Ratusz looked up, the sharp blue of his eyes piercing the American like the sudden cut of a blade.

'She is a pilot, can't you see?' Hana said, smiling tentatively.

'I sure am—are you?'

'I am adamanted!' Hana screamed, and the others lowered their voices. Suddenly the pub was quiet.

'We are Polish Air force—deposed. I am Ratusz.' As if expecting his audience to fall to its collective

366

knees, Josef clicked his heels and smirked, but none of the British war hcrocs budged.

'One of our pilots, a lady, is dying to get one of those things,' Jo explained to a receptive Hana. 'It would mean everything to her, to have a real Ouija Board.'

'Stella Teague—a former ballet star,' offered Mrs Bennell, her wide forehead now beaded with perspiration.

Hana rose. 'I am Bukova, daughter of Vera, the great aviatrix.'

'You must be Hana,' Jo squealed, delight blossoming on her flushed face. 'We're expecting you at Hatfield.'

Hana approached so close that her breath tickled the reddened surface of Jo's skin.

'Has my mother appeared—Please?'

'Your mother?' Jo felt cornered.

'Vera Bukova was expected in England, with a cargo of Jews from the Warsaw Ghetto,' Josef said nonchalantly, gulping from his pint of beer.

'You miss her—I can tell,' Mrs Bennell nodded, sitting on a stool. The other men had dispersed, their stooped shoulders now clustered in a smoky nook at the far end of the room. Tibbs, the former butler to Lord Truman, listened carefully to the Poles.

'I do hope your credentials are in order,' he murmured, slinking over to their corner.

'I can vouch for these two—they're legends in their own land,' Jo exclaimed.

For the first time, Josef grinned.

'Where did you guys get the Ouija Board?' asked Jo.

'It was a gift from a boyfriend,' Hana said,

fingering its smooth surface gingerly.

'Is he here?' Jo pressed.

'He is from Austria—Benno. Black Magic is forbidden by his religion, but he bought this beautiful one from a gypsy and gave it to me for my birthday. I only met him three or four times. His father used to visit relatives in our ghetto. They say it is very luxurious inside that place, by the way.'

'So I hear,' Jo said, her eyes meeting those of the English landlady. 'Real Ritzy and all that jazz.'

'We intern foreigners now.' A voice had broken in, and all four turned sideways. Tibbs had perked up:

'I was responsible for the capture of a German-speaking spy.'

'What was his name?' Hana asked, folding the board and smiling provocatively.

'Pavel Wojtek.' Tibbs hesitated. Had he said too much, bewitched by her remarkable eyes? 'That is believed to be a false name, however,' he added. 'The man had stolen his lordship's wallet. Apparently he has something to do with aircraft back in Germany, according to the papers. It's good that we caught him.'

Jo was looking at her watch, knowing that her forthcoming ordeal in Upavon would require a bit of homework.

'Please come back with us,' she said, taking Hana's arm.

Josef had risen to his full height and was eyeing Tibbs strangely. Jo wanted them to leave as quickly as possible—the atmosphere had made her feel closer to the enemy than had any trip alongside an unexpected Luftwaffe fighter.

'We have been sent from place to place,' Hana said, as the foursome left the pub. 'Every time we are moved somewhere I am promised a rendezvous with my mother, but it never happens.'

'I've long given up on ever seeing a mother,' said Jo. 'Mine died when I was a few days old. My father is a pilot with ATA.' Now they were outside, and Mrs Bennell was walking behind the others. She still wanted her Ouija Board.

'What was that man talking about—interns?' asked Hana.

'People are being interned here,' Mrs Bennell asserted, moving up alongside them. 'But you needn't worry. Poles are regarded as a better risk than Jews, my dear.'

'This is true,' Josef boomed, smiling broadly. 'The question is—what does one do with Polish Jews? Are they Poles? I don't think so.'

'America has loads of Jews,' Jo remarked. 'My aunt says they aren't real Yanks. And they sure aren't Polish.' She paused and grinned at Hana. 'How about that Ouija Board?'

'If we are all working in the same place, and we look after it, I don't mind,' Hana said, her mind racing through a flip album of images of Benno and the ghetto and her father's business there. She handed over the Board and Mrs Bennell beamed. They were near the perimeter of the airfield and a giant of an aeroplane was coming in to land . . .

Out of it emerged Delia Seifert.

'That's Delia and her Hind—non-operational, of course,' Jo said, as they stopped to observe the aircraft, like a gigantic Tiger Moth, being serviced. 'It's got a sixty-four-horsepower supercharged Rolls Royce Kestrel engine and can cruise at two hundred miles per hour. It climbs at fifteen hundred feet per minute. Nice, huh?'

* * *

When they arrived at the Stone House the lounge was empty. Jo was happy to have Hana at Hatfield. She had a strong compulsion to pursue the search for Vera Bukova, on Hana's behalf, and hoped ATA might give her some extra time off to go to London and make enquiries. She chuckled to herself. What would the senior men in the Ministry make of a teenager from the American backwoods descending on Whitehall? It irked her to think that because of the cultivated accent she had acquired by listening to Valerie, Cal would be a hindrance if she were to bring him along on such a trip.

'Find your mum, darling,' Mrs Bennell was saying, touching Hana's arm. The Polish girl's hair seemed incandescent despite the chilly edge to the damp Hertfordshire air, the yellow glowing against the dull background of the conservative boarding-house layout like fresh daffodils in a Poor-Law hospital ward.

'I'm going to help her,' exclaimed Jo.

'How you do this?' Hana asked, as Josef walked to a corner and pored through a sheaf of papers.

'I'm going straight to the Air Ministry,' she replied.

'London is in a pretty bad way, I hear,' Mrs Bennell shouted from the kitchen.

'That won't stop me,' Jo said, smiling at Hana.

'Why did this pilot friend of yours want a Ouija Board?' Josef piped, looking up from his papers.

Mrs Bennell emerged abruptly, her hands

370

dripping.

'She wants to contact a relative of one of our other girls,' she said, wiping her hands on a newly-pressed white apron. 'This young woman has two brothers in Spain and she thinks they're dead, but if she can't reach them in a séance they must still be alive. It's a load of cobblers, but these two enjoy it. As I said, one's a ballerina—this other is an actress.'

'They both fly?' Hana asked, her eyes widening and her hair seeming to glow even more against the fading light.

'Both are aces,' Jo said, moving to the door. 'Angelique Florian and Stella Teague. Now you can meet them. Come with me.'

As if following a senior officer's command, Hana and Josef fell in with her stride as she marched to the front door.

'I want to see how Delia managed on that Hind,' she said. 'If I pass at Upavon it could be mine next.'

Mrs Bennell stood in the doorway as the three pilots waved, like children on their way to school, and her hand moved to the elaborate Ouija Board sitting on the small coffee table. Soon it would be nightfall and London would be suffering. How glad she was that she had no close relations—only her 'Spitfire Girls', as she called them, whose numbers were increasing all the time, and whom she now feared would soon be disappearing as profligately as the men. It was chill now, but she could not be warmed by tea or by the artificial heat of the tiny electric bar she used so sparingly. Jo had told her of the huge log cabins with raging fires and plentiful delicacies strewn across tables in her strange homeland. Mrs Bennell did not want the faces to disappear, and as she looked at the bizarre Ouija Board her chill was insurmountable.

49

'What a bloody ordeal.' Delia Seifert threw her delivery paper on to the table and her Operations Officer smirked.

'Just think what comes next,' hissed Barbara Newman. She adored her new position, now that Nora had graduated from Ops to being CO Hamble. 'You get a small rest and then you have to go up with Amy to Silloth. From there you are into a Hart and on to Sealand. Lucky lady!'

'Thank you.' Delia collapsed on to a chair. 'Are you interested in hearing what happened? I had to get a man to crank up the engine, then all of a sudden the airspeed indicator was showing a hundred and fifty miles per hour and I was cruising at fifteen hundred feet. For this charming situation I picked zero boost for no special reason because, frankly, I had no idea what to do. Then I opened the mixture lever—the crank man said I must do it or terrible things would befall me—and the engine faltered. Somehow I got here. Am I dead? Is this heaven?'

'You're here,' said an American voice. Jo clapped Delia on the shoulder, Josef and Hana in tow. 'These are our Poles—here at last.'

Barbara shook hands with the pair and gestured towards the common room.

'You'd better start learning how to play cards,'

she said. 'The routine here is simple. We are paid to be safe. You get a chit and do your job. There are no pilots' notes, so one has to be an instant learner. Our acting CO is a man, Sean Vine. That's all you need to know, except perhaps that we are all in advanced stages of lunacy.'

'Lunacy?' Josef asked, stonefaced.

'Other women are safe as houses during this war,' said Delia.

'Houses are not at all safe,' said Hana.

'It depends where are you, my dear,' said Barbara, leading them into the smoky room where Alec and Marion, Jim, Amy and Hamilton Slade were talking quietly. 'Later on you can meet the CO. Now I have to prepare for my upgrading.'

As soon as the Polish pilots had entered the common room, Jo grabbed Barbara's arm and pulled her back into the main operations area.

'Listen, honey, that girl knows all about Valerie's guy,' Jo bubbled, hardly able to contain herself.

'How do you know?'

'She mentioned something about a fellow in Poland who visited the ghetto with his son, then today in the pub some weird man said he had turned in an alien who'd worked in aeroplanes. To me it all sounded like the same guy—that Pavel Wojtek from the newspapers. Maybe we could find him for Valerie.'

'Would it not be more sensible if we made a concerted effort to find Valerie?' Barbara asked. 'Everyone seems to be disappearing, and the Germans haven't even invaded.'

Jo responded:

'I think this Bukova girl knows a lot about old Friedrich and his business. Maybe he is some sort of spy after all! Poor Val!' Now Jo was shouting and Sally Met had emerged from her tiny weather station.

'Are we all ready to go at the crack of dawn?' Sally asked, her expression uncertain.

'I've got lots more to do than you people realize,' Jo continued, still breathless. 'First I have to find Hana's mother, then I have to track down Friedrich, and then I bet I can locate Valerie. For all we know they're in the war zone right now.'

'Who's in the war zone?' Angelique Florian was standing in the centre of the room.

'We were speculating on Val's whereabouts,' Barbara quipped. 'Jo is planning a sojourn in London and we have cabled Hitler to suspend bombing until she has completed her business.'

'I'll go with you,' Angelique said, smirking.

All eyes bored into her at once.

'When you are back from Upavon we shall go. I need to see Harold.'

'It's Harold now, is it?' Barbara crooned.

'Captain Balfour and I have met once or twice socially, and I have given him a lift in an Oxford, narrowly missing the Warrington balloons in the process. That same Oxford was subsequently hijacked by one Edith Allam. End of story.' Angelique seemed exceptionally edgy on this early evening. The other girls knew she had cultivated Balfour, but none, least of all the childlike Jo, could determine if her motive was to gain social ranking or to climb in ATA. So far, the organization had shown no favouritism to any woman, each girl's achievements receiving individual consideration. They knew Angelique had captivated Balfour, but so had she also

374

ensnared Oscar Toland.

As the noise from the common room suggested the day was over and that death had happened elsewhere, Barbara turned and wiped from the blackboard the names of girls who had completed a staggering flying agenda that day, while Sally returned to her weather station. Delia had been taking in their conversation and buried herself in paperwork. Jo looked at Angelique and smiled:

'When I'm back we'll go to London and solve everything before 1941, okay?'

'Jo, Balfour is our key to everything, I promise you.' Angelique draped her arm around the girl's shoulder, pulling her in the direction of the smoke screen.

Now they were in the common room, and Jo pulled away. She wanted Alec to speak to her.

'Has Cal done it yet?' demanded Jo, digging her fingernail into his shirt.

'You would know that better than I, wee lassie,' burred Alec.

'Please don't joke, Alec. I need to know before Upavon,' pleaded Marion.

Alec turned and took her small hand in his own large, rough palm. 'When you're back, he'll be doing something very special. I can't say what, because it is sensitive.'

Marion glared at him.

'Does the Ministry care about sensitive people?' asked Jo, tears on their way.

'Spits are being churned out faster than we can deliver them,' he murmured. 'Cal is on to something far more pressing. He deserves this special fortune.'

Jo could detect a slight resentment in Alec's

voice—she remembered her father being bitter about young men getting into shiny new machines—his bitterness more fierce than any he had felt about her mother's demise. She moved away from Alec and Marion, walking slowly to the fresh air at the rear doorway of the building. At the back, Delia's Hind was being serviced and with suddenness her mind moved to the imminent arrival of the Australians. She had heard a rumour that Edith Allam would bring more of these girls than Americans, and that she would also be bringing her coloured boyfriend in the payload. What would she and her father have been doing had the German economy flourished and a ranting Schicklgruber been ignored? Could Germany have passed him off as a madman during a different time in its history? She yearned for a salt-water taffy from Atlantic City, but now the Hind was almost ready and Delia was standing alongside her.

'I take it up again tomorrow, or I should say, it takes me up,' she said, her voice weak with exhaustion. The Hind had been Delia's fourth ferry job that day, and she too yearned for something sweet.

'Tomorrow I go to Upavon,' Jo murmured looking at the taller Delia, whose close-cropped hair and craggy features confused the American, raised in an environment of stars and Hollywood fantasies.

'You'll pass,' Delia said, punching her good-naturedly. 'Today I was terrified—more than I've ever been in my life, Jo. For a few moments I felt as if I were watching my own demise. It seemed as natural as eating.'

'Eating can be fun.'

'So can death.'

'Not yet.' Jo peered at Delia, then looked out at the Hind, now fading in the near darkness of blackout. It seemed to be evaporating, and she craved at that moment some transformation whereby she might awaken in Main Street and be in a land where night and the streetlights burned until dawn. She had been told that Schickelgruber had made a pact with Joe Kennedy and that the Nazis would take over America calmly.

'Your boyfriend is being pushed into a special operation.'

Delia's voice shattered Jo's imaginings and the youth's heart pounded. 'I should not be telling you this, but he has progressed with stunning rapidity and the Air Ministry is giving him a big assignment immediately he goes RAF.'

'Everyone is disappearing,' Jo said, trying to hide her horror at the revelation. Why had Cal not told her himself? She wanted to change the subject. 'Right after Upavon I'm going to London to find Valerie and Hana's mother, and when I get back I'll have to find Cal.'

Delia wished she could retrieve her words, which had pierced like darts into the American teenager's slender figure. Darkness had overtaken them, the stillness of cool Hertfordshire making the war seem an absurdity to a child aged not much older than the local farm's cat. She shook, and she was frightened.

50

Valerie Cobb was also frightened.

Men had been shouting at her all day and every time one of them made another pronouncement the projection room inside her head registered an imaginary aircraft being ferried from A to B. It was her best way of keeping stable during this exceptional ordeal. When an accusation was bellowed at her she thought of a Lysander or a Magister being flown lovingly along a familiar route by one of her choice pilots from the all-women Hatfield pool. Each vision gave her a sense of space and consecutive time, preventing her from exploding into the babble of the insane repetition of her name, address and date of birth over and over and over. She was no longer Commanding Officer Hatfield, nor was she Head of ATA. Men were shouting and she was forced to listen. There was nowhere else for her to go. She had no other work.

'How is it you were not aware of these photographs being in the possession of ATA personnel?'

This one was enjoying himself, his passion spilling over to such an extent that Valerie wondered if he would have anything left for the rest of his life after her trauma.

'If I never knew about the pictures, how could I have confiscated them?'

She knew he was trying to prove that leadership had ended with Sir Henry where the Cobb genes were concerned. Now the next one was bleating:

'Are you aware that by allying yourself with Max Beaverbrook and his insatiable hunger for publicity, you have connected lady pilots forever in the public's mind with Nazis like Fischtal and sympathizers like Allam?'

'You speak as if they were brands of baking soda.'

None of the men laughed.

Where was Lady Londonderry?

'Valerie, have you no shame about Kranz and the Fulmar?'

She pitied this particular inquisitor, who had allowed his twenty-four-hour-a-day infatuation for her to ally him with her tormentors. She wished the circumstances had been more heroic—she could have flown off course and crash-landed in occupied territory and experienced the same victimization from an aroused fascist. Her plight would have been flashed across the nation's newspapers and all the men present in this room might have volunteered for an airlift rescue mission. Now she was the enemy within, and they liked it very much.

'Your association with Friedrich Kranz, which has become public knowledge and has brought some considerable disgrace upon your family name, and upon this Ministry, goes beyond a sordid immoral liaison and enters the realm of espionage.'

'*Espionage!* I do love that word!' Valerie lit a cigarette and they watched, her image meshing into the same form of fantasy that could allow Spanish rapists to pin freshly peeled testicles next to a picture of a movie goddess.

'It would be appreciated if you could refrain

379

from your Rita Hayworth pose.' This admirer had been knighted for deeds done in the last war.

'Is this a suggestion that I change professions?' she asked, smiling and puffing into his florid face.

'We expect you will, if anything, retreat from the limelight for the duration of the war and not venture anywhere near an airfield.'

'Thank you.' She was standing in the middle of the room and had been allowed to wear the striking blue uniform. Her removal from ATA had involved a swift series of events, principally her being whisked away at the crack of dawn like a spy and being kept in polite custody at a Ministry establishment until her connections with the thieving Jew could be clarified. Her father had refused to speak to her and by now she surmised he had disinherited her, possibly in public. She had lost track of the days. In the spartan accommodation she had been given by the confused military—was an ATA woman a soldier, and could she be kept under house arrest?—she could not escape thoughts of Edith Allam in Beaverbrook's ridiculous villa in the middle of the City. Here there was no elaborate bathtub, nor were there plush sofas and opulent fabrics. Someone had decided Valerie Cobb should be kept away from humanity because she had cohabited with a Jew and had become involved in his deeds. If only they would tell her where he was!

'Are you aware that aliens are being interned in this country?'

She was being questioned again, and calculated this must be the eighth hour of the eighth day. 'I am aware political prisoners in Germany are known to be victims of cruel human experimentation.'

'That is not relevant to this enquiry, madam.'

'It's "madam" now, is it?'

'Kranz stole a new aircraft with your consent and active assistance, he presented himself at a military establishment under false credentials and he later robbed Lord Truman and created a disturbance at the Truman residence.'

'You have told me this a dozen times,' she snapped.

'We will not repeat the information again if you will agree that you assisted Kranz, sign these documents, and consent to the passing over of your ATA office to other personnel.'

'Just think of what Max Beaverbrook will do with this, if he hasn't already!' She stubbed out her cigarette. An assortment of eyes allowed looks of longing to escape and then to retreat as she stared back mockingly.

'Beaverbrook is in many people's eyes as repugnant as characters like Kranz.' This time it was the knight speaking.

'Nonsense,' said Valerie. 'He's as popular as Myra Hess. Twin institutions. His newspapers, and her concerts at the National Gallery. I expect you'd think her fur coats vulgar.'

There was a silence as the men looked at each other in bewilderment.

'Will you sign?'

'No. I'd sooner stay here for the duration of the war.'

Preparing for her ninth day in disgrace, Valerie watched as Sir Francis Shelmerdine, Gerard d'Erlanger, and Tim Haydon MP filed out of the room like soiled old men from a peep show. She was excused, and could go home.

*   *   *

That evening she had a visitor.

Listening to the tap at the door she agonized over who it might be, and after what seemed an eternity she decided the person waiting patiently outside might be Shirley.

'This is a disgrace,' Sir Henry announced, standing at the entrance to the living room and not moving forward to his daughter's perch.

'Do you mean the room, or the lack of a whisky decanter?'

'Valerie, with some considerable difficulty I've managed to keep this affair from the press. Even Beaverbrook thinks you have disappeared on some heroic mission. Privately, I consider everything you have done this year, where that man is concerned, to be utterly despicable.'

She rose from the small, flowered sofa and stood, not daring to approach his enraged presence. 'The Committee, minus Lady L, seemed more worried about the horror photographs than about my involvement with Friedrich.'

'You never told me about the snapshots,' barked her father. 'That girl should have turned the film over to you immediately. This whole affair shows even more disorganization within your Pool than I had feared.' He surveyed the room. 'I do wish you would not refer to that man Kranz by his *Christian* name,' he stressed.

'Would you rather I had become a missing person—me instead of Annabel?'

'Valerie, please. I need to get through this

present matter as quickly as possible.'

'What present matter?' She looked up, her bloodshot eyes unfocused.

Sir Henry was still standing, and his shoulders drooped, giving him the look of a tired junk merchant.

'Beaverbrook has offered to give you only a good press—'

'He knows I'm under enforced seclusion!' she interrupted.

'—to tell the story of the Jew as it stands but to make you look the victim.'

'That is absurd, Henry!'

'He has the pictures, and now he wants everything else.'

'Pictures of experiments on Jewish-looking inmates, plus the tale of Kranz—that will be marvellous!' Valerie grinned broadly at her father.

'Are you being facetious?'

'It's the best news I've heard all day,' she said, rising and stretching. 'What do you have to do next—telephone Max? My phone has been disconnected, you know. The spooks have done that, as if I were a German paratrooper squatting in a country cottage.'

'That is a preposterous notion!'

'Is it?' She moved towards Sir Henry and he backed off as if she might strike him down. 'Haven't you been the prime mover behind my ordeal of the past few days?'

'That is monstrous, Valerie.'

'Of course it is, and it is also true, so do come in and be seated like a normal person, not like a beast who turns his daughter in because the constituents would want it that way.'

He remained stationary, fingering his hat and letting his uneven breathing accelerate until it could be heard in every corner of the room.

'A father who has lost one daughter would not turn in another.'

'I've heard of worse, in Euripides and . . . other places,' she said, curling up into the sofa. 'Tell me more.'

He looked at her for the first time and his breathing had come under control. 'The men on the Committee want you to sign a small statement, Valerie, and I too ask you to do this.'

'What would Mother have said?' she asked brightly, staring back at him with a vision that seemed to bore through him despite her bleary, red-rimmed pupils. 'Do I get burned alive afterwards? Do you suppose that's what's happened to Annabel?'

'Heaven forbid,' he muttered, moving into the room.

'It's likely—fascists make you sign, and then you burn.'

'You won't miss ATA, Valerie.'

'Good God, Father—take my blood!'

'It isn't the end of the world—someone else can run the organization.' She had used his favourite word and he felt uncomfortably close to tears.

Valerie rose from the sofa:

'Just at this bloody moment, there aren't half enough girls to go around to replace the men being siphoned off for active service. D'Erlanger sat there today vexing me but he knows I have access to hundreds of pilots who are holding back from applying to ATA because they don't want to see me wronged. There is a war, and yes: there is an

384

enemy, but right now we are behaving in this country like imbeciles, imprisoning brilliant Jews who have escaped to this ruddy so-called island haven with Hitler at their heels, and removing me from a vital operation just when the Battle for Britain has been unfolding. Please listen to me, Father—all of this is happening because of one stupid man wanting to save the remainder of his family, having paid Vera Bukova's lot a fortune to rescue his closest loved ones, and because this man pinched a precious Fulmar, stole somebody's wallet and loved me.'

'People associate you with enemy aliens—that camera film implies you have had dealings with Nazis.' Sir Henry's face was expressionless as he spoke. 'Enough is enough, Valerie.'

'Gerard is in love with me and wants to see me homebound—I believe they call it bondage.'

Sir Henry was silent. He looked around the room from his spot in the shadows and smiled.

'Would you be interested in some gossip?'

'I love gossip. Do sit down.'

He did not move.

'Angelique Florian has done the unthinkable,' he murmured, fingering the rim of his hat yet again.

'She crashed?'

'She's pregnant.'

'Is that all?' Valerie slumped into the corner of her sofa with an irritable twitch.

'To me it is quite something.' He smiled. 'Had you information she was planning to do something worse?'

'Not at all.' She smirked as the thought of Angelique's proposed mission made pregnancy pale in comparison. 'Is it your child, Henry?'

He stopped smiling.

'There has been speculation about Balfour.'

'Oh—good! A member of the Committee disgraced! Let Beaverbrook get that one!'

'I must be going,' said Sir Henry. 'Please remember that if you sign those papers, the repercussions may subside, and you may be reinstated. A year from now, Kranz will be shipped back to one of those places we saw in the photographs, and you will be back as Head of ATA. Mark my words.'

'They are indelibly stamped on my forehead!'

'A father's oath has been made to a daughter.'

'Many a fatality, in classic literature, has followed upon such oaths.'

'We need to get Kranz out of the way and then things will be fine,' said her father with a pleading look.

Valerie stood up. 'Where is he?'

'I cannot tell you.'

'Please.'

'He is being packed up ready for shipment.'

She was standing next to the father and his hat. 'What if I'm carrying his child?'

'Valerie—for God's sake!'

'What if I am?'

'It's not possible!'

'Am I so plain as not to be able to make dough rise, asked the maiden?'

'You can't be having that man's child, Valerie.' His breathing was doubling in rapidity. 'When you have these notions you remind me of your mother. Anyway, there is nothing growing inside you, Valerie—when there is a seed growing, a man can tell, especially when the vessel is a daughter.'

With that Sir Henry moved to the front door and Valerie looked at her watch:

'Good heavens! The spooks will be bored stiff waiting for my gentleman caller to leave the premises,' she said.

'What are you talking about?'

'They are keeping a twenty-four-hour watch—as you well know, Henry.' She snatched his hat from his cold, loose hand and placed it atop his balding head. 'You arranged it.'

'I did no such thing. I have merely advised you of the Ministry's demands about your comings and goings.' His eyes seemed to dart from place to place. 'It was never my intention to have you watched.'

'On the contrary—perhaps you should run over and say hello. Or would you like to bring them a cold sausage? I've one just here.'

'Valerie, please think about me, and about your sister, and about Mother.'

'I spend most of my time thinking about Lysanders and Spitfires.'

He left her, and as he moved down her path in the pitch dark she chuckled.

'Don't forget my greetings to your spooks!' she hissed.

He did not turn back, and in a few moments he had disappeared into the night.

Closing the door firmly Valerie thought of Friedrich and of his heated urgency and of his exploding entry that had made her erupt inside and continue to smoulder every moment ever since their last insane coming together. She leaned against the door and ran her hand along her abdomen, begging some supernatural being to reveal his whereabouts and to relieve her of the unbearable urge that was beginning to obliterate even her worries about the pilots' pools. She was throbbing and felt ashamed, pressing herself to the door as if the cold wood might absorb the rhythm of her frustration. Her torso rigid against the flat, there was a sudden pounding and she jumped back.

Could it be him?

Might Friedrich have been released?

Would she hold him tonight, on the soft carpet in this room, letting him take her then and there because she could not endure the eternity of labouring up the stairs and entering the good manners of a bedroom?

Valerie turned, aware of the perspiration on her back that had pasted her dress to the door, and she reached behind her to pull the fabric away. There was that terrible pounding again. She turned the handle and opened the door, very slowly—and out of the dark came the face of Amy Johnson.

51

All during the night the country's youngest female ATA pilot had been thinking about flying Lancasters and wondering how one might commandeer a bomber. Eventually Hamble's best heaved a giant sigh. There simply was no way, for there surely would be a flight engineer on the Lancaster who knew girls were still prohibited from bombers; and God help anyone if that flight engineer was Slater.

End of story.

Was it possible that ferrying Spitfires had become routine for the men, after all the expectation and build-up? What the women would not have given to fly operational craft . . . Angelique Florian thrust her head into the musty pillow and tried to sleep.

As sleep eluded her, she rehashed the polite tea with Balfour. He had been alone at a smart London address, and his awkwardness suggested he had borrowed the location for the sake of this meeting. Angelique had left Nora Flint scowling on a day when Hurricanes were leaving the huge Hawkers factory at Langley faster than male pilots were available to transport each of the £100,000 machines. ATA women were needed for taxi jobs and no-one could be spared. Her uniform had looked exceptionally smart that day, although she could sense Nora's disquiet about her destination, and about her bulging waistline in these times of deprivation.

'Better she should think me guzzling chocolate from the black market than in a condition she would abhor,' she remembered thinking to herself as the Commanding Officer had granted permission for four hours' leave from her duties. That leave would have to be made up for some other day, and Angelique knew that day would have to be soon. Nora had distanced herself from Gordon Selfridge, and like so many women in positions of power, had eliminated what she considered unnecessary elements in her life. If Gordon had to go, Nora would lock him out of her life with as little concern as she had cancelled deliveries of biscuits to the base. The girls were astonished when Gordon disappeared from their midst, while some were even more incensed about the biscuits . . .

* * *

Now her baby was shifting again, and Angelique sat up on the sagging mattress. It was black outside and she hoped the Germans would attack other places tonight.

Where were Zack and Paul? Sarah Truman and Annabel Cobb? Where was Valerie? Imagine being Sir Henry!

She jumped from her cot and walked to the window of her tiny room, stepping lightly so as not to awaken the other girls whose tomorrow would likely include several confrontations with the Birmingham barrage balloons. Skirting death was becoming a constant, reflex-sharpening practice for every man and woman in ATA, but the terrors only heightened their desire for tougher assignments, some pilots now doing three complete round-trips a day; all perilous and often in once-only-tested machines. Tomorrow the Toland brothers would be ferrying a pair of Beauforts from a new shipment. Both men were fully recovered, and she smiled to herself at the thought of the two vicars in sheepskin boots, goggles and bomber jackets. One of them had shed his boots and his vestments and when he had taken her in this very room she had been terrified Mrs Bennell might burst in as he slowly peeled the cream blouse from her young shoulders.

'What do you want with *him*, when you've got *Balfour*?' Marion Harborne had shouted as they

390

flew over Slough in an Anson on the way to Hawkers, with Amy in the rear. They had giggled at the fact that she always kept her parachute at the ready when another ATA pilot was in the cockpit. Angelique's complicated personal life had become the focus of their chatter, while Amy had drifted into a sad daydream from which neither girl could hope to rouse her until they had reached the entrance to the Hurricane factory. The two Americans had fascinated the women pilots, not so much for their moonlighting as ministers but because their colleague had become, literally, a guardian angel to both men after their near-fatal ordeal. She had stood by when an enquiry had been held, and had comforted them in their typically backwoods bewilderment when Noel Slater's behaviour had been excused by a distinctly anti-American Adjudicator.

Oscar Toland would be a friend for life but she knew Martin, with his tall, lanky figure and thick, curly brown hair would be her lover. He had taken her for coffee after the enquiry, and the smell of soap, which seemed to emanate from all the Yank men, excited her in a way she did not understand. She also knew Balfour had been beside himself with infatuation for her ever since their brief encounter in the ladies' changing room during a VIP tour, and she hoped to play upon his fascination when word got about ATA that she was readily entertaining Toland the Ordinary.

'Don't be frightened,' Martin had said, his gentle personality suddenly coming to life as he drew her to him and kissed the one breast he gently took into his left hand. His right hand somehow relieved her of the bottom half of her uniform and she half

391

wanted him to stop, but now his warm, inviting mouth left not one inch of her flesh dry and still he stood, holding her like a giant ice lolly that melted but never shrank. He had placed her on the bed and as she watched his ridiculously long fingers release his strong body from the ATA uniform, she felt an urge to run down the dark, wooden stairs and go to work, naked, in Mrs Bennell's scullery.

Now Angelique could sense the approach of the same phenomenon. As scenes of her childhood in opulent surroundings amongst obscure European royalty paraded, crammed within a six-second space of thought, Martin was now lying beside her, strangely quiet and controlled. Her royalty faded, and her childhood link with the approach of death disintegrated. She reached out for the ordained minister from Virginia, who at this moment was erect as the fires of Hell, and kissed his forehead. There was no possibility of retreating to the scullery, the expert hands making her want to give everything up and perhaps do this for the rest of her life, his first entry into her churning newness like a killing during which she would weep and ask to be slain again . . .

It had left her with a baby.

Angelique found the entire situation amusing. Martin had come to her many times after that first encounter, which had lasted three hours until the sounds of pilots and beer and tea had begun to waft up to her room. As usual, it was Amy who had helped her smuggle Martin out of the girls' wing of the boarding house while Mrs Bennell had been distracted by Jim's drunken ravings. Now, standing at the window, Angelique worried about Amy.

Amy could only be happy when in the air, and

Shirley's new status as a ferry pilot had helped her fight off suicidal urges, brought on by the reality of Valerie's enslavement to orgasm with someone of the opposite sex. It all seemed so idiotic, Angelique thought, returning to the bed. In the few minutes in which she had left its warmth, the mattress had become unwelcoming and she snuggled back under the covers as if to comfort the bed. She always thought of a bed as a he, not a she. Angelique had Catholic Jesus to comfort her, and Martin had Protestant Jesus to comfort him, but what could *they* offer, in this time of global hate, to comfort *him?*

Angelique could not sleep.

Tomorrow, and the days leading into 1941, would be so important for everyone: she would see Balfour again, Martin would ferry his new Beaufort with Oscar alongside in its imported twin, and Jo would travel with her to lobby London about poor Hana's mother. Since arriving, Hana had thrown herself into ATA work, transporting up to three different aeroplanes a day. Ratusz had been just as tireless, his total lack of humour excused by all when he turned in chit after chit in every kind of weather, and in every kind of peril, be it anti-aircraft fire, balloons or simply a terrain completely alien to his experience.

And soon the Americans and Australians who wanted to help ATA would be arriving in force.

Beaverbrook had come under terrible criticism in the aviation press, but Angelique looked forward to meeting Edith Allam again. Imagine having a coloured boyfriend! It was something for which any English girl would be disowned by her family, her peers and the architects of her livelihood—in this case ATA.

Look at Valerie!

She had encouraged the overtures of a Jew, and her destiny had been fractured . . . What, she pondered, would Hitler do with Armenians? Had any of her relatives been taken to those camps?

* * *

It was 3 a.m., and Angelique thought she could hear a distant thumping. She rose again, holding her abdomen as if to support her child in its own slumber, and as she approached the window again she could see flashes of light. Germany again, she pouted. They would be daft enough, and cruel enough, to bomb Britain in the small hours. It might, of course, be the Northern Lights, and some thunder to accompany the colourful show. Even with the daily rush from sunrise until last shadows, to collect and disperse aircraft for a desperate RAF, she did not have a burning sense of war.

Where were these hordes of Nazis? What did they look like? Did their men behave any differently when in the throes of basic passions, like her Martin, out of his uniform and driven by his eager, wanting member?

Fear seemed to be the common emotion pervading as the girls spent day after long day waiting over chess and bridge for their next ferry assignment. Angelique stood at the window, watching the occasional burst, and reflected that, like fighter pilots, they too could never know the outcome of a journey: whenever an ATA pilot was lost, the name was wiped from the large blackboard and those underneath moved up—the gap must never be allowed to remain or morale would crash like the victim it mourned. So far only men had perished but she sensed the women would soon start losing their lives.

Moving to her small chest of drawers, Angelique drew out the Ouija board Mrs Bennell had coaxed from the Polish girl. Hana had stopped visibly fretting about her mother, though all Pool personnel knew how distraught she was inside. She must not have used the Ouija board, Angelique reflected, unfolding it upon her bare thighs. She ran her fingertips along its bewildering array of symbols and wished it would reach out and speak to her. Someone had said the boards were of no use in the hands of one person—there had to be two or more present to initiate a seance.

What about those poor souls in Marion Harborne's pictures?

That roll of camera film had created a sensation—the first photograph of Nazi doctors experimenting on Jews. Had any of those Jews sought guidance from the occult? Certainly their regular God had got lost somewhere else. She stared at the board on her knees and let the flashes of light play upon its shiny surface. Every new illumination meant another death. By talking to the board, she mused excitedly, could she stop the war, right at this moment? Hana had told her that on her first night in England she had sat at a window and watched a light show and had vowed never to take shelter in an air raid. Indeed, Delia had threatened to go up on the roof of Hamble and watch the next bombing of Southampton Docks.

Angelique had the life of a child to cherish, and

the thought of putting oneself at peril for something as silly as a bombing raid now seemed perverse. Delia Seifert, like Shirley, hated life. Perhaps, Angelique muttered to herself, most women felt that way, deep down inside, even in the best houses, even in the best clothes, even at Ascot in the best hat . . .

Looking down at the Ouija board she realized the light show had ceased. Angelique wanted information about Zack and Paul and would consult the supernatural anyway, even without a companion, save her unborn infant. Closing her eyes she kept her hands spread across the board and concentrated on images of Spanish countryside and of Franco, whose visage had lately been featured in so many magazines. Some of the women pilots had joked that *Time* magazine might make him Man of the Year, with Adolf Hitler and Neville Chamberlain reserved for other covers. She concentrated, and soon the birds, not weakened by rationing, were beginning their energetic dawn chorus.

It was cold in her room but she had to force herself to be oblivious to the elements: Zack and Paul, Sarah and Annabel, all of whom she knew must be in Spain, would emerge in her mind's eye very soon, and lead the way to her navigational enterprise. Tomorrow Balfour would have to agree to her mission, otherwise she would defy every rule and do something the RAF and ATA would consider unforgivable and insane.

Natural light was beginning to creep in and Angelique felt energetic despite having allowed an entire night to pass without slumber. Her mother would have said this could be fatal for her baby, but, barely into her twenties, her strong constitution kept her mind alert and her thoughts reverberating with the prospect of a prohibited mission. Closing her eyes she mumbled to herself again and begged the images to appear . . .

*   *   *

Zack and Paul were evading her plan: Annabel and Sarah seemed to float in and out of the darkness behind her eyelids as shades in white sheets. Her heart began to pound as minutes passed and she could not bring her brothers into the picture that was set against the blackened screen. She threw her head back and begged the spirits to enlighten her about the boys' whereabouts. Letting her head fall forward, she kept her eyes shut and gradually an image emerged in tandem with the two girlish shades: was it Amy?

She carried a suitcase and had Hamilton Slade in tow. They were about to enter a bright new Oxford with confidence and waving at the shades, whose hair had turned grey.

Angelique concentrated, wincing as she kept the eyelids tightly sealed, for fear that the images would be cursed and slain should she open up and see light too soon. Her head was still bowed and her hands still spread across the smooth, hard board.

Amy approached, smiling and looking relaxed, a state of being she had never displayed since joining ATA. She held an envelope marked TOP SECRET and Hamilton, his smile seemingly pasted to his square jaw, waved again. The grey-haired shades stood in front of the Oxford and scowled like small children not wanting their parents to leave them with a nanny.

As Amy and Hamilton approached the aeroplane someone's voice shouted to them to stay away, and soon Angelique was crying out. She wanted them stopped, and as she shouted the shades disintegrated like worn candlewick, their remains now a small powdery pile next to the aircraft, the Oxford's shiny silver now turned instantly to black.

Is it camouflage? *she shouted.* Is it camouflage?

Amy and Hamilton stared back at her, their expressions glazed. Now she screamed as the black machine began to ooze a white goo that wiggled like caterpillars through cracks in the fuselage and fell upon water that sizzled as each blob hit. She cried because Amy and Hamilton were gone and the Oxford was heaving, its body contorted and swelling, swelling, about to burst. Angelique could not move, and thought she would be crushed; indeed she had begun to suffocate, her voice gone. She gasped as the Oxford grew big enough to explode and out of the bulging cockpit window she saw Amy clawing to be set free.

Angelique's mouth had dried and she wanted to help but her body was being pushed against a steely wall and her baby being obliterated—

* * *

'You crazy mongrel slut!'

Sally Remington was dressed all in white and Angelique jumped from the chair, her stiffened neck sending a sharp pain down her side and through her shoulder.

'Why are you all in white?' she gasped, terrified.

'Don't ask questions,' Sally replied, pushing the chair against the wall and picking up the Ouija board from the brightly sunlit floor. 'Mrs Bennell thought you were having hallucinations.'

Angclique looked at her watch and was grateful her seance had put her to sleep and allowed three hours of rest. It was 7.30, and she had promised to drill Jo, Sally and Barbara before they tested at Upavon and before she set off for London.

'I had a terrible dream—a nightmare.'

'When I was playing champions like Alice Marble,' said Sally, 'I had nightmares too. Always the same one: balls flew past me because my racquet kept bending over like a soggy leaf.'

'There were two girls in white,' murmured Angelique.

'We were required to wear white.'

'I meant in my dream.'

'Especially at Wimbledon.'

'Are you hearing me, Sally?' Angelique's voice had returned, and she wanted to strike her fellow pilot.

'I haven't time to chat, Ange,' Sally snapped, moving to the door. 'Get dressed and be ready to go at eight.'

'Have you forgotten that I am your superior in rank?'

Sally smirked.

'You're pregnant,' she said, and with that she was gone.

Angelique heard loud voices. She would have no time for a bath—an aspect of wartime deprivation she had hated since the beginning of the conflict— and now she would have to go to Balfour dirty. She would have loved a day off, hugging Martin and reassuring him that the Scriptures had allowed him this sinful alliance. Nevertheless reality had to take precedence and, as Bill Howes so often said, 'things were moving.'

Today was crucial for so many flying folk: 1940 had been a year of month-by-month accelerations and now, after this day's ordeals at Upavon for Barbara, Sally and Jo, seventeen of the girls would likely be eligible for advanced assignments. Jo might soon be able to track down Vera Bukova, and the Tolands would be moving Beauforts for Britain. Poles were being joined in the sky by Czechs, and soon suntanned girls from Australia and New Zealand would be distracting the pale Slavs.

Angelique wanted them all to be happy, but her baby was growing and she had her own mission to perform. The country's youngest female ferry pilot bit her lip as she contemplated Captain Balfour.

52

Amy had changed her surname back to Johnson by deed poll in 1937, and in every sense had now parted from Jim, but that did not stop him from hounding her at places like White Waltham.

And now Valerie listened as Amy told her of Jim's incessant visits to her home, and of the demands he would make, divorce or no divorce. Valerie's yearning for Friedrich, which had driven her near to madness in these recent days, seemed trivial beside the problems of poor Amy, who could go nowhere without her privacy being shattered.

'How did you ever work out I'd be here?' Valerie

asked, glancing at the hands of her carriage clock. They registered two o'clock in the morning. The women saw each other in shadows, the blackout forcing them to sit by the barest of light.

'It seemed the most logical solution,' Amy replied. 'Wasn't it Edgar Allen Poe who said people always overlook the obvious? I theorized that, with all the wild speculation about your mysterious disappearance, you would be in familiar surroundings. Perhaps I am a mind-reader. Angelique Florian claims she can predict the future, you know.'

'She hasn't tracked me down.' Valerie poured preciously rationed coffee into a small, elegant gilt-rimmed cup.

'The *Sunday Express* claims Jim and I are together again.' Amy's hand trembled as she tried to lift the cup. 'Valerie, did you know he had remarried?'

'Good God!'

'Heaven knows who she is—thank God she isn't a local girl, or I should become violent.'

'Does that mean you're jealous?'

'No!'

Valerie was delighted she had provoked Amy, generating the potent cure for depression that was anger.

'He bores me stiff!' Amy complained, her grip on the heirloom nearly faltering as the cup rattled back on its saucer. 'What does make me jealous is bloody ATA, Valerie!' She jumped up from the sofa and paced the room, her pasty skin casting a death-like glow in the odd shadows of the enforced darkness.

'Dear God, Amy, what's been happening while

I've been away?'

'It's nothing you could change, even if you were on top of things. Jim walks in and gets seven hundred pounds a year, and the women get four hundred and fifty for the same work. Most of the men are amateurs. You know damned well there isn't a woman pilot in this country who isn't ten times as professional as these aging boy hobbyists.'

'That's true,' Valerie said, gleeful at Amy's passion.

'The men even have a marriage allowance! They're raking in the pennies while a first-class instructress, who would fail him on his first circuit, gets less than half as much.'

'We can try to change things when I'm out of this mess,' said Valerie.

'It will also please you to know', continued Amy, 'that I've my own personal gunner—a man, of course—in an Anson full of eight female pilots, but the Ministry is still making a fuss about our girls ferrying unarmed Hurricanes on little trips to aerodromes for storage.'

'We will need to agitate.'

'Dear God, Val, you know how desperate these girls are to fly more advanced machines! Here are those men—some barely able to handle *one* type— allowed to ferry *anything*, and yet we have learned one hundred different aircraft from back to front, some of us for twenty years as instructors. But we are women, and the Ministry says we may not step inside the things.'

'I think we will be transporting everything by the year's end.'

Amy sat again, hesitating at the thought of meeting Valerie's earnest gaze. She could feel the

Commanding Officer's eyes boring through her blue Second Officer's uniform.

'I hate ATA, Val.'

'You hate Jim.'

'How can I fit into a girls' dormitory and be a cog in a giant operation? How can I cope with catty gossip and stupid regulations?'

Valerie leaned back and closed her eyes, her arms now crossed about her neatly tailored jacket.

'Because there is war,' she said, measuring her words minutely, 'women are being allowed to perform a job they have never done before. They were instructors after the Great War, but never before have they been issued uniforms and treated as equals on bases and been granted commissions as Commanding Officers, for Christ's sake.' She was astonished that Amy could be the one to enrage her so. 'Churchill is talking about fighting from the streets and from the hills and Christ knows from where else, so concentrate on the astonishing reality that is being a woman, flying for her country during the Battle for Britain.'

'You know I love it when we have a lot of machines to be taken all over the place.'

Valerie leaned forward, her face level with Amy's. 'You want to bomb and to fight. You want to be the Spitfire pilot who leaves the canteen and at the end of the day is wiped from the blackboard. You want to drop English arms of cast iron made by English housewives, and you want to drop them on Nazi housewives with Nazi arms of flabby flesh lifted heavenwards, their fists raging at your cruelty. You have no pity for their babies, nor they for yours, and you want to be part of death. It's natural, but only for men, because we are told this

403

is so. Content yourself with transporting machines. You're still ferrying death and that's good—that is very good.'

There was a thudding many miles away and the women were staring at each other.

'Time for a light show,' Amy murmured. 'I'm so glad to be here, and not at home.' The illuminations danced amid the weird shadows.

'What about Hamilton?' Valerie asked.

'He's busy at White Waltham, with Jim and the rest of the men. He feels ill most of the time.'

Valerie smiled broadly. 'I would love to hear all about him,' she said.

'He hasn't the energy to make love,' Amy said, her head bowed. She heaved a deep sigh. 'I miss my parents so much.'

'What an odd image—your tired man, and you in pyjamas crying for Mummy.'

'Hana Bukova misses her mother too,' mused Amy.

'She's a child.' Valerie felt a peculiar urge to weep. 'Tell me all the news, Amy—please.'

'Jo Howes and Sally Met are going with Barbara to test at Upavon. Jo loves Cal March. Cal loves aeroplanes and will this week be full RAF. Josef Ratusz is transporting a record number of aircraft and Noel Slater is being beastly because more girls are entering ATA. He flew into a rage when he heard Nora Flint was made CO Hamble and he's hardly recovered yet. Shirley—' She paused.

'What about Shirley?' Valerie's voice squeaked uncontrollably.

Amy stopped, looking into Valerie's anxious face. 'She talks of suicide.'

'When?' Her mind seemed to be teeming and

thumping, in rhythm with the bombs falling on the horizon.

'Frequently—all the time,' Amy babbled. 'I shouldn't have told you. It just popped out.'

'She talks of death, and Churchill talks of death, and we are ferrying thousands of vessels of annihilation.' Her voice trailed off.

'There are different sorts of death, Val.'

'Tell her where I am!' she shouted, realizing that for this entire evening she had not once thought of Kranz, except when her loins had wanted a sudden burning and she had leaned against wood that had stayed cold.

'If she came here, she would achieve nothing,' said Amy. 'She has been tormented ever since, in her eyes, you deserted her for a man.'

'I did no such thing!' Valerie cried, her stinging tone echoed by a sympathetic ringing of the crystal on the sideboard.

'She loves you, Valerie.'

'Like a sister.'

'Like a woman.'

'I have never touched her.'

'Oh, dear God, but you have, Valerie—you have.'

'Yes, of course—figuratively speaking,' she murmured, 'but now Shirley must let the flying machines touch her heart as I could never hope to do.'

'I don't think you understand how deeply you have affected that girl,' said Amy. 'If only Jim had ever loved me half as much as she adores you, Valerie . . .'

'We have never slept together,' Valerie whispered, a tear dropping on her taut thigh.

'That is a pity, you know.'

'Why?'

'Somehow it would seem as gentle as my misery with Jim is not.'

'Tell Shirley where I am,' murmured Valerie.

Amy rose, and as the clock struck three the light show played a game of patterns on the carpet, and she wondered how many houses were awake this night, contemplating the colourful enchantment of a bombing raid.

'Edith Allam will be back soon,' Valerie said, walking her to the door. 'She has a coloured lover.'

'He will be dead within the year.'

'For what cause?'

'My mother used to say black men always perish when they take a white woman's flesh.'

'Amy! What rubbish!'

'She'd read it somewhere.'

'This man is beautiful, and he will fly for us.'

'How beautiful?' Amy was bemused.

'An Adonis. Edith is mad about him, and when she brings him here I will keep them together,' said Valerie. 'I suppose their relationship will have to be kept under lock and key.'

'Have you any hope of leaving captivity, my dear?' Amy looked around the room—at the neat antimacassars, and at the ashtrays and at the tarnished vessels from which Restoration men had drunk bumpers before their nightly profligate fucks.

'I'm beginning to enjoy anonymity,' Valerie replied, now standing at the door with the famous aviatrix.

'I shall see to it you are freed from this mess and are back on base by next week.'

'Don't be absurd.'

'You may be the daughter of an MP, but I have the press—and that can change men's minds in time of war.'

'Take care of Hamilton,' said Valerie, as Amy stepped out to the damp walkway. A cool breeze swept past them, the fringe at the bottom of the sofa tossing in its wake.

'I have lots of machines to take care of—loads to go to Scotland,' Amy said, as if wanting her deposed CO to believe she loved, not hated, ATA. 'I seem to spend my life inside Oxfords. They should give me a degree.'

Valerie smiled and they hugged. Amy strode away, her friend knowing she would walk the punishing miles back to the house where Jim might await her, having tired of his new wife. Valerie shut the door and flopped down on the sofa, numbed.

Walking down the path and into the main road, Amy was staggered. Why had Valerie never spoken of Friedrich? She had expected that he would be the main topic of conversation, but Valerie had let her ramble on about Jim's intoxicated perversions, patiently listening to her tales of the humiliations that had often crippled her on the eve of important flights. Valerie had listened to all of this. Inside she was suffering, but with colossal bravery.

Did Valerie really love Kranz?

Perhaps she did love Shirley!

Amy panted as her step accelerated along the moist gravel path that crunched under her strong boots.

What was so astounding was that she had come to tell Valerie the news for which the MP's daughter would surely kill: she had found out where Friedrich Kranz breathed life. Yet through this whole absurd evening, she had never told her!

Should she turn back now?

Amy stopped. In the distance fires were raging, and she agonized. She would tell Valerie next week—after she had delivered the stockpiled Oxfords.

Why did they need so many?

Oxford, Oxford . . . she hated it all. Her friend should have had the information about her lover: it was the one subject that left Valerie crazed . . . Could it wait until next week? She turned to go back to Valerie's house. There was a thud some hundred miles away and Amy could almost feel the searing pain of the person who had died at that moment. She walked on, towards home. Next week she would come back, after the Oxfords . . .

The legend walked on into the night, elated that for once she was alone, and free, and not being photographed, and not being harassed. The small hours, with their teasing mist and smiling clouds of passing foggy shadows, were kind to her, and she smiled back at them.

53

Jo Howes and her father had lived in a caravan since they arrived in Britain, but with the onset of a bitterly cold 1940–41 winter Bill had accepted the offer of accommodation near White Waltham, while his daughter entered the world of Mrs Bennell at the Stone House, Hatfield.

All concerned had been amazed by Jo's rapid maturity, and her progress up the ranks of ATA had rankled a few of the older women, now in their twenties, who had been flying at the expense of their daddies for ten years or more. Now Jo was to go to Upavon for the Central Flying School conversion course, and she would be at the forefront of war activities if her time there was a success. In recent weeks when he had arrived back at the caravan exhausted and white as a sheet, Bill had fallen asleep before his soup had cooled, and she had daydreamed about the autumn sunshine across America, where the Battle of Britain would have seemed remote. Congregations in Iowa and Utah might even pray for the Spitfire pilots who went up with a flash and came back in ashes, but for those churchgoers evening still meant long walks and cocoa, not blackouts and telegrams read and re-read a hundred times.

One evening in October, Bill had come back agitated, his weariness trying to take second place to a need to disseminate gossip.

As soon as his white-haired head had passed through the small, rusty door Jo could sense his restlessness and she placed the bowl of chicken broth on a side table as he sank into their one and only easy chair.

'That damned fool Sean Vine hasn't got enough to do so he's gotten everyone he can think of all riled up,' he said, his breath coming in spurts.

'So what else is new, Dad? He and Noel are always making trouble.'

'They call it "stirring it up" in this country, you know,' he said, doing the same to his soup. 'First he said Alec's gal Marion stole some valuable pictures that Valerie Cobb had gotten from some Nazis she shouldn't have been talking to in the first place, and then he upset Angelique something awful.'

'Finish your soup, Pa.'

Bill placed the spoon down on the tiny wooden table alongside, and folded his hands in his lap.

'Angelique has been talking a lot of nonsense herself lately,' Jo said. 'She's gone in for wee-gee boards and crazy black magic stuff. Thinks that way she might track down her two lost brothers. If you ask me they were nuts to go to Spain. Who the heck goes to Spain?'

'That's what I want to tell you.' Bill sipped the soup and looked at her gravely, his colour a strange grey, with a yellowing around his temples that seemed to glow.

Jo sat. 'Oh, God, don't tell me she's crashed—'

'Listen to me, girl!' he shouted.

Jo fell silent. It was the first time he had raised his voice in anger since they had arrived in this strange, overcast island kingdom. 'Something's happened?' she murmured, unable to move.

'Goddamned Sean Vine found out about Angelique's brothers and he blabbed to every goddam person about it except to the poor gal herself. She and Delia had just done three ferry trips over three days and nights in a row, all through lousy weather, and she comes back to Hatfield to find the whole place buzzing about Zack and Paul.'

'Where are they, Pa?'

'It seems that Vine took the now-famous roll of camera film to Tim Haydon, who then had Sean as his guest at some kind of Committee meeting—I bet you Vine's in for a big post—and he heard about the Florian boys then and there.' Bill bent over as if to tie one of his ATA issue boots, but his hand merely traced the shape of his foot and went back to his lap.

'Are they dead?'

'I can't tell you, honey—it's not nice.'

'If you aren't going to tell me, one of the girls will.'

'How come you didn't hear about it?'

'I had a few hours off. Mrs B asked me to go with her to find a Wee-gee Board. Anyway, these girls don't tell me inside stuff. Now that we've been working weekends and all, they hardly talk to me about anything. Fancy that—everybody knowing about Ange's brothers, except her and me.'

'You're both foreign, baby, and don't ever forget that.'

'Angelique is deposed royalty.'

'She's foreign.'

'They think Barbara Newman's an alien, come to think of it.'

'Sure thing—she may be a Lord's daughter but she's Jewish and that's why, child. Foreign.'

'What's happened to those two Florian guys?'

'Don't worry yourself about other folk.'

'Angelique is a friend, and she's having a baby, too.'

Bill stooped his face to his soup, slurping hungrily. Then he said:

'You ought to be thinking about taking less time off—some of those other gals are being promoted.'

'I'm just a teenager.'

'Angelique isn't much more than that.'

'She isn't a novice pilot.'

'If you want to be with that boy all the time, then you might as well forget about flying, girl.' He looked up and smiled.

'What boy?'

Bill did not speak as he scraped the spoon around the bottom of the stoneware and placed the empty bowl on the table.

Jo watched him quizzically and could feel herself reddening.

'You know who,' he said.

'I'm expecting him here any moment.'

'That's that, then.'

*   *   *

Later that evening, when thoughts of Angelique's brothers and of Spits falling from the sky had drifted away, a man and two children talked about life and ate delicious Selfridges' salami in darkness. Cal March had dreaded this visit, but as soon as he had entered the eccentric American's caravan he felt elated, the same sensation he experienced on his first solo flight in a rickety Puss Moth. Bemused by the curious closeness of the man and girl, Cal found himself rapidly enthralled by the pair's rapport.

Three qualified pilots had spent that twilight gossiping and the two who were children had learned that Amy was no longer Mrs Jim, and that a new ATA boy called Anthony Seifert had arrived from the Isle of Man overflowing with stories about the interned Germans and shocking everyone by claiming to be Delia's long-lost brother. Bill Howes had gossiped relentlessly that evening, entertaining the child pilots with tales of Alec Harborne's latest quirks, which had included doing circuits around Prestwick with a pet goat inside a Master because there had been no-one left at the airfield to look after the creature . . .

'Alec says Noel Slater is a male witch,' Cal had chirped, making his favourite girl laugh.

'Some of the pilots say he's cast an evil spell over that meat-market man,' Jo added.

'Meat-market Man is turning into a damned good pilot himself,' Bill grunted. 'What you two kids don't understand is what brings two people together. Sam Hardwick and Slater get along because Noel is the smart son he never had. Noel's told me all about his folks. They're worth forgetting.'

'What's wrong with them?' piped Jo.

'They're long gone, but when they were alive he was trash.'

'Why's that, then?' asked Cal, sitting upright and staring grimly at the burly American.

'He had a bad time, and accomplished nothing—got thrown out of schools and was no good at sports because he was a little bit crippled like Roosevelt—then when his folks dropped dead, one right after the other, he just took off.'

'I can't imagine Noel Slater having a mum,' Cal said quietly.

'That's because he's never missed her,' Jo asserted.

'How do you know?' asked Bill.

'It shows.'

Cal rose and walked to the narrow, partially obscured window that seemed forever overgrown with moss. Jo had often enjoyed scraping the green substance from the corners of the panes, and marvelled at the rapidity with which it grew back.

'Could I take Jo for a little walk?' asked Cal.

413

'Don't go anywhere near Slater,' Bill said, flustered. He rose from the chair, struggling to lift his heavy frame out of its worn, sagging interior.

'Noel's in Scotland anyhow,' Jo said, helping her father. His arm felt like a thick tree branch emanating rippling warmth. 'We're all sitting waiting for the Ministry to let us get near operational planes, and creeps like Noel are fighting Hitler with chits for every kind of aeroplane. He even gets to sit alongside Sam on almost every trip: imagine how Alec would love being next to Marion all the time!'

'He's a crack flight engineer,' said Bill, eyeing Cal carefully.

'He causes accidents, sir!' Cal exclaimed.

'There's never been any proof,' Bill countered.

'What about the Toland brothers?' Jo interjected.

'Slater is destined for something big,' Bill said, stretching his ample frame and letting his arms fall on to Jo. 'He's shrewd, passing all the qualifying for twins, and soon he'll be running his own aircraft factory. Mark my words.'

'Sam Hardwick took me up as an assistant in a Hudson,' Cal offered, smiling weakly.

'That's no big deal, Cal!' Jo exploded. 'Every goddam Air Training Corps cadet has to go up with a pilot in a Hudson—let's see if I can remember my notes:

'"If both traditional methods of lowering the undercarriage fail, the poor old ATC cadet's last job before oblivion is to help his pilot apply negative G by pushing the nose downwards and employing the hand pump. Most of the time you've got no intercom, so—when the flight engineer's duties take him to regions out of sight of the pilot and the pilot wishes the flight engineer to report back to him for instructions—he will convey this by momentarily increasing pitch of all engines to maximum permissible revs and then back to cruising revs. On hearing this the flight engineer will immediately report back to the pilot." '

'Now I'm going to bed,' announced Bill.

Cal stole a look at Jo. Her father's stamina had been sapped by the tasks of recent weeks, when Britain had fought to keep Germany at bay and his countrymen had continued sipping coffee at Chock Full-o-Nuts. He wandered off to the corner in which he slept, leaving the young pilots to examine the mist that hung in the night air.

'You'd never know half of the world was bracing for war, would you?' Cal asked, leading Jo by the arm with awkward assertiveness.

'I feel it all the time,' she said, pulling away from him as they confronted the cold air outside the caravan.

'It mustn't end before my chance comes,' he said.

'What—to be swallowed up for ever?' Jo demanded.

'My chance—Mosquitos,' the boy murmured.

Jo stopped and studied the boy. They were in pitch darkness and the only sound was of distant thumping. Sounds of death. She smiled.

'In a few months, you will be full RAF and then you will go out in your beloved Mosquito,' Jo said, facing him. 'There won't be any more Noel Slaters to torment you, or bunches of us ATA girls and old men lining up to get their chits. Some don't come back. Some ATA people never come back at all— they get eaten by balloon cables, or by weather, or

415

by faulty crap that hasn't been tested.' Jo bowed her head and walked on.

Cal shivered in the damp, still cold and had a momentary, subliminal flash of a squadron of Mosquito pilots flying in formation and all dropping out of the sky.

'I'm frightened, Jo!' he whispered, seeing her figure retreating.

'Come here,' she said, turning and fixing him with a steely expression.

He moved towards her and they were in the middle of a paddock, surrounded by silence. She did not touch him.

'That film Marion gave to Sean Vine', Jo said, 'is going to be printed in newspapers all over the world. It shows what remains of handsome men and pretty women who became the victims of Nazi experiments.'

'Are they still alive now?'

'Right at this moment?' Jo's breath steamed into the night, passing across Cal's face. 'Who knows? I've been told a secret—and don't you blab—that some Nazi doctor does a hundred experiments a day on the prettiest women—and then kills them.'

'So they're dead.'

'There are always more—endless supplies of gorgeous dames for him to use. I've got photographs from just one half-hour's session. The Nazis do experiments on children too.'

Cal was feeling miserable now. 'I'd love some sweets.'

'Stick around me, Cal, and we'll lick this sugar ration. Shirley Bryce says it's bad for your flying brain to have no sugar, so ATA may be letting us have a bar of chocolate.'

'I love you. Little American bird.'

'Don't be stupid.' She thrust her hands into the deep pockets of her flying jacket.

He moved closer and wanted to press her down on to the damp, leafy ground and be buried alive with her for a long, long time.

'Why are you hating me so much tonight?'

'There are little voices inside my head, Cal. They're telling me your future. That's made me hate you.'

'What do your voices say?' He was holding her arms but she sensed not the slightest excitement in his firm grip.

'You'll be sent a long way from home, that's all.'

'ATA doesn't send people far away, ninny!'

'It will—soon.' Her mind was drifting to her father, whose lone slumber she wanted to guard inside the lonely, battered caravan, reversing roles as girl protected man in a strange land.

That night, when Cal had kissed her lightly on her mouth and walked away feeling ashamed before she could shout to summon him back, she had realized how much she would hate her birthdays when her father had died, always wondering exactly when and in what conditions she had been conceived in clinging ecstasy by two people who no longer felt. Cal had gone away and she had gone back to her tiny corner in the caravan, wanting so much to recreate that clinging ecstasy . . .

*   *   *

Now Jo was living with the other girls at Mrs Bennell's Stone House and Bill had gone to White

Waltham, their caravan taken over by a queer little man claiming to have been Lord Truman's gardener until not long ago. Amid one of the worst winters in living memory Jo would go to Upavon tomorrow and if seventeen girls could advance upwards, the thousands of aircraft needing to be delivered from the factories would have female pilots drawn from the nation's ranks and forcing the Ministry to create new centres for their activities. Already Hamble was becoming a vital location, and it was commanded by a woman . . .

Jo allowed her fantasies to drift to an RAF run by females and to big Boeings being transported across oceans by beautiful young aviatrices doing the job for a living. Her goal was to be commandeering twin-engined aircraft all over the place by the end of the year, and to cap 1941 by tracking down Hana's mother. She had studied hard for tomorrow's test, and when sleep arrived fantasy became the mutation of dreams in which Jo's brown-skinned mother was piloting a fighter and leading a formation of Spitfire girls to glory over the twilight of the Reich.

54

'I've never understood why the daughter of a millionaire aviation manufacturer should have to be tested for ATA,' complained Kay, stretching her bronzed figure across a towel on the bright, sandy beach. Only a short distance away was Magnetic Island and Kay luxuriated in the special beauty of her native Barrier Reef.

'Father has always bent over backwards to make me work for what I get in life,' Lili countered, sitting upright and looking through binoculars toward the island.

'Well, if Edith Allam ever does bother to make her way here, *I* am not being tested,' Kay asserted, looking around at the neighbouring sunbathers, most of whom were women whose husbands and lovers had begun to drift away to the war.

'Edith never even sent an apology,' Kay continued, unfolding a large London newspaper that was ten days old. 'Now I'm reading here that more ATA girls are being seen at a place called Upavon, and the press boys are taking pictures of them. There's a tart from Warsaw over there as well—I gather the Polish boys have been flying with the RAF. We're missing it all because of that stupid Yank bird.'

Lili frowned and laid the binoculars on the towel.

'Actually, I had a dream last night,' she said, fingering a heart shape into the sand. 'We were on a big airship dropping bombs, and all around us were aeroplanes of every description, all manufactured by my Dad, with beautiful women pilots inside every cockpit. Suddenly we were landing in the middle of a gorgeous field next to a glorious mansion with those landscaped gardens you only see in England. Amy Johnson greeted us—just you and me—and then she went up in our balloon. That was when my dream ended because I had banged my head on the bedside table.'

'What boring dreams you have, mate,' Kay muttered.

Lili played with the sand and then looked out to the sea. 'God, I miss having you in my bed,' she

419

said, playfully dropping a grainy handful on Kay's ankle.

'Wait until we can get away from home again,' Kay said, lying back and closing her eyes. She was feverish with the urge to tear away from home, and resented the adventures being had by the European girl pilots.

'Don't you miss men any more?' Lili asked, her tone hushed.

'I'm homebound, so I try not to think about anything, Lil.'

'They're talking about stopping air joyriding, Kay—that means we can't even fly for fun anymore. All the civil aircraft are being earmarked for the war effort.'

Kay feigned sleep to stop Lili's chatter, thinking about their overwhelming physical minglings that had left Kay tingling and helpless for weeks after they had left Brisbane for home . . .

*   *   *

Edith had never come to Australia to administer the ATA tests, and the girls had had to return to their anxious parents, but Lili had been unable to settle into family life. Her father had had to take long walks after midnight to find his wandering daughter, her gaze fixed upon the Reef under brilliant moonlight and her mind distracted by something he knew was not conventional.

Her mother had asked if she had found a young man, but Lili was jumpy when such questions were asked, always running from the spacious mansion and not stopping until she had reached the threshold of Kay's front door.

420

The Pelhams were always polite and plied her with beer until she was dizzy, but Kay had looked bored. At night Lili could not sleep, her hot, searching hand running down the length of her own body and hungering for Kay's strong, controlled lovemaking. Now, alone with her polite parents and the gentle servants, Lili wondered if Kay's nights were scorched with this same desperation, cured only when Lili could run into the darkness and let the seas drench the conflagration that danced around her nipples and erupted along her ripe contours . . .

*   *   *

Lili's dream had been more specific than the version she recounted to Kay: though she had never met the American, Edith Allam was clear as a day of Townsville sunshine, her smile friendly but not beautiful and her entourage just one single man, a hulking blond. Lili had been disturbed by the dream because Amy had risen above the crowd in the giant balloon, which all the girls assumed could not be retrieved.

When she awakened Lili felt depressed to be languishing in Australia. If dreams could be harbingers, however, Lili hoped the imagery might come true and she could fly away to England with her most beautiful possession and make love in a tiny room at the top of a country hotel.

She too had read about the daring ATA girls being tested at Upavon in a county called Wiltshire, and had followed all the scandals that seemed to dominate the pages of the newspapers, war or no war. Lili and Kay had willed Valerie

421

Cobb to overcome the hypocrisy of the characters who had sent her into exile, and had laughed together at the insinuations about Miss Cobb and Miss Bryce . . .

War was, after all, incidental: Lili had come to terms with the fact that she could never stop thinking about Kay, and as a sixth sense told her the balloon dream might soon unfold before their eyes Lili let the sea envelop her burning flesh before desire might drive her to insanity.

55

Upavon village, on the banks of the Wiltshire Avon, was home to Central Flying School. Jo, Sally and Barbara had been flown there by Amy Johnson, and the trio moved into rooms set aside for them in a house by the Avon River. Amy had flown on to Prestwick, where, she explained, three men including Alec required transport back to White Waltham. Jo, Sally and Barbara had winked at one another, knowing Amy was destined for another encounter with Hamilton Slade. She was not a good liar, Valerie always said, and now the girls knew what their absent CO had meant. Amy was so nice, and her melancholy dedication to ATA duties, desperately dull compared with her previous life of glory, made her a disarming companion for all the women in the organization.

No pilot, male or female, could endure the nerve-wracking CFS course without a few fleeting moments of wanting to abandon ferrying to return to their wartime gardens. After her successful completion of the course, Delia Seifert had returned to Hatfield spluttering to the others about having to come in to land at a speed to which they had, until then, been accustomed for cruising.

Confidence was tested by throwing a pilot into an aerobatics routine and then demanding endless solo take-offs and landings. Knowledge of constant-speed propellers, retractable under-carriages and cooling gills had to be gained with rapidity, and, most exciting of all, the girls had to learn to cope with two engines. Only a year before, Valerie Cobb had had to fight every step of the way to convince the Committee that a tiny band of females should be allowed to transport trainer aircraft short distances. Now the gap was narrowing, and in a matter of twelve momentous months Valerie's dream had crystallized; in fact, the ATA women were progressing up the ranks faster than anyone had envisaged. The country simply could not do without the services of these immensely capable aviatrices: Germany's folly had made a dream a reality for the women lucky enough to wage war in uniform up in an airy space.

Several men had arrived at Upavon for the course, including Josef Ratusz and Anthony Seifert. Sally had talked to Anthony all afternoon, intrigued by his stories, which included a claim that his mother had sent him away to be fostered and would be shocked to see that he had amounted to something. During his infancy his father had been a menacing force sodden with alcohol, and the boy, who had always doubted his true paternity, was sent away 'for safekeeping', as his mother had said, meekly surrendering him to a small home in

Southampton. He had yet to tell Delia of his claim, but he had watched her from afar and admired her brilliance in the air and wondered if it had been a blessing that she had been allowed to grow up in her own home as a son within a daughter's body.

Ratusz had found the whole Upavon exercise unbelievably humiliating and refused to speak to anyone the entire first day of the course. When told he would be expected to fly with an Instructor on a Master he had exclaimed, '*I* am master,' and stormed off, only to be reprimanded by the base CO and giggled at by a bevy of WAAFs who made jokes about Seifert and the Pole . . .

*   *   *

A chill in the air seemed to herald the beginning of a destructive winter, and Jo Howes cursed as she climbed to a suitable altitude in a Master and realized her window was stuck open. Her instructor smiled and when they returned to the ground Jo felt she would die from the crackling cold that sapped into her bones and diluted her ability to think clearly in the air—while her instructor seemed totally unaffected. Some time had to be spent mending the window and Jo became impatient, her irritation increasing at the nearby sounds of Sally and Barbara chattering to Anthony about tennis, as they waited for their course to commence.

On this, the second morning, Jo returned with the other ATA pilots, their smart blue uniforms and splendid talents attracting mixed expressions from the faces of WAAFs. Jo was pleased to be going up again, on her last flight with an instructor before her solo testing. The pair resumed their labours in the Master, its window now tightly shut and the snugness inside giving Jo a feeling of security she had never felt inside her father's caravan or in a room at Mrs Bennell's. She felt a little thrill when they were airborne again. It would be a good day, she knew, and as Sally and Barbara watched the Master become a pinprick in the sky, the WAAFs envied the other girls' special magic. Glancing down at the ground below, Jo experienced a swift pang of guilt at the thought of enjoying flight better than an afternoon in her father's company. She knew she had outgrown his clumsy attentiveness and was grateful to have been ordered to Hatfield. Glancing down again she thought she could see his grey head gazing up, but before she could adjust her focus the figure had vanished.

Soon Barbara, Anthony, Sally the tennis ace and *I, Ratusz*, as Josef called himself, were airborne. Each did a dozen solos, landing at high speeds, and were exhausted by the end of their test day. They went on to twin-engined Oxfords, their tests including spinning and the perilous single-engine flying. By the time the students returned from each flight their confidence had been shaken. Only Josef endured the comprehensive course with aplomb, at one point in mid-flight feigning sleep while taking his instructor through quite terrifying aerobatics. Every one of the pilots knew they had to pass through the course if only for the honour of Valerie Cobb. Ratusz had given first-hand descriptions of the Nazi terror to his ATA colleagues, and Valerie's plight as a prisoner of misplaced zeal had irked him because he saw her

425

as the profoundly persecuted heroine of female aviation in a war of personalities remote from the real global apocalypse.

Raging through the skies and feeling that the finger-light touch of heaven was not far away, Ratusz left his instructor in awed silence, smirking to himself at the thought of British arrogance being cowed. Both Josef and Hana were bewildered by the islanders' humour and only their dedication to flying kept their spirits alive. He was disenchanted with the characters he had encountered so far, and Hana had abandoned any thoughts of carnal satisfaction with an Englishman for the time being. Now, Ratusz was ready for what everyone in the world had come to recognize: the possibility of a prolonged conflict in which ordinary love, daily habits and small commonplace deeds were to be abandoned for extraordinary acts in a timescale that could end in annihilation to the music of Wagner.

Blazing alongside Josef's Oxford, Sally was concentrating on every detail of the flight, her first solo on the course. After so many months with ATA, alternating between being Sally Met and a regular pilot, she had lost any fear. Today, however, she had quaked at the whole prospect of her future hinging on what she saw as a few idiotic sojourns she could ordinarily do blindfold. Tension mounted to a pitch she had never before experienced within her slim body, a terror she had never felt in even the toughest centre-court match at a major final. As her Oxford levelled off and the cold but clear environs whistled past her window, she knew she could afford to relax. Sally took the aircraft further afield than regulations allowed,

Barbara's aircraft now only a dot in her peripheral vision.

Sally's mind jumped to Stella Teague, who in passing this same course was now on to Mosquitos and Hurricanes but whose attention had been drawn most recently to the plight of her former dance master. As the air screamed past and the ecstasy of flying overtook her, Sally had a sudden realization: this war seemed a succession of brave girls losing the most important men in their lives but being too loyal to ATA ferry chits to go searching for them. Then again, she told herself: Hana had lost track of her mother, and Lord Truman, like Valerie's Dad, was in search of a daughter. Two more diverse characters she could not imagine: Hana and his Lordship! Hana had already evinced a certain animosity towards the natives despite the kindness with which she had been treated. It was the charitable side of the English personality that had allowed Hana Bukova exemption from this very course, squeezed in at great expense before Christmas.

Turning around, Sally headed back and prepared for her first solo high-speed landing. She knew Jo would need reassuring if her head became filled with any further thoughts of Cal March and his celebrated mission. Everything had become secret in this war, so that a boy from a slum could not speak to his loved one about a task to which he had been assigned that could change the course of their Empire's history for ever. Jo had wanted to join Hana in London to track down the bits of paper that revealed the whereabouts of Vera Bukova, but Sally wagered to herself that Jo would be rushing off to White Waltham in pursuit of Cal.

Now Sally was approaching the hilly grass and she could see Josef's Oxford, his unmistakably daring aerobatics spellbinding to even the experienced eye. She would have to do a circuit of the airfield because he was now making a landing approach and in the distance she was pleased, and to her own astonishment, relieved, to see Barbara and Anthony on their way back to base.

Close enough to Sally to discern the colour of her smart goggles, Anthony Seifert was savouring this solo flight, the Oxford seeming to content itself with his delicate, and as yet uncertain touch. He knew he should not be ruminating but the special solitude that was flying had always made his brain tingle: never did he think so extravagantly as when airborne. Delia's awkward figure rampaged across his mind, and he wondered if she would accept him as a brother and perhaps become a girl at last. Had his mother done the unthinkable and made her only daughter into a surrogate son and husband? He had loved the girl as soon as he had seen her getting out of a Tiger at Lossiemouth.

Now, as he approached the charming field that still boasted green patches of autumn grass, the vibrant engines of the aircraft reminded him that human contact would be minimal in this conflagration. Now the immediate task at hand was the bringing of distinction to Valerie Cobb's prestigious organization, without which the RAF would by now have fallen on its face.

Anthony's height made visibility excellent and he could take in the movements of every chum on this course: there was Barbara, followed by Sally, and the crazy Pole who was so famous in his own land. As he positioned himself for an approach,

428

Anthony realized that from this war he wanted a commodity about which hc had never thought until ATA had brought him back to his family's doorstep: that commodity, he told himself, was love—and with that he raced on to the somewhat uneven landing strip of Upavon and screeched past a clutch of wincing WAAFs.

Delaying her approach and embarking on a circuit, Barbara watched Anthony Seifert blister Upavon's landing patch. She relished this chance to fly solo in a new machine that had become second nature to the Angeliques and Edith Allams of this world. What was it about Allam that made her rise above any normal pattern for a girl of her generation? It was bad enough that she, Barbara Newman, had departed from the perpetual tedium that had been the destiny of every woman in her family's, but for Edith it must have been a catastrophic event. Barbara's father had always detested Americans but she felt he would not repudiate Allam. Guiding the Oxford back towards the deceptively short path that was an excuse for a wartime runway, Barbara gasped and for a moment came close to losing control of her aircraft. All she wanted now was to land and be done with this exercise: she looked forward to the arrival of Edith and the colonials and to hatching a plan that would bring Valerie back into glory. Glancing briefly to the side, Barbara could see Josef Ratusz showing off. She prayed for his safe landing, not so much for the sake of his wellbeing as for ATA's reputation.

Polish and Czech pilots were taking Spitfires into air combat and men like Ratusz, now roaring into Upavon at an excessive landing speed, were also praying. They beseeched the Almighty that Valerie Cobb might be back in leadership soon and that more of the supremely talented women fliers would be taking over as Commanding Officers across Britain. Her team of aces would be brought in on the strength of their own merits, not as a publicity exercise 'to release more men for the RAF'.

As he taxied, Ratusz was committing the cardinal sin of ignoring the instructor, but his mind travelled forcefully to thoughts of Kranz the Jew and to the gossip the Poles had already heard concerning Shirley Bryce, Amy and Jim, and Gordon Selfridge. Hana had been told that Selfridge had departed Britain desperately in love with Nora, who, it was whispered, had no real interest in men. Josef laughed to himself and the instructor glared. His mind still chattered as his Oxford slowed, manoeuvring past Barbara and Sally, each in a Master. Shirley had not been home to see her mother for six months, and this had horrified Hana more than anything she had heard in the Hatfield canteen. Amy and Jim had been the victims of alcohol, a situation that left Hana and Josef bemused: what pilots would drink so much schnapps that they would be renowned for their habits rather than for their achievements?

His engines now stopped, Josef's instructor was barking at him and a group of WAAFs were standing beneath his window like the crowds who had awaited him when in his previous life he had been greeted as an ace. He waved, half listening to the instructor, whose words suggested Ratusz was now qualified to fly any single- or twin-engined war machine to which the Ministry cared to assign ATA

430

fliers.

When the WAAFs returned to their desks the only person left on the airfield was the Polish ace who had requested three days' leave for the sake of a fictitious funeral, but whose real intention had been to conquer staggering feelings of dread that, for some inexplicable reason, and for the first time in his life, had overwhelmed all his other emotions.

56

Harold Balfour could hardly contain himself.

Events in Europe were catastrophic, but all he could do was quake at the prospect of the dark-haired vision crossing the threshold of his elegant London residence. During the months following the fall of France, the vision's frequent visits had cheered him and now he awaited another magical meeting. She had always been in uniform and an aide had always been nearby—his fear of accusations of improper behaviour were acute—but now that her condition was beginning to show he knew this would be their last contact.

Fingering the rim of a particularly fragile piece of crystal from his town collection, Balfour wondered if this was one visit too many—should he have stopped the meetings last month, when the Kranz affair had broken? There was a tinkling in a corner of the house and he came alive, striding to the door and smoothing down his own uniform.

'It won't improve you, Harold,' chirped Angelique as she bounced in from the corridor. 'All the medals in the world would make no difference.

To your friends you're always Dear Old H.'

Balfour could see the butler peering in and focusing on the girl's ample midriff.

'Please leave us, Denison,' he said, his voice stiff with tension.

Angelique turned and grinned at the butler, but he had vanished. 'They do move so fast,' she said.

'Who do?'

'Butlers.'

'So do babies grow,' murmured Balfour, smiling and motioning for her to sit. 'How are you feeling, Angelique?'

'I feel horrid—rotten in fact. You will be amazed to hear the reason is not the wretched baby at all.' She moved to a sofa upholstered in a vivid floral pattern and for the first time in all her visits noticed that each bloom on the fabric had a bee nosing into its heart. Balfour watched her with fascination, the endless thoughts he harboured away from her company now a mass of confused sparks circulating within his being.

'You're unbelievably agitated,' he said, remaining standing at the far end of the room.

'In one day I've given coaching and moral support to the latest group for Upavon, and I've been to see the Toland brothers, who are on four trips a day, and finally I've been to see Cal March, our ATA cadet, who as you know is earmarked for destiny.'

'Have you been to see Valerie?'

'No, Harold. Please let me speak.'

Balfour watched her carefully as her eyes roved round the drawing room.

'Has the war got to you?' he asked quietly.

'Good God, Harold—one would have to be living

432

on the moon for the war not to be "getting" to one. But what's really getting to me is the message I have been receiving from my Ouija board.'

Balfour sat down stiffly on the sofa, leaving as much space as possible between himself and Angelique. 'Are you joking?' he asked seriously.

'Listen to me,' she continued. 'My brothers are in a dreadful bind in Spain. The board says Annabel Cobb and Sarah Truman are there as well.'

Balfour rose and moved behind the sofa. 'Surely you haven't become a spiritualist?' he demanded.

She turned around and looked up at him, her face drained of colour and stark against the blue ATA uniform.

'It also told me what Cal March is up to,' she said. 'I want to go on his mission. It would mean I can seek out my brothers and secure the return of the two girls. Honestly, Harold, Franco is so disorganized compared with Hitler! The Spanish are like the Italians—offer them some good wine and food and they let you do anything.'

'You know nothing,' Balfour muttered.

'I'm just an ignorant woman, am I?'

Balfour leaned back against the sideboard. 'In all of our little meetings, Angelique, you've told me about the problems ATA has been having, and you've told me the gossip. I've heard about Noel Slater pushing you around, and Amy and Jim's divorce. I know that Martin Toland fathered your child and that Marion Harborne wants some credit for the concentration camp pictures. Everything you say, and the way you say it, enchants me. None of it leaves this room except to dazzle me in my dreams at night. Something you have never grasped, however, is that my sort of mind will not accept voodoo of any sort.'

'Why have you never made love to me?' she demanded.

Balfour was stunned.

'It's something that bothers me intensely, Harold.'

'Ask me again, only more loudly, so Denison will know the child isn't mine,' he said, smiling.

Angelique had become more comfortable on the large sofa, but her face remained a pallid mask.

'Your duties will be expanding within ATA,' he continued, seating himself on the sofa and reaching for her hand, 'and I don't want any of you going off on tangents with black magic, or with peculiar habits.'

'You must help me get to Zack and Paul,' she blurted suddenly, fighting back tears.

'Not possible,' he asserted, squeezing her hand, its clammy lifelessness making him shudder. Cutting into his palm was a ring that had not been there before—its stone a sharp gem giving him a physical pain that hovered in his abdomen and made him feel ashamed because he was jealous.

'Two things, Harold. You must help me get an aircraft across the Channel, and you must get Valerie reinstated.'

'What about the child?' he asked, still squeezing and letting the stone dig into his heart.

'You can't do anything about that, my dear,' she said, a bit too loudly.

'Dammit, woman—how can you fly to Spain pregnant?'

Angelique leapt up from her seat. 'The mere fact that you've suggested I might fly to Spain means we're there. Do it. Now.'

At once Balfour was set alight by the fire she had ignited within his bloodstream, a red-hot maelstrom he had known from the moment he had first spied her in the locker room at Maylands. Angelique's blazing eyes put his thoughts into disarray and he felt he might give her his house and all his worldly goods at this moment for the sake of one much longed-for coupling.

'You were talking about reality, Harold?'

She was speaking, but he was travelling at breakneck speed over a giant mountain that had left his chest pounding and his loins urging him not to think but to do.

'Will we ever make love, do you suppose?' he whispered.

'We might,' she replied. 'for the time being I suggest you keep your mind on serious matters at hand, Captain Balfour.'

But Balfour was devouring her with his eyes, and she could not move.

'I love you,' he murmured. 'It too is unforgivable, but I love you, Angelique, bastard child and all.'

'Martin's baby will be born in Spain,' she asserted, grinning at Balfour.

'Did you hear what I said?'

As they stood facing each other the only sound was the occasional shout from a newspaper vendor, motorcars now a rare presence in the dark times of the London siege.

'Go to the airfield where Cal March will be commencing his journey,' he said slowly, 'and there will be help provided for your escapade.'

Angelique's colour had returned. 'You would do this for a first generation Armenian who communes with Ouija boards?' she piped.

'I would do this for a face that God must promise will come back to me.'

'God isn't doing much currently for those poor people in the death camps.'

Balfour held her hands and kissed them, the maelstrom returning to his flesh and the veins all round his body.

But Angelique was already miles away, wanting to depart for a terrible land of which she knew nothing. Balfour was holding her now, and she let him embrace her with a kind of desperation she knew could only be spawned by war. As her breath came in spurts and he held her to him the voices inside her head announced that she would be embracing her brothers within the week and that Valerie would be free when the time came to welcome Angelique back from the fascists.

57

'I've a priceless cutting for you,' Alec Harborne announced, his presence inspiring a group of ATA women to look up from their chess board in the common room at White Waltham.

Shirley Bryce excused herself and went over to him. 'You are a noisy bugger,' she said, ushering him into a corner.

'Speak for yourself—this place was quiet until they started letting females fly with us.' He unfolded a piece of newsprint as they sat on a bench attached to the faded wall.

'What on earth have you got there?' she asked, reaching for the cutting.

436

'Blood Libels are alive and well in Norfolk. Have a read.' Alec sat back and rested his head against the plaster.

Shirley quickly became engrossed in the piece, her hand tightly gripping the paper. 'Where did you find this?' she asked.

'Sam Hardwick's old lady collects newspaper cuttings. Keep it.'

Shirley folded the clipping. 'How is Marion?' she asked.

Alec's expression changed instantly, his cheerful bounciness now smothered by a frown:

'We thought she was to have a wee baby but it was something else.'

'Something else! Why haven't any of us heard about this? She's been trooping back and forth on Hurricanes and Masters every bloody day, Alec. She never said there was anything wrong.'

'Her dizzy spells and all that—did she never mention them?'

'Never, Alec.'

'It was her female system—she had a horrendous session with a quack doctor—he did cure it, though.'

Shirley felt a wave of anger rising inside. 'Does that mean—no babies for you?'

'Most likely, lass.' He looked at the chess group, who had begun chattering over cups of coffee. Shirley's voice broke in:

'Never mind—that new CO at Weston Longville says our job is going to be doubly taxing this coming year.'

'What new CO?' Alec asked sharply.

'Charlie Buxton—in fact he's the first airman in the family. They've all been adventurers and clergymen through the centuries.'

'We've all been adventurers in the Harborne line, and I'm no CO as yet.'

'Your day will come.' Shirley knew Alec had resented the promotions being heaped upon other men. Though he had run his own business and his own life against unspeakable odds before the war, his flamboyant personality had never pleased the brass since the outbreak of world conflict and even Valerie had found him hard to take at times.

'So what does the illustrious Commander Buxton say?' he asked.

'He made a special point of coming down to tell the girls based at Hamble and Hatfield that our ranks would swell.'

'You must miss ground engineering,' Alec commented quietly.

'That's my other news. The RAF has come around full circle and appointed me its first full-time woman Ground Engineer.'

'Well, I'm dashed—this is historic.' Alec put his arm around Shirley and she did not have enough time to shy away. He kissed her on her temple and her thick hair felt delicious next to his rough skin.

'Give my love to Marion!' she spluttered, pulling away from him and jumping up from the wall bench.

'We haven't finished talking,' he said.

'I have.'

'We all love you, Shirley, and we're proud of your achievements.'

She was watching her colleagues at play. They had taken no notice of the pair's meeting.

'None of it means anything without Val,' she mumbled.

'What does your mum think?' asked Alec.

Shirley turned to face him. 'Valerie is my life!' she shouted.

The others looked up.

'Calm down,' murmured Alec, his hand close enough to hers to take it in his own.

'I've not seen her for three months, Alec.'

'I've not seen my wife for three nights—that's dangerous, lass.'

'Be serious,' she pleaded, standing over him, her hand still in his. She was perspiring and the wetness of her palm seemed to flow into Alec's cool skin like pain departing a dying body. 'Who can I talk to? My mother thinks I'm sick, and the world around me says so as well.'

'It's not incurable, Shirley.' He held her hand tightly and she felt her focus swim. 'Let go of me, Harborne!'

Alec released her and she felt her equilibrium return.

'This article would interest Stella,' she said, unfolding the newsprint and motioning to the chess players. Stella was amongst them, and Alec smiled as she approached.

'Hello, ballerina,' he sang, rising from the bench.

'My God—Alec Harborne being chivalrous!' Stella exulted. Her tiny figure was clad in the newest winter uniform and the dark ATA blue was startling next to her rosy cheeks.

'He's brought me this piece from the newspaper,' Shirley said. 'It's all about the Blood Libel. This chap says here he is directly descended from one of the Jews converted in the twelfth century in Norwich. If I were him, I wouldn't be waving a flag about it.'

'Why? Are you afraid Hitler is going to make it here after all?' Stella demanded.

'I can't imagine why this man would want the whole world to know that his ancestors were Jewish.'

'Are you ashamed?' Alec asked, sitting on the bench.

'Not at all,' Shirley responded, 'but as soon as people know this one particular fact about someone, they start treating you differently.'

'Right!' exclaimed Alec. 'Now I shall treat you differently by taking you off into an office I happen to know is unoccupied, and ravishing you mercilessly.'

'Three nights away from Marion and all he can talk about is his libido,' Shirley said.

'His what?' Stella asked, looking up from the newspaper article.

'It is a new word for romance—I read it in a medical journal.'

'You are peculiar, Bryce,' Stella said, tapping her with the cutting. 'May I send this to Grunberg?'

'You know where he is?' they both shouted in unison.

'I've only just heard from him,' she replied.

'Where?' Alec demanded, suddenly alert.

'They've put him in an Internment Camp. I'd written to him months ago, care of Cambridge U, but heard nothing. Now he appears—out of the blue, florid handwriting and all—full of news and names and anecdotes. It sounds more fun than this place.'

There was a commotion in the main reception area, and all three pilots did an about-face.

'Bottoms up!' shouted Sean Vine, escorting a

group of men into the common room. Bobbing alongside the crowd, which included Bill Howes, Noel and Sam, and Hamilton Slade, was little Cal.

'That's what I'm here for,' boomed Alec, grabbing Cal and lifting him off the ground.

'This is Cal March's last day with ATA,' Bill said, placing a bottle of black-market vintage champagne on the chess table, where Delia had lingered.

'He's going off to an undisclosed location, to be groomed for an Air Defence Cadet Corps that's due to start up in February,' Bill continued.

'Where do you get all this top-secret gen, Yank?' shouted Noel, who was not smiling.

Bill cast him a withering glare and pressed on:

'Cal has in fact been sworn to secrecy about the exact details of his attachment to the new squad, but we all wish him well. During the first year of ATA we boys and girls of all ages, and of all nationalities, have ferried thousands of aircraft around this country for delivery to the RAF. Now you are about to become one of us. Fly safely, boy.' Bill opened the champagne and with the bang of the cork an air of levity engulfed White Waltham as another punishing ATA workday, overshadowed by appalling weather, came to an end.

Cal was surrounded by ebullient colleagues but his thoughts were hovering some distance above the din, as he suffered the absence of Jo Howes on this crucial day. Because Jo was still at Upavon she would not see him again before he was taken away from ATA. He had not had time to send a message to Upavon and, even if he had, Cal wondered if news of his sudden departure might not have ruined her chances of passing the course.

441

'I'll tell Jo you said goodbye,' one of the girls was whispering.

Cal emerged from his torment to see Stella Teague standing beside him. 'You're all so kind,' he said, not knowing where to put his spindly arms. Champagne was being thrust at him and he grasped the glass by its neck.

'It's not a chicken,' Noel said, taking the boy's hand and manoeuvring his fingers up the crystal. Cal felt a curious tingling down his spine as Noel's eyes met his momentarily and he could sense himself reddening.

'Where did all this posh crockery come from, then?' asked Alec.

'We raided the local manor and raped the women,' Sean shouted.

'Does that mean we are so undesirable that you need to seek satisfaction elsewhere?' piped Delia.

Laughter filled the room but Cal could not rid his mind of Jo, and Shirley fought a temptation to scream:

Why was Valerie not here?

How could people be frivolous when the greatest woman of their generation was under armed guard for loving a man?

Shirley looked at Cal, whose emaciated physique mirrored the condition of her soul. She wanted to protect him from love, and from obsessions, be they aeroplanes, comics or American girls. Watching him daydream while the others revelled, she decided she would take the leave days to which she was entitled and try to renew her own faltering will to live.

Did Cal have such a will to live? she asked herself.

But perhaps he had not lived long enough to want more.

Champagne glasses were chinking and Shirley left the building to run out into the dark and scream into the night.

58

Emerging from the mews in which the strange little doctor had his private practice, Angelique walked gingerly along the elaborate cast-iron railings of Harley Street. She had spent two days in London and was enjoying the looks attracted by her still shapely figure inside the superbly tailored uniform. A thin layer of ice now coated the pavement and the searing cold was making Angelique weaken. She had wanted to walk to Whitehall to hear Balfour speak but her resolve was evaporating. Taxis were rare, and when one eventually trundled down the slippery street her attire dazzled the driver at once and she was on her way to the House.

When the taxi drew up into Parliament Square the driver hesitated:

'Free ride, miss, if you'll tell me I'm not hallucinating.'

'I'm not Hedy Lamarr, if that's what you thought.'

'No. It's the wings, miss.'

Angelique stepped back, nearly losing her footing on the treacherous glaze as she looked down at the emblems on her uniform.

'My wings are ATA,' she said, smiling. 'Air

443

Transport Auxiliary.'

'You're a WAAF then?'

She resisted losing her temper. 'There's nothing wrong with WAAFs, but *I* am a *pilot*.'

'Get off—you're having me on.' The fixed grin the driver had kept up throughout their ride was fading.

Angelique rummaged in her bag and drew out a diary. 'A Wellington from Brooklands to St Athan, and, my God, another chit for a Beaufort out of bloody Chobham, and—would you believe it?—a Spit to Lichfield. Why can't I have a Hurricane this week?'

'You're a bloomin' actress, you are,' he said, switching off his motor.

'Indeed I was—until I became a full-time pilot for the war effort, my man.'

'What was that you was reading from?'

'Just a diary I keep—I listen to the other girls talking.'

'There's more of you?' he spluttered, his eyes bulging.

'Good Lord, yes. In fact, I am responsible for *Are you pregnant?* being written into the RAF medical as a routine question.' Angelique was freezing alive, but with the relentless determination that had made her an actress, she persevered.

'Listen to me,' she said. 'Three days ago I got out of a Hind, and because my tummy was bulging more than I wanted it to, the male CO shouted, "What is that woman doing flying an aircraft pregnant? Did no-one notice at her Medical?" I replied, "Nobody ever asked!" and from that moment on, *Are you pregnant?* was written in to the RAF rule book for examining doctors.'

444

'You mean they ask blokes?'

'They ask blokes.'

He had started up his engine, and before Angelique could replace the diary and fish out her money he had zoomed off. She chuckled to herself at the memory of recent events, which now seemed so remote in the harrowing bustle of blitzed London.

'You shouldn't be revealing classified RAF information to men on the street.'

Angelique swung around, and if she had been kissed by the King she could not have felt a greater wave of excitement than at the sight she now beheld:

'Dear God—Valerie!' she screeched, throwing her arms about the tall, striking woman.

'You didn't see me,' Valerie said, kissing her on the cheek.

'What have they done with your uniform?' Angelique asked, looking her Commanding Officer up and down.

'Something wrong with this?' Valerie stepped back, opening her coat to reveal an exquisitely cut dress fit for a duchess. 'What are you doing in London? You should be helping to fend off Hitler.'

'Yesterday I saw Balfour, and today the doctor. I thought I would pop in to hear Harold address the House.'

'What did the doctor say?'

'I'm healthy enough. What about you? Do we get you back? Are you free?' Angelique felt faint from her sense of astonishment and joy. Until now, she had never realized how much Valerie's presence had affected each girl.

'No. And I could be stashed away in mothballs

with my uniforms for the duration of the war, if anyone were to see me here.'

'What the hell is going on, Valerie? Can you not walk the streets of your own country?'

'Apparently not—at least for the time being. Anyway—I saw you from that window over there and just had to steal away. Why did your taxi linger?'

'He thought I was an eccentric dressing up as a man.'

'Did I hear you telling him about being pregnant?'

'I suppose I shouldn't have—what do you expect from an actress with a big mouth? Valerie—did you know Amy and Jim are divorced but he drops in on her?'

'That's what I mean—loose talk loses reputations, let alone wars.'

'You're so patriotic, Val.' Angelique felt a foreigner in these surroundings.

'After what's happened to me, I'd advise everyone to be very careful,' said Valerie. 'The safest people in this world are Church of Scotland crofters.'

'Amy misses you, Val.'

Valerie did not want to reveal that Amy had visited her—she could trust Angelique with the information but her ordeal had made her reticent and frightened.

'How is Martin?' Valerie cast a furtive look at the window of her father's office.

'He's fine—starting on those Beauforts and things. He and Oscar operate as an ATA team, a bit like Sam and Noel. Are you anxious to get back inside, Val?'

446

'Walk with me.'

The two women went into the imposing building and stopped in the foyer.

'Valerie, I can't believe it's you!' Angelique enthused, throwing affectionate arms about her once more. 'Some of us thought you were dead.'

'In an odd way I have died, you know.'

Angelique had never before seen Valerie Cobb cry, but now she could detect a catch in the other woman's throat, and a reddening about her eyes.

'What about the girls?' Valerie asked. 'Is everyone all right?'

'Marion and Alec are very happy, but she always looks as if someone has taken all her blood for the war effort. Sam and Noel are getting terribly chummy, and Shirley Bryce misses you terribly.'

'Does she make a career of it?'

'Valerie—she cares deeply for you. It isn't her fault you abandoned your friendship with her because Friedrich fell out of the sky.'

'The last thing I want is Shirley making a spectacle of herself. What was that you said about Noel and Sam? Chummy?'

'Perhaps I should rephrase that,' Angelique said, studying this remarkable woman's fiercely intense eyes and understanding why Shirley might miss her so much. 'Sam and Noel have become . . . inseparable—people do talk, you know. His wife is distraught. Alec Harborne went to visit her and she's taken to all sorts of weird habits, like piling up newspapers in her drawing room.'

Valerie listened quietly, bowing her head.

Angelique continued:

'I think you miss Shirley, deep down inside.' The words had popped out, and she regretted them at

447

once.

'I miss *all* my pilots!' stormed Valerie.

'Please don't be cross with me, Val,' Angelique said meekly, wanting to hug her once more. 'Seeing you is like a dream.'

'It is wonderful to see you too.' Valerie had calmed down and spoke in hushed tones, gulping at the lump in her aching, sad throat.

'Is there anyone to whom you want me to say hello?'

'You were not meant to have seen me, my dear,' she said, smiling. 'I ask just one thing: if you should learn of a definite address for Friedrich, please, please let me know—'

'Valerie!' A brusque voice interrupted them.

'I'm coming, Dad.'

Sir Henry Cobb bowed briefly to Angelique and before she could say goodbye to Valerie, Hatfield's Commanding Officer and the founder of women's Air Transport Auxiliary had vanished down a corridor with her father. Momentarily Angelique wanted to run after her, but then emotion overwhelmed her and sobs surged into her mouth. She tried to muffle her gasps, but her weeping reverberated through the sombre chambers. She stumbled back out into the fiendish winter and a taxi took her away from Harold and the House and the expensive doctor who had said it was too late to kill the foetus. She would head towards White Waltham, where she would find a way of getting airborne and forgetting Martin Toland's child until it had been born in Spain. Her taxi pulled away from Whitehall as, from a window above, Valerie Cobb saw a blur that was Angelique but whose form was too obscured by a flood of the

448

Commanding Officer's own uncontrollable tears.

59

They had waited what seemed an eternity for Barbara Newman to arrive for tea. In this part of Norfolk guests were expected to behave impeccably, even in time of war—and especially if the guest in question was a top officer of the Air Transport Auxiliary. Indeed, Barbara would be interrupting a punishing schedule of Hurricane deliveries to journey all the way to Weston Longville. Lord and Lady Truman had no staff for this grim winter of 1940, and their financial state had crumbled further when their only useful land was taken over by the RAF. The local base was being expanded and now the Trumans lived alone amid the noise of a war they had hoped to escape in this remote wedge of East Anglia.

'Do you suppose she's been distracted by those men?'

Truman looked at his wife and frowned. 'What men?'

'This girl is a pilot, and she would have been intrigued by what's going on in our grounds.'

'If you've seen one installation, you've seen them all,' he grunted, scraping at the bowl of his pipe.

'I do hope nothing terrible has befallen her,' Lady Truman fretted, her slim figure making a perfect L shape as she sat upright in what her husband called her 'anxious before lunch' position.

'Do you remember that chap I told you about— the one who stopped here for a bath?' he asked, resting his pipe on a knee clad in thick wool trousers.

'Oh, good lord! That awful dark man from Vienna?'

'Didn't know you knew him.' Truman dug in his jacket pocket for a tobacco pouch.

'He came to see Tim at the House,' she said curtly.

'Well, that Jewish scum has wrecked poor Valerie Cobb's life.'

'I can't see what it has to do with us, darling.'

'It has *everything* to do with us,' he barked. 'I feel responsible for her plight. Tibbs and the gardener made such a song and dance about the man— you'd have thought he was the devil himself come to enslave Christian England. In the end I had to give in and tell all to the police. As it turns out, the miserable wretch was part of the same gang who stole my wallet. Fagin lives.'

'Why are you telling me all this now?' Her face was pinched, but the beauty of a debutante still peeped weakly through her tired features.

He had tamped the tobacco into the splendidly carved wood and was holding a light over the fragrant concoction. 'Virginia leaves—imported. Same as those poor airmen.'

'What on earth are you talking about?'

'Americans—the ones who they say just died.'

'Who?' His wife's face was immobile.

'They were sent to deliver some new aeroplanes. There was a great hoo-hah because the aircraft had made it through U-Boat Alley on a freighter from Virginia. It seems the blasted flying machines were faulty. Two chaps went down one after the other. Terrible mess.'

450

'How did you hear?'

'Charlie Buxton—Commandant at our new base here—told me the whole story. They crashed a few minutes after leaving the factory. If you ask me, those ATA people shouldn't be allowed to muck about in new aircraft. Think of what those two things cost. My God—it doesn't bear thinking about.'

'Perhaps that's why Barbara is late.'

Truman puffed away furiously, a grin on his face.

His wife gazed at the smoke curling up into the still air of the quiet sitting room and let her eyes wander to the view beyond their front window. 'Just imagine how the families in America will suffer.'

'What families?' he asked, squinting.

'Those two men—the vicars—surely they have families.'

'Lord knows. Anyway, I'm getting fed up with this waiting.'

'Have you any idea what she wanted to talk about?'

'She said she had what is known as a multi-pronged plan of some sort.' He paused. 'Her plan relates to our Sarah.'

'These young women are remarkable!' But mention of her daughter had little effect these days; she was ashamed to admit that feelings of detachment had begun to creep in when people talked of her lost child.

Now Truman was scowling. His pipe had gone out. 'Valerie is the most remarkable of them all,' he said, fumbling with a match. 'I want to do something to get her name cleared, and in return I shall ask for a place on one of these ATA committees.'

Lady Truman observed her faltering husband drop match after match to the floor, and she could not dispel the feeling of disgust that had crept into her in recent months. His increasing infirmity, which left him almost completely immobile, had made him flabby and irritable. Staring out of the window she could not help admitting to herself that she was finding her London job a stimulus to the fiercely sensuous female that still dwelled somewhere within her polite exterior.

'I can't imagine what Newman's girl would know about our daughter that I haven't already gleaned from the Ministry, but it's worth a try,' Truman said, managing to light one matchstick and thrust it into the pipe clenched tightly in his jaw.

Smoke curled once more.

'She is forty-five minutes late. I've mince pies to prepare.'

'Bloody mince pies.'

'You've always liked them.' She hated the smoke, and his unpredictable complaints. 'It was my turn this year for the Church and with all those airmen moving in, we'll need dozens more than usual.'

'If you make it too obvious that we've stockpiles of sugar and flour, my love,' he growled, 'those uncouth fliers will be raiding us in no time.'

'You will be pleased to know I've advertised the fact that these will be made with substitute ingredients due to rationing.'

'Ho-ho! They'll taste too bloody good. No-one will believe you.' He grinned at her and puffed furiously. 'God help us if the Yanks come in on this fracas and start bringing their peasants over here.'

'Why ever should they do that?'

'What—join the war?'

'Bring peasants.'

'Well, to be truthful, my dear, neither is too likely. Old President Rosenfeld is too busy trying to please his Congress, and even if they did join our cause their peasants wouldn't pass military exams. These mixed races are a disaster—full of physical shortcomings.'

Lady Truman glared at her imperfect husband. 'I shouldn't harp too much on that, if I were you,' she murmured.

'And what is that supposed to mean?' Truman's eyes blazed.

'Nothing.' She looked at the floor and noticed the smoke had stopped. 'Is it true Liverpool has had eighty-odd consecutive days of bombing?'

He was silent, pipe in hand. Then, 'You don't like me much, do you?' he asked.

Lady Truman rose, avoiding his gaze. Moving to the frostbitten windowpane she craned her neck for any sighting of an ATA lady pilot on a bicycle.

'*Liking* each other has never entered into our world, darling,' she replied, fingering the curtain. 'Perhaps it is more important to those peasants you were talking about just now.'

Truman sat back, his unhealthy colour making his wife shudder.

'I don't suppose she's coming,' he said, closing his eyes.

'Something awful has happened, I just know it,' she fretted, staring out at the leafless branches of their large grounds, the neatly landscaped look now gone for ever with the departure of the gardener. Focusing on one branch close to the icy window, she wondered if leaves would ever sprout again—if enough bombs fell, and enough fires were started, life on the planet might disappear.

Did people on remote exotic islands know there was a war on? she pondered. And what about those poor Britons stuck out in places like Singapore?

It was now one hour since Barbara Newman had been due to visit, and Lady Truman's throat was constricted with a raging, painful dryness as she thought of another mother missing a daughter. In Tim Haydon's briefings she had begun transcribing reports from Germany about medical research carried out in death camps. One experiment had involved a mother and daughter, both naked, strapped into seats facing each other. According to these sketchy details, disseminated by some valiant means to make their way into the Houses of Parliament, mother and daughter were ordered to press buttons to inflict electric shocks upon each other, the voltage increasing with every new push of the button. The Germans thought it interesting to determine the death threshold of young versus old and used the method ten to fifteen times daily.

Lady Truman had become ill and Haydon had sent her home early that day, but now, as she thought obsessively of Barbara Newman's mother, she realized that even in England a new way of making war had dictated that girls would no longer be girls and that shock thresholds would never be the same again.

60

Amy had been infuriated to learn that two of the newest girls had made it through the appalling weather. Though conditions had worsened, she was determined to carry out the demands of her assortment of chits earmarked for this weekend. She had hated having had to spend Christmas stranded at Prestwick but had been able to make her way to Hatfield where she had been astonished to encounter Valerie Cobb. Without so much as an explanation, Valerie had appeared in her midst, handed Amy her orders and spoken a few clipped words about dinner and twenty new ATA ladies.

Had she been reinstated as Commanding Officer and as Head of ATA?

Because the two women had not had time for a chat Amy knew she would have to wait until after the New Year to hear the lowdown on her friend's odd, sudden reappearance. Amy had known for some time of Barbara Newman's absurd plan to threaten some highly-placed associates of her father's with a scandal in order to secure Valerie's release, but this had come too suddenly for that. Amy had not seen Barbara since delivering her to Upavon and, in fact, she had not seen anyone in ATA for weeks.

She had been in the air, it seemed, for ever.

Exhaustion was now her conqueror and for once she wondered if her tenacity had metamorphosed into folly. Her brain was not enjoying this exercise and the cold of uncaring clouds pierced through to aching wrists and throbbing knuckles.

She suspected she would have to 'smell her way' to Kidlington. Amy had laughed when the engineer in charge at Prestwick had strapped her into the Oxford at teatime that January afternoon and had been so cheerful despite the perishing cold of his assigned location. It had been nice to stop in Blackpool and see her sister, but now as she headed for Kidlington she wondered about Hamilton. He did look so ill, and Amy decided that as from today they would spend more time together. She did not think her family would object to Hamilton, despite his quiet scholarliness lately overshadowed by an unhealthy pallor. Valerie Cobb had promised Amy an extravagant dinner in London at L'Écu de France to celebrate her own astonishing return, and to toast the approval by the Ministry of twenty more top women for inclusion in ATA. Amy would bring Hamilton along to that dinner—and sod the press, she told herself. As from today . . .

*   *   *

All the girls had had such phenomenal experiences since the inception of ATA. Amy loathed the organization at first, but after having got to know characters like Angelique Florian and Sally Met she had come to love the eccentricity that seemed a trademark of a ferry pilot.

If one could not fight, one could ferry . . .

It reminded her of her own marriage. Jim often raged at her to stop worrying so much about the lives of the other ATA women; when, for example, she had given money to Marion and Alec, and helped Stella pack a special gift box for the Jewish

456

men in the British internment camp.

'If one could not fight, one could ferry . . .'

She pondered the saying as the two engines of her Oxford told her they were oblivious to the thin icy air they cut through. If one had been prohibited from fighting, she told herself, one would have to let off steam in some other manner. Or else one could curl up and die. ATA had been a kind of death for her, but now she was beginning to revel in the kindness and companionship of its membership. Where else in the world could one get a job with an organization whose leading players were actresses, ballerinas, meat market clerks and ground engineers, who were also the nation's foremost flying instructors for the RAF and majestic pilots in their own right?

If men had prohibited women from fighting, they could ferry . . .

Was it not like her marriage?

She was confusing herself and wished the cloud would thin.

January, 1941 . . .

Amy repeated today's date to herself and tried to recall what she had been doing five years ago. She was sure she had been airborne, but not in such conditions as these. It was a day cruelly cold with icy snow showers and a gnashing wind. She flew above the clouds and let her mind wander back five years.

January, 1936 . . .

Was it Australia?

God, I was hot, she remembered, and Jim was impossible. Why did women want to be known by their husbands' names? Who had started the tradition? The prophets? Islam? The Greeks? She was glad she had changed her name back by deed poll, and joked to herself that she would want her obituary to say nothing about Jim.

What was happening?

Amy could feel the Oxford juddering and she fretted at the possibility that an emergency might befall her at the tail-end of an intolerable fortnight. On this hellish Sunday morning she had told Squire's Gate airfield at Blackpool that she would be flying over the top, and was delighted to have been allowed air-to-ground communication, usually forbidden to ATA ferry pilots. Now, she thought she was nearing Kidlington but had chosen to remain above cloud.

Was it possible?

Cold air screamed by and she had no idea of her location. Her fuel gauge had dropped to near nil and she knew she would have to come down.

At seventy-five feet she could see a convoy of naval vessels but the Oxford had died long ago. All Amy could do was read the lettering on the side of the vessels as an unbearably agonizing cold gripped her legs like frozen tongs, and she smiled as the prospect of a dinner at L'Écu de France loomed hot in her hopeful mind's eye . . .

Part III

Service of the Heart

61

Every night before bed Edith had hugged the tiny doll before placing it on its own little pillow. On this morning in January 1941 she had been excessively loving, because the evening before had been its last bedtime in Philadelphia. One of these days, she would be able to return it to its rightful owner in Germany, but for the time being Heinkel—as she called the doll—would have to content itself with being the American aviatrix's mascot on a round-the-world tour.

Edith had given Raine her word about delivering the doll to Frau Fischtal, but that day of promises now seemed a hundred years ago. Having spent a delightful Christmas and New Year at home, Edith was beginning to lose interest in the task to which she had been assigned by Beaverbrook. Since the mysterious disappearance of Valerie Cobb she had felt inclined to give up flying and sit out the war in Fairmount Park, with Hartmut by her side. Occasional twinges that reminded her of that night with Errol had given her more than one uncomfortable night's sleep, but now she could only speculate about his progress in the world.

Hartmut, by contrast, was here.

At breakfast her father sat glumly scratching away at a pile of papers with a newly sharpened pencil. It amazed Edith how little the European war affected her parents, whose daily routine had gone virtually undisturbed even when the Battle of Britain had put all perceptive minds on alert. Selecting marmalade from an array of freshly made preserves, Edith broke a roll in half and smiled across the table at their permanent house guest. Hartmut had agreed to stay within these four walls until Edith was airborne again, but that agreement had now stretched to months and the German was on edge. Kitty Allam had been enchanted from the first day he had arrived on Florence Avenue, and had convinced her husband, after a momentous verbal battle, to stay silent about the presence of an alien in their household.

'He's Jewish. I've seen!' she had cackled, but that only provoked Julius Allam further.

Chewing on the soft roll, Edith giggled to herself at the thought of her mother being Hartmut's geisha in the bathroom.

'What's funny?' Her father had looked up from his documents.

'Nothing, Daddy,' she replied, smiling at Hartmut.

He looked at her and then back at his newspaper. 'There is something here I think that you should read,' Hartmut said, his face unusually tense and his breakfast uneaten.

'Bad news?' Kitty asked, leaving the kitchen sink to move behind the German. 'We need this first thing in the morning?'

'I've always said they should print the lousy things to come out at lunchtime,' Julius muttered, returning to his sharpened pencil. 'By noontime nobody cares what's happening.'

'Look.' Hartmut pushed the newspaper towards Edith. She could hardly believe her eyes:

FIRST JOB BACK AT WORK
ENDS IN DISASTER FOR VALERIE COBB

462

Feelings of urgency, of a need to rcturn as quickly as possible to England, overcame Edith, and she felt as if she had awakened from a pleasant dream to find the real world an inescapable nightmare—as she read on . . .

'The celebrated aviatrix Amy Johnson sent out on an ATA mission by Valerie Cobb on Val's first day back, and now Amy has gone missing,' she muttered, scouring the newsprint at breakneck speed.

With increasing disbelief Edith read that Amy had gone off in appalling weather conditions to deliver an Oxford to Kidlington aerodrome from Prestwick, and that White Waltham had reported to Valerie that a similar aircraft had been seen crashing into the Thames Estuary—with Amy's papers having been recovered from the water. According to the Admiralty, the Naval trawler 'HMS Haslemere' had tried to rescue her and what was thought to have been her male passenger, but in attempting to do so the ship's commanding officer, Lieutenant Commander Derek Wells Fletcher, died of extreme exhaustion and exposure.

A polar explorer, he had made an heroic trip to the Arctic at the age of twenty-seven, his death following soon after when he was only thirty-four.

Edith looked up. Her father had shown no interest and she wanted to strike him. She read on:

According to reports filed by newspaperman Nick Elton, who happened to have been on board one of the naval vessels, Amy's Oxford had fluttered out of the sky and landed on a wave. He thought he had seen a parachute . . .

463

'Do you have to go today?' asked her mother.

'Damn right I have to go,' Edith said, stuffing the paper under her arm. She rose from her chair and stood in the middle of the room, still reading the appalling account of the ordeal suffered by a fellow flier. She could just imagine the common room at Hatfield when Valerie—she was back!—would have emerged from the office to tell the other girls of Amy's disappearance. Amy had become so deeply loved amongst ATA ranks, and the letters Edith had so gratefully received from England implied ATA and its folk had saved Amy's sanity.

Now she was one of the missing.

Edith could see the empty space on the blackboard, the names of other pilots being moved up as quickly as possible to avoid a breakdown of morale. A whole nation would be praying for the sad-faced lady to be found . . .

Julius was saying something to his daughter:

'Mommy thinks you should stay with us for good. Forget this Beaverbrook craziness.'

'There are things happening now that need people like Edith,' Hartmut objected. 'What American city is being bombed eighty days in a row?'

'Are you wishing it on us, Hartmut?' Kitty asked.

'Yes, in many ways I am—if it meant jarring this country into some sort of action.'

Julius left the table and put an arm around Edith's shoulders. 'And the rumours about the death camps?' he asked. 'There are pictures of these things?'

'Of course,' said Hartmut.

'Pictures or not,' observed Kitty, 'we just think

464

our daughter is irrelevant to airplanes, and to the airspace of a strange land.'

'I want to breathe all kinds of air, Mommy.'

'Your mother meant airs, like stuffy Britishers—like anti-Semites in kilts.' Julius gave her a patronizing hug.

'One of the most dreadful things you could possibly dream of has happened back in England,' said Edith flatly, her eyes glazed.

'Tell us,' Kitty said.

'Read it,' she snapped, her vision recovering instantly as she thrust the newspaper at her mother. 'Remember Amy?'

Her parents huddled over the small print, and Edith felt a wave of excitement and dread as Hartmut's massive frame left the table and moved to her side. Even now—amid her anxiety about Amy's fate—an urgency inspired by his Teutonic muscularity enveloped her body, and she wished her father would return and hug her again. In the early morning she could feel crazed with love for the German, and yet by nightfall in her quiet city she would bite her nails with the unease of Errol's absence. Through all these months no-one had divulged his whereabouts, and she had pestered Molly and her new husband Learco for news of the handsome Negro's last destination.

When Kelvin Bray had told her of Errol's brief incarceration she found the whole episode so distressing that she laughed, not wanting her friends to see a pilot cry. In private she had defied the belief that one must never weep for so small a thing as a coloured man, and Hartmut cheered her with the story of the première of *Arabella* in Dresden, when his beautiful mother had entertained Hitler's entourage in a box owned by her Jewish banker husband. In those days, before the Third Reich, being rich and Jewish had been fashionable, and many a Nazi had wooed an unsuspecting, grovelling financier. Then Mr and Mrs Weiss disappeared. Hartmut had lost track of his parents, but because he had been born blond and blue-eyed, Germany had not yet caught up with him.

'You'll need to get ready.'

Edith felt the soft skin of her mother's arm against her own and her heart fell over itself as Amy's catastrophe multiplied a thousandfold her urge to depart. Now, Edith could not wait to take the controls of the Oxford that had been impounded for so long by the unpleasant government authorities who were infinitely more hostile than any German she had ever known. With the money Beaverbrook had provided she would prove that there were women other than Jacqui Cochrane capable of crossing oceans from their native American shores and ending up in that dim little island on which firestorms now raged.

Burt Malone had never forgiven Edith for losing Raine's canister of film, but she had an otherworldly feeling that somehow they would all meet again in cataclysmic circumstances, not on this continent or perhaps even in this life . . .

It was time to go.

62

'It is hard to believe twelve whole months have passed since our operation began. This has been a year of grief for millions and the tragedy does not lessen. I fear we are in for a long siege. However, our achievements have been called "staggering" in this letter I have just received from the Board of BOAC, under whose banner ATA continues to operate. Some of you may have heard that there have been some small battles going on between the Corporation and the Ministry of Aircraft Production—we are so popular that our superiors are fighting for the privilege of saying they own ATA. We rise above it, of course—literally.'

Cold air, like a petty thief oblivious to war and ideologies, crept through the tiny cracks of the small church in South Audley Street, Mayfair. In recent weeks it had begun to be used as a place of worship for a meagre band of Americans, whose ranks were swelling in direct proportion to the number of Congressmen shocked into an awakening from hibernation. This was the second anniversary of the opening of the men's ferry pool and Commodore Gerard d'Erlanger had assembled all personnel for a gathering in this location, so special to his American flock. ATA people from various corners of Britain had cried with joy at the sight of rain. Weather had allowed some of them time to get to London, and now the familiar voice of the Commander-in-Chief of Air Transport Auxiliary warmed them in this darkest of winters.

'All of us,' droned d'Erlanger, 'were so dazed at Christmas 1940 as to have entirely forgotten the holiday. So much happened to us that there was barely time to breathe. Then, when we lost Amy, the whole nation mourned with Air Transport Auxiliary at all the stories that came out of that miserable day. Now she is one of the war dead and we wish her well in pilots' heaven, which I think we will all agree is probably much too noisy and smoky for Amy's liking. Like all of us, she wanted a death in harness, and for all we know she may still be up there somewhere—back in harness once more.'

Valerie Cobb fidgeted in her front pew seat, tormented by the information to which she had been privy concerning the last moments of Amy's life. Now, as a senior Commanding Officer, Valerie had the highest degree of responsibility within the RAF–ATA structure and would live with those secrets to her grave. Her own reinstatement had come as a shock when, on the day she had encountered poor pregnant Angelique wandering the streets of Whitehall, Valerie had been told her exceptional qualities of leadership and her resourcefulness were simply too badly missed by ATA for her to be kept in isolation any longer. Now as she listened to Gerard, her thoughts returned to her father's last comment before she had been freed:

'You are not exonerated. You are just needed.'

She was deeply gratified to be back amongst her pilots, and wondered if all fliers were born wanting only to be with other fliers. Her ears perked to the resonant voice bouncing off the walls of the church and she studied the handsome face of the man in uniform.

'Martin Toland's loss was a tragedy that has, at the very least, made ferrying a safer job to perform,' continued Gerard d'Erlanger. 'We are aware now that those wretched Beauforts all had the same fault, and we sacrificed one life and the disappearance of another pilot, to discover this awful technical imperfection. Should Oscar Toland ever be found, we hope he will forgive the makers of that flying machine. Pilots are always ready to forgive—basically, we are all softies at heart. Two brothers who had given their lives on earth to the service of God are no longer with us—one we know is gone for ever from the cheerful card games at White Waltham.'

Sitting in the quiet chapel and paying tribute to the selfless few who had defied the isolationist wave to help Britain, Nora Flint recalled Oscar's last words as he headed for his Beaufort. He had reminded her of Angelique's condition and said Martin was best left strapped in airborne, or the whole of women's ATA would cease being operational. Nora had taken his remark with a straight face and made a brief retort about the hundreds of Spitfires requiring transport from Vickers Supermarine.

Oscar thought he was in for a long war . . .

Now, Nora was wiping salty moisture from her weather-beaten nose, and wishing she had not taken a prominent seat in the room. She had never told Angelique about Oscar's quip because no-one had ever seen the actress pilot again after she had stepped into a taxi at Whitehall before the eyes of a newly reinstated Valerie Cobb.

That had been one hundred years ago, Nora told herself.

She had risen to the top of ATA and become an idol to the boss she now called Sam and who in turn was required to call her Ma'am. He was sitting next to her, deprived of Noel. Nora could not recall any time in the past year when the two had been apart, and she surmised Slater had manufactured some excuse for his absence today. He hated gatherings because gatherings meant people, and like Hitler he hated religion because religion meant caring. She could feel her nostrils moistening again and bowed her head. Inside her skull an organ was playing the same hymn she had heard at the memorial service for Amy Johnson held in St Martin-in-the-Fields, when Valerie had given a moving sermon amid the darkest winter ATA had ever known.

Then it had snowed and runways had frozen. All flying had stopped. And when it had begun again, death followed . . .

*　　　*　　　*

Nora looked up and her eyes met those of Alec and Marion.

D'Erlanger stood erect and his voice seemed to melt the frigid air circulating amongst the pilots:

'We all remember our other American, little Jo Howes.'

There was a cough in the corner of the assemblage; Bill Howes had not wanted to attend today but Hana Bukova had talked him into attending the anniversary meeting, if only to share in the group's remembrance of his only child. Hana had been alone in England for over a year now, and she was glad to be Bill's comfort after the calamity. Here amongst her new friends she watched him closely and placed her palm on the top of his hand as Gerard's words resonated around the four walls:

'In the months since her loss we have had more freak accidents, but in no way could they diminish the magnitude of her passing. Like Martin in the Beaufort, Jo's sacrifice enabled us to correct the heinous carelessness that had allowed carbon monoxide fumes to envelop her tiny cabin. She never had a chance to complete her course at Upavon, but the others have gone on to enormous achievements. One can't help thinking of our tiny, beautiful Yankee lass taken from us at the beginning of her life—smiling down at us now as we fly perfect aircraft she will never touch . . .'

Valerie had allowed her mind to wander yet again. She was utterly exhausted; only yesterday, the sixteenth consecutive Saturday on which she had worked, she had ferried a Percival Q.6 from Broxbourne for delivery to the Royal Navy at Lee-on-Solent. With its slightly aging electrically-operated variable-pitch propellers, she had had a disturbing time on her approach to Worthy Down, where all pilots had to land to obtain clearance to enter the defended southern coastal area. Jiggling levers, she could not get the rpm right and when she managed to press on to Lee she was gratified to be relieved of the creature on arrival at the foreshortened runway. After the cold of the flight and the disturbing fear the faulty machinery had caused, she was enraged to discover that the Percival was not meant for Naval communications work at all but for a senior officer's personal use: Duncan Worsley had been a motor racing

471

champion and had it not been for his enormous personal charm Valerie felt she could have murdered the man on the spot.

At that moment, Mosquitos were coming out of the factories in droves and her women were desperately needed for delivery of every kind of operational aircraft. Beaverbrook was becoming irritable with a debilitating asthma and some said he would soon resign his post as Minister of Aircraft Production. He had started it all, and she had not forgotten. Valerie was furiously proud of her girls, whose numbers had quadrupled in a year and whose nationalities now spanned five continents.

Though pride had never been a Cobb family vice, she could think of no other emotion to match her regard for these talented women. Looking across the nave Valerie allowed a minuscule smile to crease her mouth at the sight of the gorgeous Kay Pelham and her equally ravishing friend Lili Villiers. Australians seemed to possess a permanent suntan—their skin retained a vitality that glowed even in the dullest London street corner. Valerie was glad Edith Allam had been able to fulfil poor Beaverbrook's wishes, even if he was now too ill to appreciate the Antipodean beauties Edith had imported for ATA. None of the ferry pilots could believe the saga of the American's intercontinental journey, nor could they comprehend the paradise she had described upon landing in England. Edith had never seen anything so breathtaking as the magical sunsoaked heaven Kay and Lili called home. She had arrived in Australia exhausted, short of funds and embarrassed to the point of deep shame. She had

472

been astonished when upon her long-overdue arrival an assortment of enthusiastic Australians and New Zealanders had flocked to her side to do what Kay Pelham had called 'ATA auditions'.

Kay and Lili were striking beyond all criteria of physical grace, and their talent as pilots was equally superb. They were playfully rude about her delayed arrival, and Edith could only marvel at the girls' electrifying rapport.

Lili's industrialist father had produced piles of cash in exchange for a promise from Edith that she would endeavour to break the record for the number of Spitfires ferried around Britain, and that she would look after his little daughter. Lili had been nonplussed that her tragic dream of the hulking blond accomplice had come true. Unfortunately her dream of Amy had also become reality, news Edith had solemnly relayed on her arrival in Australia. Walking along the perfect beach and breathing in the pure air that seemed so charged with health, Edith had familiarized herself with box jellyfish and sea wasps in the baking January of the Great Barrier Reef, its unspoilt islands of mangrove swamps and rainforests staggering to behold. She had vowed to return some day, and if Kay and Lili were a microcosm of the stunning bodies running along the edges of Daydream Island, Edith knew she would have to pray hard for this war to come to a speedy end.

Now a year had passed and this was cold Mayfair in the depths of global conflict. Her ears registering the pleasant, unwarlike music swelling from the organ loft, Valerie marvelled at the possibility of her having recruited the cream of the entire crop of the world's women pilots for 1942

ATA. It had been a great pity, Valerie had thought privately, that lovely Hartmut had been snatched from Edith Allam's embrace by the British authorities upon her arrival, and that he had been deposited in an internment camp—when the blond Adonis could have been of such great use to ATA.

D'Erlanger had stormed at Valerie not to intervene on behalf of the dashing German after her Kranz débâcle, and Valerie had stormed back about the blond blue-eyed Adonis being a Jew . . .

*   *   *

Philadelphia's most famous daughter, the girl who had flown around the world in defiance of her nation's refusal to enter the European war, and who had triumphantly delivered the finest of the colonies' pilots on England's doorstep, now sat pale and rigid in a rear seat against the faded back wall. Edith's eyes seemed to have lost their incandescence in the short time she had spent back in Britain, but watching her Valerie could see the almost crazed determination that would make the girl such a vital element of the ATA working structure. Now that the United States had entered the war in the wake of Pearl Harbor, Edith seemed fired with delight in the present worldwide conflagration.

Music had come and gone inside Valerie's head as she too recalled a flash of Amy's memorial service, so hastily organized amid a winter of despair. Now, she noticed Edith's expression changing as the American watched with interest the arrival of a civilian couple who were taking their places at the end of a draughty row. Gerard's

474

voice was entrancing but now he was stopping to make way for the newly returned Gordon Selfridge.

'And so it came to pass', Selfridge was relating, 'that every Saturday afternoon all through that first year of ATA, a special bunch of young guys was brought to the airfield and handed cleaning cloths. These fellows shined every available surface to such excess that they were soon put on to Ansons to help our pilots in winding the undercarriage. I went away for half a year and when in February 1941 I came back to this land, your Air Defence Corps was taken over by the RAF and cadet training had begun.'

Edith Allam half-listened to Selfridge, her attention drawn to the incongruous pair who had moved into the row facing, and who seemed so uncomfortable in the company of flying people. It was only then that it dawned on her there were no ordinary civilians present. It might be, she theorized, that the sea of uniforms intimidated this shabby couple, whose grim hostility to their surroundings could be felt yards away. She had seen the man before, but a long time ago, before she circled the earth.

'ATC recruits were given wonderful uniforms,' Selfridge continued, 'and in their capacity as pilots' assistants they started flying in school Hudsons and Albemarles. Our most outstanding product was selected because of his exceptional energy and was meticulously trained for assisting in the first communications flights to the Continent. None of us will ever forget how he came back with Amy Johnson from France, full of the stories about Hurricane pilots recognizing her in the bar of the

Hotel Lion d'Or and showering her with champagne. Her young escort went on to be so damned good we lost him to the RAF and then as we all remember so darkly, a few days after receiving his commission, on his very first flight, we lost Cal March to the great Commodore in the sky . . .

Gordon's voice trailed off and Shirley Bryce, exhausted and distracted by the fact that she had not seen her mother in over a year, remained dry-eyed while others around her wept quietly. She felt unmoved by the whole ceremony, which she saw as a huge production number.

Why bother to celebrate two years of anything?

Why wallow in death?

Shirley's emotions bordered on shame as she spent the major portion of Gordon's homage to Cal March letting her mind wander to that magical moment thirteen months ago when she had reported to Hatfield just after dawn and been greeted by the sight of Valerie Cobb engrossed in paperwork. Magic had been extinguished when the two embarked upon their first conversation since the CO's exile. Valerie wanted to talk only of Friedrich, and even requested Shirley's companionship on her first visit to the internment camp, the location of which she was determined to extract from the authorities.

Could one believe it?

After registering Valerie's request, Shirley had slunk into a dark corner. Was there no end to the woman's idiocy? How could she continue to pursue destruction incarnate?

'Friedrich is a walking disaster area,' Shirley had hissed at a July dinner party, and Valerie just

476

laughed. Held to defy the devastation that had been heaped upon Southampton, the party had been at Hamble, where Shirley observed the intriguing repartee on the lips of Valerie and d'Erlanger. Some of the girls boasted over a lemonade that they had survived the bombings despite having watched the *son-et-lumière* show from the roof of Hamble aerodrome, and Stella told them to shut up before Val and Gerry, as she called them, threw her out of ATA.

After a more potent drink, d'Erlanger had said:

'I suppose there isn't really any reason why women shouldn't fly Hurricanes,' and Valerie jumped in with an opportunistic, 'Fine—when do they start?'

Every girl present at that soiree had been astonished by the steely magnetism that won Valerie every new deal for her ladies. In a few short days the Air Council, who would have been horrified at the idea in peacetime, approved the final arrangements and the women of ATA were cleared to fly every type of operational aircraft including all models of the famous fighter coming out of the Vickers Supermarine works.

At that moment women's ATA passed into an historic phase, and the Women With Wings had become Spitfire Girls.

*　　　*　　　*

Shirley had been more concerned that in the absence of Friedrich Valerie was not devoting more time to renewing their closeness, than in the progress of operational assignments from Battles, Harvards and Kestrel Masters to Hurricanes,

477

Mosquitos and the cherished Spits.

Now, on this February day, Shirley had cancelled yet another trip to see her mother in order to be near the glamorous Commanding Officer. Once more she would go back to her Hertfordshire lodgings depressed and longing for one of Angelique Florian's classic monologues full of extravagant mannerisms. Angelique was now only a memory and Shirley wondered if she was alone in missing the actress pilot. Kay Pelham boasted endlessly about joining the country's most illustrious Shakespeare Company and it was at these times Shirley wished Angelique had been there to silence the abrasive Australian.

'A few headlines in the paper and then they forget you. That was Amy's favourite expression.'

Hamilton Slade was speaking over the soft tones of the church's modest organ. He was thin and pale, his tall physique now skeletal inside the ATA blue. When he lost Amy the pilots had been awkward but he had devoured sympathy when it was offered. Most men hated pity but Hamilton's thinning body had no desire to reject the offerings.

'We have a few headlines inside our brains that flash by daily as we whizz through the skies in between balloons and dogfights. ATA remembers Cal March and Jo Howes, Martin Toland and his missing brother Oscar. We say hello to Amy and remember that in this past year our pilots have jumped in and out of over 15,000 aircraft. And we know that, wherever she is, her face is green with envy.'

Edith was staring at the civilian couple as the organ music swelled and abruptly she remembered Joe March the chauffeur and that odd day on the

Isle of Man when Hartmut's first love letter had been placed in her hand. Seeing him again after such a long gap reminded the American aviatrix of her bath at the Beaverbrook villa and of Errol Carnaby. Since then she had loved Hartmut Weiss. His sturdy torso had lain across what she had always thought was her unattractive body, but he had wanted her in a mild sort of way, making passionless love in the detached, mechanical manner she had somehow expected from her first white man. So little time had been spent with Errol that Edith had never memorized the contours of his chest, his belly, his fierce penis that scorched like an iron. She had never rested her face upon the smooth buttocks of which her tiny hands had been vaguely aware when he had gouged a molten dwelling place inside her, and from which she would have been powerless to extricate him in the crazed height of his ecstasy.

But she had had time to memorize the contours of her German. He had been pink and white all over, the crest of his manhood dusted with a fluffy cloak of blonde hairs. Edith had teased him about being a collector's item, but he had not understood her joke about the only circumcized towhead in the Luftwaffe. After great contortions of a cerebral nature, Hartmut would eventually achieve an erection, the inexperienced girl finding the effort boring and bemusing. He would enter and remain inside her for a while and sometimes she would experience small explosions of almost resentful pleasure. Now that he had been taken from her, however, she felt lonely, irritable, and glad when the memorial service meeting in the little Mayfair church had come to an end.

There was a large part of this Sunday left to live, and Edith wanted to tear away from the gathering and from Cal March's distraught parents, from the English pilots who had known Jo and Martin and Cal and Oscar, and who were now overcome with an almost unbearable collective grief. Edith wanted to leave this place and head for base, where aeroplanes waited for the weather to clear and where she could forget her uncomfortable longings. Valerie Cobb had been bitterly disappointed when Edith arrived in Britain without Errol in tow, and she had said something about war making women lose track of their men. Edith responded by saying she had lost track of her favourite woman, and Valerie walked away before Edith could finish saying:

'Raine Fischtal.'

Making her way down the front steps of the church, Edith knew she could never have attempted small talk. Hamilton and Gordon had the bug-eyed look of men trying to thwart the onset of tears, and Sam's had already come. The women were languid on the pavement, anxious for a cigarette and dabbing at their faces with handkerchiefs. She noticed Nora's smart monogram and wondered if any of these girls would invite her to their family homes. Her Australians were hovering away from the others and as Edith headed for Grosvenor Square, Gerard d'Erlanger gave what she thought was a small salute. Her pulse quickened for a moment and she contemplated the possibility that Florence Avenue might never see her again.

480

63

It was bad enough, thought Mrs Bennell, that girls like Shirley Bryce chose to leave their mothers' cosy homes to live in lodgings, but to put off visiting for a year was unnatural. Cleaning the latest room full of neatly accumulated ATA memorabilia, the landlady of The Stone House placed her hand on a large chunk of hardboard, which had been leaning against a wall and gathering dust. Angelique's Ouija board had been appropriated by Shirley after the Florian girl's departure—which some had called desertion. Shortly after she had left, Noel Slater stopped by to drink in The Stone House bar.

'In the regular services she would have been court-martialled,' he shouted. 'Fancy walking out of ATA.'

'Actually, she *flew* out of ATA,' said Josef Ratusz, his bleary eyes the product of a relentless year during which he had had five days leave.

'Don't think it has escaped our attention', Slater continued, 'that Florian went off pregnant in a perfectly serviceable aircraft.'

'None of us could do that, so it makes her special,' Josef said.

'*Bollocks*, Joe.' Slater was becoming noisy and Mrs Bennell emerged to glare.

'Why do you hate her so much?' Josef asked, rubbing his furrowy forehead.

'Yes. What has she ever done to hurt you, Noel?' asked Mrs Bennell.

Slater studied her before he spoke. 'BOAC

should never have let d'Erlanger bring in his girlfriends. Women haven't the co-ordination to handle aircraft in a pressurized situation, and one of these days a whole factory-load of things will go down in flames because some stupid ATA girl has let her mind wander to her last amorous encounter.'

Mrs Bennell's hand hit Noel's face hard, and her hard palm left an angry weal on the flight engineer's pasty complexion. He had smiled afterwards and she felt a marked woman. As he left the bar with a sheepish Josef, she knew he would be back again, his contempt needing constant release.

She withdrew to her kitchen that evening, still numb from the job she had had to perform earlier in the day. Her first loss through fatality had left a large collection of ATA paraphernalia in her room and it had to be turned over to the Commanding Officer. Having received the unbelievable news that Jo Howes had departed this life through asphyxiation, her first impulse had been to run, apron flapping in the rainy wind, straight into the Hatfield Ops room and register a formal accusation of murder. Mrs Bennell had seen Noel Slater admiring the lean figure of Cal March, the boy's unworldly clumsiness being a source of fascination for the very senior ground engineer. Some of the girls had told her of his unhappy life, but she was never one to value past histories and had informed them he had been born wicked.

It was time now to re-let Angelique Florian's room, but Mrs Bennell had heard that a new women's ferry pool was opening. Her ATA girls would be reporting to places other than Hatfield and White Waltham, and the empty rooms might not be filled. Carrying a large pile of *Theatre World* magazines out on to the landing, she looked back into Shirley's room and smiled at the tidiness of the ground engineer, who was of late bringing her sex so much distinction as the RAF's most-sought-after technician. Any aircraft could be placed under her jurisdiction and she would adapt to its specifications, remedying faults and rendering the machine airworthy in time for its next sojourn into death games.

'Are those up for grabs?'

Dropping the magazines on the wooden floor, Mrs Bennell watched as they spilled across the landing, several copies slipping down the stairs as if the beautiful faces on their covers were propelled by some inner spirit.

'They belonged to Angelique,' she answered, the newcomer's accent now familiar to the landlady's ears. Kay Pelham's bronzed beauty was disquieting, as she lingered on the landing and studied Mrs Bennell's face.

'Could I have them?'

'If Angelique returns, you must give them back.'

'Noel says she's gone for a Burton.'

'What a terrible expression that is,' the landlady muttered, going to her knees to collect the scattered *Theatre World*s. 'Why can't flying people just say someone has passed on to their reward?'

'Noel Slater tells all the good jokes, you know,' Kay said, bending down to help.

'I should steer clear of him, my girl,' Mrs Bennell asserted, their faces close and Kay's thick chestnut hair brushing the other woman's cheek.

'Our relationship is—intense,' Kay said quietly.

Rising slowly, Mrs Bennell felt a tightness in her lungs that seemed to slow her train of thought. 'Whatever "intense" means to an Australian, I expect you are implying he has made overtures.'

'God almighty, Mrs B.'

'I've never known him to like *flying* alongside a woman pilot.'

Kay looked up from the floor, where she had spread the magazines at the woman's feet.

'This has nothing to do with being up in the air,' she chortled, giving Mrs Bennell one of the smirks the other girls so dreaded.

'People do say things about actresses, Kay.'

'Blow me—I don't have to be an actress to get Noel going!' Kay collected the magazines all at once and rose, her smirk fading as their eyes met. 'Did you know I met him in Brisbane? He was over on a secret mission, out of uniform. I nearly died on the spot when I turned up here and there he was, all kitted out to be a flight engineer. Let me tell you, Mrs B: dressed like a businessman, he's okay.'

'Noel's never been of interest to any woman from the day he materialized in flying circles,' Mrs Bennell observed.

'Bachelors are fun to disarm,' Kay said. 'Don't you think men are fun when they're under you and they're like moaning puppies, in your control because you suck and drain away their power until they cry?'

Mrs Bennell glared at Kay.

'Try going down on Noel and you'll see a fiend become a pup.'

'Thank you very much but the prospect leaves me cold,' said Mrs Bennell. 'In any case what

484

you are suggesting is shameful for a respectable spinster.'

Kay reached to pinch her landlady's cheek.

'Pilots are poets, Mrs B! They have no shame—it's a waste of time when you spend your life inside a tin deathtrap.'

A clatter on the stairs startled the pair.

'That last bit was rich—why did you have to stop?' shouted Stella, clumping up the stairs in ATA boots and trousers.

'What is that you are wearing?' Mrs Bennell demanded.

'Valerie Cobb does it again—she's arranged for trousers to be standard issue for flying,' Stella announced.

'Noel will just hate all that,' Kay said, pushing past them as Stella and Mrs Bennell exchanged looks. Marvelling at the resilience of the young pilots, the landlady reflected on the rapidity with which her consignment of girls had sublimated grief. They had thrown themselves into ATA ferrying with redoubled vigour upon their return from the memorial ceremony. Though Mrs Bennell knew their lost fliers had not been forgotten, the girls had laughed and eaten and smoked for several days afterwards in between perilous flights across winter and balloons, while their landlady wept incessantly over the empty beds.

'How's your sex life, then?' asked Kay, running long fingers through rich hair. Stella wondered how many men she had touched with that delicate, superbly manicured hand.

'I'm afraid that has never entered into my realm,' Stella said, blushing at her own fantasies. 'Perhaps

485

I shall steal Gordon Selfridge from old Nora,' she continued. 'Did I tell you I've finally had a letter from my old ballet master Grunberg? I've written him once a month for a year and this is the first reply. I wonder if any of my correspondence ever got through to him.'

'Where is he, then?' Kay asked, standing in the middle of the stairway.

'Detained—the government arrested all the German-speaking people they could find and poor old André was one of them. It's all so bloody stupid: when you think of what Hitler is doing to Jews over there, and here they are in Britain under suspicion.'

'This is the craziest country!' hooted Kay. 'Men in red jackets howling their heads off because some frigging fox is running loose, and spending weekends in freezing cold houses because a couple of old geezers want to shoot birds—crazy!'

Following the Australian back down the stairs, Stella thrust her hands into the smartly designed pockets. 'We've a busy day ahead because the WASP is still surviving off Malta and she wants a new supply of Spits,' she said. Her minuscule figure seeming to swim in the flaring trousers.

'God, I'd love to do a Malta run,' Kay said, still laden with the magazines. With her free hand she raided Mrs Bennell's precious biscuit ration and headed for the front porch.

They marched briskly to the airfield, and as a timid sun began to spread a white halo upon the gleaming aircraft, the girls shared an unspoken thought: once more, fire from the sky had not fallen upon their beloved Hatfield.

'We're all moving into Hamble,' Stella said.

486

'Mrs B hardly sees any of us now, and after this week we'll only be here for brief postings when we come up from Southampton.'

'Is this because of Malta?' asked Kay.

'Absolutely,' Stella responded. 'Pilots at White Waltham are being despatched to collect those Spits from the Maintenance Units in Prestwick, and at some point the planes have got to end up on the WASP. Anthony Seifert tells me they had to abandon a plan to take the Spits by road to Glasgow because of a narrow bridge that got in the way! Now it seems our lot are flying them in to Renfrew.'

'God Almighty!' exclaimed Kay. 'Renfrew's got a teeny-weeny landing run, for Christ's sake. The approaches are hell even when the wind is is on your side.'

They had reached the main building at Hatfield Ferry Pool and walked briskly into the common room. Lili Villiers and Marion Harborne were already kitted up for a flight.

'After the Spits arrive,' Stella continued, 'they are put on Queen Mary lorries and taken to the George V docks, straight on to the carrier's deck. The worst bit happens when the poor Yank sods sail to Malta with our best of British fighter planes: I've heard the runways on the island are booby-trapped by the Germans.'

'Charming,' Kay said, approaching Lili and slapping her on the back. 'We're talking about your magic family aeroplanes.'

'My father's artwork is being hammered in Malta,' Lili said, not looking up from the chit she grasped in an already gloved hand.

A large collection of ATA women hovered near

the Ops Room. The weather having lifted, they awaited their ferry chits eagerly. They had spent a series of interrupted days and were furious at being unable to get back to Hamble, which now served as their permanent base.

'Hell's bells—it's charabanc time,' Shirley Bryce shouted, as the group realized their brief was to board a taxi Anson and be transported back to Hamble.

The squadron raced to the runway and clambered into the trusted aircraft, their designated pilot Stella Teague. Lately she had become prone to mishaps and the girls had been wearing their parachutes at the ready when forced to fly as her passengers. On a recent ferry job in a Hurricane she had been forced to belly-land; convincing the Accidents Committee that she was not at fault had been more perilous than the flight itself. On another occasion she had trouble controlling a Boston and had only been saved from crashing by being caught in tennis court netting along the approach to the airfield runway . . .

'It's the witch again,' muttered Marion, swinging her kit into the generous space behind the pilot's seat. 'For the benefit of anyone who hasn't yet had the privilege of flying with Stella, she has a habit of landing in people's fish-ponds.'

The early arrivals waited for Sally and Barbara but soon the Anson was full and the familiar sound of its twin engines drowned out conversation as Stella took it skilfully into the air. As the most senior officer now attached to this group, Shirley sat next to the pilot and Stella released one hand from the controls to give the ground engineer a friendly punch as they roared over the Hatfield perimeter. In the rear, Marion turned pale green as the aeroplane gained altitude, her expression one of dread.

'Don't you dare be sick on me,' shouted Kay, facing her in the row of heavily-kitted lady pilots.

Marion looked away and shut her eyes.

'Do you think we ought to turn back?' Lili asked, her fingers pressing into the arm of Marion's thick flying suit.

'I'm pregnant,' Marion said, turning her head to the side and wincing.

'That's good news!' Kay exclaimed. 'Let's drink to it.' She reached inside her kit and produced a half bottle of choice champagne. Five pairs of eyes gazed with astonishment at the contraband.

'How the hell did you get hold of that, Pelham?' asked Stella, turning around to see why her cargo had become so restless.

'Mrs Harborne's in the club,' Delia Seifert replied. All at once the girls were rocked by turbulence and Marion covered her face with her hands, only to be jolted once more by the champagne cork popping.

'You could cause a catastrophe doing that!' yelled Stella, scowling.

'Who gives a shit, mate?' Kay bellowed beck. 'We'll have to drink straight from the bottle, chicks.' She passed the magnificent nectar around, its cheerful foil neck losing its allure as Marion pushed it away with trembling fingers.

Levity was short-lived as Stella was forced to manoeuvre the Anson away from what she thought were enemy aircraft straying into outer London airspace. They had left Hertfordshire behind, and as she took her valuable cargo away from danger

489

Stella wondered if this had been their last visit to Mrs Bennell's for a very long stretch of time. She groaned to herself as Kay's resonant voice broke the welcome silence:

'Make room, you lot of Sheilas!'

Kay stood in the crowded Anson, and as the others watched she began to disrobe. Sally pinched Marion's forearm and for the first time she opened her eyes, offering a vague smile at the sight of Kay's striptease.

'This is what's known as taking emergency action,' Kay said, now down to her brassière and panties.

'What is she doing now?' Stella demanded, turning quickly but straining to keep her aircraft on a safe course for Hamble.

'I've got a big date at the other end,' Kay announced, pulling a delicately stitched party dress from her kit. Stepping into it, she adjusted her bra straps. 'I may have to do without this.' She began to remove her brassière.

'Look out!' Shirley screamed, as a sudden, deafening roar of fighter engines shook the giant Anson like a peapod suspended over a maelstrom.

'Dear God,' Marion said, gripping her abdomen.

'Hold tight!' Stella shouted, as the roaring drowned their voices and made the heavily laden transport plane shudder.

'I'm staying right where I am, Teague,' warbled Kay, slipping into the dress as she struggled to maintain her footing.

'You are being ordered to do so, Kay,' Stella snapped.

Their voices were barely audible as Barbara Newman leaned forward to steal a look outside through the plane's windows, which, unusually, had been cleaned to perfection before take-off by an Air Cadct.

'We've an escort, for Christ's sake,' she screamed.

Outside, a squadron of RAF fighters had come alongside the Anson, its crew straining to get a better view of Kay's striptease. Delia waved through her tiny window, her heart thumping at the sight of Britain's foremost air warriors whose humanity, she reflected, had made them seek a brief moment of folly, but whose presence made her feel indestructible. She turned to Shirley and grinned. Looking out of her side window once more, Delia waved again and realized the men would stay by her side until Hamble, whatever their ultimate destination, including oblivion.

With a thumbs-up, the aviatrix wished them Godspeed.

64

An April snowfall had covered the British Isles and as Stella's cargo tumbled out of her Anson she glanced angrily at the layer of grey cloud overhead. Her approach to Hamble had been harrowing as visibility deteriorated, and now she calculated it might be a day before the girls could move on with their ferrying allocations. Pilots were handed sandwiches and a flask and were expected to sit in draughty huts at factory airfields while the snow and ice melted, waiting for that moment when visibility might rise above twenty yards. Stella had delivered the longest-standing members of woman's ATA and hoped Nora Flint would be able to manufacture some witchcraft to alleviate the weather wait.

'We need Angelique's Ouija board,' Barbara said, walking with the others to the main headquarters of Hamble Ferry Pool.

'Perhaps the weather is a blessing,' said Sally. 'I gather Anthony Seifert has come down from Number One Pool with a surprise for Delia. I don't think she has yet registered the fact they share the same surname.'

'There are loads of Seiferts in the world,' Barbara said testily. Her image of Anthony, intoxicated beyond all recognition after the death of Cal March, came sweeping back and she wanted to alter the course of the conversation.

'Delia knows him only as Anthony,' Sally continued, her hair now cut short, accentuating her striking features that were covered in a reddish glow brought on by the cold mist. 'After all this time she hasn't twigged.'

'*What* hasn't she twigged?' demanded Barbara.

'Everybody has come to think that if he isn't a long-lost relation, he must surely be in love with her, the way he follows her about the pools,' Sally replied triumphantly as they walked on.

Barbara felt a sense of relief as the image of drunken Anthony, staggering around her father's house on a Sunday afternoon, came in waves to her mind's eye. He was invited to tea but Lord Newman had been called to an emergency meeting of Ministers and Anthony broke down in her lone presence. She had plied him with brandy and soon he began unravelling a story she found horrifying and at once attractive in its sordidness. After five stiff drinks he divulged a secret he must have kept bottled for nearly quarter of a century, and she had wondered ever since why he had chosen her as his confidante. Then a memory flooded back: just before her death her mother had told her about a little boy-child born in her house on Sabbath Yom Kippur . . .

An American accent broke her train of thought:

'Ready for the long endurance test?' asked Edith Allam, her small figure looking plump and bulky in the heavy winter flying suit.

'What endurance test?' queried Barbara.

'I'm sure you know about the waiting time at the factories,' Edith replied.

'Of course—I thought you had organized another round-the-world expedition and were expecting us to accompany you,' Barbara said, smiling at Sally, who was walking alongside.

'Sean Vine tells me that film you lost has been sold for thousands to Beaverbrook,' Sally said, falling into step with the American.

'Yes, well, I have an important visit to make soon,' said Edith, 'and I think it has something to do with taking pictures. Somebody very high up in the RAF—a real big shot—wants to see me and I bet he needs an aerial photographer extraordinaire.'

'Your modesty would flatten the Luftwaffe,' hissed Sally.

They entered the Ops Room and Nora Flint looked over her reading glasses at the aviatrix from Philadelphia.

'Did I hear you say you had to visit someone?' Nora asked, her voice resounding with its usual chill.

'Yes, but it's nothing important,' Edith replied.

'Is it ATA business?' Nora pressed.

'No, CO Flint, not that I know of.' Edith smiled and wondered if Nora had forgotten her days as a meat-market girl. Since Cal March's death, Nora had become even more cold and distant, her sexless gait causing collective giggles when Gordon Selfridge tagged along behind his beloved CO.

'You look too happy for this mystery journey to be classified as business,' Nora commented.

'Oh, Nora, give the girl a break,' chimed Lili Villiers, smoking in a corner.

Edith walked up to Nora and stood so close as to feel the Commanding Officer's breath.

'Dear old CO,' Edith began, 'what I have to do could be explosive. I am told it is Top Secret but I can reveal that I have been summoned to meet Wing Commander Charlie Buxton in Norfolk and I do not intend letting the guy down.'

'We have a siege on our hands,' Nora said, removing her spectacles as the din of newly arrived girls filled the room. 'You are needed, Edith—for God's sake, Sally says that when the weather lifts we may have a clear pocket for three days, and that means Spits being rescued from mothballs.'

'Please let me go now,' Edith said solemnly. 'I will be back in twenty-four hours, I promise.'

'Wait until next week, then you can go,' Nora said, watching her pilots crowd around the big Ops table. 'I shall notify the Wing Commander that you will be released as and when.'

Turning away, Edith shut her eyes and tried to imagine the village of Weston Longville, where Charlie Buxton had begun to negotiate with the

494

Americans a massive plan to turn the area into a major centre for RAF–USAAF operations. She pictured a vast field with one stately home situated in its centre, the inhabitants remotely aware of a war and of the local ramifications it now held in store. Edith was awakened from her imaginings by a voice she had not heard in months of non-stop flying.

'I ate this bloody sweat-and-trickle pudding!' Hana Bukova had settled herself in the canteen.

'Any news of your mom?' asked Edith, settling into an adjoining seat.

'Nothing,' Hana replied, her mouth brimming over with custard. 'That man who paid for her last trip is in this country, you know. I am going to find him.'

'How the Hell do you know that, honey?' Edith asked.

'Honey—honey—I wish I had some!' she exclaimed, looking down at the pudding. 'Listen, Edith—Stella Teague has a letter—it's from her ballet master—the one who disappeared. In roundabout way this guy is my last link with Momma. I have not heard from Poppa in a year, but this man Grunberg—he knows Kranz.'

'Kranz?' Edith asked, sitting up. This man had to be Friedrich.

'Yeah—Kranz used to do business with my Poppa in the Warsaw Jew Settlement, and as I say, he arranged the airlift when my Momma piloted his family.'

'I think they call it the Warsaw Ghetto in these parts,' Edith said, cringing at the imagery of skeletons and cousins she would never know. 'What was this guy's full name?'

'Friedrich Kranz—his son was my friend.' Hana drew the photograph of Benno from her pocket. It had frayed but the corner markings were still distinct. She handed it to the American.

'Fischtal—Berlin!' shrieked Edith, gripping the snapshot lightly.

'What this is?' asked Hana.

'I know her—she's an old friend of mine, but I've lost track of her, and of Zuki,' Edith said quietly.

'Who are these people you talk about?'

'Friends,' Edith replied, handing back the photograph of the hauntingly handsome boy. She knew by now his dark eyes would be seeing atrocities to last him a lifetime. 'Do you know the whereabouts of this man Kranz?'

Hana pushed away the now cold pudding bowl. 'You must understand I have been told to tell nobody, not even Valerie.'

'But Valerie! . . .' exclaimed Edith.

'Yes?'

'He's her boyfriend.' As the words left her mouth, Edith knew she had spoken too freely, and Hana was appropriately mortified.

'He is Benno's father! He has a wife—Momma was rescuing the whole family.'

'Maybe I'm thinking of someone else,' said Edith, smiling at the Polish pilot as her heart pounded at the prospect of Valerie's joy if such information were ever to reach her ears. 'Can you tell me where he is, just as a matter of interest?'

'He has been taken from the Isle of Man to some place in Norfolk.'

'Where in Norfolk?'

Hana rose.

'Please do not ask me any more questions,

496

comrade,' she pleaded. 'Now I go play cards.'

Watching her stroll away, Edith observed Hana's lack of confidence, which communicated itself in the Polish girl's awkward gait. Edith vowed to herself she would extricate the information about Friedrich—if only to make Valerie happy for the rest of a cruel war. Hartmut had been interned and it had never occurred to Edith he might be lying in a bunk alongside Friedrich. ATA had come to accept the theory that Kranz had been separated from other internees and was uncontactable, hence Valerie's inability to trace his whereabouts. Some of the girls thought it cruel that Sir Henry, whose connections would have given him access to such information, had withheld the facts from his pining daughter.

'Did you hear about our escort?'

Edith looked up at the pale countenance looking down.

'We had a squadron of RAF boys alongside the Anson,' Delia explained. 'It all started because the Aussie took off her flying suit and changed into a dress in full view of the heavens.'

'I wish I had been there to watch,' interjected Anthony Seifert, who had seated himself at the table and appropriated Hana's cold leftover pudding.

'Would anyone know if Stella Teague is still around?' Edith asked.

'She's off in a Spit,' Delia replied.

Edith rose without a word, her mind now fixated on the village of Weston Longville and the secret of Hana Bukova. As she left the canteen, Anthony gave a mock salute.

'Don't you like our Yank?' asked Delia, sitting

down with reluctance.

'It doesn't matter,' he responded, taking her hand. He had never touched her until now. Delia could see snowflakes in the window, and she was pleased. It meant she could stay and he could keep talking.

65

Shirley had left Mrs Bennell's during a light snowstorm and walked through slush to meet the Commanding Officer before departing for London. When she had told Delia she would not be proceeding to Hamble for the Malta transports, the girls who were eavesdropping on their conversation whooped with laughter. It was assumed Shirley would finally visit her mother when she had run out of cash, and as the ground engineer kept a close watch on her collection of bank notes, this news had brought mirth to Hatfield Ops Room. Now, all the girls had moved on in the big Anson, its innards having been checked by Shirley herself before they departed.

On this cold, misty morning she felt the emptiness of the airfield in the absence of the ferry group.

'Angelique would have loved these new Mosquitos,' said Valerie Cobb, giving Shirley a rare hug around her shoulders.

Standing alongside a giant map of Britain and Europe the two women felt a tension between them that had accelerated since the Commanding Officer's reappearance and reached a peak during this weather-bound fortnight.

'Tell me about them,' Shirley said, overcome by the scent that was unique to Valerie and to which she had grown so accustomed during their happy caravan years.

'We've only been able to get our hands on a few but they look very versatile. They're being used for target marking, and in a couple of cases for bombing. I am told they can carry a four-thousand-pounder. In one section of RAF they're deploying Mossies as long-range fighters, day and night. And some of their boys have been sent out to do aerial reconnaissance photography. I'll wager our Edith Allam would love to get herself ensconced on board with a camera.'

'Don't encourage her or she'll pinch a Mossie—like the way Angelique scarpered,' Shirley said, moving away from Valerie's closeness.

'Angelique did not scarper—she had some sort of Ministerial approval for her bizarre mission, whatever it may have been. God be with her.'

'Are these Mosquitos coming out in swarms? asked Shirley.

'Not like Spits,' Valerie replied. 'And they do have drawbacks. You need to be a concert violinist to master the throttle on take-off. Maximum boost is eighteen pounds per square inch.'

'What's the bomber version like?' asked Shirley, leaning against the table and wishing this day would stretch into eternity as she noticed the deep creases above Valerie's determined chin and the eyes that had become even more piercing with age.

'Mossie bombers', Valerie continued, 'have a two-handed grip on the control column. Lord help you if your take-off acceleration is poor—it needs a fiendish lot of power to keep it in the sky when the undercarriage is down.'

'Where are the buggers?'

'They're expecting to churn out several hundred down the road, here at Hatfield, my love,' Valerie said, studying the giant map. 'So—are you ready for the mother-daughter débâcle?'

Shirley had grown accustomed to the sudden changes of subject that invariably peppered a conversation with the woman she still regarded as her partner.

'I'd love to see one of these new Mossies before I visit Mum and hit reality head-on,' Shirley said, willing her eyes to twinkle.

'You just want to put off the visit until it's too late.'

'Rubbish, Val,' retorted Shirley. 'This Mossie business is making me drool. What sort of engine does it carry?'

'Two Merlins.' Valerie eyed her quizzically. Had the girl lost all sense of emotional attachment, even to the extent of not missing her own mother? 'Incidentally,' she continued, 'it was a Yank— Ambassador Winant—who saw the first demonstration with me. He wants a few hundred to be made in Canada by Packard! It was all highly secret until a few months ago.'

'What a pity you can't be privy to information about Friedrich's whereabouts,' Shirley said quietly.

'Believe me,' Valerie said, 'I would trade a top-priority demonstration of Mosquitos for a lead on my darling.'

'What nonsense!' screamed Shirley, throwing her kit to the floor. 'How can you refer to him that way? The man is nothing to you. After all this time, he ought to be a blank page.'

'After all this time, are you so devoid of feeling?' Valerie demanded.

'Devoid of feeling!' mocked Shirley. 'Pilots are flying all over the place at this very moment, in plenty of horrific, heart-stopping, death-defying predicaments, all at your personal behest as head of this organization, but all you can do is sit at a desk and dwell on some oversexed married man.'

'That is an outrage!' Valerie shouted back, her voice out of control. 'I feel you ought to know that it is being put about that you and I have most definitely had some sort of unusual relationship, and do you know why?'

Shirley's face was aflame.

'There isn't any place you go,' Valerie continued, 'where someone doesn't pick up on your alleged pining for me, and I want it to stop, Shirl.'

'I've intimated nothing.'

'You've said enough and moped enough,' Valerie murmured, her heart racing.

'Career is your sole concern, Val, and if I have to be thrown by the wayside, you'd do it for your own advancement.'

'If I were that sort of woman, Shirley, would I have got involved with Friedrich?'

Silence fell over the room.

Then Shirley said:

'Mum has never forgiven me the crazy suicide business, Val.'

'Go now, and give her a happy time,' suggested Valerie, her hair glowing even in the dreary light of a misty April.

'It's been more than a year—the last time I had

quality time with Mum was Marion Harborne's wedding day. Everybody was still alive then.'

'Don't think about our losses—I've thirty more women joining and it looks now as if the sky's the limit.'

'Promise me a Mosquito, Val,' Shirley said as they walked from the building on to the quiet forecourt. It was not yet eight o'clock and ice covered the landing strip. Shirley hated arguments, but Valerie was the only person she had ever known who could generate such uncontrollable rages within her soul. Stella Teague had told her that Grunberg knew Kranz and that Valerie's lover played word games with him every night. It was something Shirley would not divulge. Now, she looked at the fiercely attractive woman and laughed to herself. Recently thirty-three members of the male crew at White Waltham had been polled in a rare moment of mirth. To a man, they had said they would rather be stranded on a desert island with Valerie Cobb than with Rita Hayworth.

'You'll have your Mosquitos,' Valerie then said quietly.

And suddenly Shirley knew that was the most her partner could ever offer.

66

Watching Shirley depart on the first leg of her journey to London, Valerie ruminated about Friedrich. Had she *really* wanted to see him, would she not have found a way? On that last day in exile, when in the presence of Haydon and Shelmerdine her father had lain down conditions for her return to service, she had left Whitehall determined to locate her lover. One of Sir Henry's conditions had been to prohibit Valerie from seeing Kranz, the thief and madman, until the war was over. She had pleaded with Cobb to reveal Friedrich's whereabouts but Haydon had interrupted them, fuming on endlessly about individuals dangerous to national security and she had abandoned her desperate quest. Now, alone at Hatfield, she had put thoughts of Friedrich aside as ATA mobilized to move its women to Hamble, her job that of figurehead more than squadron leader.

Suddenly there was a distant roar and Valerie turned around to see an Anson approaching.

'This is some sort of cock-up,' Valerie said, watching the taxi aircraft doing a circuit. When it had made its final approach she braced herself to witness a crash but the skilled pilot mastered the treacherous surface and skidded to a halt several yards from the main building. Valerie marched to the aircraft and strained to identify the emerging pilot.

'Sorry to arrive unannounced,' shouted the thickly clad flier from above, the height of the Anson making disembarking a major undertaking.

'This is highly irregular,' Valerie shouted back.

'Who are you?' demanded the pilot, removing fogged-up goggles from a heavily wrapped head.

'Commanding Officer Cobb.'

'Valerie—shit!'

As she descended Edith Allam was followed by a skeletal man, his ATA uniform grotesquely baggy and his gait pathetically limp.

'Why have you brought back the Anson?' Valerie

503

asked.

'It was a special mission,' she replied, offering Valerie a good-natured form of salute. 'Do you remember our old buddy Hamilton Slade?'

Coming up behind her, his steps laboured, Hamilton looked a hundred years old, his hair white and eyes sunken into cavernous gullies.

'You've been in one of those death camps, haven't you?' asked Valerie lightly.

Silence followed.

'I'm on my way to see Dame Dazzle,' Hamilton then said weakly.

'For God's sake, why?' the CO asked as they walked from the Anson towards the shelter of the common room.

'This is home for me, and I'd like to end my days at my local hospital,' Slade replied.

'All you need is a meal, for goodness sake,' said Edith, stopping at the front entrance.

Valerie turned to her and placed a hand on her waist, squeezing and letting go. 'It's good to see you again.' Valerie said, her eyes not leaving those of the sturdily built American. 'Shirley is off to see her mum, you know.'

'About bloody time, too,' Hamilton said.

As the threesome entered the common room of Hatfield Ferry Pool, Edith grasped Valerie's wrist.

'I've contravened my CO's orders, Valerie, and I am AWOL from Hamble, to be honest.'

'I thought you had done this for me, old girl,' murmured Hamilton.

Edith held her grip on Valerie.

'You and I are going to see an aircraft manufacturer today,' said the American.

'Whatever for?' protested Valerie, extricating

herself from Edith's grip.

'He calls himself Pavel Wojtek.'

67

Hamilton was astonished when a sea of young male faces looked up at him from their hospital beds. Dame Dazzle had walked with him from the specialist unit and had assigned him a bed between two badly injured patients.

'Because they are not RAF we are allowed to treat these chaps,' said the Dame, supporting Hamilton by the arm and leading him to his assigned bed in the ward.

'Who are they?' he asked.

'One is called Sam and the other is Ludo,' she responded, her stern expression not having changed since the day Hamilton had had his cricket injury treated twenty years before.

'What sort of a name is Ludo for a "chap", as you call them?'

'He's Romanian.'

'I've not come across him in ATA.' Hamilton had begun to undress, fingering the pyjamas neatly folded on the bed.

'We are told he drifted in to Britain, as they say.'

'Does he speak English?'

'He speaks enough English for our girls to have determined he is lovesick for one Hana something-or-other.'

Hamilton was sitting on the side of the bed, his legs protruding like a pair of knobbly gentlemen's canes in a corner of a quiet London club.

'We've a Hana in ATA,' said Hamilton, struggling to raise his limbs up on to the bed.

'Oh, heavens, yes,' the elderly matron murmured. 'That Hana is one and the same.'

'Is she indeed? Why has no-one contacted the ferry pool?' Hamilton asked.

'Someone did—several times, but the girl insisted she'd never heard of him and put the phone down. I was half tempted to bill ATA for the cost of the telephone connection. This is wartime, you know.'

'As if I didn't, my dear,' he said, wanting to sleep. 'Do the patients still refer to you as Dame Dazzle behind your back?'

'Please sit up,' she said, ignoring his query. 'You're due for an injection.'

As Matron left him he settled back against the sweet-smelling pillows. Closing his eyes, Hamilton could see the controls of fifty different types of aircraft glowing brightly against a dark background. During the past year he had completed more ferrying jobs than any other man in ATA including Josef Ratusz, who ran a close second to Slade's record. In one month he had delivered sixty-one aircraft, the majority operational, having spent twenty-four hours and thirty minutes airborne. He had to forget Amy, and if marathon ferrying meant obliteration of his finest memories, he would continue tackling the Priority One delivery orders while other pilots dropped with fatigue.

The loss of Amy had dealt Hamilton a double blow: he had been the recipient of scathing jokes about the mystery man she had been alleged to have carried in the doomed Oxford, and his private grief was a constant, throbbing despair compounded by the cruel insinuations. Was it possible she had taken a passenger? It irked Hamilton that Valerie Cobb had not insisted on more accurate information from the highest authorities. Did she know something to which the rest of ATA must never be privy?

Hamilton wondered why his injection was taking so long. He opened his eyes and looked at the men on either side: there was dear old Sam Hardwick, obviously drugged to the earlobes and seriously injured.

Hamilton's bony face creased into a smile as he thought of poor Noel pining for his best mate, and then chided himself for concocting lewd accusations that were as groundless as those heaped against Amy. Was it human nature, he reflected, that made people want to damage those who had never damaged others?

There was Hitler, massacring millions, the vast majority of whom had done only good works their entire lives. There was his very own Amy, having brought distinction to her sex, her profession and to her country, now vilified because she might not have died an innocent. Hamilton had known affection and loyalty from the women of ATA after the tragedy, with not one of the Spitfire girls—as he so loved to call them—creating fictions about Amy's last moments. In this year he had yearned to be sent to Hatfield, where on brief stopovers he could laugh at the permutations Hana Bukova imposed upon the English language, and commiserate with Delia and the other lady pilots on the technical shortcomings of one hundred types of flying machine.

With the men he could not be so mirthful, and it seemed odd to him that in the wake of his loss he could find solace only amongst females in the same profession. Delia's dismissal of the rumours about Amy, and the other girls' condemnation of a wartime press obsessed with an aviatrix's sexual habits, gave Hamilton Slade the will to continue to live.

'Sobibor?'

Hamilton turned to the other bed alongside to find a staring Ludo.

'Slade, Hamilton, ATA White Waltham.'

'Oswiecem?'

'Oh, God, bring my injection!' Hamilton turned away.

'You have suffered?'

'Great Scot—you do speak English,' Slade exclaimed.

In the bed on the other side, Sam stirred and issued a small groan.

'Look, what is your name, old fellow?' Slade asked.

'Name? Ludo—just Ludo, please.'

Hamilton could see Dame Dazzle approaching with a small tray on which were arrayed tubes and needles.

'You think I've been on the Eastern Front?'

Ludo waved a hand at him weakly and turned away, his face pale and miserable.

'Time for a little discomfort!' announced Matron, flashing the dazzling smile that had given her the twenty-year-old nickname.

'I say, Ludo,' Hamilton said, sitting up and leaning towards the Romanian's bed, 'do you know Hana Bukova?'

508

Ludo looked round and the colour seemed to return to his face at once.

'Hana—Vera—yes!' he gushed, moving to leap from the bed.

Matron set the tray on the bedside table and pushed the hulking soldier back under the covers.

Hamilton laughed.

'Tell me about Hana and Vera while I have my injection,' said Slade, his voice gentle but demanding.

'Vera and her Jews—Sobibor.'

'Hold still,' Matron muttered, preparing Hamilton's thigh.

'Who the devil is Sobibor?' he asked, wincing as she inserted the needle.

'Vera was taken—and her Jews—they would have gone to Sobibor. I want Hana to know this.'

There was a silence as Hamilton fought off an urge to scream at the pain of the endless serum tearing into the delicate vein that lived under a pathetically thin layer of his sensitive flesh.

'Just relax,' Dame Dazzle murmured, still holding the agonizing object in place. Hamilton's colour had faded in rhythm with the course taken by the invading liquid.

'Please relay this man's information to Hana Bukova,' Slade gasped, his entire body shuddering as he resisted the onset of unconsciousness, brought on not by the serum but by the excruciating ordeal.

'Vera would never have gotten to England,' Ludo continued, staring straight ahead. 'People are being tortured and they give up. They drop beans.'

'*Spill the beans* is the expression, I believe,' said a male voice. Sam Hardwick had been listening.

'Torture comes in many manifestations,' Hamilton croaked, his torso going limp as Dame Dazzle at last removed her needle. He turned to face his neighbour. 'What are you in for, Hardwick?'

'I've had an arm off, my friend,' Sam replied lifelessly.

'You'll still be able to fly,' Hamilton said, brightening.

Matron was watching him intently.

'I doubt it,' said Sam, his face a grid of age and guilt.

'How has your wife taken it?' Slade enquired.

'She knows nothing—it's better for her, poor love.'

'Mr Hardwick lost his arm in a rather unusual way,' Matron commented, sorting through her paraphernalia and rising from the edge of the bed.

'How did you do it, then, Sam?' Slade asked.

'Our idiot Yank, as Noel likes to call him, tripped me up in front of a prop. Unfortunately the prop happened to be rotating on full power at the time.'

'Have we such idiots in ATA?' demanded Hamilton, irritated by the disparaging reference.

'Bill Howes,' Sam said quietly. He had acquired an edge of sarcasm under Noel's influence, and all in ATA had lamented the demise of his former personality.

'That poor sod!' Hamilton spluttered. 'He's had enough unhappiness in his career to last a lifetime—are you certain it was Howes who tripped you up?'

'According to Noel, it was Howes,' Sam said meekly, his former self temporarily returning. 'I was knocked unconscious at once.'

510

'At least Slater isn't blaming some poor female on this occasion.'

'Oh, no—according to him it was Howes.' Sam's head sank back and his eyelids drooped.

'I'm truly sorry about the arm, old boy,' said Hamilton, Dame Dazzle standing over him.

'Try not to overtax yourself,' she said, patting Slade's hand.

He smiled. 'Please get this Romanian chap's information to ATA, will you?' he asked, gripping her hand tightly. He thought her eyes showed pity.

'I shall do my best for you lot,' she said. 'God knows where we'd be without ATA—probably in one of these camps Ludo keeps rabbiting on about.' She gathered up her instruments and moved away, Hamilton's hand falling limply by his aching side as he watched her stride along the busy corridor. Looking to his left, he could see Ludo fading into a deep sleep.

'Ludo's AWOL,' Sam whispered. 'He was Army but I gather he learned to fly and made a miraculous escape to Switzerland. Can you believe he risked life and limb to meet some girl over here?'

'Some girl', Hamilton snapped, 'is our very own Hana Bukova.'

'She's not one of Noel's favourites,' Sam remarked.

'What woman is?' Hamilton said, closing his eyes once more.

'He has one he rather likes.'

Hardwick and Slade faced each other, their heads resting wearily on creaseless pillows.

'Who on earth might that be?'

'She's a tomboy,' hissed Sam.

'One might say that could be expected,' Slade remarked, winking.

'I beg your pardon?'

'It would stand to reason your mate likes those sort of women, if he likes any.'

'I'm afraid I don't follow, Slade.'

'Let me explain tomorrow. I'm shattered now.' Hamilton could see Sam's troubled face slowly turning away and a wave of compassion swept through his emaciated breast.

'My sons are all on one ship,' said Sam, talking to no-one.

'That can't be an ideal situation for your wife.'

'One American family has five sons in the Pacific,' Sam reflected weakly. 'I read about it in a newspaper. The ship is called the "Juneau". The Sullivan family. Three of the boys have the same exact names as my lads . . .'

Sam's voice was droning, and Hamilton could no longer listen. A strange stillness had begun to overtake his mind, images of Amy now more vivid than at any time in the past year. Noises from the hospital corridor became loud and intrusive as Hamilton begged slumber to rest his painful limbs. His last vision, as he drifted into dreams, was of Angelique Florian, determined to rescue her brothers from the jaws of Europe, and Amy pleading with her to abandon the mission. He had spent his life around courageous women and wondered if Angelique would ever be seen again. Amy had been horrified that a pregnant girl could contemplate a near-suicidal flight, but deep down he knew Amy would have done the same . . .

His fading mind saw Amy's frail figure draped across his once-strong arms as he placed her on his small bed and fell on his knees to worship an angel he had loved so completely. Pain was throbbing through his lifeless arms, but he could still feel her warmth. Hamilton smiled at the memory of their last coming together, when his manhood had not yet withered and climax after climax erupted all night long and all next day to remind them how they both still raged with life.

Nothing in him stirred now, and as Sam the cockney snored, and Ludo the Romanian babbled quietly about Sobibor, Hamilton Slade sank into a deep and welcome rest.

68

'You can't be seen with him—it's outrageous!' screamed Lili, her expensive bomber jacket covering the regulation ATA-issue flying suit.

'Noel stops me from feeling frustrated,' Kay asserted. She had put the finishing touches on her evening attire, the cracked mirror of Hamble ladies' lavatory reflecting an image of fierce sexuality.

'There's something queer about the whole thing—why don't you wear makeup when you date the pommy creep?' demanded Lili.

'By now you should know how much I hate lipstick and war paint,' Kay replied, standing back from the small glass. 'Everything you lot say about him is exaggerated. People seem to forget he is the organization's top flight engineer and he knows every damned aeroplane from tit to ass.'

'Well, all I can say, Kay, is that it's a shame he

has to know *you* from tit to ass. I wish you'd never gone out that first night in Brisbane. I asked my uncle what creepy Slater was doing sniffing around Australia in the middle of this war and to this day he hasn't been able to come up with an explanation. He's probably a double agent. It's a great pity you're wasting yourself and that you give licence to him to know you intimately. He diminishes you.'

'Why?' shrieked Kay. 'Is it my fault that except for what you and I did together you insist on staying pure, you old bag? I've even got his mind off boys. This is the real thing, and it's normal.'

'What we did together, as you choose to call it, was special,' Lili said, her voice cracking and her heavy flying boots feeling like lead weights on the harsh lavatory floor. She sat down on the small wooden ledge jutting out from the tiled wall that had once been a men's urinal. Their last night in Australia—so many centuries ago, it seemed—had been a prelude to frequent and relentless lovemaking in their uppermost room at The Stone House, Hatfield. Always demanded by Kay, the exquisite couplings had left Lili feeling removed from herself, Kay's strong, broad-shouldered figure bringing her to a frenzy as she possessed the delicate blonde like a hungry cheetah. Her beauty could not be measured against the faces of her age; Kay's features were a photographer's dream, her Grecian profile offset by pert dimples and rich, unruly hair. Lili had set out for England in search of a husband but in the year that had now passed she often chuckled at the totality of her passion. Never once had any suitor attracted Lili's attention; she thought only of Kay and suffered in

514

silence on nights when ferrying jobs left them apart at different ends of the British Isles. She knew Kay did not suffer: pining was alien to a personality obsessed with its own advancement. Lili had promised her financial backing for the films in which she yearned to star, and had been bemused when Kay had accepted the offer as if it were part of a business agreement—not as the generous outpouring of love that Lili had intended.

'He could destroy your career,' Lili said, still sitting on the ledge. 'Everybody who meets him is antagonized. Just think if you get into a great theatre company—no-one will want to know you after a while.'

'On the contrary—being with him, I'm learning proper pommy English, and I intend taking him with me everywhere, buying him a house and a motorcar, and tying him to a chair until he writes the charter for his new airline corporation.'

Lili scowled in silence as Kay's elegant fragrance wafted through the dank air and seemed to warm the atmosphere like a tropical sunbath.

'I suppose I should find a bloke to marry, and have a baby,' Lili mumbled.

Kay whirled around.

'Lil, are you crazy?' she shrieked. 'Your career is going to be hot stuff—after the war you'll be producing all my films.' Kay paused and looked back into the mirror. 'If you get pregnant, you're fucked!'

Kay had made Lili laugh. Suddenly Delia Seifert entered the lavatory, her skin white and blotchy. Before Lili could offer her a seat, she ran to the lone cubicle and vomited.

'If she's in the club I'll eat my dress,' Kay

muttered. Emerging from the cubicle, Delia went to the basin and washed her face.

'Are you ill from our flight?' asked Lili.

'I've just had some disturbing news,' Delia said, leaning over the basin and grimacing.

'It's the Immaculate Conception—you're pregnant,' Kay warbled, gathering up her evening bag and fur wrap.

'If I may say so,' Delia said, recovering her composure, 'you do look the height of tartiness—and no, I am not expecting.'

'What has happened?' asked Lili, her arm encircling Delia's narrow waist.

'I've been put forward for Class 5 conversion to four-engined planes,' Delia replied, taking a deep breath.

'Is that why you puked?' Kay asked, her hand on the exit door.

'No—it's Anthony. Did you girls know his surname was Seifert?'

Lili looked puzzled. 'You related?' she wondered.

'Yes, that's pretty much it, as they say,' Delia replied.

'I still don't see why that would make you throw up,' Kay persisted.

'Perhaps I should go,' Delia muttered. As she pushed past the two beautiful Australian girls Delia knew her own future would hinge less on being one of the women on armed four-engined bombers than on the information her brother Anthony had imparted over a cold Hamble pudding.

516

69

'Wake up, you dozy bastard!'

Hamilton Slade rolled over painfully, the remnants of a flying dream—was it a Halifax?—circulating in his head as he tried to focus on the figure beside his hospital bed.

'I've brought you cigars, chocolate from Selfridge and Co, and a dirty comic,' the figure continued.

Hamilton left his dream behind and the uniform of an ATA officer emerged, silhouetted against a bright morning sun.

'Are we in pilots' heaven together, sir?' Slade asked earnestly, trying to identify the silhouette.

'Fucking hell, man, pilots don't go to heaven.'

'Alec Harborne!' Hamilton exclaimed, sitting up and smiling. He could see Alec's grin, which was fading now, as more of Hamilton's deteriorating physique emerged from the white sheets.

'What's wrong with you, lad?' asked the Scot, sitting on the bedside chair.

'Dame Dazzle knows,' Hamilton responded, his hand outstretched.

'We've all met her at one time or another,' Alec said, gripping Hamilton's bony fingers. 'Have you got a good doctor?'

'I suppose all doctors are good,' Hamilton replied, looking to each side. 'Have you seen who I've been given for company?' He gestured towards a sleeping Sam and a babbling Ludo.

Smiling at the skeleton that had once been an ace, Alec felt an urge to grasp Hamilton's hand for a long time, as if his own life force might be transmitted to the human shadow on the bed. Marion had told him she thought Hamilton had been destroying himself with grief over Amy. Looking at the pilot who had brought honour upon the RAF and now upon ATA, Alec knew this was more than grief.

'Marion sends her love,' he said, uncharacteristically subdued. 'She's due to have the baby this autumn and I'm off to move Wellingtons. Delia Seifert has offered her a room in the family house and I moved Marion into the place yesterday. Old man Seifert has given up the bottle—some people say it's because his daughter has given him so much pride. If you ask me, he's pleased to have a son in a girl's body. Incidentally, Ham, I'd have come to see you sooner but I've been stuck in Hurricanes for a week.'

Hamilton's colour had begun to return at the news and at the names—pilot gossip made his heart come alive.

'By the way, there was a rumour our Delia's to be put on four-engined bombers,' Hamilton said, feeling a clamminess creeping over his trembling hands.

'She's already airborne.' Alec's voice travelled the length of the ward but Hamilton's head was facing the other way and he chose not to hear.

Dame Dazzle stood in a corner of the ward, and at this sad moment was motioning for Alec to come to her. He stroked the side of Hamilton's face and moved from the bedside, walking gingerly on the hard floor. Now he stood alongside the Matron. 'Get our Hamilton back in the air,' he said.

'Hamilton is past caring—about living,' she said.

518

'We all know why, of course. Grief is recuperation's most fiendish enemy, but if you can help us get him to the Canadian Hospital, he might just have a chance.'

'That could happen tomorrow if he could only cheer up,' said Alec.

'Mr Harborne,' she murmured, 'Hamilton is gravely ill. Nonetheless he could possibly be saved by this new cure.' She paused, the dazzle in her eyes dimming. 'Has he any next of kin?'

'He has no family we know of,' Alec said, subdued. 'I will arrange for him to be taken to Taplow—I'm Commanding Officer Air Ambulances and if I have to I'll fly him there myself.'

'That would be wonderful,' she said. 'You and I can make it our personal mission. I've often thought Mrs Mollison is looking down from above and willing him to live.' She smiled at Alec, and he thought he could discern an unprofessional moistness in her eyes. 'What has happened to Jim Mollison?'

'Who knows? Who cares?' Alec retorted, straightening up. 'I'm off now, and I'll get you an Anson straight away if I have to stop the whole bloody war for ten minutes. God bless.'

Turning her back on Alec, Matron appeared to vanish as she slipped along the corridor, leaving Alec alone amongst hastily stacked crutches and wheelchairs.

How he yearned to go back and drag Hamilton Slade from the white bed. Standing in the middle of the passageway, Dame Dazzle's words reverberating in his head, he remembered his wife and his child and the life that would be there to live after this war. For the sake of Hamilton and Amy, Alec knew he would have to throw himself into ATA as never before, and he stormed out of the hospital thinking only of Wellington bombers and of the German tyrant still striving to conquer the world, and of the most important ferry trip he would ever undertake.

70

Making history, and performing exceptional deeds, had been the job of circus acts, Delia told herself as the press tormented Commanding Officer Flint on this bright afternoon. April snow gone, and mammoth ferrying tasks now dominating the whole of ATA, Nora had wanted as little attention as possible given to her top girl's latest assignment in a four-engined bomber. Having been recommended for the Class 5 conversion course by Commanding Officer Sean Vine, Delia had been etched into aviation annals, the magic of this recommendation being the fact that it had come from a man.

Delia, however, was unconcerned and felt a keen sense of irritation that her full-time job was becoming a source of publicity. Amongst the near one hundred girls who now flew for Valerie Cobb's organization, there was a common feeling that this was a form of employment, not a showcase for women's rights.

'Oh, let's get on with it, for God's sake,' shouted Delia as a photographer insisted on her posing next to the giant Wellington bomber before she

520

took it on an urgent delivery flight to Number One Pool, White Waltham. Already on this day she had ferried two Spitfires and a Hornet Moth sandwiched between a Mustang and a Mosquito, and now, as the exhausting day drew to a close, her big moment had come: she was to take Wellington X9707 from Castle Bromwich to White Waltham.

'History is made at Castle Brom-witch,' sang the photographer, his assistant fussing with film and dropping a plate on the muddy tarmac.

Delia laughed. 'Are you American?' she asked, still smiling.

'Burt Malone,' replied the photographer. 'This is Stan Bialik.'

'What would make you want to spend your teatime at Castle Bromwich?' she asked, preparing to enter the massive aircraft.

'We were offered on-the-spot jobs in war-torn England, so here we are,' Burt replied.

Stan fretted.

'Asshole,' Burt whispered, tearing the plates from Stan's unsteady hands.

'Don't you think your colleague ought to be doing something else for a living?' Delia asked, her tired spirits lifting.

'He ain't used to gals dressed up like guys,' Burt replied.

'Can he not speak for himself?' she demanded, staring at Stan.

There was a pause.

'I believe they call this the European Theatre of War,' drawled Stan.

'Well done—it talks,' Delia exclaimed, climbing into the cockpit.

'Idiot—this isn't Europe, and it sure as hell ain't

no theatre,' Burt growled, collecting up his equipment.

'Do you think what we heard is the truth?' Stan asked, his thin figure a pinprick next to the majestic Wellington.

'Why wouldn't it be? I gather anybody named Buxton in Norfolk doesn't tell lies. They say three families own the county—and they're all Catholics, too!'

'I'll be damned,' Stan said, his face brightening.

'That's not exactly how I'd put it,' Burt mused.

'Does being Catholic make them more truthful?'

'Ask the Pope,' Burt replied. 'You think up the dumbest questions, Bialik,' he added, watching Delia in the cockpit. 'I wish I had my telephoto lens—wish those goddammed shitasses hadn't confiscated it for the war effort when we arrived. Some Limey squaddie will break it his first time out.'

With a great roar Delia had the engines alive and the huge bomber taxied away from the Americans. Looking down at the men she waved: their manner had disarmed her. As she manoeuvred her enormous aeroplane along the runway she was surprised that nerves had not entered into the task: Sally Met had bombarded her with weather information, and some of the other girls had shown a rare apprehension when hearing of her assignment. She had not even bothered to tell Marion Harborne that she was tackling Wellingtons: Marion had become edgy in her pregnancy, and Delia had dreaded the thought of upsetting Alec's beloved.

Her Wellington had a wing span of eighty-six feet and was virtually double the measurements of a

Blenheim, yet much less responsive on the controls. Delia had been told this was another case of reading one's notes and getting on with it, and having done some homework amid her parents' nonstop chatter the night before, she felt comfortable in the flying machine that had a geodetic basket-weave infrastructure. This bomber had been designed with the shape of the airship R 100 in mind, and was so flexible the pilot could feel the fuselage flexing when he or she pulled on the controls. Now, as Delia took her very own Wellington into the air, the gusty weather Sally Met had predicted took hold, and she could see the wingtips moving up and down. Too much strain, she knew, would break the elevator trim.

Delia prayed for no mishaps, and as she roared along the magnitude of the occasion began to creep into her psyche. It was just a job, she kept telling herself as her tiny figure commandeered the powerful monster through the heavens, but it was thrilling.

*   *   *

Before departing for London and her long-suffering mother, Shirley Bryce had told Delia that the first girl on four-engined things might be landed with any one of a number of types of Wellingtons: some tended to swing to the left on take-off, she had warned Delia, and some to the right. Some told the pilot the undercarriage was up when red lights flashed, while others had red lights to say the monster was airborne. Delia had marvelled at Shirley's instant expertise—she had a photographic memory and in recent months, had been seconded to the RAF enough times to make Nora and Valerie apoplectic with frustration, but all the girls were aware that awe was at the heart of their exasperation.

For Shirley was indeed the pride of ATA.

Every lady pilot had been amused when Shirley emphasized the importance of brute strength when explaining manual lowering of the undercarriage. It was perhaps for this reason, the girls theorized, that the RAF had been reluctant to allow ATA women on to the largest bomber in the force. As she roared on towards White Waltham, Delia recalled the ground engineer's comments about the port engine: if its hydraulic pumps failed, one might have to land with the wheels retracted, there being no time to perform the umpteen strokes of the hand pump required to lower the undercarriage manually. Delia was pleased this aircraft had searchlights and radar for communication with ships. Now, as the minutes ticked by and she felt at one with the raging quartet of engines, she yearned to operate the Wellington that had aerials for detecting submarines, or the version that could explode mines from the air.

Cruising steadily, Delia was acutely aware of the need to concentrate, but her mind had begun to review the extraordinary events of the past fortnight. After twenty-nine years she had met her half-brother for the first time. Anthony had kept her father's name, but the astonishing facts about her mother's liaison with Lord Truman had so confused Delia as to make her ill for a week. When her mind had assembled the story, she realized Anthony had a claim to one of the ten largest estates in England. Anthony had told her that their mother had nursed Truman upon his return from the First War and, though already married to Seifert, had tasted passion for the first time and from this had come a son.

How had he discovered the truth?

Delia had been suspicious of Anthony's story, but she had to admit that their physical resemblance was uncanny. She had pressed him for evidence and he had told her the even more remarkable story of his birth: their mother had been compelled to leave the family home when Seifert had become insane with alcoholism. Lord and Lady Newman had taken her in on a Friday, the eve of their most sacred holiday, Yom Kippur, and had told her a child born on Sabbath Kol Nidre would have good fortune all his life.

And Anthony had indeed arrived during that night, after hours of agony for his mother. Certain of her impending death, the Brigadier's wife had confessed her transgression and begged them to tell Truman he had a son. She survived, however, and with the passage of a day was beseeching the kindly couple to keep her secret intact. Life with Seifert became intolerable, and the baby boy became wild and uncontrollable. Without money, and her mind a shambles, Anthony's mother had surrendered him to a children's home, her psyche too filled with shame and uncertainty to have considered the possibility of the childless Newmans adopting the boy. He would have been raised in the Jewish faith, and that would have damaged his future, she told herself. Late in life, the Newmans had a child of their own, a daughter, and when Barbara had come of age her mother had related the story of the baby Anthony, who had been born in their home on the Holiest of Holy Days.

Delia's Wellington surged on.

She hoped her brother would keep his story to himself. He had a propensity for animated and effusive narrative and she had asked him to exercise discretion. They had agreed it would do their parents little good to discuss the matter, and now, as the weather cleared and her bomber sailed along with glorious power, she vowed to swear Barbara Newman to secrecy. Life as a champion athlete had made the girl over-confident, and Delia wanted her family story silenced for ever. Brigadier Seifert had become benign in direct relation to the number of flights Delia had completed for ATA, and she did not wish to disturb his quietude. She was glad mothering and romance never entered her train of thought. After all, Angelique's life had become painfully complicated due to her desires. Marion had had to leave ATA at the height of war, and Delia could see this as a result of silly desires.

Why did people marry?

She herself would be satisfied in the pilot's seat until she died.

Out of the corner of her eye Delia was startled by the approach of another Wellington. For a moment she thought it was a mirage or a weird optical illusion reflecting her own X9707 through one of the windows. Gradually the image grew more distinct and she remembered Alec Harborne having threatened to provide an escort, his chits requiring Wellingtons to and from various Maintenance Units all day. Delia was delighted

526

and waved excitedly, but she could not be sure it was Alec or if in fact the pilot could see her happy gesture. Heavy weather was closing in, and following one of Shirley's thousand pointers, she veered away from the other bomber, only to see him in hot pursuit seconds later.

Delia's relaxation melted into a sweaty unease but she pressed on towards White Waltham and begged the Almighty to prevent womankind's first major four-engined-bomber assignment from ending in disaster.

71

'By any stretch of the imagination, the whole thing is monstrous,' fumed Brigadier Seifert, his wife cowering on the edge of the dreary grey fabric that covered a well-worn sofa.

'My darling, you were not meant to know—but the boy is on his way, and I want you to love him as I do,' she said, shaking within.

'I would never be able to find love for human filth.'

'He is a beautiful boy—so Delia tells me,' she said. 'This is wartime. For God's sake—people reveal all their secrets when whole cities are burning before midnight. What does it matter, anyway? This was thirty years ago.'

He moved to the whisky decanter. 'You were always an unloving slut and you bred me an unnatural daughter who behaves like a boy.'

'Delia is your reason for living—you adore her!'

'Could I ever be seen at my club, I ask you?' he

boomed. 'Dare I present myself at the Parish Council as Fleet Street's favourite cuckold?'

Listening at the door leading to the drawing-room of the Seiferts' sparse residence, Marion Harborne had heard the saga of Anthony unfolding and wondered if Delia had been exposed to any portion of the story. She had wanted to sleep, but the sounds of shouting awakened the heavily pregnant pilot, her stamina decreasing with each passing week of April 1942. She wanted the new life inside her to eclipse even the fever of war.

She thought of Delia in the Wellington. Alec had told her of the girl's historic first, and she was baffled by Delia's secrecy. Perhaps she had not wanted anyone to worry; Marion knew the four-engined bomber could be a daunting prospect and in unfamiliar circumstances could place the flier in great peril. Marion had moved down the stairs one by one and stopped outside the room in which Delia's parents raged: she could grasp a scenario about an affair on which Marion knew this withered woman had had every right to embark, her withering having started long years ago. Brief but unbridled, this affair had produced fruit equally volatile: talkative and violently energetic, Anthony had set sparks alight amongst all of women's ATA.

Passion, Marion theorized, was passion's inevitable product.

Had Hitler been conceived in rapture, she wondered?

Now the beauty and prolonged ecstasy of the Brigadier's wife had been putrefied by the newspapers during a war in which scholars were being hung on meat-hooks to die.

There was a sudden loud knocking and Marion stirred. She hadn't time to mount the stairs, and she watched wearily as her hostess moved slowly to the front door as if walking to her beheading. Anthony entered the hallway briskly, holding his cap and projecting an earthy, intensely masculine presence as his purple eyes surveyed the staircase.

'Marion Harborne,' he exclaimed, striding to the figure crouching along the wooden banister.

'I wasn't eavesdropping, Mrs Seifert, if that's what you were thinking,' she said pleadingly.

'It's all in the press anyway,' the older woman said, turning away.

'The woman's a slut!' Delia's father shouted from the drawing-room.

Marion looked on quietly as the boy and his mother, meeting for the first time in thirty years, embraced—her thin figure engulfed by his tall, robust newness. They remained in each other's arms for what seemed several minutes, and Marion feared the Brigadier's temper, which growled aimlessly a few feet away.

'There is something I need to tell you, Mother,' he said, holding her face and studying it, his colourful expression bringing a pulse to her deadened veins. 'Would you excuse us, Marion?'

Lifting her heavy abdomen with her hands, Marion rose from the steps and Anthony moved to help.

'I'll be fine,' she said, mounting the stairs.

Mother and son entered the drawing-room and Marion stopped once more, settling on a middle step. There was an eerie silence—no explosion from the Brigadier, just a strange stillness. She could barely hear Anthony's voice, and the urge to eavesdrop compelled her to move without standing, sliding down on her bottom until she had reached the base of the staircase.

'Two ATA Wellingtons collided—it was all very quick, and there was little suffering,' she could hear him murmuring. Her heart began to race with blind alacrity and she could no longer hear the unbelievable because Mrs Seifert's hideous sobs were drowning out her own as she cried out for:

'Alec, Alec . . .'

72

'This is going to ruin our word games,' said Friedrich Kranz, packing a large suitcase full of books.

Watching his movements, Raine Fischtal focused and snapped a photograph. 'I think it is very unjust,' she said, winding the film to the next exposure.

'You just hate the idea of Jews being freed and real Deutsch being kept imprisoned,' he asserted, grinning.

'May I keep your old neckties?' Zuki asked, rummaging through Kranz's detritus.

'Of course,' Kranz replied. 'Just think: someday you will be offered British citizenship and on the day you are sworn in you will be seen wearing a Cambridge tie. Mark my words that this will happen.'

'Nonsense,' Zuki said glumly, 'we are to be exterminated very soon.'

'The British would not be so stupid,' Raine said,

still snapping from different angles. 'We will be given important jobs and perhaps the Americans will buy our freedom.'

Grunberg listened in silence, ecstatic that the day had finally come. His gargantuan project on the Blood Libel was nearing completion, and he was hopeful of a publisher. His months interned had passed without trauma because he had been allowed to exercise his brain. This had not been the case for Hartmut Weiss, whose internment had been a nightmare of boredom; he had fought daily for permission to be freed to fly for the RAF, or at the very least for ATA, but the authorities had scoffed. His brawn had been assigned to haulage duty, and he had begun keeping a record of the number of bags of camp garbage his arms had lifted in thirteen months of captivity.

*   *   *

Throughout their time in the Isle of Man detention centre, Raine and the four men—Hartmut, Zuki, Friedrich and André—had developed a rhythmic relationship in which waves of bad temper were overtaken by periods of intense humour, characterized by ingenious word games and political debates the Nazis always won. In one of their most heated arguments, Raine had predicted Britain would be the next location for a National Socialist regime. A camp guard had joined this organized affray, asserting that foreigners and African tribesmen would colonize the British Isles and by the 1990s ruthless money-grabbers would rule the Kingdom and hordes of young neo-Nazis would terrorize the streets. Friedrich always became hysterical at these debates, his truculence making the others laugh as he predicted a gentle England overrun with university towns and human rights organizations, neutral like Switzerland but quaint as a giant Norfolk . . .

*　　　*　　　*

'You have visitors,' a guard announced, reaching for Friedrich's suitcase.

'I suppose this is goodbye until we meet in Utopia,' Raine said, smiling.

Friedrich had grown fond of the Nazi film-maker, her yearning to see Edith Allam manifested in the small snapshot she had kept pinned to her headboard through the long, frustrating months. Hartmut had asked Raine for a copy, but he had been unsuccessful and could often be found staring at the faded likeness for whole afternoons, and evenings, and mornings before sunrise.

Grunberg's picture of Nijinski had been removed by guards shortly after his arrival, but Zuki's portrait of Hitler had remained in place. When a small contingent of detainees had been transferred to a location on the English mainland the close quintet had been overjoyed that the authorities were not separating their group. Sadly, however, Grunberg had stopped receiving letters. He became convinced his mail was not being forwarded from the Isle of Man and had vivid imaginings about news from Stella being incinerated.

'It's an entourage,' muttered Zuki, peering out of a barracks window.

They had not been given the location of their

new encampment, but Hartmut's calculations, based on the length of their transfer trip, placed them in East Anglia. This had been confirmed when copies of the *Anglian Press* had begun appearing around the compound. Their luxury accommodation was a country house, and Friedrich had asserted on the day of their arrival that they were on the verge of liberation.

Friedrich became apprehensive as voices approached. He had been informed only the night before that he was 'to be released along with the other Jew'. Britain had decided they could be of better use as free men, despite their German origins, and Grunberg had invited Kranz to Cambridge. Hartmut wanted to escape to the nearest airfield to fly once more, and now all three men waited anxiously for the truck that would transport them to freedom.

'Ready to go?' asked a pompous voice. Tim Haydon had arrived ahead of the liberation party, a photographer at his heels.

'I take pictures—why do you need him?' smirked Raine, scrutinizing the man's camera.

'This is a Leica,' said Stan Bialik, moving to let her have a closer look.

'Probably the one stolen from me when I arrived in England,' she said.

'I'm from Philly, honey,' he said meekly, 'so I couldn't have stolen your stuff.' He looked at Raine more closely. 'I remember you! Raine Fischtal!'

Raine stepped back and her face flushed. 'You were the projectionist?' she said. 'Do you know what has happened to Edith Allam?'

'I'm here,' said a voice. Edith's smartly

533

uniformed figure entered the sedately furnished room and offered a gloved hand to the dishevelled German film-maker. Raine felt ashamed, her hair having gone grey and her clothes in tatters as she had forgotten real life in the endless months of nothingness.

'This is a surprise,' Raine said politely, her heart racing.

'What do you think of Stan, huh?' asked Edith. 'Both my guys are here, and now they tell me Molly and Kelvin are here with the first of the US forces. It's the whole Philly crowd back in one place!'

Raine became subdued, her face acquiring an odd, glassy stare as she listened to the vivacious aviatrix.

Edith turned to face Hartmut. She was mortified that nothing stirred inside her, his taut, muscular presence only made her want to avert her gaze. He had not moved from the far end of the room, and she let her eyes return to Raine. How strange that the small German still inspired excitement, Edith reflected; she regretted her task, which would leave Zuki and Raine behind and bring Hartmut back to the real sex he craved. Edith was not sure she could fulfil his needs and she let her eyes roam once again, letting them fall upon an *Anglian Press*.

'Have the others arrived?' asked Tim.

Edith was engrossed in the newspaper.

'Miss Allam?'

Edith looked up, her face white as snow. 'Please let me read this,' she said, as more voices closed in.

'Friedrich.'

Valerie Cobb stood at the door and Kranz was transfixed. She moved towards him, her father in

534

tow, and Friedrich felt the same fascination that had intermingled with the sting of wanting he had known on that first meeting in the little hut. His mind reeled with images: Hunstanton, the caravan, and Shirley's talk of Blood Libel tumbled into visions of Valerie at the edge of his ecstasy in a small bed that could barely contain their pulsating nakedness.

'We must not make this into a production number,' Sir Henry Cobb crackled, pointing to Grunberg's bags and snapping his fingers at a guard. 'There will be a few photographs when we leave the building—in front of the lovely grounds.'

Valerie and Friedrich had not unlocked their minds, and as bodies moved about them she could feel his mental imagery penetrating her own brain, their cerebral meshing a cauldron that obliterated her year of joyless solitude in one flash.

'Hope you don't mind!' shouted Stan, his camera snapping.

'I thought you said outside,' Hartmut mumbled, pushing him aside and nearly knocking him to the ground.

Valerie glared. 'Stella Teague was to have joined us,' she said tersely, 'but she has been ferrying Spits for Malta. She sends you her greatest love, Mr Grunberg. I give you my love, too.'

Sir Henry glowered, his anger at the simple nature of the revelation of Friedrich's whereabouts—a letter from an elderly ballet master to a former student—still churning inside his abdomen. Haydon had decided the exercise should be a publicity stunt to demonstrate British compassion. Cobb and the Ministry had reluctantly agreed it was time Kranz was set free and his

535

expertise in aircraft production put to national use.

As for Valerie, all she wanted was the help of Hartmut, peace for the ballet master, and—in parallel with the nation's requirements—the expertise of her lover. She hoped Shirley would be able to handle the renewed presence of the man for whom Commanding Officer Valerie Cobb would die.

'This is awful,' said Edith, immobile.

Slowly, the men and women present turned to the girl, her face a mixture of agony and confusion. On the front page of the *Anglian Press* was a blown up close-up of Errol Carnaby, and the banner headline:

Hideous Crime: Negro Held

73

Information was not disseminated in the Spanish prison, and news of the war arrived only with a fresh inmate. Incredibly, this new captive had smuggled a newspaper into the compound, and ten faces crowded around to read over her shoulder. Of various nationalities, some of the victims retreated when they realized the print was in English but a small cluster of women devoured the information with relish. They were unguarded today, having been brought a breakfast of roach-infested figs and water, and since then no captors had reappeared. Figs were dreaded for the terrible cramps they produced in the scorching heat, but the offerings had to be consumed since, as each day passed, one never knew if food would ever arrive again. In recent weeks torture had subsided and the prisoners were often left alone for whole afternoons and evenings at a time. Judging by the testiness of their senior tormentor, some of the recipients of figs suspected a change in the direction of the war.

Generously circulating her precious *Times*, the new woman allowed it to leave her sight when a male inmate passed her on her way back from the only torture session she had endured in her first week. Usually, the first few days when the skilled sadists tried to break foreigners were the ones some did not survive. Even when this latest arrival was introduced to the crude removal of fingernails, the men performing this initiation ceremony seemed distracted and lacking in the glee with which they had inflicted agonies for years. This sublimely excruciating act, which had left their most recent acquisition wanting to die, caused the new woman to plead with them to chop off her hands because she thought it would lessen her torment. That night she could not think, sleep or read the newspaper and her excrement soiled her bedding. Gouging of one's fingernails had become a dim memory for the women around her, most of whom were mutilated to the point that they would be unrecognizable to an old friend. Their new cellmate could not sleep, and they were annoyed by the anguished noises she was making.

In the next corridor along, the male population had decreased in the past three months, no new arrivals having been available for the sport their captors called 'forced rape'. With the women left, for once, to keep their legs unspread and to feel their wounds healing, a certain quiet had settled upon the prison and for the first time in three years a sense of hope began to permeate their reeking habitat.

'Pacific—paradise under siege—what an incongruous scenario.' One of the men had seized the coveted newspaper, the front page of which showed a terrifying wire photo of naval vessels engulfed in blackness and flame.

'This means Roosevelt's in it at long last,' said another inmate, scratching at the hideous rash that had spread from his knees upwards into his anus, as if following the path of a giant tentacled insect within his limbs. 'It's been so long since I caught up on the history of the Far East,' he continued, scratching furiously all the time.

'That itch will eat you up in the end, my friend,' said his companion.

'Do you remember when we were at school and I got rushed to that hospital where Dame Dazzle looked after me? Her face keeps coming back to me at the oddest moments. It's been twenty years since that day.' He gesticulated wildly with his hands as if to make the other man understand him more fully.

'Perhaps your life is passing before you in small spurts. As bits of you are taken away in the torture chamber, you die proportionately each time.'

'It was Hertfordshire—1922.' He had not been heard.

'Did you say 1922? We weren't born yet.'

Both men tired when they talked, their frames making minimal shadows on the slippery floor. Other men slept, and their bodies stank, but the newspaper had kindled hope in this pair and they fought off slumber to read that the United States had entered the war at last, although there was little detail.

What had been the provocation?

Both men were intrigued. Had they been able to chat to the new girl who had slipped them the paper, they would have learned that the American base at Pearl Harbor had been attacked on 7 December by the Japanese, causing catastrophic damage to the fleet and countless casualties.

Their minds had begun to work in unison after having been confined together for so many years, and now the pair looked at each other knowingly. This new woman had delivered a ragged, yellowing newspaper and they calculated that, if America had taken up arms in December 1941, months of transformation would already have taken place, and by now the conflict might be turning in their favour. They read of the siege of Malta and of the island winning the George Cross. It appeared Roosevelt had released the US aircraft carrier 'Wasp' at the personal request of Winston Churchill. Fantasizing the absurd possibility of liberation in 1942 and an end to their horrendous ordeal, the men shook skeletal hands and spent the rest of the night combing the glorious pages and learning about Shirley Bryce. In a human-interest story they were told that Miss Bryce, Britain's most valued ground engineer, had gone on leave from the Air Transport Auxiliary for the first time in a year to visit her mother near Cannon Street, London, but unfortunately an enemy bomb had made a direct hit on her mother's house and both women were killed instantly . . .

When the men were awakened unusually early the next morning the newspaper had absorbed excrement and urine from the floor and the inmate riddled with rashes tried to salvage the adored black-on-yellow pages. A hovering guard pulled the man away, leaving the other half of the team tearing out pictures and advertisements and making a small pile of foul-smelling cuttings. An hour passed and the other men in his cell had been taken away. Something was definitely afoot, he told himself, and wished his rags had pockets for the collection of choice news items. He was the last to be taken away, dragged up off the floor, his booty scattering everywhere. He cried out but the newspaper was gone for ever. Led into the sort of bright and cheerful room he had not seen for a year, he was given a small plate of fresh-smelling food.

'I've heard of the last feast before the execution, but this is a bit much,' he said, grinning at his minders.

'They call you the idiot here, Florian,' said one of the Spanish fascist thugs.

'For a death banquet this is better than most.' Paul ate, the food making him dizzy as he wondered where his brother had been taken. Unbelievably, he was handed a carafe of good wine. 'Surely you are too kind,' he said, fighting off the nausea of a dead body being revived.

'We have had some interesting revelations today, and the boss is feeling in a generous mood. All the prisoners are being fed and bathed.'

'Are we being visited by the great man himself,

the Generalissimo Francisco Franco?' Paul asked.

'Oh, much better than that,' replied the guard, leaving the cell.

Paul's nausea was increasing and he sank down in the chair, his head slumped. When the appalling sensation had subsided he moved to the neatly made camp bed, and when his guard returned he knew he had been nourished in order to be alert in his performance of a series of sexual acts upon a creature who had been brought in and was now banging, banging, banging its body against the bed frame, grunting in a voice so ugly as to chill but which Paul could not hear. Cries that he could not hear were cascading down the corridor and permeating his new palace, their agony making the creature curl into a little ball whose head rested against the spotless mattress.

As Paul drank the wine, he reflected that when he and Zack next talked in their cell they could fill the empty days by learning sign language. Belching loudly, he caused the female torture victim to look up for the first time, and when he saw a face he had known a lifetime his eerie scream reverberated all the way to the interrogation room, where Zack Florian's mutilated testicles had been pinned to the wall next to the rapists' favourite picture of Rita Hayworth.

74

Errol had been asked to clean a rifle for a newly arrived Air Force man, the weapon having been meant not for war but for games. Lord Truman had invited the handful of American officers to his shoot and it was left to Errol Carnaby, of the coloured brigade, to ready shotguns for the pheasant weekend.

In this part of rural Norfolk, Hitler's war seemed remote and the trickle of Americans had not yet reached invasion levels. Errol, his book of Blake's poetry tucked into a small haversack, resigned himself to being excluded from the outing. Albion was now his home but he mused that entry into Jerusalem was more complicated than he had envisaged. On that day in Philadelphia when he had begged the Recruiting Officer for shipment to Britain, his vision of Blake's kingdom had excluded the criteria necessary for membership of the local shoot. Errol had laughed when a fellow Negro soldier suggested he was possessed of more natural elegance than any of the other men assembled with Wing Commander Charlie Buxton for the exclusive gathering.

Errol's trial was several months old and 1943 saw a build-up of the American presence in Britain. Much attention was being paid to the Carnaby cause célèbre because the base of the 466th Bomb Group, Eighth Air Force, Second Air Division, was gaining strength in Truman's parish of Weston Longville. Errol had loved Attlebridge when, in the twilight of 1942 he first arrived from Fort Oglethorpe, Georgia. His group was photographed in the centre of the Norfolk village, and for some reason Errol's likeness was earmarked for a centre spread on the front page of the *Anglian Press*. At the time his comrades joked about the British photographing the arrival of tribal warriors from one of their African colonies. Errol hoped the bizarre publicity would attract Edith Allam's attention; in fact, Charlie Buxton summoned her to the new base to meet the entire American contingent, who included Molly and Kelvin and a hulking Military Policeman, Frank Malone. On the day Edith visited, Errol had been called to cleaning duties and told the white platoon was off limits for the time being.

Inexplicably, the picture story was never printed by the *Anglian Press*. It was only on the eve of the trial that Errol's face was plastered across Norfolk, Suffolk and neighbouring counties. Seeing his black self displayed like a WANTED poster across a county, his memory was jogged back to the days in Fort Oglethorpe: there, the coloured lady soldiers were called Waccoons and the sole Jewess in the white WACS was ostracized for not taking part in a marathon drinking weekend that left the whole of the base unconscious. Life in the fort was desolate and he thought of Edith ceaselessly throughout the misery of basic training. Here in Norfolk, however, Errol had got to know places like Shipdham and Wendling and he also got to know Lady Truman very well indeed.

They had become friends when her ladyship asked Charlie Buxton if he could recommend a good editor to evaluate and correct some prose Tim Haydon had written for an American publication. When the handsome black man first appeared at the front door of the Truman residence she had been horrified and extremely frightened, slamming the door and gasping for breath. Running out of the rear door of the large mansion, she stumbled through half a mile of undergrowth until the new air base was in sight, and begged Buxton for assistance: his Lordship, she babbled, was up in town, meaning Norwich, and she was defenceless without staff! The Wing Commander had calmly reassured her that her sinister intruder was the American editor she had requested.

Tim Haydon's prose was dutifully evaluated for the American wartime market and Errol began keeping company with Lady Truman whenever his Lordship was up to town. She worked in London three days a week and this coincided nicely with her husband's sojourns to Norwich on the other two days of the working week. Always in the back of her mind was the fear of an unexpected visit from a villager, producing the inevitable accusations of eccentricity, or even worse, immorality. 'Keeping company with a coloured man!' they would shriek, and she had lurid fantasies of being dragged through the town to be vilified as a witch and an outcast.

It was impossible not to like this young man from Philadelphia, a city he described as a bigger version of Cambridge. After a month she had forgotten his colour and admired the immaculate uniform of the United States Armed Forces and the books of poetry he selected for each Tuesday and Thursday. Lady Truman, thin and proper, and bound by centuries of moral dogma, thought of Errol as a tribal phenomenon sent down by the Lord to test her Christian generosity. Jesus, she reminded herself, accepted all races, and now she had been summoned to rise above the fears and hates of generations of East Anglians in order to cultivate a new member of the community.

Unfortunately Errol fell in love with the much

older lady, her rosy cheeks and soapy smell mesmerizing him whenever they chatted about Enitharmon and Orc. 'What a crazy man he was!' she would exclaim as they laughed over Blake's verbal inventions, and Errol wanted so much to love this woman, but was fearful. She would tell him about her husband's ill-health, and about the missing daughter whose absence diminished his spirit, but Errol could only watch her lips moving animatedly, wanting to unpeel the delicate silk blouse that barely hid a still alluring womanhood. He would sit quietly, his other, invisible self jumping out to kiss the fleshy ripeness divided by a welcoming cleavage that seemed to deepen and deepen for his probing urgency.

Each night he would think about her ladyship and when he slept he would dream of Edith's young, pulling wetness and after many weeks he thought he would go mad, throwing himself even more deeply into his poetry readings. Charlie Buxton no longer administered the small American force, and Errol's detachment was now under the command of the Unites States Air Force Attlebridge, with men like Frank Malone keeping an eye on the niggers.

Errol Carnaby had never set eyes upon Lord Truman in his life before he killed him. Sadly, his American comrades did not believe him, and even the coloured soldiers—brought over like him to perform the most menial tasks for white warriors—rejected his plea. When the shotgun exploded in his hands and the man in boots and tweeds lay fallen at his feet, Errol cried out in terror. Blood spurted across the small courtyard in which the handsome Negro had been cleaning the white men's rifles, and more blood seemed to pour endlessly from the writhing figure of an English country gentleman. His pipe leaned grotesquely against his engorged mouth, and his ears oozed over his stiffly starched collar.

Errol had never looked upon death, and all he could do was stare.

War took second place to the biggest local story ever to inflate the pages of the *Anglian Press*. A black GI who was helping out at the local air base and had an accident with a rifle was not the stuff of front-page headlines. Rather, here was a Negro who was keeping company with the wife of the Lord Lieutenant and who slaughtered her husband in cold blood. Much was made of Errol's relationship with Lady Truman; she had denied intimacy but had to confess to their close friendship when asked to take the stand. He had been tried under British justice, and marvelled at the eloquence and detachment of the barristers trading syllogisms under the gaze of a scandal-hungry press.

When Errol had been taken into custody he was quickly beaten to a pulp by Frank Malone in the Philadelphia cop's unofficial capacity as base thug. Errol praised his Maker when handed over to the British civilian authorities and when Edith Allam appeared on the base, having been summoned by Charlie Buxton. The RAF Wing Commander, worried that Errol would be victimized by the white soldiers, thought a visit by the famous American aviatrix could defuse the situation. For all the bewildering weeks afterwards, Edith had kept Errol company in between exhausting ferrying jobs. Air Vice Marshal Sir Arthur Harris had been making enormous demands and every type of operational aircraft was now being transported by the men and women of ATA.

Valerie's Spitfire Girls had become Mustang, Typhoon and Dakota girls as well, their numbers increasing as quickly as she could find competent fliers. Soon there were one hundred and eighty, including Jacqui Cochrane's American squadron.

Despite the bruises inflicted by Frank, Errol had laughed heartily when Edith described her pathetic return from Philadelphia to England via Australia with only Lili, Kay and Hartmut in tow. Beaverbrook had not wanted to greet Edith, and he called the human cargo of pilots her 'motley crew', but the Townsville girls were to prove valiant in the service of ATA. Edith made Errol smile again when she recounted the story of Kay, who when stranded in Barton in a Battle meant for Silloth, was moved to cable her ferry pool about her predicament. Her message, 'Nobody wants my beautiful Battle, so wedded are we until Barton us do part,' was picked up on 41 Group RAF signals and relayed to the Air Commodore—who was not amused.

Errol had rocked with amusement when Edith declared Kay a true menace to women's aviation, having set the cause back twenty years as far as the Air Commodore was concerned and despite Gerard d'Erlanger's effusive assertions that such talent should be put to use confounding the German signal scramblers . . .

Passion came to the surface when, on the fifth day of Errol's trial for murder, Lady Truman pleaded for mercy and stressed the black man's intellectual brilliance. She likened him to Paul

Robeson—a scholar and an athlete, an artist and a philosopher all rolled into one—which only inflamed the courtroom atmosphere further. Complications arose when Fleet Street joined the uproar and reopened the festering wound inflicted upon the Trumans when the Anthony Seifert story broke. Ever since the revelations leaked to the newspapers, the Trumans had drifted apart, his lordship spending countless hours brooding about his lost daughter, and her ladyship devoting more and more time to Tim Haydon's office and to her black American companion.

Lord Truman did not want to meet his son and heir and repudiated the boy's claims through his own, very powerful Fleet Street connections. Nevertheless, the Anthony saga left Truman prone to terrifying fits of temper; when Errol Carnaby walked into her Ladyship's life, her day-to-day existence was already a series of frightening confrontations. Secretly, she wanted desperately to meet Anthony Seifert, and though her moral upbringing dictated she should regard the boy's mother as a profligate, she could not suppress a fascination with the liaison, which by now seemed of another century.

Anthony's sister Delia had been making banner headlines with her achievements; Lady Truman read with alacrity the story of the girl's first four-engined bomber flight in a Wellington from Castle Bromwich: ATA had given her up for dead when two of the monsters collided in mid air shortly after take-off from Castle B. Delia's mother, the woman to whom her Ladyship's husband had gone for satisfaction thirty years before, became hysterical with joy at the sight of her daughter alive and well. Delia would go on to ferry scores of four-engined bomber aircraft, armed with gunners onboard. Lady Truman nursed a secret desire to meet this girl, though after much soul-searching she still could not pinpoint her reasons why, nor could she fathom why she no longer missed her own Sarah, her own flesh and blood.

'Accidental! It was an accident!' screamed a reporter who tore down the steps of the Old Bailey to a large awaiting crowd. Errol Carnaby's story had attracted national attention by now, as had the constant companionship of his ATA heroine Edith Allam. Local people in Norfolk had come to sympathize with the black GI, who, like the American girl, had come over to Britain to help the war effort ahead of time. Though the popular newspapers chose to cheapen the nature of the pair's rapport, Lady Truman's dogged loyalty to her Negro made a deep impression upon the community of Weston Longville. Its villagers developed a degree of compassion for the soldier whose country, founded on the principles of life, liberty and the pursuit of happiness, forced him to serve in the niggers-only detachment of a segregated army.

'Accidental,' was the verdict on the killing of Lord Truman, and a small congregation of ATA girls clung to Edith as the courtroom spilled out on to the sunbaked London pavement. She had been grateful for the company on the judgment day, and was touched by the sudden humanity of Nora Flint in allowing four of her best pilots one full day's leave to attend the last day of the trial. Tears came quickly to Edith and the women celebrated in a fashionable restaurant, their flying pay now on a par with the men of ATA.

Errol had been taken back to his base, waving from the army vehicle at the bevy of attractive uniformed ladies gathered along the pavement. Watching him depart, Edith felt a mixture of relief and sadness, her true depth of feeling for Errol only having risen to the surface during this ugly trial.

Was this a form of jealousy aroused by the passion of Lady Truman?

Had Edith loved and forgotten Errol at a time when she had needed to dominate, hence the attraction of sweet, dumb, passive Hartmut?

'. . . the progressive destruction and dislocation of the German military, industrial and economic system . . .' was the joint message relayed by the British and American Bomber Commands, and now it was time for Edith to return her mind to the work at hand. This was the year of the Halifax, and the volume of ferrying tasks was staggering. Edith wanted Errol to be seconded from the United States Army to ATA but she doubted even Charlie Buxton could persuade the Americans to release their useful tribe of workhorses. Her only wish now was for her Negro lover to be happy; she knew that he adored her, and she would beg Wing Commander Buxton to protect Errol from the danger his exoneration might engender.

75

Mutual Broadcasting had sent its star radio man from New York to London when Errol Carnaby was freed. Eddie Cuomo was thrilled to be in a war-torn country and had spent hours staring at the bombed-out ruins of irreplaceable English architecture that had survived for three hundred years until the arrival of the German Luftwaffe.

Eddie's first assignment entailed a visit to Norfolk and Suffolk where American Bomber Command was descending on villages and establishing major bases of colossal size and population. Watching the country settings being transformed into military strongholds, he wondered if the county might become a new American state at war's end. His tour had ended at Weston Longville, where he was instructed by a gruff military policeman to wait in the outer enclosure for the British Wing Commander.

'I'm not actually in charge here,' Charlie Buxton said, his cheerful, roundness greeting the equally effusive Italian American. 'Our American Commanding Officer is meeting the Ambassador today.'

'That doesn't matter,' said Eddie. 'I want to see Errol—this story is hot, you know.'

'We'd all like to see it evaporate,' Charlie said, leading Cuomo to a dirt pathway. Shirtless black soldiers were building rounded bomb shelters amongst the thickly overgrown fields of the Truman estate.

'This place seems kind of wild,' Eddie

commented, looking out across the uneven foliage.

'Ever since the scandal', Buxton explained, 'Lady Truman has let things fall into neglect. She's an odd old bird. We've offered to help with the landscaping but she wants no men anywhere near the house.'

They walked along the path to the coloureds' barracks and a lone soldier stood to attention.

'We are looking for Carnaby,' Buxton announced.

'Corporal Carnaby is visiting with some local children, sir, or so I believe,' said the GI.

'Now I've heard everything!' Eddie exclaimed, grinning.

The soldier remained impassive.

'Was this sanctioned?' asked Buxton.

'I don't know, sir—we were told he was to go to the village hall to read some poetry to a group of kids.'

'Thank you,' murmured Buxton, taking Cuomo by the arm as the black man saluted. 'This seems odd—I'd been told most of our coloured men were detailed for building work today.'

'Is that what they do with their time?' asked Eddie.

'Is this a journalistic exposé or are you asking me man-to-man?' demanded Buxton, stopping at the entrance to the compound.

'If you ask me, it looks like a Southern plantation here,' Eddie replied. 'My question is man-to-man.'

'Your American military', Buxton said, resuming walking, 'chooses to separate white from coloured, and it is clear the Negroes are given the most awful jobs to perform. One could say somebody has to do these tasks but it is a pity these men will never see

552

combat. We have women flying four-engined bombers in this war, but strapping men like these are kept in the background.'

'Do you know if Carnaby's lawyer is still around?' asked Cuomo.

'Kelvin Bray has gone back to Pennsylvania,' Buxton replied. 'He was a brilliant chap, but the whole thing left him exhausted and now he is on extended leave.'

'That doesn't leave me with a whole lot to do,' complained Cuomo.

After ploughing through underbrush the two men emerged once more at the RAF base. Three uniformed women were hovering by the main door.

'Eddie Cuomo!' shouted Edith Allam. 'The voice of the Hindenburg disaster!'

'Do I know you, honey?' asked Eddie.

'Seven years ago at Lakehurst, New Jersey? I was there with Raine Fischtal,' Edith replied. 'What brings you here, Mr Cuomo?'

'I'm supposed to be doing an exclusive on the Negro boy, Carnaby,' he responded. 'So far I've found an empty barracks and not found an army lawyer who apparently has battle fatigue. Who the hell are you, anyway?'

'These are Flight Captains Delia Seifert, Barbara Newman and Edith Allam,' Buxton announced, smiling.

'God Almighty,' shouted Eddie, 'you're the great Edith herself! I didn't recognize you in the uniform. Flight Captains—well, I'll be damned! That's a news story if ever I heard one. Holy shit.'

There was an embarrassed silence as Charlie exchanged pained looks with the two English girls.

Decent as Eddie was, Edith did not want the intrusion of a New York radio station, in search of sensation, at a time when Barbara Newman was spearheading the most delicate amateur negotiation ever undertaken by a close unit of ATA friends. Originally, Barbara had wanted to use the information Anthony had divulged to her regarding the whereabouts of Sarah Truman to coax his lordship into acknowledging his heroic son. Indeed, the information Anthony had extracted from Kranz on the Isle of Man regarding cells of Resistance workers had already been communicated to Sir Henry Cobb in his search for Annabel, but Barbara wanted Truman to give something in return. Eventually she had had to abandon the scheme because a war demanding a 365-day year from ATA pilots had intervened.

Now, Edith had agreed to accompany Barbara on a visit to Lady Truman, with Anthony and Delia in tow. Edith had begun her own crusade to secure the release of Zuki and Raine from internment, their talents now sorely needed by Bomber Command. Edith knew that amongst British and American military scientists there was great interest in the advanced technological expertise stored inside the brains of German fliers.

Though Raine had had peripheral experience of rocketry in comparison with Anke Reitsch, her exposure to the inner Reich would be useful.

Regarding her familiarity with new kinds of aerial photography, linked to heat rays, she had been interrogated when she first arrived in Britain but the remainder of her knowledge had lain dormant in the stupidity of incarceration. Zuki too was supremely talented and it was believed he could be compelled to work—under tight supervision—for the Allies. Edith doubted either German would betray the Fatherland, but it had become apparent to her in recent weeks that Kranz and Grunberg had carved deep impressions into their hearts and had turned the pair well away from Nazism . . .

'Everywhere I go I meet Yanks,' Eddie said, unable to take his eyes off the highly ranked American aviatrix.

'It is a form of invasion,' Delia said glumly, 'but long overdue.'

'May I interview you two girls?' he pressed cheerfully.

'We are not allowed to talk to the press,' Delia growled. She did not like this owl-like little man.

'Maybe after you have seen Errol,' Edith said tactfully, 'you could come down to Hamble and see what we do. So far in this war ATA has transported nearly 16,000 Spitfires and Seafires alone. Has anybody seen Errol, by the way?'

'He has gone to entertain some local children,' said Buxton.

'Do you know this coloured boy?' Eddie asked sharply.

'They're both Philadelphians,' Barbara said, smiling broadly. 'End of story.' Retreating, the three women saluted and Charlie Buxton winked, the warm sun baking into the quiet, sandy pathway—far away from bombs and cruel slaughter.

'I'll be keeping track of you,' Eddie sang as the attractive trio walked briskly down the path towards the Truman estate.

Waiting along the main road was Anthony

Seifert. Nervous and hot, he was relieved to see the girls emerging.

'Where is Errol?' he asked as they approached.

'He's entertaining kids in the village,' Edith said nonchalantly. She knew she would have to wait until nightfall to see him.

'This mission ought not to be undertaken without Errol,' Anthony moaned.

'Perhaps it's a blessing in disguise,' Delia said, as they headed towards the mansion. 'We want her to be surprised and pleased to meet his lordship's rightful heir, and I could never see why Errol's presence would have helped.'

'He relaxes her,' Edith said quietly.

'Don't let's forget this whole production was my idea!' chimed Barbara.

They had reached the long entrance pathway leading up to the house and Edith felt giddy and ill-prepared for the imminent meeting, an event she had been anticipating with fascination and dread for days. Planning the first meeting had involved Valerie Cobb herself, the Head of ATA having allowed Anthony time away from the crucial Halifax transports to accumulate courage for the meeting. Involving herself in the Truman affair had salvaged Valerie from despair; all her girls had been relieved when her seemingly inconsolable grief for Shirley had at last begun to ease as she became embroiled in the layers of the scandal.

'We should have brought old Aunt Valerie along,' remarked Edith, staring at the neglected structure that once had teemed with servants.

'She's too busy rehabilitating Friedrich Kranz in secret,' said Delia. 'At this rate he'll soon be a

Commanding Officer.'

All four pilots shared the same thoughts as they walked on: Kranz had risen through the ranks of ATA with staggering speed, Sir Henry having had to cave in on his demand that Valerie be banned from Friedrich's presence after Balfour had recommended that the Austrian be allowed to manufacture in Britain. It had transpired that Kranz had known for two years the whereabouts of Valerie's sister, but his hatred of Sir Henry had sidelined his goodwill and he had kept the information to himself. Now, he had chosen to reveal the data and a search party had been despatched to Spain. Within a day of his revelations, Kranz was awarded a contract to make aeroplanes in Norfolk, and his elation at the ire of Sir Henry Cobb, when the prototype bomber was named the 'Valerie', thrilled Kranz so much that he became insanely drunk for the first time in his life.

Valerie the woman, sadly, had decided with steely determination to lock physical involvement with Kranz out of her life for the duration of war, leaving her lover bewildered and deeply frustrated. Both had thrown themselves into their work, Valerie never allowing Friedrich more than two minutes of her time even when his eyes pleaded for the renewed consummation without which he felt he might go mad.

Had Shirley in fact meant more to his mistress than anyone had suspected?

Kranz had asked himself this question on the day the 'Valerie' aircraft was unveiled in the presence of Commodore d'Erlanger, when the woman after whom the magnificent bomber had been named had not attended. Still, her ATA boys and girls

557

loved their head lady, who had been made an MBE in the New Year Honours . . .

'Barbara would do anything for me,' blurted Anthony Seifert as the group of fliers neared the Truman residence.

'They call it love, I think,' said Edith, grinning.

'Shut up, you lot,' said Barbara, her voice beginning to shake from the onset of nerves.

Stopping to stare at the mansion that could soon be his own, Anthony fingered the wings on his uniform and lamented the deformity, a scoliosis, that had excluded him from the regular RAF. It was only during the Errol Carnaby trial that Lord Truman's physical handicap had come to light, his wife's alienation a result of his inadequacy. At once Anthony had pitied the man and hated him as well.

'Time to go in, kids,' murmured Edith. 'Let's hope that radio guy hasn't followed us.'

They walked slowly but purposefully toward the house where Lady Truman was spending another afternoon in solitude. Waiting for the time when Errol would resume his visits she fought off images of her husband's hideously deformed ghost, a spectre that would not stop crying for the daughter he had lost and the crippled son he could have embraced.

76

Errol could not deny the overwhelming feelings of envy he had experienced when in the canteen the group of white airmen had recounted tales of heroic skirmishes in gleaming fighter aircraft. One of the men had described the disaster that had befallen an RAF base at which all arriving aircraft, delivered by the ATA, had punctured tyres. Eventually it was discovered that a convoy of dump trucks had deposited a huge covering of dirt over the runway, the load filled with forks, knives and nails. Much speculation led to the conclusion that the lorry drivers were Germans hired from the camps . . .

RAF men spent an afternoon attempting to sift the metal sabotage from the dirt load, but eventually a giant magnet had to be dragged over the runway . . .

In the village, teachers were fascinated by the black GI who was a Blake scholar and today Errol had been invited to talk to a small group of children who seemed safe from death in the remote rural setting. Errol had walked a short distance from the base but was ordered back by an agitated Frank Malone, who escorted him to the white canteen. Astonished to be allowed into these hallowed premises, Errol remained standing, but a small group of airmen invited him to sit at their wooden table. Talk of Defiants and of Mustangs distracted him but after an hour he was beside himself at the prospect of disappointing the schoolchildren in the village. He became even more alarmed when Malone entered the canteen and summoned him with a greasy finger.

Outside the compound, Errol and his guardian moved to the rear of the canteen, where a group of boys in civilian clothes hovered amongst potato peelings and other catering detritus. Dreading the possibility of a day's secondment to kitchen duty,

Errol scowled at Malone but dared not speak—he knew the combustion point of the ex cop and chose to reserve his passion for a positive activity; perhaps this evening he might be able to see Edith alone at last.

Pushed to the stinking garbage heap that festered on the edge of high grass, Errol was bewildered by the disinterest of the quiet congregation of young men. With Malone keeping a close watch on his every movement, Errol sat down on a small pail and waited for orders.

At nightfall he was allowed to rise from the pail, elated that Malone had disappeared and flattered when the friendly hand of a white cook came to rest on his shoulder.

Had this been a dream?

Another hand, and still another, helped Errol make his way in the twilight and he felt moved by the warmth emanating from the men's touch. Soon he would be with Edith, he told himself. He walked on with the young men clinging, and in their company Errol thought of Jerusalem and as darkness descended he felt at one with Albion.

77

'Money has not been able to save the lives of those Jews in the death camps,' Anthony Seifert said harshly.

'You have none of your own,' said Lady Truman, 'and I would be hard pressed to believe you want your title without an allowance.'

'Anthony has enough to live on,' Delia offered,

her trousered legs crossed across the edge of the late earl's favourite chair.

Her ladyship had been astonished by the forthright conversation pouring from the mouths of the four pilots. They had described the love affairs of numerous members of the ATA, and suggested morals had changed since the First War. She had objected that morals were nonexistent in flying circles, or so she had heard, but her words petered out as the memory of Errol came flooding into her aging but still restless loins.

'ATA has sent a party to rescue Sarah, your daughter,' Barbara announced. 'One of our immoral ladies, Angelique Florian, went out to Spain over a year ago on a similar mission sanctioned by Captain Balfour. She flew off to find her brothers, who I believe knew your daughter very well. Angelique was heavily pregnant at the time, by the way.'

Something about Barbara's tone made Lady Truman laugh.

'We are a fertile bunch,' Delia remarked, wondering how Alec's Marion was coping with the child and with a ferrying workload doubled by Delia's absence from her ATA pool. 'My colleague Marion Harborne had her baby on the day ATA ferried some eight hundred and seventy aircraft in twenty-four hours.'

Voices droned on as Lady Truman continued to debate the issue of Anthony's right to his title, lamenting the absence of her solicitor. Her three female guests had a sharp comprehension of the law and she wanted the ordeal to end. She had begun to like the boy, who reminded her so much of the man she knew Errol Carnaby had set out to murder.

Delia had begun to tire, and she closed her eyes as the others pursued the debate. Marion was now a permanent member of the Seifert household, her unbearable personal tragedy having rocked ATA for months and having jolted Delia's father into a period of alertness and generosity. Half-listening to the voices in the Truman drawing room, Delia reflected that no-one in ATA—not even Noel Slater—had been unaffected by the events of April 1943, when Alec Harborne volunteered to transport Hamilton Slade from Hatfield to the Canadian Hospital at Taplow. On the return journey via Prestwick, where medical supplies were collected, Alec had manoeuvred his Anson through appalling weather conditions, something he had done so miraculously on previous occasions. On this mission, however, his luck expired. Somewhere above the Irish Sea, in low cloud and precipitation that merged into a cold and horrible morass, the Anson plunged into oblivion with Alec and his accomplice, Dame Dazzle, lost to eternity.

Delia would never be able to erase from her memory the sound of Marion's cries when the pregnant woman's second fright in the space of three days—the crash of two Wellingtons having been her first—was confirmed as truth in the form of a telegram. Marion's sobs had torn into Delia, their poignancy all the more searing because the couple had had such a terrible argument before his last Anson trip. One by one, each member of the Seifert family read and reread Marion's telegram, its coarse and jagged type detailing the valour of her husband's last mission . . .

'How on earth could a child have the right sort of upbringing with a pilot for a mother?' Lady Truman demanded of Edith Allam.

'Or a pilot for a father?' Edith asked, grinning.

'Marion Harborne is doing very well as a full-time pilot and mother,' Delia remarked, her eyes puffy and bloodshot from weeks of marathon ferrying. She looked toward the unkempt gardens of the Truman estate and her mind moved agonizingly back to the day Marion and Alec's baby had arrived, the tiny girl born six weeks before her time and delivered by a member of the ATA Medical Staff—a nurse whose husband had died in the Wellington crash. Marion and the nurse had campaigned for Air Traffic Control to be set up within ATA and shortly afterwards the first Controller was appointed at White Waltham. Marion's baby, named Alexandra, had become Delia's adored obsession.

'Who the devil cares about all this paternity business anyway?' scoffed Barbara, jolting Delia from her thoughts. 'I was the one who got excited about Anthony's rights, but does it matter?'

All eyes were now on Barbara.

'If Hitler wins this war, half the occupants of this room will be exterminated—you, Anthony, for having been born in a Jewish household, Edith and myself for being daughters of Abraham, and you, Lady Truman, for having associated with a Negro.'

'Does an alcoholic father count with the Nazis?' Delia asked meekly.

Anthony bowed his head and sighed. 'I only wanted to make your acquaintance,' he said calmly, rising from his chair and taking her ladyship's hand.

563

'You are mine, somehow.'

Lady Truman had spoken. She held Anthony's young fingers, pressing them to her face. 'Stay with me,' she said.

'I have my own mother,' he whispered.

His hand was set free. 'Go to her, then,' snapped Lady Truman.

'You come too,' suggested Delia, suddenly alert.

Lady Truman's expression turned thoughtful. Secretly, she longed to be flown to the village in which her husband's mistress lived. She longed to be transported by one of these remarkable young pilots but she also longed to be transported by the sounds of Errol Carnaby's voice. Talk of Anthony's parentage, and flashes within her mind of that night of carnal fusion between Truman and Delia's mother a generation ago, had made her strangely restless. If only Errol were here! She knew that upon their next meeting she would have to submit to the terrible wanting that had pushed her along a relentless course to the planning and execution of the killing, to be known by posterity as Carnaby's accident.

'Will anyone be seeing Errol today?' asked Edith.

'I may be doing so, in the village,' her Ladyship replied.

'May I leave this for him, madam?' Edith asked, producing a small book of sonnets.

Barbara caught sight of the book's spine and glared at Edith. 'Why trouble her ladyship?' she demanded. 'Can't you give it to him at the base?'

'I hate that base,' Edith replied. 'Burt Malone's brother Frank is in charge of policing, and he gives me the creeps.'

Lady Truman had opened the small volume of

love poems and her face was expressionless. 'Why are you asking me to give this to Errol?' she asked slowly, her eyes boring into the soul of a child.

'I wanted him to have them, and I thought he might like to read them aloud to you,' Edith said solemnly, rising from the sofa. 'This war is getting worse, and I've decided to jettison certain encumbrances. Sonnets are a prime example—like love, they seem absurd juxtaposed with human experiments in death camps.'

Lady Truman studied the American closely. Her guests had moved to the doorway, as if avoiding a confrontation between two rabid dogs. Edith had expected this to be her only meeting with Lady Truman, but as the silent group walked to the front entrance, she was disturbed by a strong feeling that the two of them would meet again, perhaps over a book of sonnets.

78

Nothing had been resolved, but Edith knew Anthony Seifert had generated a firestorm of conflicting emotions within Lady Truman's breast, and she left her colleagues to drink in the RAF club before embarking on the next step of her day's journey. By now Edith had grown accustomed to the ATA routine: regulations provided that each pilot worked thirteen consecutive days followed by two days off, with a fortnight's leave in summertime. White Waltham had doubled in size, and here in Norfolk Edith and her fellow pilots observed the total colonization of the countryside by the military establishment. Everywhere one turned a base was shooting up, and as Edith made her way to the tiny motorcar, she remembered a comment made by Eddie Cuomo about England becoming an American military outpost. The war had lasted for four years now, and for Edith's British associates the end of the conflict had stopped being a point of conversation; war had become a way of life, and some even dreaded its conclusion.

Inside the car, Molly sat ready to chauffeur the flight captain to her next mission. The two friends buzzed along the peaceful minor roads, the newly arrived WAC corporal reticent in the company of one so superior in rank. Despite ATA's non-combatant status, all participating forces regarded the organization's officers as the elite of the nation's civilian flying corps. Edith reminded Molly about petrol rationing and then gave up any attempt at further conversation, Molly smiling in silence and gazing sideways at the imposing ATA uniform crowned by its majestic wings.

Soon the large country house, also known as the last of the internment encampments, came into view. Edith motioned to Molly to stop the car well away from the imposing edifice and marched along the immense gravel walkway until she had reached the front door. Here, she was to meet a contingent who would endeavour to see the last of the three inmates released.

'Is this an RAF headquarters?' Molly asked timidly as they entered the glorious main hallway.

'You're kidding!' hooted Edith. 'This is where they kept all the foreign Jews and Wops before they realized they were good for Britain.'

'Like concentration camps?' Molly asked, wide-eyed.

'Not really,' Edith replied, scanning the room for her entourage. 'It's not in the character of Britishers to spoil their routine for some crazy kind of extermination business.'

'What routine is that, Edie?'

'They have their season and their fox hunt and their shooting parties, and the Glorious Twelfth and Henley. It's all kind of stopped for the war, but not altogether.'

'Somehow I picture Hitler and Mussolini loving fox-hunting,' Molly observed.

'Next time you meet them, don't encourage it,' Edith countered. 'Remember, they're just across that little channel of water, sweetheart.'

'Isn't it a shame Kelvin Bray had to leave us so soon after the trial?' Molly asked.

'He was never cut out for the service—the guy's a softie,' Edith replied.

'Do you think he's a coward, Edie?'

'Goddammit, Molly—what a dumb question!'

'Mario, my husband, thinks he's a sucker.'

'Mario, your husband, is a tough dago,' rasped Edith. 'Kelvin Bray could never be called a coward—he defended a Negro.' As Edith spoke, Hana Bukova and Josef Ratusz came through the door with the American press contingent.

'Where is Hartmut?' Edith asked, looking around anxiously.

'He got called back to special ferrying duty,' Hana said glumly. 'You know how good Valerie thinks he is on those Hudsons.'

Edith knew Hartmut had been taken on by ATA as an aerial reconnaissance pilot, his unique skills

567

invaluable to the small team of photographers employed by the organization. Hudsons were used for the flights and Hartmut had shown exceptional skill, working in shifts with his team-mate Ludo, who had shown similar talent on the surveillance assignments. All the pilots had felt great amusement in the light of Ludo's total infatuation with Hana, a passion that had so far gone unrequited. Hana had never even been willing to speak to him, and as his English was appalling none of the ATA men took much notice of his pleading, garbled requests to tell Miss Bukova about her mother and the Kranzes at Sobibor . . .

'We have a new arrival here,' said a guard, shaking Edith's hand. 'We have reason to believe he may be the genuine article—he speaks the King's English. Unfortunately the man knoweth not from whence he cometh nor will he divulge a name. He had a phoney passport—the sort that were used by those refugees escaping through Romania some years ago.'

'Did you say Romania?' Hana piped excitedly.

'This chap is definitely not Romanian, miss,' continued the guard. 'We think he may be a Nazi operative. He gets on beautifully with our Germans: Raine and Zuki.'

'Could I meet him?' asked Hana, forgetting her reason for being on the premises.

'We have a publicity stunt to perform, my dear,' said Edith, smiling at Hana.

'This man might know something of Hana's mother,' speculated Josef.

'What's happened to your mom, then, honey?' asked Molly.

'She was supposed to be here—almost two years

568

ago!' Hana said animatedly. 'Her job was ferrying refugees from Poland and the German-speaking countries, through Romania and then on to England. She had my favourite young man in her cargo.'

'There would be no harm in Hana's meeting this new inmate,' Edith said. 'I'd just appreciate it if you press guys would stay outside,' she added sharply.

Burt Malone and Stan Bialik exchanged amused looks.

Leading Hana, Edith, Molly and Josef inside, the guard walked briskly down a ghostly corridor and soon they arrived at the end of a hallway, where a neatly dressed grey-haired man seated in a rocking chair looked up at those assembled.

Edith could feel Hana's heartbeat somersaulting at the sight of the gentleman who was not her father or Benno Kranz, but whose unearthly expression held her spellbound.

'This lady thinks you might know something about her mother,' said the guard brusquely.

79

Valerie Cobb had wanted to get away from her spacious new office at White Waltham to attend the publicity exercise in Norfolk. At the back of her mind she wondered if the mystery man newly interned in East Anglia might, for some reason that bordered on the psychic, have information about her sister Annabel. Having left Barbara Newman and Edith Allam to defuse the Truman affair in order that Anthony's claim to a title might attract as little publicity as possible, Valerie had been able to concentrate on the staggering demands of the accelerating Allied war machine. She reflected on the tragedy of Lord Truman: the man had emerged from the Carnaby trial as a generous philanthropist, and the fact that now those within ATA who knew about Anthony lamented the fact that the old man had never met his rightful heir.

Lady Truman had seemed so tragic at the Old Bailey spectacle.

What of her daughter Sarah?

What of Annabel Cobb?

Intelligence services were searching, but there was little hope.

Valerie had come to love her headquarters at White Waltham, where women now worked on a par with men and the male and female ranks of ATA had grown to six hundred pilots and over one hundred flight engineers. Stella Teague had been made a Commanding Officer at one of the smaller ferry pools, and it was no longer necessary for Valerie to fight the Ministry for jobs suited to her girls. Today, she had sent three of her best girls— Kay Pelham, Lili Villiers, and Sally Remington— on Halifaxes along the now standard Marwell–Radlett–St Athan–Holmsley South route, which the pilots said they could handle blindfolded. Another of her best had taken a Percival Proctor: Marion Harborne had become a part of the Seifert family and her baby was cherished by the Brigadier and his errant wife. Marion had worked tirelessly for Alec's legacy, the Air Ambulance Service, and was on her way to becoming a Commanding Officer for Number Five Ferry Pool. On Hudsons, ΛTA had requested Hartmut Weiss and the man known as Ludo, to pilot the ATA photographers, and secretly Valerie hoped Raine Fischtal too would be taken on by ATA, since her work was so incomparable.

On this day, Valerie had been delayed because Hamilton Slade, with Noel Slater as his flight engineer, had been given the honour of flying Churchill's Skymaster to be photographed from the Hudsons. Various complicated arrangements had to be made, with the Churchill aeroplane being flown out of Northolt. Everyone in ATA knew Slade had only a few weeks to live and though one-armed Sam Hardwick had shown disappointment in not having been selected for the Skymaster flight, the men understood the magical moment Hamilton had been granted.

Kay Pelham was finished for the day, and she smiled broadly as the two women met in the middle of the newly widened White Waltham landing strip.

'What a day!' Kay exclaimed, her skin as radiant at the end of the ten-hour day as in the early morning mist.

'Duncan Worsley is joining our crowd,' Valerie said. 'We should have quite a turnout for this little show.'

Kay had been organizing a poetry reading for some days, the unbelievable pressures of Bomber Command sometimes making her project seem an impossibility. She had wanted Errol Carnaby to share in the reading of Blake and Milton, and had been overjoyed when it appeared likely her ATA group might be able to converge on Norfolk for the special occasion, an event she liked to call warstopping.

'I think you and Duncan are a number,' joked Kay, walking with Valerie to the large Operations Room. 'Is it his racing-car past that excites you, old lady?'

'He is a charming man, but his interest in my work is purely professional,' Valerie replied testily. 'Those two Germans in the Norfolk country house, the so-called internment camp, could be ideally suited to an intelligence operation he's undertaking for the Navy.'

As they spoke, Worsley emerged from the canteen, his trimly tailored naval officer's uniform accentuating the tall, square-jawed figure whose knowing, masculine expression sent a tingling sensation down Kay's legs.

'We've one hell of a contingent,' boomed Worsley. 'Perhaps we should take out extra insurance on this flight—it will be carrying the best and the brightest of ATA.'

'If I'm not mistaken,' Valerie said without a smile, 'war suspends all insurance claims.'

'You *are* looking cheerful, my girl,' Worsley said, his large hand coming to rest on Valerie's arm.

'I'm worried about this Anthony Seifert business,' she said. 'Perhaps I should not have got involved.'

'Rubbish!' Kay exclaimed. 'It's great for publicity.'

'Speaking of publicity, I think we should be on our way,' Valerie said, looking around the Ops Room with concern. 'Where is everybody?'

Unusually quiet, the room seemed to have acquired a pall as it dawned on the trio that several uniformed ATA men and women were standing glumly about the chalk board. The Ops Officer had emerged and was studying a sheet of paper. One name had already been erased, and now two others were about to disappear.

Valerie wanted to leave the room and the building—perhaps, she groaned to herself, she could leave the planet—as a collection of pilots walked in circles, lit cigarettes, whispered and tried to hide the unbearable sorrow that had suddenly struck them at the end of their day.

'Who is it?' Kay asked, moving to the board. 'Who have we lost?'

There was no reply as personnel scurried away, as if the mere act of looking at the list of names might tempt the hand of fate.

'Oh, dear God,' said Valerie. She had registered the "PP" alongside the empty name space.

'Are they your girls?' Worsley asked, his hand holding her arm once more.

'One of my best,' she moaned—knowing, now, that Alec Harborne had willed his beloved back into his kingdom.

80

'Eddie Cuomo should be here for this!' exclaimed Edith. 'Where the hell is our crowd anyway?'

At the internment mansion, Burt Malone and Stan Bialik fussed excitedly as their cameras flashed into the faces of Raine Fischtal, Zuki and the mystery man, Paul Florian. A local reporter from the *Anglian Press* interrogated Angelique's grey-haired brother in the greatest scoop of his journalistic career.

'You would confirm, therefore,' droned the press man, 'that the photograph you saw in the *Times* newspaper in a Spanish jail showed Miss Bukova, Miss Bryce and other members of ATA, and that this jolted your memory?'

'That is correct,' Paul responded slowly. Never as long as he lived would Paul reveal that he had broken at the sight of Zack's torment and had revealed to the Fascists the Vera Bukova airlift operations financed by Friedrich Kranz.

'Was your sister Angelique pictured in the *Times*?' the reporter asked.

'She was there.'

All at once the room went silent. Raine and Zuki had taken a back seat to the proceedings and were listening as eagerly as the others present.

'You mean she was in Spain?' the writer pressed.

'I held her in my arms, and then she was taken away,' Paul murmured. 'Someone hit me very hard after that, and my hearing came back, but my sister was gone.'

'When were you released?' asked Malone.

'I escaped when they left all the doors open one morning. Just like that—the guards left us unsupervised and we went.'

'Who is we?' asked Edith.

'Some girls—I don't remember their names,' Paul murmured, rubbing his scarred forehead.

'This man needs rest,' Hana interjected, moving her gaze to the senior security guard.

'I think he should be taken to the base,' said the guard. 'The RAF can make some enquiries about his sister.'

574

Edith was shaking with distress. Her visit to the camp had lasted thrcc hours, and now it was dusk and her entourage had still not arrived. What had become of Valerie and Duncan Worsley? Most of the ATA women were due in the village to attend tonight's poetry reading, and Edith wondered if Kay had arrived at Weston Longville.

'Would Mr Florian be allowed to attend a little performance this evening?' asked Edith, smiling sweetly at the guard. 'Technically he is a British citizen and should be a free man.'

'What about us?' asked Raine, looking sorrowfully at Edith.

'You and I can catch up on lots of stuff later, Raine,' Edith replied. 'You and Zuki aren't free and that's life, baby. These press guys are here to show how humane the Allies can be—you should be getting good jobs with the British as from tomorrow but you won't be free until Hitler is demolished. Then you can deliver your little doll to your mother, and come home with me to Philly.' She winked at Raine and the German woman blushed deeply, fingering the frayed photograph of Edith tucked neatly into her flying-suit pocket.

'Raine took a picture of Benno Kranz,' Edith continued, tapping Hana on the shoulder.

'You knew my friend?' shrieked Hana. 'How? Where?'

'The Kranz family used my portrait studio in Berlin,' Raine responded, still casting a sideways glance at the American girl she had grown so much to love in her solitary confinement.

'What has happened to Kranz?' asked Paul, his voice agitated.

'He manufactures aeroplanes for the British,'

piped Josef Ratusz, bored. 'I, of course, will fly only Polish Mustangs.'

Edith moved to the entrance and watched the clouds overtake the setting sun, the voices of the group reverberating through the now empty house.

What would this evening bring?

She had a terrible urge to see Errol, and she beckoned Molly as the guards moved Raine and Zuki to a waiting lorry.

*　　　*　　　*

It had been decided that the poetry reading would proceed as planned, and when Valerie arrived with Duncan and Kay, Edith breathed a sigh of relief. They had flown in to Weston Longville and had been due to be wined and dined in the luxurious officers' dining room, with Charlie Buxton their gregarious host. A relaxing meal had not taken place: the group was grief-stricken at the loss of Marion Harborne and Valerie seemed unusually distracted by the reality of a parentless ATA infant waiting at home for the pilot mother who would never return again.

By eight o'clock Edith was anxious because she could not locate Errol, but the rest of the group had departed for the village. She knew the reading was to commence at half past eight before blackout reduced light to a minimum, and finally she gave up her search for her former lover. Molly drove her to the small village hall, where a collection of polite ladies had managed to organize light refreshments in a time of harrowing shortages.

Kay began her reading, but Edith could not concentrate. By now it was assumed Errol had shied away from the performance because of last-minute nerves arising from the Truman affair. Edith watched the light fade and saw that Valerie was sobbing quietly against Duncan Worsley's shoulder.

Edith did not feel moved by death this evening. She was cold, the hooting of an owl making her shudder as the old ladies listened to Blake. Words of Jerusalem and evocations of Albion oozed from Kay's lips, and Edith could only tremble.

81

Kelvin Bray had been infuriated when his tour of duty as a lawyer for the United States Army became twisted into a gazebo-like detour culminating in his return to Philadelphia.

Errol Carnaby's trial had prevented Kelvin from seeing his friends, all based in England, and when the protracted Old Bailey spectacle had come to a conclusion he had felt no joy upon the acquittal of his Negro client. It had been the opinion of the Army that Kelvin tired easily, and indeed he had to admit that having to listen to an English barrister fight his battle had been more exhausting than taking centre stage himself. His banishment from Britain, he felt, had deeper connotations, but the second-generation Irishman was too weary to decipher the machinations of the military machine.

July had been hellish and Kelvin looked out at the stillness of the centre of town, William Penn seeming to perspire between his masonry features atop City Hall. Gazing along the length of

Benjamin Franklin Parkway, Kelvin could see the sun just beginning to swing around, its scorching rays bouncing off the exquisite golden filigree along the roof of the Art Museum. He thought of his parents, and of the poor men saved from the brink of starvation by the innovations that had burst forth from Roosevelt's New Deal, including the programs like WPA that had used the talents of artisans astride the Art Museum's edifice.

It was nearly a year since Errol Carnaby, named after a street in London his slave grandparents had never seen, had blasted Lord Truman to oblivion on the eve of the Glorious Twelfth. Kelvin chortled at the thought of Englishmen stopping in the middle of a war to celebrate the ritual slaughter of defenceless birds.

Mutual Broadcasting was interrupting Kelvin's favourite radio show. He was too hot to rise from his chair and raise the volume on the wireless. Eddie Cuomo's voice shouted excitedly and when the name 'Errol Carnaby' crackled across the room Kelvin leapt to his feet and grabbed the volume control.

'From Norfolk, England this is Eddie Cuomo reporting,' announced the voice, now deafening.

Kelvin ran down the steps of the army legal department at the Customs House and strode into his superior's office.

'Has there been some news about Errol, sir?' Kelvin demanded, saluting the Colonel.

His Colonel looked up from an uncluttered desk top. 'Sure thing, son—sit down.'

Kelvin felt a wave of sickly heat reaching out like an unfriendly palm across his forehead.

'Your Negro boy hanged himself,' the Colonel

578

said, a tiny smile trickling across his face.

'Errol Carnaby . . . never!' shouted Kelvin.

'Keep your voice down, Bray,' barked the Colonel. 'We knew about this incident a couple of days ago but that goddam Eddie Cuomo stuck his ass into things and got the story over on Mutual Broadcasting.'

Kelvin's eyes had glazed over. 'He was not suicidal—he had everything to live for!' he cried, hearing his own voice shrilling against the walls of the old colonial building erected in the shadow of Thomas Jefferson.

'It seems,' the Colonel continued, 'this fellow was found hanging from a tree near the base, and he'd left a note saying something about a guy called Blake or some such shit.'

Kelvin turned and moved to the door.

'I didn't give you permission to leave, Bray.'

'I apologize, sir.'

'Carnaby's note,' crooned the Colonel, 'said something pretty personal about that Jewish gal Edith Allam—the flying dame who works for goddam British Air Auxiliary.'

'With all respect, sir,' said Kelvin, 'you make the British sound like our enemies.'

'Watch your step,' snapped the Colonel. 'And I want your solemn undertaking, Bray, that you won't go snooping into this business and trying to make it look like it ain't what it seemed.'

'I can't imagine it being anything other than what it seemed,' Kelvin replied calmly, his stomach churning.

'You said just a minute ago you thought the nigger wouldn't have hung himself.'

'That was speculation, sir.' Kelvin could feel bile

579

rising in his gullet.

'Do I have your solemn undertaking?' the Colonel asked quietly.

'What if I don't give you that?' asked Kelvin.

'If you don't,' said the Colonel, 'we'll drum up some nice little story saying you and the Negro were fucking each other, and secondly you'll be kicked out of the army on your ass—and be disbarred.'

Kelvin knew he would be sick in a moment. 'I won't interfere, sir,' he muttered.

'At ease—you're excused, Bray.'

Kelvin darted from the office and down the endless, winding steps into the enormous lobby, barely reaching the Chestnut Street pavement before vomiting violently on the cobblestones. When he had composed himself, Kelvin walked to the waterfront, the Navy Yard busy with wartime operations. A newspaper stand had just received its delivery of first editions, and he looked with dread at the photograph of a smiling Errol Carnaby in the *Philadelphia Daily News*. Folding the paper, Kelvin walked back to the Customs House and as he settled in his office a WAC arrived, holding out a V-Mail letter officially stamped Norwich, England. Grasping the neatly handwritten communication, he closed his office door and drank cold coffee from a paper cup.

Reading Edith's carefully worded sentences, he was astonished that her message had not been censored by the army in wartime transit. Obviously it had arrived on an Atlantic ferry plane, but the news was already three days old. As he read, Kelvin perspired, and as the reality of Edith's meticulously couched phrasing sank into his

580

tortured insides, hc knew his Negro should never have been left at the mercy of Frank Malone.

Kelvin looked up as the bright July sun poured into his humid office. Errol Carnaby had not hanged himself—he had been hanged. No-one would ever know who had performed the task, a grisly act incongruous against the wartime setting and enacted while villagers listened to Blake being read in the dim light of blackout. Lynching had now been exported to Britain, by the descendants of those very same villagers.

There was nothing to do now, Kelvin told himself. He could feel sanity leaving his soul and wished Edith could be there beside him to talk him out of his next act. She was far away, as were Molly and Burt and Errol's corpse—which, according to the V-Mail, had been hideously mutilated. Somewhere in this city a faceless Negro family begged for information about their lost son. Kelvin felt an inexplicable wave of guilt for Errol's lonely, horrible demise, wishing he had fought to be allowed to stay behind to remain guardian to the remarkable Blake scholar.

The Delaware river sparkled in the distance, and, as Kelvin left the building once more, he knew his war was over.

GATE OF REPENTANCE

Angelique Florian could not believe how many babies had been born during this war. Lying on the spacious sofa in her father's London flat, she counted the children of conflict inside her head: first, there was little Alexandra Harborne, now three years old and destined to be an actress if her adorable histrionics were to be regarded as a signpost. Marion's bitter parents had suggested the child was 'by some other chap', and had signed the papers allowing Delia Seifert and her new husband adoption rights.

Luxuriating on the sofa, Angelique thought of the next batch of war babies. Left in the care of their hapless father Duncan Worsley, Valerie's beautiful twin girls had eventually been given to her sister Annabel, debilitated though she was by her ordeal in Sobibor. How sad, thought Angelique, that Valerie had never lived to see her sister again.

'What stupidity is engendered by destiny,' she muttered to herself.

Valerie had married Duncan not because she loved him, but because ATA had been wound to a close and she had been beside herself when Friedrich Kranz had left, so suddenly, for Austria. How ironic, Angelique reflected, that Valerie, who had ferried 3,300 aircraft in the ATA years, should expire in hours of prolonged agony because modern science had not yet devised a solution for 'childbirth with complications', as they called her heartbreaking form of death. She had lain helpless and pathetic, life draining from her beautiful face as two little women burst forth from her useless, ebbing womb.

In that wonderful year of 1944, Angelique recalled, the Normandy Invasion had kept the Spitfire girls working without respite, and the excitement of the European Liberation had been heightened when women pilots had been officially assigned the Continental routes. Angelique would never forget the look on Delia Seifert's face when the ATA flight captain arrived in Brussels in a twin-engined Mitchell and had found her lying underneath a defective Boston, her baby playing on the landing strip. Delia had wept for the first time in her adult life, babbling uncontrollably to Angelique about the organization having given her up for dead and having awarded her a special medal posthumously . . .

When Angelique returned to Britain she was astonished to find her brother Paul alive, and had decided never to tell him that she had found Zack's name on a list of men executed by the Fascists.

When Angelique returned to Britain she had joined the other girls in the hazardous flights to Amiens in Mosquitos, to Courtrai in Dakotas, to Istres in Wellingtons and to Brussels in Spitfires. Indelibly imprinted on her memory was the image of Kay, Sally, Barbara and Stella stepping out of Spitfires at Colmar, along the foot of the Vosges Mountains, on the eve of VE Day, 8 May 1945, and of the delicious brandy Kay had smuggled over, courtesy of Gordon Selfridge . . .

Now, Kay was to begin her career with the Old Vic Company, playing Queen Margaret in the

Henry plays. Angelique had wanted the part very badly, as had many other English-born actresses, but Kay was determined to land the role of a lifetime at the tender age of thirty-three, and she succeeded. As the rain began to patter against the windows of her family home, Angelique laughed at the memory of Kay sneaking away to rehearsals of *Henry VI, Part I* between ferry trips to France in the summer of 1945. When she had a near-fatal crash, Nora Flint cursed Kay for losing a valuable RAF Dakota and reminding her that her contract with the soon-to-be-disbanded ATA was exclusive:

'Shakespeare or no Shakespeare,' as Nora so succinctly put it.

Angelique remembered the evening of Kay's opening in *Henry VI*, when her husband Noel Slater had been unspeakably rude to Lili Villiers. Everyone in ATA knew that Lili had talked her father into backing Kay's film career, the first cinema effort to dramatize the story of ATA. Noel had screamed at Lili in the presence of the Duke and Duchess of Gloucester, and a very drunken Kay had compounded the scandal by suggesting her former lover ought to abandon her new-found career as a film producer and be a lesbian call girl.

Somehow, Angelique reflected, women like Kay always got away with such outrageous behaviour, but then again, the postwar world had no time for gentility . . .

She had been ordered to rest until the birth of her next child, and Angelique was enjoying her weight gain, although she missed aeroplanes with a desperate kind of anxiety. She worried that the new generation of flying machines, like those pressurized Boeings about which she had heard so much, might prove beyond her scope, but she vowed not to be deterred. Noel had teamed up with Sam Hardwick and Friedrich Kranz to start their new commercial airline, and the Spitfire girls had agreed amongst themselves to boycott Slater Airways when he refused to hire lady pilots.

Friedrich, Friedrich . . .

Every ATA girl had been mortified when Kranz returned from Austria, having given up the search for his lost family and determined to marry Valerie. Everyone knew he had always loved her passionately, and the girls had been mystified when she left the Closing Ceremony of ATA in 1945 and walked straight to the registry office to wed Duncan Worsley. Friedrich wept openly when he arrived in Britain and discovered that Valerie had died two dawns before, her tiny babes still screaming in a hospital ill equipped for peacetime prosperity. The Spitfire girls knew Friedrich would never recover from the tragedy, and when Worsley refused to let him visit the girls Kranz had thrown himself into his aeroplanes, becoming as cold and calculating as his new business partner Noel Slater.

Without Valerie to lead them, what would happen to all the lady pilots? Angelique wondered.

When ATA had been officially disbanded, men like Josef Ratusz and Bill Howes had found exciting work, some quite secret. Other men, of the calibre of Ludo and Zuki, had stayed in Britain to pursue the airborne women they had loved in wartime and who were now forced to remain grounded. Britain teemed with Americans, but Edith Allam and her Philadelphians chose to go home.

Would Kelvin Bray have committed suicide,

Angelique wondered, had he stayed in this green and pleasant land of England?

Edith left flowers on Errol Carnaby's Norfolk grave, the villagers of Weston Longville having claimed him as one of their own. This was the birthplace of the Blood Libel—and now the natives were burying their deeply ingrained prejudices to accept the corpse of an African into their soil.

In the end, the ladies of ATA had been instrumental in the ferrying of over 57,000 Spitfires, 29,000 Hurricanes, 26,000 Wellingtons, 10,000 Lancasters and thousands of other aircraft including flying boats—the grand total, Angelique had been told, amounting to over 300,000 aeroplanes. She had kept her logbook, although the Air Ministry had ordered the Spitfire girls to turn in all ATA property when the organization was disbanded. Now, she sat on the sofa and browsed through its poignant pages. When she had used it, so many faces had not yet faced death . . . Delia Seifert had told her that the Ministry was shredding and burning any remaining piece of evidence of women's ATA, including the wonderful giant wall map in White Waltham Ops, the rationale being that the annals of history would condemn Britain for having had to resort to using female pilots during a world war . . .

And now they could no longer fly for the RAF.

Angelique pitied girls of the supreme excellence of Delia Seifert and fretted at the possibility of Nora Flint and Hana Bukova being left with no livelihood whatsoever. The ATA men and women had been refused a place of their own in the Cenotaph Ceremonies, having been ordered to march with the London Transport bus

587

conductors—'You *were* transport workers,' the ATA had been reminded—or never to march at all.

They had chosen not to march, men and women united in defiance.

Angelique admired Hana Bukova for her dauntless determination to find her mother. The girl was convinced Vera was alive even after Friedrich's fruitless searches across the grisly wasteland of 1946 Europe.

So many faces passed in front of her mind's eye as Angelique awaited her husband's arrival. She would have tea today with Stella Teague, star choreographer of the Royal Ballet, and they would listen to their guest of honour, André Grunberg, raving on and on about the Blood Libel, the subject of his hugely successful book. People said he had shown superb timing, devising a volume that would coincide with the liberation of the souls they called Holocaust victims. Angelique had heard Britain was refusing entry to these refugees and that Sarah Truman, herself a survivor, had been fighting Sir Henry Cobb and Tim Haydon on the plight of these human skeletons who had once been scholars and doctors and scientists . . .

Tomorrow was the day the Spitfire girls would have their first reunion, and they would troupe to Hamilton Slade's tombstone on which had been inscribed:

I Don't Give a Damn.

Sally Remington would go off to play tennis at Forest Hills in New York, and Barbara Newman, crippled in a Blenheim bomber crash, would watch other women playing hockey, the game at which she had been national champion before Hitler and before the Spitfires . . .

It was said that Edith Allam had already created a nationwide clamour in the USA. Now an officer for the United Service for New Americans, she had used the press to expose the unbelievable policy against Holocaust survivors. How could she send such people 'back home' if they did not meet the criteria for becoming 'New Americans'?

Angelique felt honoured to be seeing Edith again—a woman who was doing something of use for the remnants of humanity, numbering millions left over for a postwar world to deal with, God having yet to come out of His coma.

It would be tomorrow—Angelique would pay her respects to the memory of Martin Toland, the father her beautiful little girl would never know.

What had happened to Oscar? she often wondered.

And tomorrow . . .

Tomorrow, the Spitfire girls would pay their respects to the memory of Amy and Marion and Alec and Jo and Cal and Valerie, and then Angelique would settle in to await the arrival of her husband's first progeny.

His Lordship wanted a boy, of course, to continue the Truman line.

Angelique did not love Anthony, but he had made her a Lady.

589